T0383315

"*Above the Circle of Earth* skillfully incorporates themes of faith, sacrifice, and family in a taut tale that will challenge and convict readers . . . Burnett's meticulous technical expertise and passionate theology combine beautifully in this riveting hard sci-fi adventure!"

—RONIE KENDIG, award-winning author of The Droseran Saga

"Those with a love for the Gospel, a heart for the lost and missions, and a love for Christ's church and the Five Solas will bond quickly with this story and pursue a well-crafted and lofty tale, one that challenges our calling in the face of our weakness against terrestrial adversaries and the vastness of space. Fast-paced and engaging, yet imbued with wit, theology, and the fantastic ESB turn of phrase. *Soli Deo Gloria!*"

—MARC SCHOOLEY, author of the Carol Award–winning novel *König's Fire*

"This action-packed story has a lot to say, not only about Christians struggling against the world, but also against the tensions that often exist within our churches and communities. It's a clash to define what it means to live faithfully, no matter what the frontier."

—JOSIAH DEGRAAF, fantasy author, writers' coach, co-founder of Story Embers

"Filled with action and intrigue, this novel offers readers an exciting look into a future of missions that could take believers beyond the limits of this world."

—CLINT HALL, author of *Steal Fire From the Gods* and *Echo Nova*

"This space-age tale takes humanity, and the Great Commission, beyond the Earth. An inventive fusion of space pioneering with lived religion, *Above the Circle of Earth* is a profound examination of the ties and trials of a shared faith."

—SHANNON MCDERMOTT, author of *The Time Door*

"Are you a fan of both *Star Trek* and Jesus? Hop in and buckle up!"

—JAMIE FOLEY, award-winning author of The Sentinel Trilogy

ABOVE
THE
CIRCLE
OF
EARTH

ABOVE THE CIRCLE OF EARTH

E. STEPHEN BURNETT

For the Lorehaven crew,
for my true love Lacy,
and for the Creator and Savior of all worlds.

1

BROCK
04:37 LMST, HALL 17, 44 (SYNDIC)
ARES VALLES

CRIMSON LIGHT FLARED IN THE DARKNESS, BEATING WITH THE emergency tone that pulsed in Brock's head. He drew himself out of the warmth, facing quadrupled flashes that silently cried out *e-mer-gen-cy, e-mer-gen-cy*. Dim hovering text summarized the call for help. A new dome in Xanthe Terra was leaking air, one percent in the last hour, cause unknown.

Atop the blankets, he shivered. Temperatures out there would be even colder.

Alicia lay still beside him, undisturbed by the alert, her soft cheek emanating warmth.

He drew his clip from its dock and whispered, "Stay safe, love."

Quietly he shut the bedroom door. For five days he had waited on a new job. This one would pay 300 yun—enough to cover three days of home life support and Daniel's diapers.

In the chilled corridor, Brock donned his gray jumpsuit and found his warmest jacket, the navy one, then glanced into the boys' room. Daniel and his older brother, Adam, slept well. So did Emma in her own room, shielded from his departure noise by the running furnace.

Brock fixed his clip to the bridge of his nose. Viz shone into his eyes, able to reflect grainy feeds from the home monitors. When he entered the utility bay, he saw no movement back in the skiff. None of his children stirred as he climbed into his quad-environment vehicle and depressurized the bay, then retreated from the small chamber and closed the gate.

Brock set course over the dismal deserts of Mars.

Nearly two hours later, his destination rose over the ridge—a pale and glowing bubble, stuck to the land, like a new half-moon against the frigid night sky. Autodrive adjusted for that direction. Dual headlights cast leaping black shadows over desiccated rocks.

Both his pinhead-sized bronze eartags were already charged, able to create eight hours of audible earspace. "Reyes Syndicate, this is your freelance repairman. What's your access point?"

No response. Did they think he could use his secret repairman powers to get inside this place, or wield magical science to fix everything from a distance? Someday, perhaps.

Using sight commands, he re-checked the alert. Yes, it came from a real person.

A cello note strummed his left eartag. "Project manager."

The voice was human and sounded new, not a rarity among settlements with population nearing 850,000. Based on the dialect, this man might even be from Brock's homeworld.

"This is Brock Rivers. Please send me all your data about the leaking—"

The man's voice drifted away, speaking to another. *Legacy* received a new map. Brock tapped a glyph to refocus autodrive, coursing over the ridge, then descending.

Here it was. Just below the crater's rim and slanting 20 degrees on the eastern slope, Reyes Syndicate crews had manually laid their new base. Shallow piles driven into land secured a circular foundation. From there the dome had nano-generated its own frame. This process formed a half-globe structure about 60 meters wide, paneled with black squares that glowed white against the night, filled with the silvery translucent web that insulated the interior and conducted heat and oxygen. Those spec-formed fibers would turn opaque twelve hours after formation, meaning this dome must be newer than that.

One small desert channel, a *rille*, reached across the land and vanished into the crater. Centuries ago, Earth scholars had called these *canals* and filled them with legends of living water. Workers here might honor that mythology by using the channel for new utility lines.

There waited the dome entrance, an arching passage protruding from this composite igloo. Outer bifold gates drew apart like a theater curtain.

Lord willing, Brock could finish this job within the hour.

Legacy glided into the airlock, keeping her port and starboard fins comfortably distant from the walls. Crimson viz data revealed AIRLOCK PRESSURE: 0.97 ATM.

Another two percent lost. If that pressure fell beneath 91 percent, Martian law called for evacuation. Just last week Brock had pored over his home oxygen, seeking ways to conserve air without insisting the children never run in the house.

When he was a boy, his parents could send him outside. This land's outside would kill people.

Inner airlock doors also unfolded. While his craft auto-glided into the dome itself, Brock moved to the cabin's pull-down bed/workbench and clipped tools to his belt. From the corner lavatory/storage closet, he retrieved his spec paintbrush and sonic array.

They were quiet out there. "Reyes dome? I still need your structure data."

Brock tagged the rear door stat. Latches released, allowing dusky light to shine inside his cabin. Both doors pivoted outward. He stepped into lower gravity that drew his heels onto loose regolith to bounce and settle. Voices echoed in this shelter, real and human.

Vox crackled. "Almost ready," the project manager said.

"I also need to meet you first, in person."

"Ahm . . ." Of course the other sounded surprised. "In a minute."

Even holding at 97 percent, this air *felt* plentiful, tinged by scents of cold dust and metals.

He blinked against the roof panels' warm white light and dry heats, then surveyed the site. Here came a dark-haired woman in green coveralls, leading other workers down the slope. He could smile at the sight of people with new faces . . . and yet, even this early, they were trudging. Were they already working a shift, and without emergency suits? Brock's own atmoskin was still piled on his home workbench, awaiting the delayed arrival of membrane patches and new batteries.

Two officials stood near a forged modular office—a large plastic-like box with rough edges hewn by spec formation. Their armbands bore the red R-shaped logo of Reyes Syndicate.

There was the *rille*, passed through this crater, its twisted diameter bisecting the dome floor. Workers had used a ladder to climb down into that channel. Instead of utility lines, were they preparing foundations for an energy pylon or oxygen tree? Then why use a ladder instead of a levitator?

Viz data refreshed: 0.96 ATM. Did these people see this?

Here at last came more data. Schematics revealed this dome did lay along a planned utility corridor that ran west to the Syndicate's new Residential Enterprise District. That would attract more immigrants. As the capital city grew, Reyes and its member company syndics were fighting to build colonies ahead of newly taxable land.

"*Bienvenidos? Yokoso?*" A man hustled up the slope. His dust-laden gray sleeves bore only the old Reyes insignia, with no other accessories, and he might be 35, slightly older than Brock. "*Dobro pozhalovat?* Welcome? I'm project manager."

Brock shook his hand. "Glad to meet a fellow American. Where from?"

The man stared back.

Well, many people came here to escape their old lives. Brock switched to his professional voice. "I need your name, plus your crew manifest."

"Devonn, and—why?"

"Just in case I need to know my neighbors." Brock put on a smile as he recited the line. Settlers with steady jobs had higher-class professional networks, leaving freelancers to make their own connections. More importantly, these neighbors needed support only he could provide.

"Mr. Rivers, your inspection won't take that long."

Why speak so casually? "Mr. Devonn, your site has lost three percent oxygen since I arrived. You requested emergency inspection. Do you want to change the work order?"

"No, sir. Just . . ." Devonn stepped forward. "Not so loud, so early, 'ey?"

He must have onsite supervisors. Brock gave a single nod, keeping this slow and careful. "Speaking of which, I need you to suspend the noise while I take interior sound clips."

"Suspend. How long?"

"Fifteen minutes for leak tests, longer if you can't clear the soundscape."

"We can't stop the work."

0.95 ATM, truly? "Air loss could stop that, Mr. Devonn."

The man stepped back. "I will send any project data we can."

"I'll take that, but also, what is the goal of this project?"

"This will be a utility junction site. Anything more's proprietary."

Brock could guess the rest. "So you're doing an ancient-life survey."

For growing settlements, Reyes Syndicate would lay water and power lines across new lands. But for lines installed near specific land features, old Martian laws required astrobiology tests. Of course, any oxygen-pressurized dome like this would only pollute the soil; today's settlers, unlike their forebears, honored that old law by letter alone. By now even Premier Alaimo had gently mocked suggestions of sentient Martian life.

Devonn fingered his sleeve. "I'll send you everything."

"Thank you." Brock tried a smile. "Don't add people to mess with my sonic prints."

"*Pfsh.*" Devonn headed back for that modular office. "We're not the Cause."

He meant either CAUSE, the collective regime over all space settlement, or *the Cause*, its secular philosophy. Over the last year, Brock had seen more CAUSE ships and those tiny survey drones—the "spirits" of Mars—than vehicles from the Syndicate and other private corporations.

Brock uncased his sonogram. By sight commands, he told that device to get five-second noise samples. Without a clean sonic print for this new atmosphere, he would try comparing real samples with simulated noise, based on data from a virtual dome.

Beyond the airlock gate, three brighter lights shone from approaching vehicles.

Devonn was adding people to mess with his sonic prints.

Soon the frigid sunrise would fade across the east, possibly bringing a shift change. Each new vehicle docking and exchanging air pressures could worsen any leak. Thirty years ago, Reyes Syndicate could get away with such hazards. New frontiers needed people to risk their lives like pioneers. Now hundreds of immigrants arrived monthly in Port Ares. CAUSE's distant and titular government would soon secure real authority over all the red planet. Their laws, beliefs, and even calendar would later supplant all others. Within the next five years, Reyes would need to change its practices, or else be frozen out of its own grand expansion plans.

That threat awaited in Brock's future. For today, this was his calling.

Seven years ago, he and Alicia had traveled 200 million kilometers of dueling orbits. Without his basic engineering experience, they would have never survived, and these workers were likely much greener. Even if he never spoke with them, he could help them in his own way.

Back inside *Legacy*, Brock unloaded his brush and switched out the cartridge. His forge cabinet's downstream would finish in five minutes.

The crew manifest arrived. One tiny musical note brightened at top viz. Side cards showed tiny dossiers with photos of the first dome worker. Brock's favorite narrator read, "Ivan Fernando. Levitator specialist. Born 2102, age twenty-three. Emigrated 2123."

Ivan looked so earnest. *Creator of worlds, remember Ivan in this dry and weary land.*

Dome pressure held at 0.93 ATM.

Brock strode to the dome airlock's left side. His brush shot a horde of tiny swirling specs that formed a palm-sized gray circle upon a web panel, two meters over the ground. After two strides, he added another brush spot, then another, descending the crater slope.

"Justine Bach," his vox said. "Born 2090. Age thirty-five. Emigrated 2117."

Justine looked much younger. She was the dark-haired woman in coveralls whom he had seen earlier. *Jesus, strengthen Justine, after many years of wandering.*

He glanced down the slope, where two more workers descended the ladder into the rille. Near them on the ground lay two curved packages encased in transparent foam, along with two meter-wide polarizer discs. Techs would later assemble those parts into a human-sized levitator.

"Sayed Lytton. Retired farmer. Born 2085. Age forty. Emigrated 2112 . . ."

Sayed looked so meek and content. *Holy Spirit, preserve Sayed, for now and forever.*

Brock ascended the crater incline. With every brush stroke, he interceded for more names until he returned to the airlock's right side. There he fired his last burst and waited. Viz revealed all specs unified, each spot serving as a tiny nerve cluster to measure oxygen sound and tell him the results. He halted the manifest narration.

New text arrived: TEST COMPLETE. OXYGEN LEAK POSITIVE.

0.91 ATM.

Brock sighted sonogram returns. What was the leak source?

Viz drew a solid red line. INCONCLUSIVE.

This couldn't be right . . . unless there was no *single* leak source. The leak was everywhere.

Dry breezes tugged his jacket as structural pressure fell to 0.90 ATM.

Now his viz flared a crimson alert, but the dome kept its steady light. No warning tone? No evacuation order? Brock had been too optimistic, and Devonn was obviously much greener than Brock had assumed. But the man could no longer handle this problem quietly!

No time to repair this, either. If the officials weren't acting, Brock could try.

Back in *Legacy*'s cabin, he retrieved several RedMed emergency kits and a pen-sized vox transmitter. This dome ran a standard Reyes OS. With a few familiar and legally dubious commands, he overruled the OS, and held the pen steady under his rough-bearded chin.

"Good morning." His voice echoed outside. "This is your repairman. Over the last thirty minutes, your air pressure has fallen by ten percent. Ask your project manager for direction."

Now he had done his duty . . . and forced them to do theirs.

Crew voices lifted into shouts. Two officials ran toward the modular office, where the single door whipped open. Devonn emerged and landed hard on the soil.

Brock intercepted him. "Manager, your oxygen leak is everywhere."

"What—"

"Either your foundation isn't level, or it's not bonded to the land."

0.89 ATM.

Devonn's gaze darted up and down. "In the office. We have maybe . . . ten masks."

"Not enough." Brock started opening RedMed kits. "What about atmoskins?"

"They're arriving later. Guess we can handle the cold till it's fixed."

Brock held his voice steady. "That is . . . not possible. Your site is compromised."

"Well, try patching the leak as best you can."

He knew nothing! Brock could push further, but technically this man could fire him, even delist him from the Reyes job boards.

This great Syndicate should be responsible for its own people.

Brock pivoted back to his vehicle. His legs drifted for moments, then settled back to the land. *Oh, Lord, help them.* And yet Ivan, Justine, Sayed, all those other workers whose names he had prayed for . . . they needed more than his wishes to be warm and filled with oxygen.

He reopened vox. "Attention. Your atmosphere has dropped under point-ninety."

Devonn swore and lunged.

Brock sprang out of reach, leaving the man five paces away and staring with shock.

"We have emergency masks! Find me near the blue-and-silver vehicle by your airlock."

"We . . ." Devonn was thinking. "We can try to get people in there. But the modular . . ."

That was better. But yes, the interior structure was reserved for Syndicate officers. "At full depressurization," he announced, "one emergency mask will not keep you alive for long."

At that point a person might have twenty seconds before unconsciousness. This was in a best-case crisis. Last year, he had seen his worst situation, thanks to a salvage order for the survey ship crashed in Valles Marineris after a synthetic gravity failure. Brock had never learned the names of those three scientists. Interior gravity cushions had preserved them from impact, but the ship was torn apart. Within minutes, the desert had frozen them into victims of Martian spite.

Christ preserve me. Don't take me from my family.

Three workers arrived to retrieve masks. Brock should keep one for himself.

He secured *Legacy*'s doors, but should he consider offering space inside?

Devonn stood beside him, finally ready to help. His own voice popped onto dome vox. "Stay calm. Walk to any secure area, but avoid the modular shelter. It's already full."

Each lower percentage decreased oxygen and increased damage to human brains and bloodstreams. Low pressure reduced the boiling point for sweat and any bodily liquids, including blood. Anything below 0.50 ATM would soon kill a man; anything below 0.25 ATM sped the execution. If only Brock had trained for higher altitudes as well as higher gravities.

Brock handed out two more masks. Not everyone was here. "Where are the novices?"

0.87 ATM.

"Survey detail, lowest level—wait, where you going?"

Brock cleared the crater's edge and dashed down the slope, toward that rille that spanned two meters across. He halted among tangles of dust and stared down to its floor nine meters below, between sheer rock sides without handholds. Several workers peered upward, clutching survey tools. They were so young . . . sheep with no shepherd. None wore oxygen masks.

Their rope ladder, once hooked to the canyon's edge, now lay in bent metal pieces below. One green-haired woman slumped nearby, her tiny left foot bent against her knee.

He counted twelve novices, with thin jackets and no atmoskins, nothing protective.

The dome flashed dark orange, without sound, but this was an official evacuation call.

Brock called, "You there!" One man, then the smaller woman, were the first to look up. Sweat bristled on the man's dusty beard, thinner than Brock's own. Gold paint shone around the woman's eyes. "I'm Brock. I'm the repairman. Does anyone have another ladder?"

The man swore, his accent Italian. "They gave only the one."

What else was up here? He found no climbing gear, yet beside that crane . . . were all the levitator parts here, along with a power source? Brock bent to lift the polarizer. No easy task.

"Everyone! Let's try floating you out of there. This is heavy, but I need you to catch it."

The man nodded and braced himself.

Brock released the meter-wide disc, which tumbled into the novice's grip. Next he dragged over the levitator's two curving shaft pieces, a ring frame, and the other heavy polarizer. Now to assemble a shaft, somehow without upper polarizer suspension, or a vertical guide?

That crane might provide both. Its boom of steel lattice was five meters long, and it held one lamp. Brock's viz commands linked fast. *Crane control.* He sight-twisted a dial until the crane's steel arm rotated enough to shine lamp light down into the rille. After several quick breaths, Brock tensed . . . and leaped, polarizer in hand. He wrapped one free arm and both legs around the boom lattice. Muscles trembled. Even in lighter gravity, that polarizer disc pulled hard at his right hand. A fall from this height would break more than the machinery.

0.86 ATM. This was not his imagination. Before long, everyone would struggle to breathe.

Brock hauled this polarizer alongside the crane. With his free hand, he detached the riveter from his belt. Who was the man who'd caught the other polarizer? "Mr. Sherrod! Lay your disc on the ground inside the crane light. Make the disc as level as you can. Yes?"

The polarizer pulsed green. Brock linked with the disc, watching two green viz circles. Not close enough. Sweat slid from his face. One outline jumped too far. He moved the disc right.

There! Both green circles merged. The polarizers were aligned.

With his riveter, Brock injected several bursts of 15 mm specs that hardened into visible bonds against the latticework. Yes, the polarizer held. Could this levitator generate zero gravity?

He released his riveter inside the levitator beam. The tool hovered in zero-G. He lowered himself until his single gripping fist on steel suspended his body inside the pillar of light, then dared to loosen his hand . . . and lingered in midair. Shoving at the steel, he pushed himself down, slowly, until he flipped about and returned to land beside the rille's edge.

Up there on the crater ridge, workers pressed close to the dome's airlock.

0.84 ATM. Chills raced from his shoulders to his arms.

Now for a red- or at least orange-ranked worker. "*Mr. Sayed, are you down there?*"

An older man looked up, wincing against the glare. With that sparse gray hair, he looked like that ancient Baptist elder, Dr. Samuel Morrison, from back in Brock's CIRCLE college leadership class. *Manage orderly evacuation*, Dr. Morrison would say, probably based on his experience with the postwar militia. *Give your people simple, non-optional commands.*

"Sayed, form everyone into a line. Do *not* touch the disc or we lose the zero-G field. Help lift your neighbor ahead of you, carefully in the light, to ascend all the way using the zero-G."

Viz flashed red. 0.81 ATM. *Oh, Jesus, help us.*

Vox crackled and Devonn called, "Rescue vehicles incoming. Ten minutes."

"Thank you! Can you get these people to the airlock?"

Devonn paused, then replied, "If . . . if they can get here in time."

0.75 ATM.

"Continue the evacuation." An automated agent voice crossed thinning oxygen, calm and falsely human. "Do not run. Do not hold your breath. If you feel dizzy, use your emergency signal. Breathe slowly. Seventy-percent pressure is projected to last four minutes."

0.67 ATM. Any cause could have done that—external temperature change, shifting sands, or even the natural slide of a poor dome foundation. Regardless, one-third of oxygen was gone.

The nearest Syndicate base was nine hundred klicks away. Even if Reyes sent more help, rescuers would arrive to find shriveled bodies. By their indifference or incompetence, they might prefer losing this base—and these souls—than beg help from the highest power of Mars.

That grave duty must fall to the repairman.

Brock accessed his personal black-box 'ware, and he voxed that highest human power.

This reply was less human. "Coalition, Port Galilaei, please state the emergency."

"My location is Xanthe Terra. I am an engineer inside dome twenty-one-J-B-oh-nine-four-six. We are suffering an air leak endangering thirty-three human lives, and we need immediate evacuation. Vox off."

Voices clamored down in the rille. "I'm first," one person said.

"I should be first!" another shouted.

Brock leaned down. "Let the youngest and greenest go first! Is that Mara Zeisloft?"

The small woman looked up with surprise, head framed in gauzy lime-green hair.

"Mara, can you put weight on that leg?"

"Yeah. Almost."

"Then get into the zero-G."

Sayed and another woman stepped in to guide her. With one push, she floated upward.

Carefully he took her by her frigid bare arms. "Good job, good job. Up the slope, go to the airlock. If that's full, you can find my blue-silver quev." She might not know the Earthling term. "My craft. A quad-environment vehicle. It looks like a stingray, if you've ever seen those."

Brock shared his access code, then gave her the oxygen mask . . . wait, this was his own.

0.61 ATM. Chills pricked onto his skin and now within his lungs.

His vehicle could hold six more people, besides himself, presuming he could get there.

Brock caught the Italian novice. Then another man ascended, heavier-set, but fairly easy to retrieve. Then several more novices glided up and out. This might work. In a moment, he could follow them.

0.55 ATM. His lungs scraped air. Near-vacuum shoved into his temples, aching . . .

It drove him to the ground, crying out, hands clawing at the chilled soils of an alien land.

Would the Lord really take him and leave alone Alicia and his three children?

What about the Starr family? They were still new in the faith, with so many questions.

Down in that ancient waterless trench, two last young faces stared upward. Their own families were far away. Any gods they unwittingly worshiped had abandoned them. Even if Brock died, writhing in the desert, he should awaken in a true paradise, and they would almost certainly not. They needed so much more than this life. Before his final breaths . . . he might give them the gospel. No private syndicate nor secular tyrant could punish a dead man for that.

Perhaps the Lord would grant him final breaths for this.

From the sky fell a noise like thunder.

2

THAT VOICE SPOKE CLEAR AND DEEP: "I AM THE epsilon of CAUSE Squadron Octo."

How had they arrived so quickly?

Rolling onto his back, Brock recoiled against under freezing air. High and beyond the dome's translucent squares loomed a great bird, the CAUSE vessel, hull gleaming like solid pearl in the night. Two broad wings lifted to release four smaller ships that dipped close to the dome, casting down long webbed shadows. Minute lights blinked green on the mothership, whose wide gate opened to issue smaller human figures. They fell to the dome roof and landed with three muffled thumps. Shining green atmoskins clung to their muscular forms.

Over dome vox the epsilon called, "We're sharing emergency air for three minutes."

Viz halted at 0.49 ATM. They were blasting sparks from the roof. Web fragments rained down, then switched direction to cling overhead by gravity holds. Pressure sprang to 0.60 ATM, then 0.67 ATM. CAUSE was *cutting* into the dome but restoring pressure, and they were fast. Within seconds Brock's skin no longer stung and his oxygen flowed.

"Sir!" Sayed called from below. "She won't go, she says."

With a groan, Brock turned to the crevasse. Who was that last woman? He knew her face from the crew manifest. "You are Justine, yes? I know you can do this."

"What about *him*?" She coughed, pointing to Sayed. "Only one of us . . ."

Of course. By lifting her into zero-G, Sayed would leave himself without jump leverage.

Dome alarms returned. 0.65 ATM. The Causians' air supply would not last long.

"Those at the airlock, please maintain order," the epsilon said. "You three at the rille, we promise we will try to reach you. If not . . ." Was this an audible sigh, as if showing regret? Then his tone changed, lifting and falling, as if uttering a liturgy: "Then please do not fear. Death is the natural end of every man, every woman. Your work is not in vain."

Was this man mocking them, or worse, was he in earnest?

He continued, "You fought for the human Cause. This means your name is forever . . ."

"Sayed, get up there!" the woman shouted.

Give them simple, non-optional commands. "Justine, I want you to enter zero-G first."

"What for? Maybe it *is* my time." Fear and defiance stung her eyes. "Quick and natural."

Brock could not argue. If none escaped, Reyes should pay for their deaths.

The epsilon said, "We will always remember your sacrifice."

Enough of him! Brock summoned blackware to override dome vox. He killed the other voice. Sand ground between his fingers as he gazed over the crevasse, forcing eye contact. "Listen. That's a lie. From the pit of Hell. You weren't meant to die! Fight to live forever."

". . . *Ever.*" That was his echoing voice. He'd somehow cast himself over dome vox?

Now he would be finished, air-starved in vacuum or else exposed to the Causians.

Well then, let them do their worst. Their wicked religion would kill more than the body.

"Sayed. Justine." He climbed to a crouch. "Stand back from the polarizer."

Brock bent near the canyon's edge and dropped inside, one arm and leg scraping the wall, dragging pebbles with him. But he needed this leverage. He elbowed sharp stone and thrust himself from the light, throwing hard ground under his feet, but he'd avoided the polarizer disc. Brock stood directly beside the other two, shuddering near chilled stone.

He held Justine's upper arm. "Sayed! Other side."

Sayed took her other elbow. She kept silent as they hoisted her into zero-G and shoved. Slowly the woman ascended, until she reached the edge and scrambled over.

"I can try"—Sayed caught his breath—"to lift you myself."

The older man was shorter, and his arms looked brittle as dry bones.

Jacket sleeves drew tight around Brock's arms. His heaving breaths released dry fog.

"Denied. Repairman's orders." Brock wrapped arms around Sayed's legs and strained to lift. Sayed ascended, sleeves fluttering, until he took Justine's hands and stepped over the edge.

Dome pressure fell to 0.61 ATM and lower.

Brock coughed. Clods of soil poured onto him. One large stone bounced high and punched with a *plonk*—directly onto the polarizer's battery nodule.

Two green circles turned red, cutting the zero-G.

0.55 ATM.

No time to fix that. Not even his Earth-conditioned jump could drive him that high.

Higher up, one of the dome's lumen lines bent outward and snapped loose. CAUSE might tear through that surface to airlift survivors, risking worse damage to the structure. Without air pressure, the whole place would come down.

A small black object slipped over the rille edge. Was that a cable? Sayed and Justine were still up there, working together, lowering this cable until it halted three meters down.

It might be enough.

Brock drew prickling oxygen into his lungs. With that breath, he lifted both arms, bent his knees . . . and leaped. There! His hands seized the cable and clenched tight, while he kicked at the wall, scrambling against returned weight, fighting for altitude. The others reached down and their warm hands clenched around his.

0.42 ATM.

He stood and his head fell backward, under a sky of reeling, crumpling dome pieces.

The others' voices crawled under vacuum, urging him to go somewhere.

Up there. Sayed and Justine were running. Fleeing toward his quev.

He pulled his legs as if through freezing concrete, up the slope, following them.

0.33 ATM.

Vanishing air smothered alarm noise.

0.25 ATM.

Pressure clenched at his head. His fingers stiffened. Which symptom would strike before unconsciousness? Next his sweat and saliva would dissolve, lung alveoli shriveling.

His knees could not bend. One more minute to death, his death today, not decades from now, but this moment. Soon he would see the Lord, truly and forever. He would leave his family stranded on Mars without husband or father. Adam would never be able to meet a dog, Emma would never see an ocean, and Daniel would never run through grass in the spring. In this alien land, they would age and grow brittle. Never again would Brock rest beside Alicia, enraptured by her music, holding each other for warmth in frigid nights.

What cruelty was this, making a man freeze in the desert?

My love, I'm so sorry.

Blurred viz dialed all the way to 0.14 ATM.

Do not fear, they said. *Death is the natural end. Fight for the human Cause.*

No, he would defy that. *Lord God almighty, show these people why I really fought.*

Brock bent his legs, descending against his own agony, and leaped again. Collapsing dome pieces swept lower. His body cleared the crater's edge and gravity retook him.

His trachea tightened.

Four seconds. Three.

Legacy waited with its open rear hatch. Her floor slapped up to his body and hurled him into a wall. Voices shouted. But he could move, resisting new forces. What did he need? What had he kept? There, his com clip. It showed viz glyphs for control of all quev externals. *Doors, cargo, close. Pressurize.* Light dimmed, but *Legacy*'s gates pivoted back into the cabin.

"Stay clear . . . of . . . doors!" Air shredded his throat as he fought to stand.

Brock lived. He mustn't black out now.

A woman swore. "Are you well? Are you well?"

"What's the gravity in here?" came Sayed's voice. "Jovian level?"

Heat throbbed in his chest. His bare hands pressed to the floor. Emergency heat fans burst to life, while ceiling lumen lines revealed the women's faces. They were Mara Zeisloft and Justine Bach. Their skin tones looked normal. They breathed. "Oh . . . thank you, Lord."

Dust fell from Justine's dark hair as she glanced back, then she touched his shoulder.

"I'm well, truly." He leaned against the wall. "Brock Rivers. I came for the leak repair."

Mara's dry, gold-rimmed eyes fixed on him. Her voice quivered. "Good job."

His throat caught until he let out a cough, which became a laugh.

Now even Justine allowed a smile. "Oh. They'd still better pay you."

"You first . . ." Brock winced at his throat pain.

"Not likely now, they won't," Justine said. "This your place? We safe in here?"

Yes, the hatch doors held firm. Beyond the quev windows, the dome roof continued its downward implosion, grid conduits flashing sparks, web strands twisting from their skeletal frame. All this would bury that promised 300 yun. Still, if Brock had not come here . . .

As for Sayed, his body slumped against the opposite wall, silent and pale, but moving.

Brock clambered beside him. "Can you breathe right? Any signs of hypoxia?"

Sayed shook his head.

"Your lungs? No, heart problems?" No and no. Brock gripped his hand. "Asthma?"

The man gasped out, "Long time, since Earth."

Pain stabbed Brock's knees, but he pulled himself up and wrenched at the cabinet handle until the door opened. He found one medical mask and fastened this to Sayed's face, then viz-sighted for stimulant. Sayed drew air, then burst out a long cough.

Brock turned to the women. "I need to drive."

After hesitating, Mara said, "You have first aid?"

"If you know it, use it." Brock flung himself into the quev's front seat and tagged the console. *Power. Ascend.* Gravity spectra throbbed and lifted the quev. *Infrared scan.* This would show any bodies. The dome had held three Reyes officials, seventeen upper workers, and thirteen novices. Excluding Brock, this totaled thirty-three souls.

Most of those might form that faint orange cluster, apparently safe beyond the airlock.

Brock pulled his yoke, drawing *Legacy* off the land and pointing its bow to the shredded ceiling. Torn fibers framed a new opening, ten by five meters wide, just enough. Grav cushions compensated, and he cautiously lifted the craft between crumpled materials. She passed under early sunlight that washed the sky's edges in shades of dull pink.

Brock added altitude and swung about the wounded structure, toward the new CAUSE ship that loomed over rusted land, separated from Mars by its own radiance. Adjunct rescue crafts were floating down into the dome site, mimicking their ancestor ambulances.

That CAUSE vessel might let him enter for an emergency. "Justine, can you—"

"Just talked with them and got clearance," she called.

Brock leaned on the yoke until *Legacy*'s front window was filled by the mothership's expansive pearlescent hull, bringing forth the ship's crest. Multiple solid circles, hued with bluish-violet and silver, formed two chiseled human silhouettes whose eyeless faces gazed rightward as they bounded, overshadowed by straight-edged text:

CAUSE: COALITION FOR ADVANCEMENT OF UNITED SPACE EXPLORATION.

From the great stern extended a long tubular connecting bridge, a starway. Brock floated *Legacy* toward this, then allowed linkup. With gentle impact, the starway connected, and pressures equalized. He fixed the quev at low power in midair.

Doors, cargo, open. Brock hoisted Sayed from the cabin and stumbled into the starway, where lighter gravity eased his burden. He entered the ship's vast bay, a single floor three levels high and wide enough to contain all of Brock's home skiff. Dozens of medical staff wielded scan pedestals and clad in blue-edged white uniforms showing cause squadron octo badges.

Three medics rushed forward with a gurney for Sayed.

Brock started, "He has asthma—"

One woman replaced the mask over his face, and they took him away.

Rows of advanced recovery beds allowed for one victim per station. Bed rails and wall sheets displayed vitals that could be monitored by all of these trained professionals. At a central elevated platform, three crew members managed coms, linked with the ship's bridge.

Seven years ago, similar medics on Earth had saved Alicia and their son.

Yet their most zealous leaders claimed *death is the natural end*. Who was that epsilon from earlier? And when had CAUSE blessed the Port Galilaei station with such an expensive and well-staffed new ship? Two medics in their late twenties sported black hair and finely cut eyebrows. Behind them came a woman with golden curls. Her sharp-muscled shoulders carried a slender face set with purpose.

Brock headed aft to an observation window. This revealed the caved-in dome only a few dozen meters away, like viz of a distant disaster in some other world. He could do nothing more—yet he might request his own treatment, possibly paid by those new taxable settlements.

"Mr. Rivers?" The slight woman, Mara, spoke faintly beside him.

"Have they examined you?" he asked.

"Waiting. Not serious. I did see you jump earlier, up the whole slope. You're a *carter*?"

Brock could reveal this truth, and perhaps more. "I try."

"Haven't seen many of them. Only heard. How do you do that?"

"Well. It takes hard choices . . . mostly high power usage . . . to live by Earth gravity." Brock focused on her gold-rimmed eyes. "What are you in for with Reyes? Apprenticeship?"

"No. I'm a mail-order bride."

On two occasions, Brock had heard that response from other women. Each time he had replied with *I'm sorry*, and needlessly offended two cultures at once.

"But you're *not* with Reyes," she said. "Must be nice to have that freedom. Even to help."

One medical alert sounded, and staffers responded. "I do what I can."

"That was you too, down there? *Fight to live forever.* Meaning what?"

Surely CAUSE wasn't listening. She was sincere, so he must answer. "That means—"

His earspace chimed. "Good morning. This message is for engineer Brock Rivers. We see you aboard. I am Costache Ionesco, the ship's epsilon. Please come to my office now."

3

BROCK
06:47 LMST, HALL 17, 44 (SYNDIC)
CRATER 21JB-094-1, XANTHE TERRA

BROCK HAD CLUNG TO HIS OXYGEN BUT RUN OUT
OF BREATHING room. If he ignored CAUSE and left their vessel,
they might attempt tracking him through *Legacy*. And if they already
knew Brock had jammed their death sermon, he and his family could
face unknown consequences.

New maps blinked onto his viz, telling him exactly where to go.

He excused himself from Mara and followed the new course.

CAUSE had tread more lightly on the Martian soil until new laws in
2120. Officials from the expanding palace of Port Alaimo—well, now
CAUSE called this Port Ares—regulated newly declared public territory.
Lord willing, most of Mars would remain wild land, accessible to
anyone fleeing their reach. Was he destined for such a life?

Inside a side levitator, he floated up to Level 1. A curved passage
between doors opened to a broader hall. Solid tiles spread toward
an astroglass floor that revealed rocky soil far beneath. This was the
ship's prow.

Viz led him through one final door into a wide office lined with dark
earthen-wood edges. Four staffers stood before an officeholder's desk.
Over this hung a full-color version of the CAUSE insignia, surrounded
by framed mementos and awards. One black-haired woman offered a
bow. *"Willkommen. Yokoso? Bienvenue?"*

"American English."

"I'm the new regional delta, Somchai Kamon. My epsilon is
Costache Ionesco."

This was him, the tall man beside her, holding his posture as stiff as his angular blond beard. He had lectured those victims about dying for the Cause.

"Mr. Rivers, we have your signal to thank for this rescue," Delta Kamon said.

So they had seen through his "anonymized" emergency vox. *Lord, help me.* But they had not mentioned his intentional block of their homily and his accidental defiance over dome vox.

"*Alba Columba* began service last month," she said. "Under my epsilon, we carry a complement of six command crew and fifty-six rescue officers. We patrol from Eos Chaos to Viking Point. Our pilot program should help secure Xanthe Terra by 2130."

Officially, no one had died in the dome. CAUSE had this to their credit.

"Delta," the epsilon said. "Mr. Reyes has arrived."

Why bring the Syndicate owners into this?

A man entered, ruddy face sweating over a full brown beard. He wasn't *the* Reuben Reyes or one of the sons. This was the nephew, Benjamin Reyes, who ran civilian ops in this hemisphere and might oversee the Xanthe projects. Then another man arrived—the dome project manager, Devonn. He ignored Brock and only watched Reyes. But he looked healthy.

"Welcome, Mr. Reyes," Kamon said. "This is the Mr. Rivers who called for rescue."

Reyes examined Brock. "After they summoned you to find the leak."

"That's true. I can report on—"

"Want to tell me now?"

Here, before CAUSE officials? "I found flaws in the structural ground bonding."

"My crew didn't detect that."

"Your subcontractor probably used Grundfast. It's not intended for a crater's incline."

"Seems to work fine elsewhere."

Brock must say this without sounding accusatory. "It might work in the short-term or on a level plain. But at temperatures below minus ten, newly forged Grundfast loses cohesion."

Devonn kept a vacant stare.

"Syndic Reyes." Delta Kamon spoke firmly. "This is your third violation this year."

So the man *had* been made a syndic. CAUSE had saved his crew's lives, but the Syndicate would never accept that debt. Reyes Syndicate had been developing this region long before CAUSE had outgrown Port Ares.

Reyes turned to Devonn. "What's our publicity on this?"

"We're, ah, releasing news of an incident."

"This CAUSE brief says they pulled thirty-three people from *our* collapsing dome." Reyes swore. "Nothing stays buried on Mars. No longer. What else do you have?"

Devonn's neck swelled.

"I know your name." Reyes turned to Brock. "You're still working indie. How long?"

Brock could answer this much. "Seven years."

Tiny viz shone under the syndic's eyes. "Your records look strange."

"Pardon?"

"Today, it's rescuing people from this site. Last month, I think it was? Back in Lowell—no, Schiaparelli." Reyes had forgotten his own calendar. "In that Chryse expedition, you found the sandfly. Last year, the Marineris probe? Losing that data would have set us back years."

Mars had many other indie repairmen. Brock shouldn't stand out this much.

"Mr. Reyes," Delta Kamon said. "We need to account for these violations."

"I'm getting to that. I think . . . the Syndicate can make a new position. Assistant manager of local infrastructure. Reports from Reyes to CAUSE. *He* could be suitable."

Brock had heard this right. "You want me to be CAUSE liaison for you."

"No more repair work. Forty to sixty hours a week, securing new projects along the Tharsis Bulge. You're already level. Seven years' work makes you a red."

Reyes waited for Kamon's reply. Epsilon Ionesco bent his head, like a synthient image.

They were offering a job with the Syndicate, paid by Reyes, but under CAUSE.

Still they had not mentioned Brock's signal-jamming and defiance of Causian dogma.

Delta Kamon activated a smile. "Today we saw a single failed project. But is that not the risk of progress? Of course, someone must still be accountable."

She meant Devonn, standing by with his sedate expression. Reyes would need to fire the man. Hours ago, Brock might have wished the same. But despite Devonn's initial misjudgment, he had finally acted. He also knew well that Brock had jammed the dome vox at least once. Why hadn't he exposed this? Was he covering for Brock or for his own system vulnerability?

"Delta Kamon, if I may," Brock said. "This error can't be one manager's fault. No one in Mr. Devonn's place could have known Grundfast would fail in those conditions."

Devonn said nothing, as if copying the epsilon's stoic manner.

"Also, thank you, Syndic Reyes, but my records hardly qualify me for such a position."

Let all of Mars grow lush with rainforest before Brock would work for CAUSE.

Reyes grunted. "How long've you been a repairman?"

"Mr. Rivers," Ionesco stated. "Your records show zero offenses, but no education or career path. You just helped rescue thirty-three people. That recommends you for progress with CAUSE. Please. Become more than a repairman. Be greater than a Syndicate liaison."

He spoke here just as smoothly as he'd spoken his lies into the dying dome.

"Aboard ships like this," Delta Kamon said, "our medical staff find new lives of service to the Cause. Like them, you can preserve humanity."

For seven years Brock had preserved his own humanity—and freedom. "I'll consider it."

Silent alarms pricked his ears. Even saying this may have been a compromise.

Delta Kamon resumed her seat. "Thank you, Mr. Rivers. You are released."

He turned to go, passing the puzzled Reyes and the silent Devonn without shared glances.

Easing down the corridor, Brock fought this strange sense of uplift. He mustn't let their praise affect him, even if by any rational thought he should wildly embrace this chance. Working sixty hours weekly, increasing his income and rank, would strengthen his own foundation. No more waiting for new jobs. No more panic over financial ruin.

Back in the levitator, he glided past deck openings to the lowest level.

What if this was the Lord's will? If he dared accept it, he could stay diplomatic. CAUSE might lead Mars differently than its secular regime governed Earth. Here they could be limited by settlers already accustomed to freedom. Only a fool would reject this chance to influence CAUSE from inside—all, of course, for the sake of Jesus and the gospel.

What a pleasant dream, fleeting as viz or false religion. In reality, if he ever criticized CAUSE, they would persecute him and the family he fought to preserve. Despite his records, they would find some evidence that revealed the truth:

He and Alicia had never wanted to leave Earth.

Seven years ago, his own people had cast them out.

4

BROCK SLIPPED LOWER INTO *LEGACY'S* CHAIR CUSHION, TOO close to the gash that he'd tried to repair with bonding tape. *Legacy* confirmed full detachment from the CAUSE medical ship.

He set course for home. Even at 450 kilometers per hour, this trip would last two hours.

A newer vehicle would cut that crossing by half, and without taped-together seats. With a Reyes/CAUSE salary, he could purchase better com chargers for Alicia or bulk diapers for Daniel. As for all those people from the dome, the lost souls he was leaving behind . . .

"Only the Lord can save," he murmured.

Whenever you're alone, speak first to the Person you worship. That's what Grandfather used to say. He had never been forced to confront Mars in all its deserted glory.

The crater's edge rushed higher, then jumped to the quev's rearview screen and drew away the wounded dome and CAUSE ship. The forward horizon was spread with chilled deserts and flecked with rocks and small impacts. To the left appeared CRATER XANTHE-34XN-198, labeled by his screen. Behind this rose the higher slope of XANTHE 98RF-345, and so many other craters and canyons, long since charted, measured, and serial-numbered.

Brock had once prayed for such adventures, to stay secure, but behold new worlds.

• • •

BROCK
08:57 LMST, HALL 17, 44 (SYNDIC)
ARES VALLES

Voices chorused in Brock's cabin, reenacting his people's act of worship in a faraway land: *"All nature sings, and round me rings the music of the spheres."*

There across Ares Valles awaited the best shelter on Mars—Areopagus. Alicia had named their skiff-turned-home after the famed Greek philosophers' mount. This might be the first family "church" on another planet. Congregation, five.

Legacy's bow pitched up, compensating with interior synth gravity cushions. Sheer cliff edges whisked under the quev, then slowed as autodrive switched off. Brock manually guided the craft up the slope where smoother regolith formed his trail, laid over four years. Morning light spilled from bedroom and galley windows. Alicia was awake.

Rear double gates opened so he could enter the bay, avoiding his crates and spare parts. Red flashes sped their tempo while cargo doors sealed. *Legacy* grounded.

1.0 ATM. 1.0 GRAVITY (EARTH CUSTOM).

He brushed open his pilot-side door and landed on the deck. Home physics matched those of the quev's interior, rightfully resisting him; each forward step fell with proper impact. Inside the hall, he shut the outer door for one more pressure equalization.

Inner doors opened to reveal Alicia in her green blouse. Her simple brown hair hung loose over the golden butterflies she'd printed on the short sleeves. They caught the light, unlike the tension and remnant fear slowly easing from her face.

"I . . . found the problem," Brock said. "Yes, the dome decompressed, but I'm well."

She threw her arms around him. "Thank the Lord."

Home gravity pressed upon him like a weighted blanket, yet his muscles throbbed, and his skin flashed raw. "Gentle. I'm sorry. I don't think I burst anything."

Alicia withdrew to check him, stroking his arms. "You sure?"

"Sure as you're married to a man who survived seconds of near-vacuum."

"Well. That's a resume boost."

This could be the last time she ever wondered if he would safely return.

Brock eased down his shoulders. He returned his navy jacket to the row of hooks beside the old Reyes Syndicate insignia covering most of this wall. The *R*'s curve formed half a red planet that shone out branches like light rays. For over four years this emblem had been stamped on his house like a foretelling.

His knees buckled until he leaned against her.

"Sweetheart. I've got you." Alicia led him to the galley and sat him at the counter. "Haven't you eaten since last night?" She poured a late breakfast of lime-green powder. This resembled Grundfast in micro, now with artificial sweetener.

"Cheers." Alicia clunked her plastic bowl with his.

Working for CAUSE, he could afford better food, and backup air for the backup air.

Brock shook off dried brown chunks from the bowl's edge, leftovers from Daniel's midnight snack.

"Sorry. Dishwater won't be recycled until noon."

"You started work early."

"After you left, I couldn't sleep well. So I tried ambient tracks for a new song."

She deserved the details. "You saw the news about CAUSE moving in for the rescue."

"Yes. How good for the Cause."

If he concealed his other news, he wouldn't be able to rest. "One of the Reyes family was there. He proposed hiring me full-time as security manager."

She stared at the table, replacing a curl behind her ear. "What do you think?"

"I haven't said no."

Thump, thump, went Alicia's spoon against her bowl. She might be fighting her own temptations—not to encourage him to consider this, but to feel that she ought.

A stat warbled beyond the main living space. Central air activated, likely in response to the opened cargo bay, and propelled heated currents through narrow channels in the arched ceiling. Brock hadn't needed to repair the system yet, but the skiff was ten years old.

"We could turn off home gravity. Stop pleading for the Lord to let us go home. We could seek the good here." He bent his head. "What could we accomplish with lower costs . . ."

Alicia touched his hand. "Then once you've earned a place, you can try missions?"

This felt like a rehearsal to show strength or stubbornness. "Reyes doesn't exist for the gospel. They want that big red *R* to become a mountain that fills the world."

Alicia poked her bowl, then brought her finger to her mouth.

"What are you thinking?"

"I'm thinking: Don't look at me like that. We're out of clean spoons."

The air blast shifted into fainter rattling hums. In a few hours, Mars' ascended sun would heat the window of their living area that held a few chairs and threadbare sofa.

"Maybe in the future . . ." Brock lowered his arm. "We won't need air-conditioning. We'll have wall specs that can absorb residual energy from hidden sources, air patterns, sound waves, or solar. They'll have perfect efficiency, enough to create heat like magic."

His arm struck and rattled the bowl. Alicia lifted one eyebrow. "How much sleep . . . ?"

"Last night, about four hours." The night before that, he had managed five hours' sleep, and the night before that, three.

"Then go rest." Alicia drew his hand from the bowl.

Soon the children would awaken. "It's my turn to help."

"Make up the time later."

In their tiny bedroom, Brock eased with a groan to lay on tousled sheets. Alicia pulled off his boots and outer shirt. She fixed his com clip to the cabinet port and darkened the room. Three stripes of pastel light shone from the windowpanes.

She bent and kissed his forehead. "If you don't rest, I'll send the kids in after you."

• • •

BROCK
14:42 LMST, HALL 17, 44 (SYNDIC)
ARES VALLES

He awakened under the wriggling, leaden weight of *something*. This creature had over-magnified gravity, building pressure on his head to Jovian levels.

"Say, 'Up, Daddy, up,'" came a bossy voice.

"'Up-addy up!'" a younger echoed.

Brock coughed. One of these little bodies had issued gaseous vapors. He opened his eyes to behold the sight of a full and pale . . . moon. Rolling aside, he scooped up Daniel and fought to hold the squirming boy over carpeted floor. "Licia! Our child is stripping again."

"I told him not to." Emma leaned in from the door, sounding less bossy and more concerned as an older sister should be. "He didn't listen."

"Well . . . why didn't you tattle on him?"

Emma put on a squint under her loose tangles of rust-gold. "What is a *tattle*?"

He had failed them. "All children should know how to do this."

Before the tiny closet door, Daniel pranced without a care. Oh please, please, he must *not* pee there, not after Alicia had finally removed stains left by previous tenants.

And there sat Adam by the cabinet, his only Earth-born child. An earnest calm overtook his seven-year-old features as he focused on Brock's reading sheet, putting into practice his new skill that he'd begun rather well about three grade levels earlier.

"Oh? You reached chapter twenty-seven. Can you pronounce the title there?"

Adam tried, "His-tor-ical the-oh-ries of the . . . at-one-ment."

"*Atonement*, but close enough."

Someday, one of them might grow into a professional Christian scholar.

• • •

BROCK
22:31 LMST, HALL 17, 44 (SYNDIC)
ARES VALLES

Hours later, Brock paced before the living room window and held the tiny bundle close to his chest. Soon he would try moving Daniel's legs. Then, if Brock could relocate him to bed, he would fulfill his debt to Alicia. Parenting was easier by tracking these little achievements.

A cello *plunked* his earspace, and he flinched. Who would send a message now?

Daniel whimpered, ready to break his sleeping spell.

"*Shhh.*" Brock pressed his back. "Please . . . this is the part when you sleep."

Daniel's breathing eased closer to that beautifully slower rate.

"While we wait, oh, I can teach you about my morning mission. Out there in the night, down there across that long gulf. Ares Valles. You can hardly see the other side. Further south lies the Silinka Valles. Ssssi-linka. It's fun to say. It does look serpentine. It pours into Barsukov Crater. This morning, I flew northwest of Barsukov and across Mojave to Xanthe Terra."

Daniel squirmed, then resettled, increasing his weight despite gaining no mass.

"It's so fascinating. Someday I can take you further out."

Somewhere out there were Justine, Mara, and Sayed, trying to live on this dead land.

Brock resumed his slow rotation before the skiff's window. All the valley had fallen dark under a sky of cold summer stars. No other lights shone out there—no slow-blinking low-atmosphere buoys or distant ships making their long descents toward Port Ares. No satellite winked above the atmosphere. Deimos and Phobos had hidden elsewhere.

"Time would fail me, small one, to tell of the many incredible features of Xanthe Terra. Our greatest fascination lies further west, Valles Marineris, the largest canyon on any known planet. Reyes Syndicate's high officials probably go *there* all the time. They earn two hundred thousand yun per sol, plus company housing, maybe com or travel credits. Ah yes, we've found our savior, not Jesus Christ, but man's great expanding empire on Mars."

Judging from his silence, Daniel must have agreed.

Brock stole through the dim hallway into the boys' room, where Alicia had already lowered the side of the makeshift crib. There he slipped Daniel down to the blanket folds.

Daniel whimpered, then returned to blessed sleep.

Nearby, Adam was quiet on his own bed, illuminating by faint golden lumen thread. Brock leaned into the glow. "Which book is this?"

Adam's gaze stuck to the page. *"The Black Stallion."*

"Great choice."

"You ever seen a horse, Daddy? Or ride a horse?"

"My parents took me to a farm in a Kentucky preserve. But I was too scared to ride."

"Well, I want to ride one someday."

"I wish I could teach you. Maybe when all the worlds are new."

Adam fell quiet, leaving Brock an opening to bid him goodnight and say *I love you.* As his son grew older, he would have even more questions about his birth planet. So would Emma, resting in her own smaller bed and room, her wispy curls tangled beneath her head.

At the bathroom door, Brock whispered through the metal to Alicia. "Daniel is secure."

"Thank you," she called. "If anyone pops back, I'll do first intervention."

"In that case . . . I'll try some night school."

"Please do. Can you look over my curriculum notes tomorrow?"

"I should be free . . . if the job boards stay quiet." And they probably would.

Back in their main room, the evening lights activated. He sat at the old console, long since converted to a study desk. Sight gestures linked his clip to the console and woke all systems. Pressure: one atmosphere, no deviations. Temperature: twenty-one degrees in all bedrooms, eighteen in the galley and main room. Weather: usual wind shear for a Martian midsummer. Climate radar: clear.

Thank you, Lord.

General yun showed the same as last night: 143. No sign of the 300 he was owed for the dome inspection. If he and Alicia cut more corners, they would survive five days.

Reyes boards showed no job listings.

Brock conveyed work data to overlay sheets. One sheet flickered, its lumen charge nearly gone. He ran analyses on his tools in the quev. Only the Lord knew how this morning's mess had damaged his forge and sensitive equipment. Really, he should resume tutoring prep for Adam and Emma, inspect the skiff pressure, then wrack his head over budget adjustments. Only then could he resume selfish pursuits.

Still, he'd promised Alicia he would study tonight.

Brock navigated to CONSOLE and SEMINARY. Two skiff repair manuals switched covers to his church history book and Scripture commentary. He readied his Bible. For his next data downstream, he might queue a second edition of the apologetics course.

Viz showed a message from Grandfather. Brock could check it, then ignore distractions.

He summoned playback. Before the skiff's outer window, Grandfather appeared, twice life-size, hovering over the night like an ancestral spirit. Lumen specs like magic dust formed the man's thick hair that fell like silver waterfalls around his dark eyes and wrinkled ears.

Grandfather leaned back toward great bookcases on his office wall. One narrow crimson wedge snapped out of his left coat sleeve, thanks to bad spec emitters.

"Evening, Brock. I wish I could see you. It's busier than usual back here, planning the fiftieth conference. Sure wish you and Alicia could rejoin us." He sat forward and glanced away. "We miss you. Seven years. That's been too long a tribulation."

Next, his grandfather would say he had no updates about their potential return.

"I think I'll break our tradition by avoiding vague promises from Legal. Still, I praise God for your faithfulness anyway. Yes, that's a platitude. It's also true."

Brock braced one elbow on the console's soft edge.

"Today I'm speechwriting. Want to help me?" Grandfather's next keynote would provoke his audience's spiritual passions. They would say *amen* and feel inspired. They would reenter the same classes, only to return home for their much simpler lives.

"First question: You seen any attempts up there to start religious preserves?"

Brock flicked his palm against the air and froze the image.

Why ask this? CAUSE barely tolerated preserves on Earth, and certainly would not expect them to grow on any other world. If anyone tried starting any church, synagogue, mosque, or non-humanistic, non-corporate faction, CAUSE would object—at least if the corporate Alaimo administration didn't first break up the new party. Neither of those prevailing systems would make room for older religions exported from the homeworld.

No one gets baptized in the rivers of Mars.

Brock restarted viz. "Second, we've done some . . . excavation at Heritage House." Grandfather's voice caught, and he smiled. "There's still a place for your own section in the family exhibit. Can you let me know what keepsakes you have? And share a few pages about their meaning in your life, to encourage and challenge others?"

Brock paused again. For any other leader, that "pastor voice" might be a professional posture. But Grandfather spoke just as earnestly as the day Brock had last embraced him.

Review his story to help for other Christians? What nonsense.

For that great Savior, whom he still loved, Brock was a defeated evangelist.

5

BROCK
01:30 LMST, HALL 18, 44 (SYNDIC)
ARES VALLES

SOMEONE DOWN THE HALL CRIED FOR HELP. BROCK
charged into the corner bathroom. The tiny sink faucet gushed precious
liters, while Emma stood by the toilet.

"Emma! Save the water!" One hand twisted shut the spout.

She had spilled more than that on the toilet. This wasn't her fault;
this seat was much too big for her. Brock used as little tissue as possible
to clean up.

"Back to bed, sweetie. I'm glad you woke up." They needn't wash
her sheets again.

Emma whispered, "I heard you talking in the main room."

"I was recording some notes. I'll try to stay quieter."

She toddled off, clutching her toy dog and trailing her thick
nightgown.

Alicia padded into the chilly corridor, wrapped in her flannel robe.
"I can take the next need. Aren't you tired? It's nearly midnight."

He knew his own mind. Despite his misgivings, Grandfather's
prompt might keep him awake for hours longer, even to speculate
how one *could* plant churches in the dead Martian soil. "Got some
homework. Grandfather knew to mark the anniversary."

She glanced down. "That's kind of him. But those dates don't matter
much here."

Hours passed. Brock tried to let Alicia's warmth and the comfort
of bed lull his mind into rest. Instead, his thoughts kept scattering
against the dark.

For all his insistence on never forgetting Earth, he might be going
native. This was missional drift. As the family "captain," he had been

derelict. Alicia didn't need to hear his despair. She also shouldn't need to tolerate his fatigue tomorrow.

Gray viz hovered half a meter from bed: 03:39. Not in weeks had he stayed up this late.

Grandfather may have assigned homework only to make Brock feel included in ministry work. Well, why not? Brock could enjoy the pretense, and perhaps even help Grandfather feel included in the life of a Martian pioneer. To do this, he should finally open the memento crate.

• • •

BROCK
03:52 LMST, HALL 18, 44 (SYNDIC)
ARES VALLES

There it waited, in the corner of the bay, sitting beside the metal sheets Brock had fastened together to form a worktable. Apart from some disastrous leak, this silver-walled octagonal box, one meter wide, should have resisted repeat exposures to the atmosphere.

Brock shivered as he climbed past his grounded quev.

One ping confirmed his ID. He clenched the upper handle and pressed . . . *click.* Pressure released. If only he could smile with affection for these packing blankets and foam capsules. Each touch of fabric stung his fingers with preserved cold. Really, these things shouldn't harm him. In truth, he had acted rather rudely, locking them up as if blaming innocent objects for sin.

This first object had been added at the last minute. It was one of *those* fine napkins. He had never meant to steal it. One white corner bore the golden letter *H* with curving sides, like a DNA segment. Another corner showed spots of old blood.

He sighed and laid this on the worktable. Otherwise it might get mixed with the rough-pilled gray blankets. These he moved aside to reveal the first ordered items—several thick white notebooks with flexible, intact covers. One spine was labeled *2095*. He opened to page one—an old digital sheet, its writing locked like a memory:

Brock had asked his first scientific question at age three. *"Why do we need air?"*

His father Stanford told him, *"Because the Lord made us to breathe. Even in eternity, we'll have good limitations. We will always need the air Jesus made for us."*

Even then, far away in the Ohio preserve, Brock had longed to see worlds beyond.

Later books conserved his oldest creations. Original artwork showed an alien planet, covered in blue crayon without land but with astronauts, possibly sailing on seas of methane. *Brock R., age 6.* From this he'd soon graduated to colored pencils, trying complex shapes and shading, ironically enough, for a planet of rust-red rocks and jagged mountains. Another sheet showed his best version of orbital waystation L5, but with three rings dangerously imbalanced.

His parents had never left the homeworld. They too had always enjoyed free air.

Beneath the notebooks was the tiny Earth that Grandfather had given for Brock's seventh birthday. Back then, the globe was already fifty years old. Its Middle East showed more countries. Japan was yet untouched, and China loomed larger—in fact, Grandfather had said the gift's first owner had worked in China for decades in that old job that none now dared attempt in the secular world, that of a *missionary*.

Grandfather had told Brock that, many years ago, missionaries left their homes to live in other countries. They worked and met friends. They started churches and taught people about Jesus. Often they suffered persecution, far different from the lives Brock's people enjoyed.

Every day the missionaries had seen new lands and peoples, bringing good news.

Going back to the days of Jesus's apostles, these faithful saints had seen adventures, miracles, healings, and all the most incredible stories of the early and medieval churches. Without them, Brock and his people could have never existed.

Brock found the tiny half-peeled gold star placed as close as possible to Cincinnati. His parents helped stick it there, marking his Biblical Christian preserve led by CIRCLE.

He flipped past his graduation certificate from CIRCLE's middle school. Then on to the plastic box frame holding his high school badge, BROCK R. They had abbreviated his last name to prevent undue attention. After all, Caleb Rivers, his great-grandfather, was the founder of CIRCLE—effectively, the Rivers clan's last missionary. Family tales and evangelical histories both told how Caleb moved to Cincinnati in the early 2060s to teach at an unaccredited Bible college. Standing at an old whiteboard, before skeptical allies, Caleb used a famous black marker to spark a new reformation, complete with a new acronym:

CIRCLE: Center for International Renewal of Christian Life and Education.

Years later, CIRCLE had become the *de facto* capital of Ohio's first religious preserve, culturally and legally guarding its Biblical Christian people from secular government, selectively preserving their liberties but forbidding their exercise in the rest of the world.

This preserve was Brock's homeworld, the air he breathed.

But sometimes new ideas would leak in from the outside. The next book held photos of the smiling Dr. Colin Van Campen beside Brock himself, a young man of fourteen, slender yet broad-shouldered, with straight brown hair. Adam might grow to look like this.

What a mighty witness Dr. Van Campen had been, despite coming from outside CIRCLE. As an academic refugee, his secular astrophysics degrees had mattered little when CAUSE caught him sympathizing with religious groups. He had joined the new Harding School of Engineering within CIRCLE. Within months, he shared his testimony before a crowd of hundreds at Brock's own high school, speaking on interstellar wonders and the gospel.

At the end, Brock stood to ask a question—not about the speaker's new-forged faith, but about quantum research.

Students were aghast. Parents complained to Brock's mother. Dr. Van Campen even shushed Brock from the platform. But later he requested Brock visit his office after class.

"I didn't know you people knew about that," he'd said, meeting Brock at his door.

You people. Wasn't this great mind one of them, a special kind of Christian himself?

Fourteen-year-old Brock said, "Do you mean . . . *quantum vaulting* is real?"

"Of course it's real. It's hardly a great secret. CAUSE is testing out vault machines. Maybe for private use. So, young man, remind me. What revolves around what?"

"Excuse me?" That question made no sense.

"What astronomy do they teach at CIRCLE? What orbits what?"

"Earth orbits Sol, about three-sixty-five point twenty-five days per revolution."

Dr. Van Campen said, "Well, thank Heaven they won't go *Galileo* on me—"

"Do you mean the Galileo persecution? Because actually the Church didn't . . ."

The professor dismissed him, sending Brock into new research about two startling truths.

The first truth? Quantum vaulting did exist. Later in public, Dr. Van Campen explained how near-instant transfer between entangled-space machines may soon become the last century's third greatest scientific breakthrough, following affordable fusion and synthetic gravity.

As for the second truth? Dr. Van Campen would rather be torn to pieces in a misaligned quantum vault than lecture at a Biblical Christian high school.

Brock's mentor had been torn from his original calling. At least he found paying work.

• • •

BROCK
00:10 LMST, HALL 19, 44 (SYNDIC)
ARES VALLES

On the next morning, Brock found no new tasks whose payments could offset a recent supply run. He was forced to transfer yun from savings.

That evening, Alicia and he quietly did their best to celebrate their love anyway.

Hours afterward, he surrendered to sleeplessness and returned to the bay. In the crate he found Dr. Van Campen's first textbook, *And The Firmament Shows*, first edition. Within weeks of meeting the man, Brock had begun exploring data about quantum vaulting and its potential for human expansion beyond Earth. Secular materials shared the human race's incredible story, led by the Cause that Brock was always taught to reject.

Here were all the notebooks with Brock's findings. Thinner books noted the duty of foreign missions that Christians had followed, centuries before CAUSE, the One Humanity Accords, and the religious preserve system that shaped Brock's world and restricted the wonders of any other lands. But his ancestors had solved that problem simply by obeying the Great Commission. By serving as missionaries, they could keep their own world while beholding other worlds. Who could take up the forgotten way of the old saints?

Why, Brock himself.

Full of this youthful zeal, he had no choice but to share his beliefs in public.

Beneath more filled notebooks, he found that old viz of his sixteen-year-old self, in his old bedroom, pronouncing big ideas to his high school network.

Mom and Dad held their own frustrations with CIRCLE. That had probably led them to their abrupt move the year before Brock's exile. But if his parents had ever seen some of Brock's opinions, they would have challenged him to be gracious, or else warned him about his zeal.

What excitement that would be. Brock wasn't wandering from the gospel, but from the sheltered people of CIRCLE! He only wanted to restore a biblical truth they had missed.

Brock turned another page and found himself at age seventeen. The younger Brock had moved from his bedroom into a borrowed church classroom, for a memorized speech.

"We live in God's world. Science is His idea. If we study science, we're studying God."

He needed no audio to recall each word, complete with that classroom echo.

"None of this weakens our faith. These help us know God better. So why doesn't today's Church care about this truth? We neglect this truth just like we neglect all creation. It's like we've made our tinier worlds and rested from our labors."

"Such a clever young man." Brock's real voice fell into the bay with one flat echo.

The first page of *CIRCLE School of Rhetoric* held photos from the Senior Social. He had asked Alicia Beth Hyatt to join him there, and she said yes. Her parents were long friends with Brock's parents, all on CIRCLE faculty. Even as a boy, Brock had never known anyone like her.

That very next autumn, they began their joyful courtship and their university classes: theology and engineering for Brock, English literature and music for Alicia. He gently turned to the photos of their courtship's joyous finale, dated July 27, 2116. How beautiful she looked in white raiment edged with gold, aided by her two younger sisters and best friends. On the next page stood Brock with his best man, Alexander Moore, and many other brothers plus CIRCLE leaders—Dr. Patrick Keller, Dr. Harold Templeton, with his father and Grandfather.

Not long before that moment, Alexander insisted that he quote from Acts during the wedding, reminding them all that Jesus had left His "bride," the Church, and would return to reunite with her only after her people served as evangelists. Templeton kindly scoffed at that. At first, Brock tried to defend Alexander's motive if not his argument. When Alicia and her family intervened against that diversion, Alexander held his peace.

One way or another, he must have learned Brock and Alicia were forced to leave.

Perhaps a little nepotism had secured Brock and Alicia a one-month break before they began grad school. He flipped past their paper menus from the student café, that rainy night in October, on which they'd penned their grandiloquent life statements.

Alicia had written, *I will share the secret glories of art and music with the real world, where people repeat the melodies but cannot know the true words.*

Brock declared, *I will learn God's gifts of science to help build communication in the real world, helping lead diverse peoples beyond our preserves.*

One year later, Alicia had taken her happiest test. By next summer, they would be parents. She was assistant-teaching. Brock had joined CIRCLE's media department, working better with the elders. He and Alicia were ready for a new adventure. Perhaps even to try an experimental missionary journey.

Here lay one isolated page. Like the cloth napkin, it was likely thrown into the crate at the last minute. Brock reached down with cold fingers. The page showed a printed map of downtown Cincinnati, with outlined destinations and walking paths.

If only they had not earned that bonus in March 2118.

If only they had ordered supplies from a preserve business.

And if only he had not returned to the missionary biographies, learned of Alexander's faith struggles, or had that one bad conversation with Mom and Dad in fall 2117, or—

"Aren't you cold out here?"

He was vaulted back to the present. Alicia stepped into the bay, wrapped in her blue robe.

"You caught me. And no, I'm well." He would be, if he stopped here and returned to bed.

"Oh." Alicia took the stained napkin from his worktable. "I thought we threw this away."

"It's still a memorial. Not everything about that trip was terrible."

She leaned on the table, bracing her foot on warmer floor pads. "That day before we took our tour outside the preserve, I remember you apologizing for not reserving a shuttle."

"In my defense, I was thinking of you as a missionary, not a very pregnant wife."

He couldn't laugh, but Alicia did. "Oh, the things we surrendered for ministry."

On that warm sunlit Friday in late May, they had felt so much gain. Never before had they left the preserve to enter the large secular city of Cincinnati together—not just a permissible visit for the purpose of trade, but a small act of subversion, a test "missionary journey." First, he and Alicia partook in the city's wonders. The outside world became real. Mighty towers burst upward. Glowing sharp lines resembled a viz overlay, mingled with high walking bridges, parks and ponds, levitators, ports for trains and shuttles. Spicy scents drifted over roads. Crowd clamor mixed with music from classic and contemporary genres.

All of this "dead" land was alive, a vast new world to explore.

They bought snacks. They even engaged in a witness encounter with women at the baby furniture boutique. Brock marveled at citizens who could no longer wonder at the majesty of their own world. He spotted a cadre of CAUSE officers, likely on leave from Port Cincinnati, the American Midwest's first gateway to commerce beyond Earth.

Before these people's very eyes, at cost to no one, while not *technically* defying the Accords, he and Alicia could "share" the gospel with their actions even if not their words.

Alicia was full of energy, too. Secretly, Brock had planned a surprise dinner. He took her to the Hourglass. What a perfect conversation they enjoyed on the top level of 18, surrounded by so much wealth. Brock was sharing spiritual wisdom when Alicia grimaced.

He asked what was wrong. She could only say, *"The baby."*

Brock called her mother at Samaritan back home. He paid the high bill and used napkins for desperate cleanup. Brock took her to the ground floor, but it was too late. Her labor was unstoppable. He didn't call for an ambulance; the Hourglass staff did that. Inside the craft, two medics stabilized Alicia and vainly insisted he provide her health information.

Brock tried to arrange a return to the CIRCLE preserve.

No one listened. The medics brought them to Cincinnati General Health Center. In there, secular doctors cut open his best friend and saved the life of their infant son: Adam Caleb Rivers.

But here in the bay, Brock released his words: "I nearly surrendered our child."

Alicia fingered the napkin's edges, avoiding its long-preserved blood from her own body. "I don't suppose you kept the immigration forms that man brought in."

"I turned them over to Timothy Sheldon at CIRCLE. His team wanted it all."

"Sir, I'm sorry," the hospital legal department man had said. *"This is a division of the Cincinnati public health system. You've acted outside any preserve. That means your child cannot be a preserve resident. He's a citizen of the world."*

Beside him, a white-haired young woman nodded gravely. She had seemingly arrived out of nowhere, her lime uniform and badge identifying her as a Minister. He had never in person seen someone from the Ministry, CAUSE's domestic enforcer of preserve law. And never had Brock heard anything like this challenge of their citizenship.

Alicia's parents were visiting family in Florida, and Brock's parents were much further away. His only help came from CIRCLE's highest leadership. Dr. Sheldon quickly arrived, along with two other church elders as well as Grandfather himself.

In these men's view, they had three options, each terrible in its own way.

First, Brock and Alicia could beg CIRCLE to fight this, resisting fifty years of legal precedent after the One Humanity Accords, and risking Adam's removal by social services.

Second, they could move to the secular world, suppressing their faith and parenting Adam as best they could. Perhaps they could cling to new fantasies—that they would learn to live apart from their family in the preserve, or that Adam would not be trained by all his surrogate parents in the system to be a good citizen in service of the Cause.

Third, they could emigrate elsewhere, forsaking their people but finding refuge in another world—in fact, the freest settlements in the solar system, at least for now.

In the bay, Alicia set down the napkin. "You and I had the best intentions."

And if they ever re-tried such *religious activity*, city authorities or educators would learn. In the future, Adam himself might be legally obligated to inform on his own parents.

They'd returned all their baby items and transferred every scrap of yun, originally saved for their new duplex near campus. One-quarter of those earnings granted them two costly tickets with a launch window: PINNACLE STATION 12, MONDAY, JUNE 6, 2118, 3 TO 5 PM EASTERN TIME. How those daily CAUSE updates over viz mocked him.

Even as CIRCLE prepared for its 43rd conference, Alicia and Brock packed all they could fit into three large square containers, plus the small octagonal crate.

They took a public shuttle into Port Cincinnati.

Like a great sleek ziggurat, wrapped in bands of gray and rust-red, the CAUSE migration ship towered against the heavens. Her queue lasted hours. Ceaseless viz and vox propaganda promised passengers new life on a frontier world, destined for the brave.

In moments, his old world had shrunk into a map beyond the cabin windows.

Every day became night. During most of those 24-hour cycles, baby Adam screamed.

Brock and Alicia had ignored their people's cautions and resisted their preserve limits in hopes of taking the gospel into other worlds. Now the civil magistrate—a servant of God?—had responded, punishing their foolish and likely sinful action by giving them just what they wanted.

6

THAT NIGHT, BROCK AND ALICIA HELD ONE
another in bed until the chills subsided.

No more jobs arrived overnight or the next morning. After a
scant breakfast, Brock returned to the bay and took photos of each
memento. Then he packed them all back into the crate among blankets
and foam pellets, restoring their order, with one exception. He had
placed the stained napkin on the crate's very bottom, with their old
summer clothes.

Seven summers ago, Grandfather and the elders had generously
paid for open coms, so they already knew what happened after Brock
left Earth.

By the record, the voyage lasted two months. Brock could not
imagine attempting this without plasma propulsion, synthetic gravity,
and whatever small luxuries even a D-class cabin could provide.
Early astronauts, of course, had gone willingly on this adventure, and
unburdened by an infant who should have never been brought out here.

The CAUSE migration ship *Valkyrie* glided into Port Alaimo, then
disgorged its settlers into their exciting new lives in a city of insulating
nets and regulations. Brock found a consignment dealer who refused to
go lower on the least-terrible quev in the bay. By some quirk of divine
hilarity, the craft's previous owner had christened this the *Legacy*.

For two years, they survived inside *Legacy*. Alicia's writing provided
enough yun for data links and their food. Only by providence did Brock
find better work. Months later, they found the Reyes Syndicate–owned
skiff, abandoned high upon an Ares Valles embankment.

At the time, Brock felt poetic, citing Jeremiah 51 about *a land of drought and a desert.*

If Grandfather seriously wanted to start Biblical Christian churches on Mars, this skiff probably qualified as the first and only one.

• • •

BROCK
11:20 LMST, HALL 24, 44 (SYNDIC)
ARES VALLES

Five days later, the family account reached zero yun. No jobs arrived over the boards, and no reply came from Grandfather. Brock stepped up his teaching for the children, then tried to busy his body and mind with chores in the utility bay. He patched his atmoskin as best he could and stowed this in the quev. He re-checked all fluid levels, then sprayed a spec refresher on the skiff's outer gate. Viz showed atmosphere secure at 1.0 ATM.

Out of curiosity, he tried to look up Sayed. Record trails ended with the medical ship *Alba Columba*. Sometime he might try to contact them, claim to be family, and learn his fate.

Anyone in this barren world must labor for every breath. You couldn't waste time dreaming about other worlds, either on one's distant home planet or in spiritual realms. Only people granted free oxygen could afford those luxuries.

Brock set down the spec canister and clutched his forehead.

Here on Mars, the Lord provided a one-percent carbon dioxide atmosphere. Only on Earth did the Creator grace everyone with air, and every Scripture assumed Earth as center stage for God's work. Jesus would make His Church a temple before He ever returned to Earth. Where did that leave a near-vacuum frozen world about two hundred million kilometers away?

Brock checked *Legacy*'s latrine. Its water tank showed empty, but he couldn't afford to refresh that supply with any gallons from the skiff. In the latrine mirror, he glimpsed his own face. His beard had long outgrown the condition that Alicia teasingly called "unkempt theologian." These days he more closely resembled a desperate prospector.

No longer could he retreat to his studies. They were a false escape. Even free education cost data and time. What good was training for another man's mission?

Here in the real world, the God who allowed all this to happen might be guiding him toward working with some Reyes Syndicate/ CAUSE alliance. If a man could not provide for his family, how could he serve anyone else? He could no longer afford to delay his choice.

• • •

BROCK
12:20 LMST, HALL 24, 44 (SYNDIC)
ARES VALLES

At lunch, Brock found Alicia waiting for him at the galley table.

"Love," he told her. "I think returning to Earth has become my idol."

Her face didn't change. "Do you mean you want to accept the Reyes position?"

Brock's hands clenched together on the table.

"If it's not *wrong* to take the job, then . . ." Alicia set down her cup. "Let's do it. But if you want to stay indie, keeping your study time, we can try depending on my work."

Brock returned to the bay and stood beside the closed storage crate. At last he summoned a vox. Viz edges lit orange, and he took one breath before speaking. "Syndic Reyes, this is Brock Rivers. If your position is still available, how should I apply?"

• • •

BROCK
18:50 LMST, HALL 24, 44 (SYNDIC)
ARES VALLES

Reyes kept silent all day, until chilled sunlight had vanished over the western horizon and Brock's viz flashed. He left the bay and entered the bedroom to answer.

"This is Ben Reyes, about your message."

With heart pounding, Brock shut the door. "And your answer?"

"We already found a candidate."

Window glass pressed Brock's forehead, thin and cold, like this weight in his lungs.

"If you'd voxed yesterday, we could've gotten you started."

"Do you have anything else? Any other salaried work?"

"Nothing else for a while."

Viz collapsed into streaks on the blackened glass while Brock's exhale drew fog on the surface. He shut his eyes and steadied his voice. "You have nothing now . . ."

"No. Frankly, this new position was yours to refuse, Mr. Rivers."

Chilled glass pressed to Brock's hand, and he clenched fingers just as cold and hard. Oh, the ripostes he could hurl at this irritatingly professional man. "Mr. Reyes, I can prove that—"

With a buzz, Reyes ended the vox.

Brock retreated from the window and wiped his hands through viz. He must refuse the temptation of standing here, lost in anything like despair, much less unjustified anger.

Cry out to the Lord. There was an old thought, with all the simplicity of a child, or the faith of one. Only a fool would be ungrateful for the other day's deliverance. But wouldn't a second-rate fool expect two providential escapes within a week?

Well. If he did this, he must say it aloud. "Lord God—"

Another signal? Viz splashed in green, a strange sequence. "This is Rivers."

Color covered his face, a blanket of warm golds amid luxuriant greens and watery blues. Before this palette lifted a new face, showing dark eyes under wrinkled silver hair.

"Brock?" Grandfather must not have known his recording had already started.

"Well, go on," Brock muttered.

"Can you hear me?"

"Yes?" This was a live signal?

"Good. Hello! I see the top of your head. Also, you need to make your bed."

They had not talked like this in years! "Grandfather, how are you doing this?"

"This is a Q-link, fully paid by your family at CIRCLE. Keep it live as long as you like."

Even with a choppy signal, oh, how Brock ached for those seas of flowing foliage, real, living Earthen trees that grew among free and natural warmth, a whole world away.

"Wait. Are you well?"

He must have seen Brock's expression, which left no reason to hide the truth. "Sir, we are alive and breathing, so praise the Lord for that. But financially . . ."

"I will send some yun. Two thousand four hundred. It's for your contract work."

Refreshed and heated air, as if from that summery planet, coursed down from hidden vents. The cold was gone. He could provide for the warmth that stilled those fears.

"Not for the last time, you're an answer to prayer."

Grandfather leaned aside to reveal more of the headquarters' rooftop garden, washed with early sunlight. "Good to hear. We've had some shakeup here. Can't wait to share more! But we want you back in time for the conference in a few weeks. Let's hear in person, about your work on Mars."

But this wasn't possible. Not in their position, and not with—

"We can provide the travel and lodging. As soon as today, we can reserve your fare, and at least for that week, you and Alicia can come home."

• • •

BROCK
19:28 LMST, HALL 24, 44 (SYNDIC)
ARES VALLES

The vision had come to life—all of Brock's children sprawled on stacks of pillows to speak with their grandfather, interacting as best they could with this faraway visitor.

Standing in the galley, Alicia whispered, "Love, can we really just *vault* to Earth?"

"The kids can stay with the Starr family," Brock mused.

"Longer than overnights?"

Brock had messaged Michael, who was fascinated by the idea and had himself made the offer. "They've let us watch Rachel longer. I might trust them even if they weren't in the faith."

"Even if we leave the planet."

Elizabeth Starr had helped Alicia give birth to Emma. In return, Alicia helped inspire Elizabeth to leave the Port Ares medical system and become an indie midwife. She then aided with Alicia's third pregnancy and their in-home delivery of Daniel. That partnership had led to genuine friendship, and later the conversion of both Elizabeth and Michael.

But he dared not take this lightly. If only he could bring his whole family to Earth. Someday, perhaps. "We'd leave in a few weeks, for the big anniversary conference starting June twenty-first. Grandfather acted like he had some great secret." Brock shut his eyes. "I could try to be skeptical. We shouldn't. We need his help."

Daniel waddled up and lifted his arms. Alicia bent to sniff his hindquarters. "Yep."

What timing. "My turn or yours?"

"Mine. Your grandfather's donation will help stock more than clean diapers."

They would need no expenses beyond basic power and heat for the skiff. A remote utility would monitor systems.

Adam walked in from the main room. "Great-Grandest is asking for the grown-ups."

Grandfather waved to them, unaware of his arm vanishing into the viz gap. "All right, kids. Let's discuss your visit to CIRCLE. Yes, we want you to share about Mars, but I long to see you again." He glanced aside, as if distracted by a waving branch. "Either way, when you're here, I can reveal my surprise."

Alicia faced Brock with gleaming eyes.

This could be real. After seven years, CIRCLE's legal team could have won an exemption from the city government. The only greater event would be Heaven opening and Jesus returning. Without surrendering Adam as a world citizen, Brock and Alicia might bring their family back to stay with their people forever.

• • •

BROCK
EIN. 9, 44 (SYNDIC)
ARES VALLES

Two days before his homeworld's June 21, Brock readied home systems for partial atmosphere shutdown mode. Using part of Grandfather's 2,400 yun, they bought two valises and packed all their long-unused summer clothes, including Brock's old suit coat. From there, they trained the children for their first stay with another family.

Alicia carefully trimmed his beard from the status of old-prospector to kempt-theologian.

On the nights of June 19 or June 20, no one slept well.

Brock spent those evenings pacing the main room. So much could go wrong during this trip. At best, the children could misbehave in the Starr family's apartment, or at worst, say the name "Jesus" too loudly in one of those public parks for Causians. Back on Earth, Brock and Alicia would face questions, even accusations, from people who didn't know their whole story. As for the "surprise," Grandfather would likely use his keynote in Heritage Hall to mention his grandson's work on Mars, then bid him go in peace to be warmed and filled.

• • •

BROCK
6:00 LMST, EIN. 12, 44 (SYNDIC)
ARES VALLES

The day had come. Brock had triple-checked his clocks, but checked once more while he and Alicia brought their children to the skiff's bay. For Cincinnati it was Thursday, June 21, early afternoon, 16:00 local time on Mars. Adam had packed all his things, but Emma and Daniel needed help to ensure they had all clothing, hygiene tools, and small toys.

Brock verified their partial home shutdown and utility monitoring.

At 16:27, Brock confirmed all crew aboard and pressurized the quev. He opened the bay and slipped into cold daylight. Com reported balmier weather for this late summer. He dared raise the quev to a 20-meter altitude and set course for Port Ares at 700 kph.

"Can we play music?" Emma shouted.

They hadn't done this in a while. Alicia retrieved a mix of late-1900s Sunday-morning preschool classics. On such a day, Brock didn't mind their cheesy racket.

About an hour later, Port Ares crept within sight. Brock invited Adam up front to see the city, whose furthest borders swept like a crater's rim across the desert wilderness. *Legacy* approached the settlement's outer ridges, formed of scattered dwellings made of rougher native materials. As the quev rushed forward, these structures drew closer together like stones at a mountain base, their appearance growing smoother and shinier. Here and there, fine raiment of insulating fibers, like silken spiderwebs, draped between buildings, containing shared air pressures to form pseudo-outdoor environments.

By autodrive *Legacy* entered the inbound lanes of Alaimo Courseway, the dense central route between outer sprawls of brick-compression factories and prefabricated housing. Drifting maps on the quev's window margins showed alternate routes and traffic patterns. In this late afternoon, most vehicles bore the gray-blue patterns and insignias of CAUSE.

• • •

BROCK
17:31 LMST, EIN. 12, 44 (SYNDIC)
PORT ARES

One hour later, Brock told himself that he had *not* left his children with strangers. Asking the Starrs for help was a big step, yet not as significant as this upcoming journey.

That thought pinched at Brock's stomach, as if he were preparing to skydive.

He knew this area, Port Ares's cavernous central hub, yet he and Alicia struggled to walk in the lighter gravity. This causeway crossed Probe Point. Three levels below, tourists congregated on a vast floor to see the NASA memorial or the glass-encased probe itself. Overhead, a glass-segmented dome revealed the already sunsetting heavens, bedecked with 189 flags, one for each member nation of CAUSE.

"I heard Michael wants you to bring back Earth souvenirs?" Alicia said.

"Mm. A physical Bible, or materials on New Testament Greek." Here even a whisper might carry. Few officers striding these halls would tolerate such conversation.

"He seemed more quiet than usual," Alicia said.

"Licia."

"Yes?"

"Michael and the kids aren't making us worry." Their valises' wheels gently clicked on faux-marble green floors. Alicia's fingers tightened against his, while red arrows winked across her head. "Left here."

Brock led them to an array of levitator tubes, where they ascended one level and followed signs toward HUB 21. One aisle led them through wide glass doorways. Port attendants darted between three queues of people, giving instructions, checking IDs for civilians, waving CAUSE officers closer to the front.

This might look like any apartment complex, if not for the roars inside the vaults.

Fifteen years ago, Brock had learned from Dr. Van Campen about these incredible machines. Now they would actually step into a quantum vault.

Brock checked in with a human attendant, sharing the destination codes he had received from Grandfather for a Port Cincinnati center. This process felt little different from signing into any public transport, or for that matter, booking a room at a preserve hotel.

"IDed and all good," said the young female Causian. She pointed to one vault door. Brock stepped forward with Alicia at his side.

The operator stopped him and smiled. "First vaulting? One passenger at a time."

Brock couldn't protest while the operator motioned for Alicia to enter the neighboring vault. At least they could vault out together and arrive in Port Cincinnati at the same time.

Black viz numbers marked his vault door, which slid aside.

I love you, he mouthed.

Alicia whispered it back just before their hands parted.

He pulled his valise after him into his vault, following the orders, standing inside the floor's meter-wide red circle. With a hiss, the door sealed. Glass walls throbbed like a living organ, extending a circle of hand-length silvery flanges at waist level.

His earspace popped as Alicia voxed, "Jesus, please keep us together, literally."

Brock slowed his breath. "Let this experience be thrilling, not terrifying. Amen."

Their vox ended.

"Welcome to the Port Ares Quantum Travel Plex," came a male voice. "Quantum vaulting is a nonhazardous method to relocate persons between entangled space."

Instructional viz appeared in the door, showing doorways and arcing arrows.

"Once you have entered the vault, please stand in the exact center circle. Keep your hands, feet, and peripherals in this circle. Do not attempt to hold your breath. After the vaulting process is complete, do not exit the vault until the light flashes and you hear the all clear. In the event of an emergency or adverse physical reaction to the vaulting sequence, sensors will detect personal distress. First aid will be available at your destination."

Brock might be today's only traveler to watch each animation very carefully.

Red light creased over his head to his boots, then vanished into darkness. Something must have gone wrong. Their yun had not cleared, or their code was bad.

The hum shifted, throttling into a higher-pitch rushing like flames.

FWOOOOOMMM! Blazing white particles burst from the chamber flange into a shimmering, blinding cloud. They filled the vault and birthed energy strands that coursed about him, coating the floor and walls, the ceiling, his valise, his own body. Static charges crackled while tornadic roars formed irresistible gravities that pulled him up and down, casting him into this astrophysical sorcery.

7

BROCK
5 P.M. EDT, THURSDAY, JUNE 21, 2125
CIRCLE PRESERVE, CINCINNATI

TITANIC FORCES RELEASED BROCK, AND SEARING light faded to reveal a different place. The glass was darker, and the encircling flange gleamed musky copper instead of silver. The tall gate on Mars had collapsed into this smaller door. Beyond the glass, the environment had shifted to the outer wall of a small room. Roars diminished as glowing threads unwrapped his head and neck. More faint tingles darted up his legs. Particles withdrew to the center flange, which burned as the light dimmed into millions of pinpricks.

He lifted one foot. The resistance was Earth standard. Imagine it! No floor spectra simulated this force that pulled him so naturally. Here was the good gravity of home.

Brock had truly done it—experienced a quantum vaulting.

His viz shifted clocks from 17:46 LMST to 5:02 PM local time. Thanks to the Overseer of all orbits, today he had lost only 45 minutes. And on this world, despite its woes, he could escape those ten-cycle abominations of the dueling Martian calendars. Today was Thursday.

A man's voice said, "Vaulting complete," and red light speared the chamber.

"Brock?" Alicia called over vox. She must have arrived in a neighboring vault.

"I'm here, love."

"All in one piece?" the same man asked. His accent sounded like New England, almost familiar. Whoever this CAUSE staffer was, God bless him.

"I'm well. You can let out my wife first."

"Can't do that yet, Brock," the other said. "Clear out so she can vault in."

Only one vault? "Is this not Port Cincinnati?" So he left her far away on Mars?

Brock's door slid aside, and he slipped out of this much smaller vault into a wide room with low ceiling. There, standing by a tiny stat on the vault, was the tall form of Dr. Colin Van Campen, unmistakable, with that same gray beard and padded shoulders on his long gray jacket. He whirled about with flying coattails and folded his arms around Brock. "You made it."

Brock trembled in this powerful embrace. "How?"

"She's coming in, promise." Dr. Van Campen tagged the stat, sealing the vault door and restarting the machine's roughened hum. He clicked once again—

FWOOOMM. The vault burst into new roaring flame, re-entangling spaces.

Soon she would be here.

Van Campen wiped his face. "Never thought I'd ever get to help you through a vault."

The chamber barely contained its whirled lightning, but its surrounding room looked like other storms had blasted against the walls, throwing open doors and scattering old devices among palettes and boxes. CIRCLE had not changed the low, white ceiling with 2060s square patterns. Flat walls held high windows of slanted glass that spilled in . . . oh, such warm and natural *blue* light. "This is the Harding School basement."

"And kept in pristine condition."

The vault shuddered, powering down. Alicia had come. Her red skirt wrapped tight around her knees and spiral sleeves clung to her arms. She opened her hand, holding the butterfly earrings he'd managed to find for their fifth anniversary.

When the door reopened, she timidly emerged, and he took her hand.

"Welcome, daughter, to our finest in quantum transport," Van Campen said.

Alicia lifted one hand for balance. "This is CIRCLE campus?"

"I thought we would vault into Port Cincinnati," Brock said.

"And I thought your grandfather sent you instructions with the new vault code."

Brock had seen the code, but yes, he had missed that unread note glyph.

Their host guided them toward the basement's wide staircase and quickly ascended the stairs, then took them to a wider passage. Instead of leading them to the front hall, he turned to a back foyer. Two absurdly thin glass doors guarded this interior from the outside.

Alicia's hand trembled in his.

These doors couldn't maintain pressure. One small impact could shatter them, letting oxygen burst out and lethal chills rush in—

They need not fear, not in this place.

Glass panes poured warm light over the violet-polished floor, and onto a pair of shining black shoes. Silken black pant legs led up to a white shirt, under that same long crimson jacket with luxuriant sleeves and matching puff tie. Grandfather's long silver hair looked immaculate, straight in the back and curled in the front. There was his same cologne like freshly cut wood.

He embraced them both. "Oh, welcome home!"

Brock's eyes watered as the corridor reeled.

"Whoa there." Grandfather asked others, "Excuse us, please."

Two other men had arrived. Brock was caught by waves like motion sickness . . . until warmth smothered him, pressing his neck. *Stay oriented. Floor goes beneath, and golden-white ceiling goes above.* "Grandfather," he managed. "CIRCLE now has *vaults*?"

"Just the one," Van Campen said, "and best kept out of sight."

Two glass doors closed behind them, and they entered a new land.

The unbroken blue canopy spread over lush green lawns. Walls of solid silver jewels lifted to form buildings, free-standing, without domes or webbing. Mulch bases, all sculpted into circles, supported real and firm trees whose foliage colored the grass with finely drawn shadows, speckled by natural sunlight that beamed through thick branches.

Air danced over his face, so simple and free. Birds chirruped melodies and insects droned. Humans held quiet conversations, not from narrow halls or emitters, but in distant places from which their sounds drifted through air itself. In this place was so much life!

Alicia lifted her gaze to their homeworld skies, then quickly bent her head. There in the garden, a true butterfly landed. Not viz. Its shining blue wings opened and closed.

"Alexander," Grandfather said. "Take the lady's luggage?"

"Yes, sir!" The reply came from that younger man with a trimmed blond beard. Alexander? He was back with the preserve, then, and working with CIRCLE?

"Brock, you know Mr. Moore. Our new chief executive of com relations?"

And he was working here happily and successfully? "I thought you—"

"Yes. I know." That eager and firm handshake was also new. Alexander had kept his same high and enthusiastic tone, yet with new maturity, perhaps even wisdom. "I've seen lots of growth since you had to leave. Hard work of sanctification. Your grandfather's helped a lot."

The man who had once argued and disparaged the Church before church elders, including Dr. Templeton and Grandfather himself, was now reconciled to CIRCLE.

Just like that, Brock's ten years of missing their friendship may be ended.

At some point, Van Campen had excused himself, just before Brock's valise was taken by a second man, shorter and middle-aged. He gave Brock a friendly smile, yet his face was somber. This might be a council elder from CIRCLE or an affiliate college.

"And here's Dr. James Woodford, our vice president."

That name was familiar. "As of three years ago?"

"And I'll run again this year," Dr. Woodford said. "I've heard much about you."

Brock hoped he had not. "Grandfather, how does CIRCLE have quantum—"

"Ah, brother." Alexander edged closer. "Let's discuss that later."

Grandfather showed no concern. "If you can handle the gravity, follow me. We have two hours before my keynote at seven. Alexander, send their luggage to the hotel?"

"I can do that," Dr. Woodford said.

"Thank you, good sir. See you at Heritage Hall."

Grandfather led them to the central avenue. At the elliptical Pool of Reflection, this path would join the southbound trail leading to Heritage House, Heritage Hall, and the wider route to the rest of their preserve.

Brock and Alicia could visit Sola Cathedral, his childhood home, their first apartment . . .

Past the Humanities and Theology complexes, the campus trees grew further apart. Soon these gave way to CIRCLE's own "feast of booths," plain or colorful, many already finished. Browsing guests were likely summer students. They looked so young, and most of them wore less than they should. Had CIRCLE relaxed campus dress standards?

No. He was still seeing this world through Martian eyes.

Alexander approached Grandfather. "Sir, it may be quicker to walk across the grass."

"True," Grandfather said. "But this course looks more interesting."

So many vendors were the same. There were the two simple mud-brown tents for a Southern Baptist college, and one salt-and-pepper tent with royal red banners for a Presbyterian seminary. Only their purple fluttering neighbor looked like a replacement shelter for the HOLY GHOST REVIVAL TABERNACLE, complete with verse-inscribed banners and shofars.

"President Rivers?"

"Rivers?"

"Yes, that's him."

"That's the president."

One tabernacle lady shook his hand and wished him blessings.

"Thank you, sister," Grandfather told her. "So good to see you here. Mm? Yes, I speak tonight. Oh, if you disagree, just give a shout. You know I'll hear you at Heritage Hall."

More sisters laughed gaily, but Brock knew that woman by all three names. Sister Leona Maribeth Ward had spoken more prophecies than Daniel himself, about CIRCLE's eternal prosperity or else the doom its elders could bring on the Church.

They moved past a wider open-sided tent with shelves full of books. The owner held out one thick hardback. "Mr. President—Mr. Rivers. Sign here? For my son?"

Grandfather clapped that man on the back. "You're kind, but I didn't write this."

"Well, no."

"It's not even *my* study Bible."

"Take a picture, then?"

Grandfather posed for several photos. Another woman exited her tent. "Thank you for helping show us the way of love!"

Their party neared a smaller, azure-toned booth. This was BIBLE BUILDERS, complete with boxes showing a 3D jigsaw Bible. Finished puzzles filled the tables, from the cruder Noah's Ark to the better-made tomb of Christ.

"Mr. President!" Celina, the founder and owner, greeted Grandfather, dragging along three grandchildren clinging to her many-layered skirt.

So far, no one had recognized Brock and Alicia. If they did, or reacted with suspicion, he needed to love them as his grandfather did.

A gaggle of older ladies wore frilly 2090s clothing full of clashing pastels and pointed curves. They carried Bibles as well as tote bags labeled CIRCLE 2120. Further ahead waited booths for a toy manufacturer from Oregon, a children's book publisher from Florida, a health care provider from Canada, a private electrician training school in Texas.

Across the way was Insight, a Lutheran group spanning most Christian university–oriented preserves, staffed by earnest freshmen. Beside them worked Bezalel's Apprentices. Every year they journeyed from their Pennsylvania preserve to offer beautiful carved and woven creations. Alicia had once hoped to fill their home with these.

Then came fragrant vendor spaces, whose clouds of real steam rose into the sky, a pleasing aroma unto the Lord. In this amazing world, people could cook real food, and they could cook it *outdoors*: hot dogs, gyros, corn on cobs, shish kebab . . .

Alicia whispered, "That is . . . homemade ice cream."

A shimmer drew their gaze to a flat sheet, glazed with sunlight—Lake Heritage. It was the largest water body on campus, holding a startling amount of exposed liquid in one place. Closer to the lake arose a large red fabric structure with flexible plastic windows and canvas that peaked liked mountains. Aides invited passersby into the entrance labeled A+CROSS TENT OF MEETING. Three men with black suits and blue-striped puff ties approached Grandfather, who held up two fingers and followed those men inside that tent.

Alexander scurried after him while muttering something.

Well, then, fried foods and ice cream might need to wait.

Brock and Alicia ducked after him into the entrance, passing into air only slightly cooler than outside. Dozens of people knelt on cushions. Gold spotlights shone on a performer. Was that Mari Heart? She looked older, but she swept nimbly about the stage in glittery skirts. Keyboardists and guitarists followed her praises. Once Brock had thought this process almost supernatural, until Alicia had taught him the benefits of band practice.

"Twenty-four hours each day," sang Miss Heart. "Each day of this event. Each day a moment. Each moment worship. Come inside. There's room in this house."

Their tradition wasn't his own, but he could watch with respect.

A stranger's hand touched his shoulder, a kindly man whose gaze held behind crescent lenses set upon wrinkled cheeks. "Hey, brother. Need prayer?"

Brock tried to relax his upper back. "That would be fine."

Gray eyes grew wide. "Brock Rivers?"

Not now, then. "Excuse—"

"Well, let's pray." The old man lifted his other hand over Alicia's arm, but didn't touch her. "Father God. Keep our brother, and his wife. Work your will in his life. Give him courage. Give him love. Let your light shine from above. When he wanders, keep him blessed. Make him . . . strive to see your best. We know he is safe in grace. But grant him a longing for . . . your Spirit, in this sinful world, helping us return to the life that you—"

"Amen." Brock gently pushed away. "Excuse us."

He returned to fresh air and late sunshine. Sweat clung to his skin as those words with all their implications burned in his ears.

Alicia hurried alongside him. "Do you want a snack?"

"Please. Anything. Grandfather can pay."

Who else accepted the apostasy rumor? Most of the church elders should know the truth, but did they believe it?

Brock found a bench of cool curved stone near the fountain, where streams twirled and splashed, muting all other human and musical clamor, gilded with real sunlight.

These architects had showed wisdom. Nothing was fake about this intricately carven centerpiece from which the waters flowed. One swirling and tilted stone pedestal, crowned by a stone model Bible, opened to reveal ancient rough-hewn pages that artfully hid the aquatic system. Instructions wrapped the pedestal in simple letters:

LET THE ONE WHO IS THIRSTY COME.
LET THE ONE WHO DESIRES TAKE THE WATER OF LIFE WITHOUT PRICE.

"They still put those in there." Alexander approached. He rested his foot on the bench and pointed toward the pool. Specks of sun glinted off tiny gold and copper discs in the basin. "Odd habit—you see a fountain, you donate money, even the old solid coins."

He was skeptical. Brock palmed his eyes against the sun. "Where's Grandfather?"

"Back in the tabernacle. He'll be along soon."

"Even without you to push him?"

"Seems I do that a lot. Someone must. But nowadays I think it's a blessing."

Alexander spoke as frankly as before, but he looked content. Maybe he truly had grown out of his frustrations, and given enough time, maybe they could truly rebuild this friendship. "How long have you been running CIRCLE com relations?"

"Two years. Started a month after I finished my com relations degree."

"*In truth,*" Brock said, "congratulations."

Alexander grinned at the old phrase from his college newsletter subtitles. "I do better with com relations than engineering. Maybe better than my old apologetics."

"You had skills in reverse-engineering words. I told you so."

"Guess I had to learn that for myself. But I'll never know how your grandfather does this stuff every year." Alexander's shadow crossed the waters as he joined Brock on the bench. "All of *this*. After you've been away so long, this probably looks strange to you."

The water settled, its timing now changed. New arrays flipped into a sheet of liquid.

This probably looks strange? Overwhelming, perhaps. But while Brock accepted free oxygen and delighted in simple, unearned water, how could he feel ungrateful?

Alexander leaned closer. "We knew about our people's issues. But *in truth . . ."*

"Brother. We didn't truly know how worse the outside worlds can be, whether Mars, secular Earth, anywhere. In our homeworld we find *saving* grace. The outside world has none."

Alexander had grown up with his own family dysfunction and had escaped this only to encounter many CIRCLE controversies. Biblical Christians might have their quirks, traditions, and strange ideas. Some fringe preserves would even mistreat or wrongly banish a person. Unlike CAUSE, however, they would never urge you to die happily for no reason, trapped in a Martian rille. Alexander needed to know *that* truth.

Grandfather came striding up the walkway, accompanied by Alicia. "I believe we're well covered in prayer now. And if you're hungry, hold onto that for a moment until I have a chance to feed you some good news and more. Shall we shortcut across the lawn?"

• • •

BROCK
5:40 P.M. EDT, THURSDAY, JUNE 21, 2125
CIRCLE PRESERVE, CINCINNATI

Gleaming reflections of a vast white bulwark slipped under lake waters. Then from across the shoreline and beyond a tree ridge, the original structure passed into view. Heritage Hall: site of chapel services with famous orators, including Grandfather with his keynote tonight. Sunlight flashed from the Hall's towering sides of polished granite. More guests teemed before the Hall's entrance, most of whom had walked from the Ark Hotel on the furthest lakeshore.

In his day, Brock had simply walked from home to the Hall. What a privilege to see every special event and visiting luminary without cost. Others had to save months for the trip, often funded by offerings from churches or smaller schools.

A woman's enhanced voice rose over the crowd. Her reedy form stood under shadows of the courtyard oak trees. "Heritage Hall is almost full. Standing room only! Please, no children. Families can view from their hotel rooms or from guest quarters at local churches and businesses."

Alicia pointed to Heritage Memorial, the tapered stone pillar that bore etched quotations from Brock's great-grandfather Caleb Rivers and other CIRCLE founders. One enormous crimson canvas wrapped the memorial's base, anchored by pegs to the ground.

"Alexander." Grandfather pointed. "Please go join Bryony with crowd management."

"I can. Remember, we have one hour to your prep time, sir."

"I'll be there in fifty minutes."

Grandfather took them to the heart of campus, Heritage House, the remodeled two-story dwelling that had once belonged to Caleb and Christi Rivers. As a child, Brock had thought this landmark the dullest place in the world. Now he saw the house as Grandfather always had.

With manual keys, Grandfather unlocked a side door. Refreshing and cooled air drifted outward, and they stepped between wood-paneled walls that blocked outside clamor.

Brock knew every room of this place. Some time ago, CIRCLE had removed the counter-tourism fence at the door to Caleb Rivers's old study. That room still held Great-Grandfather's original desk, armchairs, and book collection. Faint orange guard tape blocked the staircase entrance. White plastic sheeting covered the hallway rug.

Grandfather lay a hand on Brock's shoulder. "Well, how did I do? With our people?"

In private, Grandfather was always self-aware about their world.

"You are so skilled at this." Brock was sincere. Not even Alicia with her many charms could have disarmed that praying brother at the tent of meeting.

"I hope the Lord can grant anyone this gift." Grandfather led them down a hall. "I'm sorry we have so little time. But what I must share, I ask you to keep quiet for two hours. Until then, only you, and Alexander, and the council elders will know this truth."

8

BROCK
5:51 P.M. EDT, THURSDAY, JUNE 21, 2125
CIRCLE PRESERVE, CINCINNATI

GRANDFATHER MOVED TO THE KITCHEN. "BROCK, please take viz, for posterity."

Brock moved into the breakfast nook and sighted the option. "Confidential records?"

"Yes, for our eyes only. And this next is for your enjoyment only."

Grandfather returned from the kitchen and handed Brock one hot package that released . . . oh, a wondrous scent, the earthly blessing of fried chicken and macaroni with cheese.

This would outdo the fragrant offerings from outside vendors.

A second paper package held biscuits, gravy, and mashed potatoes, and the third one provided coleslaw, bottled iced tea, and every condiment Brock could have requested.

Alicia accepted her own meal and closed her eyes. "American cheeseburger. With pickles and mustard. Onion rings."

"These come with one condition," Grandfather said. "Thou shalt not feel guilt."

"Where sin abounds, grace abounds." Alicia unwrapped her gifts.

Brock removed the plastic lid and released a burst of steam. Back on Mars, only Port Ares elites might enjoy such delicacies. Tonight's joy might not last, but for now, he could ignore that reality.

"Family, I've a question. What do you think of our new quantum vault?"

So this celebration dinner came with learning exercises. Grandfather's challenge was rhetorical, yet Brock should speak carefully. "I'm glad CIRCLE can move into the twenty-second century. But I know why you're keeping the vault secret."

"Why is that?"

"Revealing the vault won't serve others."

"In what way?"

This answer was truth, whatever Brock felt about it. "We honor Jesus by respecting our people, even if we think they're immature about certain technologies."

"Go deeper for me."

Of course he would say that. "Good leaders speak truth. If their people aren't ready, wise leaders wait to reveal some truth, like the existence of the vault, while staying honest."

"I agree." Grandfather began drawing lines in the air. "This is not about the two axes of good versus bad, or love versus hatred. Our third axis is wisdom. Leaders must act like parents who plan how they teach children. Or like God, reserving His secret things."

Or like Caleb Rivers' willingness to have political conversations with the early CAUSE in the 2060s. His infamous tactics had helped establish this preserve.

"You want to share hard truth with us," Alicia said.

This hot meal and Grandfather's clear-eyed sincerity might help Brock receive that truth.

"I do. But we all know that in the past, both of you—similar to Alexander before—would have thought CIRCLE leaders hypocritical for concealing the quantum vault, much less choosing not to confront people about their superstitions. I'm already sure you've changed, and even in this little way, I have seen that in you. That's why I want others to hear your story this year. Educate us. Encourage your people. Challenge us to gospel missions."

If the people would listen, Brock might do whatever he could, but Grandfather had not mentioned better candidates. "I presume Dad and Mom couldn't attend this year?"

Grandfather glanced to the table, only for a moment. "They're still hard to reach."

Technically, coms with the remote Russian theology school were even less reliable than Martian networks. Ravaged by the Last War, the area had scarcely recovered fossil fuel–based power, but was home to a few struggling preserves for Biblical Christians and other religions. Soon after Brock's and Alicia's wedding, Stanford Rivers had heard of that new remote teaching opportunity, supposedly for a single year. He and Mom knew the risks, yet they relocated to one of those preserves. At least they had gained CIRCLE's official blessing.

Brock hid his expression behind his fork. "Grandfather, we're not missionaries."

"We could share what *not* to do," Alicia said lightly.

"You know my view on that," Grandfather said. "We all had to make hard choices back then. Because of CIRCLE's reputation, we're accountable for more. Even when we choose right, some claim we're enabling sin. That could be correction or slander. I live under that burden."

Brock smiled. "So do you plan to announce a new hard choice?"

"You could say that. We've spent days in meetings. The elders have many cautions, especially once CAUSE learns what we're planning. We need a final vote by this weekend. But what I'm about to show you . . . is what your great-grandfather and our founders wanted."

Grandfather shoved back his chair and stood. "I've prayed to the Lord. I have locked my doors and lain flat on the ground. I've asked Him for courage to speak truth in every kind of love. I've even asked the Lord to work miracles." He paced near the kitchen door. "Now I can say this. Jesus answered my prayer. He truly has. Please come with me."

Brock's chest tightened as he stood.

Grandfather led them down the staircase into Heritage House's finished cellar. Years ago, this space had kept Caleb Rivers's private manuscripts and his many rumored emergency supplies from the Last War. They passed the hall to the storage room between on-fading lights. Someone had cleared boxes to reveal the man-sized corner safe Brock knew from before.

Grandfather keyed in a code. "We should have room enough for three."

Alicia pointed to the safe. "You want us to go in there?"

"Why not? Just for fun."

Brock let her step first into the gloom. Of course the safe lay empty; staff had long since moved all its contents to the CIRCLE Museum of Biblical History. They all crowded into bare space beside dusty shelves with crumpled labels, and Grandfather shut the door.

Alicia blinked for viz. "What're we doing?"

Pressing against Brock, Grandfather faced the vault's inner wall. "*Sola . . . fide.*"

Brock knew those words and the newer melody.

Slowly and carefully, Grandfather half spoke and half sang in his quiet baritone, "*Sola Scriptura. Solus Christus. Sola gratia.*" Then, finally, "*Soli Deo gloria.*"

Machinery clicked and hissed. Soft gleams shone from a wall crack that widened by six centimeters. Grandfather pulled something and moved into the light. Had he opened a hidden second door at the back of the safe? Behind this door lay another room, already brightened by warm overhead spheres.

"They're LED." Grandfather lifted his finger. "Watch the brittle glass."

These walls and floors looked like dirt, but reflected light as if treated with sealant. Alicia gazed to one wall mural portraying green fields transected by a broad blue river. Among mountain peaks lifted the golden spires of an imagined New Jerusalem.

"They built a small kitchen." Grandfather beckoned to another doorway. "There's a water closet and reclamation system. Vice President Woodford thought a person could last three months down here. That wall unfolds into three beds. In that corner is an old generator. That door opens to a closet, full of rations and fuel and 2060s era com gear."

Brock let himself fall into a padded chair and leaned back. A survivor could stay busy with those full bookshelves. "I never knew Caleb Rivers built a war refuge."

"He never told my siblings nor me," Grandfather said.

"So my great-grandfather was prepared, even before the Accords."

"And he didn't prepare for himself and Mother alone. In that desk, I found old blueprints. Even after the Accords, my father considered enlarging this space. He didn't want to act on paranoia or be caught unable to help his neighbors."

"Who else knows about this?" Alicia said. "How did *you* find it?"

"Only James Woodford, and myself, a few others, and now you. And this is how."

Grandfather unlocked a cabinet and withdrew a simple steel box. Dirt tumbled from its edges. Brock opened this box to find a single page with bent edges, encased in laminate. Printed and bold black words formed a letter. Alicia stepped closer to read it with him.

Greetings in Christ.
If you have followed our wishes as inscribed in our

Charter documents, you have opened our Heritage Memorial time capsule on June 21 in the year of our Lord 2125.

You now find enclosed a few treasures of great worth to CIRCLE's founders and the first council of elders. They include one of my first Bibles, early drafts of the Charter, the pens we used to sign this, and other artifacts. A complete inventory will follow.

Yet we hope that in the future, this capsule will be useful for more than ceremony. We have faced the judgment of the Last War, the victory of neutralists, and CAUSE. Then in February 2070 came this preserve system, which we know will estrange Christians and all other religious believers from the human family.

We have not, however, founded CIRCLE to train biblical Christians for mere survival. CIRCLE exists for the far greater mission the Church has followed for twenty-one hundred years. We pray that someday all believers will join together and shine the light of our Lord Jesus Christ into the greater world. Even more, we long for the greatest Someday to come, when the true Kingdom will fly as the prophesied stone, cut without hands, to strike the golden image of men. This stone will scatter those pieces like chaff, then become a great mountain that fills the whole Earth. In that day, "The God of Heaven will set up a kingdom that shall never be destroyed, nor shall the kingdom be left to another people." (See Daniel 2.)

If you, our descendants, long with us for that Kingdom, then we, from this last century, offer you help. We join the many sisters and brothers who have collected our resources for restored world missions. *Behind this long-awaited vision* when we shall walk on *streets of gold*, God will *safely* preserve His treasures for His glory.

> *Caleb Joseph Rivers*
> *on behalf of CIRCLE's founding elders*
> *Religious Preserve–Biblical Christianity–Ohio–1,*
> *United States, June 21, 2075*

Brock had just read long-lost words from his own ancestor, the famous founder.

"Jerome." Alicia turned on Grandfather. "You opened the time capsule weeks early?"

"Yes, last week. I'll ask my dad's forgiveness in Heaven. But we had to open it before the conference. We hoped to unveil the contents in a new exhibit."

"What does he mean by these set-apart words, like the *streets of gold?*" Brock pointed to characters hand-drawn under the letter's printed date. In black print they spelled *50*, but ink swirls over the *0* made this appear like a musical note. "Licia, that's a treble clef, yes?"

"Looks like it."

"And it seems to say *fifty*. What about the fancy zero? This means 'start the song.' So the symbols mean *fifty, five zero*, and *start?*"

"I puzzled over that," Grandfather said. "It was the best symbol Father could make up—fifty, the anniversary year for opening the time capsule, but also *five-S*, with the S drawn as a treble clef. *Start the song*. What's the meaning? Sing the five S's."

"The five *solas?*" Alicia said.

"That, along with this word *safely*, made me think to check his old basement safe."

Brock lay down the letter. "So we've found another self-memorial in the histories of CIRCLE. I don't see how this shelter counts as a great treasure."

Grandfather walked to the wall mural. "There's more."

Brock waited.

"Behind this long-awaited vision, when we shall walk on streets of gold." Grandfather tugged a handle, which divided, from the mural frame, a new surface that opened to reveal embedded shelves. Shelter bulbs cast shadows inside the vast compartment, then light sparked back from many glimmering corners.

Brock was truly seeing this.

Shelves bore long objects lined in rows. Each object looked as large as a book, hundreds of them, solid and shining. They were bars of gold.

"One gram of this secret treasure paid for your journey here."

Brock slid a finger over one solid brick, imprinted with 1 KG. How could one even measure the worth? Had CIRCLE's people already converted some of this to yun?

"Where did Great-Grandfather get all this?"

"I think he told us. Once our founders knew the world was ratifying the Accords and the preserve system, many of them sold their properties. I think we've found the proceeds."

Alicia laid her hand across the bars. "Do you plan to announce this?"

"Only at the right time. First I must share this with the elder council. I have done the research. This treasure is worth three hundred eight million yun."

Brock's hand slipped from the shelf and he stared at the mural's street of gold.

Alicia's lips parted for a silent *whew.* "Then . . . who owns . . . ?"

"Legally, I am Caleb Rivers's last heir. This house and the old camp property surrounding it are mine. I suppose, as of last week, I've become a multi-millionaire."

The old bulbs buzzed with much paler light.

Brock formed a question. "What do you plan to do with it?"

"It's not for myself. Not a milligram. But if I could give . . ."

"We don't want it." Even if he granted them the full sum, this would be wasted for one family on Mars. "Put this toward missions, real missions, for Christ's sake."

Grandfather smiled. "One mission for the glory of God alone."

"Would you really?" Alicia said.

"We can and we will. It's no longer a matter of finance. As soon as I finish tonight's keynote, every supporter will ask me, *Jerome, who pays for this project?* In summary, I will."

Brock could dare to believe it. Here waited the amount and its promise, solid as gold.

"What about CAUSE?" Alicia said. "When we're found in violation of the Accords?"

"What *violation?* We won't start churches outside our preserve. We won't preach on the streets or public com. Maybe we should, but we know the early Church fled persecution and went elsewhere, sharing the gospel and planting churches."

Brock murmured, "Causians govern Earth . . ."

"Then we will go elsewhere."

9

"GOOD EVENING! I AM JEROME, AND I WELCOME you to the Center for International Renewal of Christian Life and Education's fiftieth annual conference!"

People raised their hands and echoed their cheers across Heritage Hall. Never before had Brock taken his place on this platform. From up here, the auditorium's high and bright lights nearly obscured these enthusiastic thousands. Eleven CIRCLE elders stood from a single row of chairs to add their applause. Brock and Alicia did the same.

Grandfather stood tall at his copper-trimmed lectern, reflected in both size and sound via three large viz mirrors cast on the auditorium's rounded walls.

His grandfather's eyes glistened.

Tension like doubled gravity gripped at Brock's arms and chest. This might be manmade excitement, or a sense of divine blessing. He dared hope it would last.

Rushing acclaim faded to a trickle. People retook their seats.

"Over three thousand of you have packed this hall, with hundreds standing in the back. Please behave yourselves, or I'll summon CIRCLE Security."

People laughed. Only he could make that sound like an original joke.

"For those new to CIRCLE, this is the first religious preserve founded in the state of Ohio. Our preserve has its own security, utilities, and power. We have one hospital, seven hotels, a few dozen restaurants and shops, and thousands of homes run by the Housing Council. CIRCLE began its work in Christian education. Then the health care and engineering schools added more. So tonight, we have many eyes on us. Most of you come from other Biblical Christian preserves or allies around the world. Our live viewership is close to forty million. By the end, we should have a lot more. In fact, tonight we could make some history."

He swept an arm toward them. "Two special guests traveled the furthest to join us. Please welcome my grandson and granddaughter-in-law, Brock and Alicia Rivers."

Applause resounded, probably from visitors who didn't know Brock's reputation.

Grandfather gazed forward. "In 2118, many were led to believe Brock and Alicia abandoned our preserve. But this rumor was not true. They never wanted to leave us or abandon their faith. Instead, a single accident involving public law forced them into exile. They have spent years hoping to return."

Some people applauded louder, including a few council elders. This was the first time Grandfather had said this for the record.

"I welcome delegates from our fourteen satellite campuses around the world. And I welcome our friends from other Christian preserves of all denominations, as well as some friends from among our neighbors in non-Christian religious preserves. No matter where you come from, you may be interested to hear tonight's news."

Grandfather's image on the trio of screens looked down over three thousand people who faced the stage with curiosity or confusion. "I remember, over fifty years ago, when many of us began opposing the Accords. That's when one fancy new religion—the Cause—began work to restrict all the smaller religions, for the security of Earth. They established religious preserves in the hopes of keeping believers safe and free, dividing us from the secular world, until the old traditions naturally died and let humankind outgrow its old ways."

"Please do not fear. Death is the natural end." Weeks ago, the CAUSE epsilon had called down this lie to the dying, far above a land of false promises. *"Your work is not in vain."*

"Over sixty million human citizens live beyond the Earth. Cities and rail lines connect lunar industries and tourism. Record-setting settlements expand on Mars. Drones surround Venus. Soon explorers might go to the Jovian and Saturnine moons, powered by the great works of sustainable fusion, synthetic gravity, and quantum vaulting!

And yes, these *are* great gifts to humanity. Lest you think I condemn all of CAUSE, I certainly do not."

Startled heads lifted. Oh, thank the Lord, Grandfather would say this.

"Our Creator made science and exploration. These are His gifts to human beings. When I consider the heavens, I'm moved to worship my Lord. And if people who reject God sail their ships into the heavens, we must ask, *What is man that you are mindful of him*?"

From all of the wall screens, Grandfather surveyed the auditorium.

"Millions blamed Christians for their role in the Last War. Fifty years later, we have not challenged their system. We've joined old denominations and formed new ones. We've built businesses. We have children and form our dynasties. We want peace and security."

In his place, Brock would not sound so optimistic.

"I like my preserve too. Almost all of it! Yes, our ways can be strange. But we also build our own cultures to celebrate Jesus. Anyway, it's not like we're trapped in our lands by physical barriers. We can reenter the secular world for trade or travel. And we can share our faith with one another and avoid the wider world that rejects us, yes?"

Now the president was meddling, and he might get away with this.

"Most of our neighbors view this as good. Imagine if we left our preserves and returned to the real world. Imagine if we spoke publicly about our ancient faith. They say our old ideas would reintroduce evil to our 'peaceful' planet."

Alicia and Brock leaned forward.

"We need truth. We must see what really happens to people on 'peaceful' planets."

Over Grandfather's shoulder, a dark-haired woman's face appeared on all screens. Alexander had chosen Justine Bach's image from public records, then blurred this for privacy.

"This woman was born in Germany and cast into the social nets. In 2097, she broke out. Authorities recovered her from an underground stitch lab in Sweden. She applied for asylum and later became a novice on Mars. Most novices gain promotions in ten years. She has not. Even if she lifts her settlement rank, she can never be perfect by Causian ideals."

Another obscured photo showed Sayed, whose status had proved so hard to confirm.

"This man ran a prosperous farm in South Africa, before the changing industries forced him to sell his land. Despite his asthma, he earned a three-year astro-mining degree, and in 2112, he left Earth for Mars, hoping to find work."

Grandfather waited for the final blurred face of Mara the mail-order bride.

"Our final portrait is only nineteen years old. She has no tragic story. Instead she was raised in a decent, CAUSE-fearing home in Columbus, not far from here. She stayed active in sports, music, chess, and robotics, and she interned with CAUSE's Ministry program. This year, she chose to leave home to join a Martian woman she had never met, forty years her senior."

Brock had asked Grandfather to summarize the rest.

"One month ago, all three of these individuals were assigned work in a utility dome. Because of corporate haste to 'change their world,' that structure lost air pressure. These two women nearly died. The man suffered permanent lung damage. Today he is on life support in Port Ares. Unless some relative claims responsibility for him, his life will end within the year."

People were stirring. *Lord God, if You act, please move us to more than sympathy.*

Mara's image faded, and Grandfather led his hearers into silence.

"We can hope CAUSE will preserve their lives. But they're still without eternal hope, just like those people who taught themselves to fear the gospel, and fear all 'religious people,' fifty years ago. My friends. People I knew and loved. Entire families and states and nations were divided by boundaries between the human race."

His fist tapped the lectern. "My Bible says there is no slave or free person, 'religious' or 'secular' person. Jesus told us to *go therefore* into the world. Should we follow Him?"

Brock blinked furiously. Heritage Hall kept silent.

"Yes. We should. We will go therefore."

Gently the people rustled, and Brock held his breath.

"Heed the ancient prophet! 'Do you not know? Do you not hear? Has it not been told you from the beginning? Have you not understood from the foundations of the Earth? It is *He* who sits above the circle of the Earth, and its inhabitants are like grasshoppers.'

"Tonight, I announce the start of a new CIRCLE outreach in three stages.

"First, we will recruit men and women who believe in gospel missions. They will have training in theology and science. They will long to show Jesus to our neighbors.

"Second, we'll organize the mission in the public world. Technically this won't be a religious effort, but a for-profit therapeutic program. And for any of our CAUSE neighbors who suddenly take interest in my words—our project will fall under CAUSE Constitution Business Class, Section Eighty-Six, amendment one, which states that a for-profit or business concern can operate from a *religious preserve*. The term is clear. It builds our foundation to resist the inevitable challenge.

"Third, we will find or build a ship. Within one year of today, we will launch. This starcraft will travel beyond our homeworld, to the moon, Port L5, Mars, Jovian space, to any world that needs this gospel. We will obey our God. We will go above the circle of Earth."

This was no fleeting spiritual fervor. Heaven itself must feel like this!

Some people leaned forward, eyes wide, eager for more. A few lifted from their chairs as if preparing to walk out. Some glanced back to friends as if wondering, *Did you hear that? President Rivers seriously said CIRCLE is launching a spaceship?*

One man with a mustache, sitting near the front, mouthed, *Yes. Yes.*

"We will not ask for funds. God has already provided support from a benefactor." Grandfather paused for whispers and gentle laughter from the skeptical or covetous. "This outreach will be called The Space Mission."

Two copies of the early emblem appeared behind him. The simple circle, like an Earth, shone out light. Above the planet rose the main words THE SPACE MISSION.

Smaller script circumscribed the shape: DEUS VOCAT ULTRA ORBIS— VADE ERGO.

God calls us above the circle of Earth. Go therefore.

Applause began, then grew louder, ascending to the rafters. Other attendees sat quiet as stones, but they weren't protesting or even scowling.

"CIRCLE's council elders largely agree. Most of them see the hazards we face, if we continue as we are. They are ready for change.

Tomorrow morning, we vote on the Space Mission. All members of the deacon council are welcome to join us!

"Many have already pledged their lives to this mission, including two with whom I spoke earlier. They have responded with enthusiasm. Now . . ."

Brock's life would never be the same.

"I'm honored to present the first servants of this outreach, Commander Brock Rivers and Mission Specialist Alicia Rivers."

More applause arose, like music from the spheres.

This couldn't be true. Something would interrupt him, or Brock would awaken.

CIRCLE's elders had not yet discussed recruitment. This week they would meet for more plans. Meanwhile, Brock and Alicia would enjoy days of nothing but this impossible creativity. Could he write his own speeches? How soon could they draft a mission statement? What would Alicia do as *mission specialist*?

Down in the Heritage House shelter, Grandfather had told them, "What man meant for evil, God meant for good. We can't bring you home to Earth. But you can leave Mars. Move aboard the starcraft. Work to share the Kingdom beyond the Earth."

He had shown total certainty, just as he did now.

"Might some of *you* join the Space Mission? Have you longed to go beyond your homeworld? To meet new family in new lands? If so, pray. Be wise. Then speak with us."

When would Grandfather share exact destinations?

"As soon as we dismiss, I've asked Brock, Alicia, and the elders to answer your many questions at a media briefing outside Heritage Memorial."

Brock had scribbled notes, but had no time to confer with Alicia.

Grandfather shouted, "Leaders may leave the platform! Everyone, please wait so they can escape. I'll distract you by requesting that you pray with me. Oh, but please, pray *for* me. Without ceasing. Lord knows I need it. All of CIRCLE needs your prayers."

One older couple moved from the front row. Brock led Alicia down the steps after them, while the council elders rose from their platform seats.

"A dream," Alicia murmured. "Like a dream."

"Are you with me? Do you want this?" he asked her.

"More than anything. But I cannot believe . . ."

Brock lifted her hands to kiss them.

Remaining on stage, Grandfather lowered his arms. "Join me in prayer."

They halted in mid-aisle, turned and waited. People stilled. Some raised hands. Every head bowed.

"Lord God, thank You for Your grace. Give us wisdom to guide us. Keep us from speaking evil against one another and against our neighbors in the world. Preserve us from deceptions and arrogance and idol-worship. Build Your kingdom through us, Father, as we delight in Your purpose. Yours is the glory, on Earth as it is in Heaven."

That last syllable faded behind Brock's closed eyes and the people's quiet stirrings.

His fingers gently rubbed on Alicia's hand.

Grandfather waited at the lectern for many seconds, head bowed and eyes closed.

"*Sola fide* . . ." On the melody's fourth note, he lifted his face. "*Sola Scriptura. Solus Christus. Sola gratia.*" Jerome Rivers drew one breath to finish. "*Soli Deo gloria.*"

His platform erupted in hellfire.

10

BROCK
7:30 P.M. EDT, THURSDAY, JUNE 21, 2125
CIRCLE PRESERVE, CINCINNATI

BLAZING STORMS CAST BROCK INTO THE ABYSS.
Hot metals clawed against his face. Voices wailed. Pain pinched his legs and tore across his chest. He saw no visions and felt no divine healing. Roars blasted his ears from some great, tumbling beast—then fell under silence.

His arms were thrown over his face, buried by heaving deluge that wrapped him like molten steel. But his legs. He could feel them, steady and true.

Could he resist the weight? Throw aside the darkness and escape?

Wreckage tumbled. Dim light revealed soft panels with wooden pieces and wall sections. Brock lifted himself from the center of this mess, and he stood within Hell.

The lectern platform and supporting wall were gone, replaced by a black cavern. High ceiling beams and surfaces were blown away, collapsed at the edges, exposing night sky with distant light from nearby lampposts and other buildings.

By some miracle, he'd kept his com clip.

His right hand opened and closed on no other hand. She was gone. *Gone.* "Licia!"

"Here . . . I'm here."

His viz focused into beams. Two paces away, she lay between a ceiling board and shreds of red carpet. With trembling arms he yanked these away.

Scratches covered her face. Her blue eyes opened. "You're all right?" she said.

"I might be." Oh, she lived and spoke clearly. "What hurts?"

"Legs and bum. Lower back."

"Pain in your head? Did you black out?"

Alicia thought about it. "No. You didn't either?"

He helped her stand. Dusty crimson trickled down her foot to expose a bright slash higher on her leg, slowly bleeding, without spurts. Alicia grimaced and tore a strip from her dress to bind it. "Already ruined . . ."

This conference. Heritage Hall. Grandfather's news.

Two meters away, another man's suit-jacketed arm was torn by debris. Behind him lay stilled bodies. Taller and living forms rose over piles of wreckage.

No one here would suffocate or freeze from near-vacuum, but Brock was frozen.

"God gave us good emotions in good time." Dr. Morrison had also said this in training. *"During disasters, you let the Lord grieve. Your job? Obey Him by helping your people."*

They were Brock's family, the Christians of CIRCLE, weeping and dying.

Parts of the vast floor threatened to spill into the basement. Heritage Hall had kept half of its ceiling, held by frayed rafters and steel, but those remnants could soon collapse.

Brock clenched at his head. Rescue would come from CIRCLE Security and emergency squads of Samaritan General. Yet moments had passed since . . . whatever this was. For all he knew, no one had reported this cataclysm—perhaps the worst crisis his home had ever seen.

Lord, help them understand this. "Licia, do you have public com access?"

"I think so."

"Then send a note to Port Ares. Make it Q-link if we need to, letting Michael and Elizabeth know that if they hear of this, we're fine. Then vox Cincinnati public authorities. Tell them we had . . . some kind of incendiary reaction in preserve limits. Maybe three thousand casualties."

She began work.

Brock sighted for vox to Samaritan General, bending to check the nearest victim . . . whose arm was missing. He found no pulse in the man's neck. Black eyes stared upward. This man Brock didn't know, this beloved son, had gone to meet his Father.

Three tones sounded. "Samaritan," said a living woman.

Sweat burned at his eyes.

"Sir? Are you in trouble?"

They didn't know. "This is Brock Rivers, at Heritage Hall."

"What happened there? We just saw—"

"There was an explosion. West end, stage area. Half the building's gone. Many bodies."

"Oh, Jesus, save us. Can you tell what caused it?"

Was this a fusion reaction? What could have provoked it? "I don't know."

Lights appeared in the sky, growing in size and density, reaching for the ground. One beam swept over two stumbling men—council elders Patrick Keller and Maxwell Adams.

"We're nearly there, sir," the Samaritan staffer replied. "Keep this channel open."

Adams, also head of CIRCLE Security, growled about getting hit. Alicia met them, and they bent to help an older man, council elder Eiichiro Mashima.

More light burst into the Hall, shining from a large ambulance that hovered beyond the ceiling shreds. Two more lights emerged, cast from small CIRCLE crafts that held five medics each. Was this all the help they sent?

Brighter light burst around the CIRCLE ambulances, thrown from a vehicle twice their size. This arrival slid to the ground and tousled grass beneath its fiery underglow. Side lumen lines hurled orange-and-red beams into the Hall interior and against all three CIRCLE vehicles. Red letters shone out CARES: CINCINNATI AGENCY FOR RELIEF AND EMERGENCY SERVICES.

They had come to do the work he and the preserve could scarcely manage.

Out of the ambulance spilled a dozen secular medics, carrying stretchers and supplies. Two staffers jumped over the Hall's remnant walls, where one medic tossed up an object and paused to steer it with his eyes. The object split into two discs that threw white ripples against the ceiling, and one more object shone a faint red glow.

Lord, preserve my people.

One city medic approached Alicia. "Are you well?"

Alicia let them inspect her. They were firm yet caring. Other medics climbed over wreckage and unearthed victims. Soon they were cleaning wounds and applying bandages. From outside, more lights shone from an approaching second vehicle.

Another medic checked Brock. "Sir, can you provide data for the building?"

"I can. I'm also helping with rescue. Please share your infrared sweep." Brock summoned local info, then voiced his code and transferred. The city medic did his part. Brock sighted new data for the blast site and saw fiery circles radiating into a sea of clouded orange, with hundreds of darker red areas showing living people. Some survivors had fled outside the building. Other victims were entombed by debris.

"Maybe three hundred eighty casualties," the lead medic said.

"Dead or wounded?" Alicia said.

The woman's badge name showed LT. TYRA GOUDEAU. "We can't know yet."

"Can you find survivors?" Brock said.

Goudeau stared at him. "For a preserve, we need population records."

"We had about three thousand—"

Someone grunted from behind. Brock turned to find a young man whose black mustache was flecked by dried blood. "Brother, did *you* bring them here?"

Who did he mean, the emergency workers? "These are city medics."

"Shouldn't do that."

This man looked truly bothered. Brock touched his shoulder, then bent closer to whisper, "*Brother,* CIRCLE needs all the help we can find."

"Next they'll bring their little friends in green."

Technically, Brock had not lived here and had not dealt with civic authorities since 2118. "Last I checked, Cincinnati police and public health have no reason to . . ."

Goudeau knelt next to one fallen victim. Her viz lit green to reveal a grimacing, dead face. She touched the eyes, drawing them open, as if for a retinal scan. Brock stepped closer. "Lieutenant, local police cannot capture facial imagery or any biological—"

"Sir, I'm more than local."

Chills deepened under his skin. "What are you *lieutenant* of?"

"That's an honorary ranking. I am a Second Minister."

For the second time in his life, Brock beheld someone from the Ministry. Why then hadn't she come in a marked vehicle, or worn CAUSE's green Ministry uniform or gold badge that identified her ranking? Now she set her face as if expecting deference.

"Our preserve's still got rights," said the other man. "Why are the Causians here?"

"Mr. Rivers, and Mrs. Rivers, I could ask why you've returned to Earth. I could make a case of this. Or I could talk about the building collapse and the fact that flawed preserve structures invite the Ministry to be involved. Or else, given this crisis . . ."

Either the rules had changed, or Brock had missed something from his legal training. "This info goes to the city. No faces. No biologics. Do you keep the names stored off-site?"

"These are temporary."

"After the crisis, I want the city to *delete* all that info. Is that clear?"

"Of course."

"Thank you for upholding the Accords."

The mustached man turned away murmuring.

Brock sighted home base and conference records, waited for the scan, then found Heritage Hall's attendance. *Show names, ages, work profiles. Redact financial tags. Bundle and watermark Brock Rivers, CIRCLE. Send to Minister . . .* Brock said aloud, "Tyra Guh-*doh*."

The Minister received this and stepped away.

He mixed the infrared info with this data. Two red names said DECEASED. Orange name-placeholders numbered 377. Medics could only find them by sight or DNA scan.

"Do you see Grandfather?" Alicia said.

"He's not listed." *Send to Alicia. Standing query,* "Jerome Rivers."

Calm blue text replied, NAME NOT FOUND.

Brock made himself say the words. "He was right in the center of the blast."

"So we might need to grieve him later." She was right and brave to say this aloud.

Brock turned to the west. "Some of the elders survived. That is . . . little comfort."

Alicia touched his arms. "Be careful."

He made his way across loose wreckage. In this area . . . Heritage

Hall's platform, side pillars, steps, tall stained-glass windows, the synth organ, chairs, pulpit, and any man left standing there . . . all was destroyed. Crimson heat burned from the main crater, and odors of burning metal lashed his face. Deeper inside the caved-in floor, sculpted sides of foundation smoldered from the explosion. That was Heritage Hall's basement. What down there had erupted? Wasn't the Hall reactor installed further back, under the offices?

Brock stepped over stalagmites of outer wall and lowered his feet onto singed grass.

Three more city crafts arrived. Gray-and-red uniformed medics joined blue-and-white-clad police, aiding Christian medics to set a new perimeter. Between them stood other people, conference-goers turned survivors. Their clothes were dirtied or torn.

Here came a more honest vehicle, whose sleek fuselage flowed with light lime tones representing the Ministry, complete with sunrise-and-blood-drop-themed emblem.

Nearby stood Dr. Woodford, his bare arms and blue suit lightened by white dust.

"Mr. Vice President?" Brock asked.

Dr. Woodford lurched closer. His powerful arms enfolded Brock, and he pressed silver hair to Brock's chest. "You are safe. Thanks be to the Lord. And your wife—"

"She's well. Have you seen Grandfather?"

Dr. Woodford touched his eyelid, as if to wipe away viz. "He was up there."

Sirens cut him off. The new Ministry craft dropped and landed before Heritage House. Metals dimmed and doors opened to release new Ministers, these ones wearing the usual green.

Dr. Woodford charged forward. "Wait a moment!"

A man with slicked hair and tiny ear stubs lifted his hand. "Yes?"

"I'm CIRCLE's vice president, and this is a sovereign preserve."

"We've come to help. We have food and water and counselors."

"Thank you, but we have plenty."

Brock tugged his arm. "Sir, a word?" Dr. Woodford fell back and waited. They shouldn't be forced to deal with this now. "The Ministry has people here already. They're wearing the metropolitan police uniform, as if they're incog—"

"Of that I've no doubt." Woodford stared over the destruction. "We've heard reports of CAUSE Ministers being more aggressive. Watching the preserve borders. Issuing public warnings to our neighbors. Maybe five years ago, Congress endorsed a new CAUSE policy. Timothy with Legal thought that change might let Ministry chaplains join with local police and health departments."

And now Brock, in his great wisdom, had given them preserve population data.

When he told the vice president, Woodford shut his eyes. "They would have taken our data anyway. But would they go so far as . . ."

He was called away by CIRCLE elder Charles Montague.

Brock moved to inspect a new recovery zone, where city medics—and Ministry infiltrators—had lined dozens of gurneys that each held a victim. Medics watched viz scroll over their eyes, sourced from stat units, while inspecting their patients.

Two women lay unconscious, their chests moving with labored breath. One man's face bore scars and so much blood where his right eye had been. Darien Lombardi, another council elder, was comfortably resting.

One medic gave an all clear, and in came three public Ministers, each wearing tight lime-green blouses and pants. One woman approached the victim who had lost his eye. She gazed down, spilling violet curls from bundled hair. "May I speak with you?"

That man opened his mouth for a desperate response.

"You may be near death. I can share human comfort."

One burned arm lifted, pointing toward the sky. The Minister looked up but saw nothing.

New commotion came from the trauma zone's far side. Two CIRCLE medics and one of the elders, along with two Ministry people, had surrounded an old man who was shouting.

"Calm. Calm. Calm," chanted one Minister, his voice bizarrely loud. Brock shoved between two officers.

"Give him space, you lot!" shouted the elder. "We can help him."

"No worship of the beast. No worship of the idols." The old man gestured wildly toward one of the cots with an IV running into the arm of an even older man. "My father. He doesn't need . . . Ministry evils."

"You've had great loss," one Minister said. His hair shone white, but his skin looked as smooth as a twenty-year-old student's. "There are no idols. We are human like you. Loss and pain are normal. We want to understand. Now, will you do the same?"

Not even the CAUSE lecture at the Martian dome had sounded like this.

That younger old man stood as if dumbfounded. Brock lay a hand on his shoulder. "Brother . . . I'm Brock Rivers. The president is my grandfather. What is your name?"

The man stumbled, then lifted his languid eyes. "Micah McCarthy . . ."

"Micah, your father is already secure in Jesus Christ." Brock gripped tighter to this fearful saint. "No one can separate him from the Lord, not even the Causians."

"I've heard of you . . . your grandfather said you weren't . . . but did you call *them* here?"

Brock tried to retreat. "No, brother."

"Did you?" Micah pointed near Brock's chest. "At such a time?"

Officers advanced, but before they could act, a young man darted between them—the man with the black mustache. He drew the struggling Micah into a tight restraint, like an embrace, pinning brittle arms to his sides.

"Sir. I know." He spoke quietly but clearly. "I'm sorry. It's not right. This struggle. For years those people persecuted my old preserve. Giving us reproach."

Micah shuddered. "Where you from?"

"New York state. My people got things stolen. But we have better possessions. That's the biblical argument. Now here's a practical one. Don't give *them* any excuse to hurt you."

The CAUSE Ministers kept their benign expressions.

Somehow that mustached man sounded aggressive while speaking words of peace.

Micah kept breathing hard but gave a nod.

Brock fell back from the gathering, while Dr. Scofield and someone else moved in to lecture the two Ministers, pointing forcefully to the city officials. One gray-uniformed woman, standing over the oldest victim, carried actual medical equipment.

Brock's viz had kept the developing database. "Jerome Rivers?"

NAME NOT FOUND.

He mustn't fall into false hope. More likely, there was no sign of him left.

Out of the crowd stumbled that black-haired man, who spied Brock. "Eh. The city people asked permission for zero-pol radiator use. I can't give that. Can you?"

"Are they really city people, or Ministers in disguise?"

"Since they're asking for help, I think it's the former."

Either way, they needed to begin serious debris clearing. Brock voxed Dr. Woodford, who approved the request, and forwarded the note to a city medic supervisor.

He stepped back onto the carpet and against the crater's heat. Bare light from the hovering disc shone on the Hall's remaining roof. Another team moved in, pushing two large zero-pol radiators. They were next-gen versions, like hovering generators with wide and flexible protruding tubes used to charge stabilizing fields.

"Mr. Rivers?" the other man said. "About what I told you earlier . . ."

"It's all right. What's your name?"

"Jason Cruz."

Sight-typing the name yielded no data results. This man didn't live here.

At the crater's other side, a uniformed man with large shoulder pads shouted, "Get me a craft up there for light. Need a better thermal cam! Radiator ops, take the polarity past zero. We'll have a load of wreckage. How many suits? Get us torches, winches, cables."

"Let's move back from the circle," a uniformed Minister told his people.

One official dialed in polarity, and both radiators shuddered into pulsing hums. Two men fed the machines' outlets against the closest wreckage pile. They turned the ground into turbulent colors, refracting rays of light in several directions as distortion waves poured from the tubes.

Debris stirred and began drifting. With gravity reduced or nullified so long as the machines stayed on, medics wrapped in polarized suits slipped into the new field. Some rescuers stuck to the floor and headed straight for the newly accessible victims. Other medics lifted wreckage to one side, catching objects with grapples and fusers. Their airborne craft shot blue cables through new gaps to be snatched by others who would harness and retrieve victims. Red cables would be used by crews to secure debris.

One floating medic nearly reached too far outside zero-G, then pulled back.

Brock looked over to find white-haired Dr. Harold Templeton, a disheveled Dr. Van Campen, and Alexander Moore. Sweat covered Alexander's ashen face and blond hair. Brock could scarcely admit to himself the near-certain truth about Grandfather, but before long, he might need to share this with others, even Alexander, about the man he had followed for years.

Less than a meter away, newly lifted wreckage hovered in zero-G.

New data arrived: ATTENDANCE—2,791. IN TREATMENT—152. MISSING—208. DEAD—19.

Two glints interrupted his viz. Brock stepped closer to the field's edge, where two tiny silver sparks had locked in a slow mutual orbit. His fingers grasped them from the air, then drew back. In his palm rested two solid silver cufflinks, shaped as doves, with blackened edges.

"*Yes, they look kitschy,*" Grandfather had once said. "*But they're such a great symbol.*"

Brock slipped them into his jacket pocket. He turned and crossed the wide floor. He stepped over jagged pieces of wall. Left behind all the lights and hovering ships that had brought caretakers and enemies into his wounded family. Here the blast had found its limit. From this place, and extending to the Heritage offices behind the Hall, every structure had escaped harm and not one window had cracked.

Past the auditorium's curved exterior, only distant echoes and light could find him.

No one would see him or hear his cries. He fell to his knees and sank against the earth. Again and again he drove his trembling fists into grass and soil.

11

BROCK
8:17 AM EDT, FRIDAY, JUNE 22, 2125
CIRCLE PRESERVE, CINCINNATI

BROCK'S RAGGED THROAT FLARED PAIN WITH EACH breath. Last night he should have grieved more quietly, especially if the elders wanted him to speak before them today.

The small office foyer held a familiar wooden table with four chairs, used for any informal staff gatherings. Beyond the table's far end, one closed mahogany door led to Grandfather's old office. By this weekend, a new president might need to move in.

Alicia pressed her face to Brock's chest, and he clasped his hands around her back.

Last night at 3:00 AM, the death toll reached 36 and showed JEROME RIVERS. With no one left to rescue, Brock and Alicia retreated to their hotel room and mourned together.

They had slept a few fitful hours, haunted by fire and burning metals.

In seven minutes, the council would start its planned meeting in the vast center auditorium atop CIRCLE headquarters. They must carry on, voting to approve the Space Mission, and facing any consequences Grandfather had left them.

He'd sounded so confident about this vote and CIRCLE's chances of resisting CAUSE. Now he was truly gone, as if at the wicked hand of their distant enemy. CIRCLE Security had released no news of any investigation. Maybe they could not; after all, the Causian Ministry had moved in. And may the Lord prevent any Ministers finding their way to this meeting.

Security officers were posted below. All this top floor of headquarters rested in silence, as if Brock's people had already began holding vigil.

After the conference—if this event even continued—they would honor Jerome Rivers with an all-day memorial.

"Let's do this," Alicia said, and they separated.

Brock sighted the virtual key from Alexander, then touched two sheets on the table. They lit with versions of the same document. The will named Brock as sole executor and overviewed the estate. Most of Grandfather's condo furniture and décor were pledged back to CIRCLE, and he had specified one donation of 3,000 yun for his church, Sola Cathedral. He had dedicated smaller amounts for other groups, even to pet adoptions in the preserve.

Alicia tried a smile. "He did it. By the end, he'd given most of it away."

Grandfather and Dad used to fake-threaten Brock's removal from "inheritances." Brock could only hope CIRCLE was able to notify Mom and Dad in Russia. More likely, a human messenger would somehow bring them the news about Grandfather's fate.

That was the cost of the Lord's work. If they could bear it, then so should he.

"Here, the last page." Brock pointed to the date with different lettering: JUNE 14, 2125.

> Addendum: I have received a new inheritance. My executor and CIRCLE's council of elders know the amount. I leave this sum to CIRCLE to form a new outreach, possibly called Space Mission, care of Brock and Alicia Rivers. Jerome Rivers, *soli Deo gloria*.

Someone gently knocked on the office door.

Brock opened this to find Dr. Harold Templeton, tall like his grandfather, but a little broader. His familiar navy coat with long sleeves made him resemble a sea captain. Crimson wrist trims hid his hands, where light caught on one of his gold cufflinks.

"I'm sorry to intrude."

Templeton asked about their emotional health, like a pastor, and after their physical health, like a physician. Somehow all that time, the elder kept wearing his professional face. But there was deep pain and restrained fear in his spectacled eyes.

He coughed gently. "I'm sorry we have to do this meeting now."

Just as Grandfather once said, Dr. Templeton often apologized too much, yet somehow not enough. "Also, I wanted to tell you that in the president's absence, our preserve's liaison with the Ministry passes to the vice president, Dr. Woodford. He tells me we haven't yet heard from CAUSE."

Alicia said, "Isn't that good?"

Templeton shook his head. "They must have seen the declaration for the Space Mission. It's only a matter of time. Meanwhile, we get ready for their consequences."

• • •

BROCK
8:28 AM EDT, FRIDAY, JUNE 22, 2125
CIRCLE PRESERVE, CINCINNATI

Not in ten years had Brock visited the Epicenter. Fourteen encircling rows of plush white chairs descended into the large meeting room, encircled by cornsilk-shaded walls that were interrupted by a single arched entrance. Morning sunshine cascaded from the room's high round ceiling of triangular glass panes. That surface carried a new structure—a com projection tier, two meters high, hanging down like a silvery chandelier.

"They finally added that new tech," Alicia whispered. "And the platform . . ."

Brock nodded. Down in the middle, the new center table was made of richer cherry wood and held twelve seats. For now, five were empty, and one would remain so.

Their party descended the aisle on new red carpet that had replaced the old blue.

Clock viz showed 8:30 AM. The room bristled with whispers from over a hundred people in one-third of the seats. Warming air flowed with full strings among echoic pulses and vocals. This was *starsong*, like Alicia's creations, a genre unique to Biblical Christian preserves. On any other day, that calm and watery soundscape would soothe him.

Bryony Sedgewood, a CIRCLE mediator, jogged up the room's opposite slanted aisle toward a crescent-shaped console. Down in front, Alexander slipped into the second row.

Brock and Alicia sat next to him, and the rest of the elders arrived to take their seats.

Dr. Woodford stood on the center platform beside the table, looking poised and demure in his long brown jacket with subtle silver trims. As vice president, he was next in line to lead CIRCLE. "Let's start with prayer for the victims of last night."

Victims, as if from a natural disaster . . . or from an enemy attack.

• • •

BROCK
10 AM EDT, FRIDAY, JUNE 22, 2125
CIRCLE PRESERVE, CINCINNATI

CIRCLE's elder council voted unanimously to pause the conference, and the deacon council ratified the decision. Next came item number two, responding to the disaster.

Dr. Samuel Morrison, so aged that his signature graced CIRCLE founding documents, began by condemning a "spirit of fear" among people. "No enemy weapon formed against us shall prosper," he quoted. "That includes anything we hear from the Causians. Amen?"

A few people murmured *amen*.

Timothy Sheldon described how civic emergency workers could legally enter the campus to help with disaster relief, without violating preserve sovereignty.

CIRCLE Security chief Maxwell Adams loudly favored kicking out the Ministry.

"Even if you do," Dr. Woodford said, "the city has trained Ministers on staff."

"Then the strategy is obvious," Adams insisted. "CAUSE makes new policy to get the Ministers inside public agencies. Stalk the borders of a lawful preserve. Harass the people inside, like they've already been doing in other countries. Then they try something worse."

He halted there, leaving them to wander among their fears and imaginations.

Dr. Woodford held quiet, as if merely considering that scenario.

"Could be that's why CAUSE has gone silent," Adams said. "They're already here."

Templeton raised a challenge. "Isn't this a chance for us to love our enemies?"

Several elders chorused their protest. Dr. Woodford slipped above them to take the floor, affirming that, of course, Christians ought to act appropriately toward visiting Ministers. "Still, they are not hungry or thirsty," Woodford observed. "If they ask, we can give these. But what if they burn our crops or poison our wells? That's another problem."

"If this meeting were public . . ." Templeton paused. "What would our people think?"

CIRCLE supporters might truly believe they wanted their elders to act in the open. But in truth, if two CIRCLE leaders publicly clashed—even if they later enjoyed a private lunch—people would remember only the public dispute and think badly of both men.

Dr. Van Campen moved in, proposing a resolution for CIRCLE Security to supervise city emergency officials and the Ministry. The elders approved this, nine to two.

There was still no forthright discussion of last night's attack or its cause.

"Leaders must act wisely," Grandfather had said. *"Like parents who wait to share truth."*

• • •

BROCK
12:18 PM EDT, FRIDAY, JUNE 22, 2125
CIRCLE PRESERVE, CINCINNATI

During a long break in their hotel room, Brock stepped out into a quiet alcove on the Ark Hotel's ninth floor balcony. From the hotel's high roof hung four winged beasts, one great pterodactyl and one dragon—his favorites as a boy—and two great eagles, silently watching the ground floor. Down there, remnant guests milled about the common areas and restaurant.

Every mental image still desperately sought the old future—the now-banished world where he would have lost sleep by staying up with Grandfather to plan the mission.

Grandfather is gone. Grandfather is gone. He must repeat this truth to himself.

In that perfect and destroyed world, Grandfather would have helped him and Alicia organize mission recruits, timeline, and perhaps find a great starcraft.

• • •

BROCK
3:07 PM EDT, FRIDAY, JUNE 22, 2125
CIRCLE PRESERVE, CINCINNATI

Brock lay his fresh white sheets of notes on the nearby Epicenter chair while Alicia sat to his other side. Deacons were still arriving. A few more council elders strode down the aisle—Dr. Mashima, bearing a benign smile, and Dr. Montague, who trod much more heavily. Would these elders vote by majority—perhaps six over five—or demand a unanimous vote?

Dr. Woodford reopened the session. "Jerome would not want us to postpone this important vote. But on a personal note, I think, given recent events, he would ask us to search not just the Bible, but the signs of the times, to make our decisions . . ."

He could set the table, while Brock plotted his main course.

If they asked about the apostasy rumor, he could repeat Grandfather's explanation from last night. What if they asked whether the president should have appointed his own grandson? Then he could rely on his seven-year record of labor on Mars. And what if—

"Jerome was my friend, too," Dr. Gregory Hendricks said quietly. "He believed in the mission. But for now, his support might be good enough for me."

Dr. Van Campen stood with a curt bow. "As for me, I know Jerome would say we should engage our competition in the open space of worldviews, ideas versus ideas, rather than just hoping the humanists don't foul up the place too badly. Excuse me."

"Now, I don't often agree with Dr. Van Campen." Dr. Morrison put on a smile. "But I say *amen*. If we have some way to stand up to CAUSE, no matter what, let's do it."

Templeton was next, but he held up a hand to delay his comment for now.

Timothy Sheldon lifted his shiny-sleeved hand, like a student, though it wasn't his turn. "Rather, let's consider shrewd ways to challenge them, starting with their Ministry."

"They're pushing it," stated Maxwell Adams, fresh from his earlier ruckus. "I don't mind telling you all—I won't let more trouble in. Buying spaceships for missionary work? Is that the best answer? Our enemy's already at the gates. Or else trying to kill our people."

There it was. Someone had finally said it, and the head of CIRCLE Security, no less.

That set off a small detonation among the elders and deacons.

Dr. Woodford tried to talk them back from this edge. Why delay it? Didn't he see this explosion had torn apart Heritage Hall just after Grandfather announced a challenge to CAUSE?

"We have no evidence about the blast," Woodford said.

If CAUSE *had* somehow attacked them from within, how had they done it? Was such an attack inevitable after Grandfather's declaration?

Dr. Morrison repeated himself from before. "You gotta answer that fear with faith."

Couldn't one elder encourage them all to follow the promises of Scripture?

Dr. Charles Montague scarcely turned his head within his high white collar. "I do say this was a warning. Obviously. Whoever the enemy, whatever they meant by doing it, I take that as a reminder—that we're meant to lead a quiet life and mind our own business at home."

No, not *that* Scripture.

"People are intrigued by the mission," interjected Dr. Calvin Scofield. "The world hates us, but Jesus sends us there anyway. But is a public space mission the best approach?"

Patrick Keller worried about reactions from CIRCLE supporters but hoped for the best. Eiichiro Mashima sounded positive but hinted at practical challenges. Darien Lombardi wanted to hear more about the mission funding after the initial donation.

Sitting two paces from that table, Brock couldn't step away or vanish inside viz. In all this, the Lord might want to remind him that he was too personally invested. All his strong beliefs mattered nothing if these good men retreated from the mission. They deserved truth about the explosion and Grandfather's secret mission funds. And if Brock were sincere, shouldn't he want the same, even if those answers sent him and Alicia back to their desert world?

Dr. Woodford stayed diplomatic, thanking everyone, speaking more slowly than Grandfather. "Jerome rightly spoke of our neighbors in other worlds. The hurting people. If we see a way to bring them the gospel, well, I say we do it."

Well, if there was an election, and CIRCLE let Brock vote, he could support that man.

"Now . . . Brock Rivers? Can you summarize your idea for a mission?"

Lord, help me. Brock stood and walked to that slender lectern before the elder table.

Beyond the elders, red-carpeted ridges lifted around him like a small valley, holding the chairs for several dozen in-person members of the deacon council. From further beyond them, in space and time, generations of future church leaders might look back to judge his words.

Brock began with the Matthew 28:18–20 text, which he cast in gold onto the room's central viz, mirrored threefold. "The Bible says Jesus holds all authority in Heaven and Earth. Our Lord said, 'Go therefore and make disciples of all nations.'" Next he cast Acts 1:8. "We must be His 'witnesses in Jerusalem . . . to the end of the earth.' As we know, the end of the Earth has locked us inside preserves. They will not receive us. So, like Jesus said, we can leave that city and try elsewhere. For us, we can leave this planet. Go therefore."

He could have said that last phrase with more conviction.

What about the rest of his notes? *Evangelism by Flowchart.* He might skip that part, if his people needn't hear of their lack of results from secular "seekers" finding Christian materials on com. Brock's next note may be too informal: *Also, I can fly spaceships.*

"*Go therefore.*" Dr. Hendricks stood and buttoned his jacket. "That's true. But so's this—old Christian rhetoric about 'missions' led to problems. We assumed the world was ours to take."

Brock had never made this assumption. This was an old remedy for a cured body.

"We made people afraid, so they started locking us up in preserves," Hendricks said.

Was this a time for answering them? "My dear sir." Brock might sound too formal. "I've tried to live like Jesus, and I know you have. When did He tell us 'go therefore—unless the last generation did not do this perfectly and failed'?"

"You cannot deny the risks, either here on Earth, or for your family up there on Mars."

Of course, and that suffering made him fight harder to follow Jesus. Yet if Hendricks spoke directly about Heritage Hall, Brock could not rationally minimize the risk.

"If you'll permit . . ." Dr. Woodford stepped on Brock's rebuttal. "It's worth asking how our neighbors would react, here at CIRCLE and across the world. If they saw religious people seeming to resist world laws, couldn't this be a bad witness?"

Did he mean that for himself, or on others' behalf?

"If we try a space mission, people might see us trying to regain power," Dr. Woodford said. "The kind of power that could start another war."

"God didn't give us a spirit of fear, but of power, yes, and love and self-control!" Would they let Brock—this younger man, barely 24 hours back in their gravity—debate them? Had his Bible quote worked, or were they shocked at his outburst?

These were Brock's people, but this wasn't his world. Some had labeled him *apostate*.

But no one at CIRCLE should accept that rumor today. Grandfather had condemned it.

Dr. Templeton stood and lowered his navy-sleeved arms. "I agree with Brock. In the last century, during the Last War, some Christians chose a bad legacy. Political corruption. The FatherSons movement. But we must answer for our own sins, not another's."

"That's what Jerome would say, if *they* hadn't . . ." Maxwell hushed himself.

Other elders whispered. For some reason, none of them would speak of the attack. They might want to wait for further evidence before saying more, or they knew more of what happened but wanted to practice wisdom. Grandfather would have chosen the same.

• • •

BROCK
9:16 PM EDT, FRIDAY, JUNE 22, 2125
CIRCLE PRESERVE, CINCINNATI

That great pterodactyl drifted above indoor breezes, its muscular wings held fast to the skylit ceiling by unseen strings. Eight stories below, the Ark Hotel's late restaurant crowd slowly cleared. Brock's own full meal might help stabilize his aching thoughts.

He leaned against the balcony rail, pressing his stomach against tempered steel. A fall from this height on Mars would bring minor injuries. Not so on his homeworld.

Twelve hours from now, at 9:00 AM, he and Alicia would return to the Epicenter, likely to watch a minor storm caused by Templeton's warm rhetoric versus Woodford's cold front of caution. This dispute alone could end the mission. Moreover, if some other news broke from CAUSE or its Ministry pets allowed on campus, more elders would have sufficient evidence to balk at pursuing the mission. All this excitement would have been for naught.

How could he defend his beliefs without needlessly offending his people? Could he persuade them he wasn't doing this from self-interest? Or should he admit that he *was*? The mission would follow Christ's command, taught by churches for 2,100 years. The mission would give his family a new home between Earth and sky. Was this so selfish to want?

If the Lord knew Brock had *any* self-interest, He might respond with discipline. No, such a thought was foolish. Did not God also grant heartfelt desires to the man who delights in the Lord? What could be better than this hope to obey Him?

Brock's earspace pulsed, and he sighted a new note, sent by someone named J. CRUZ.

> Hello sir. We met last night after Heritage Hall fell. About the Space Mission, I was very glad to hear your words about the Great Commission. Please stay strong. You're encouraging me and I'm sure others. I'm new here, and I want to join the Space Mission. I am

qualified with teaching and even military experience. See my affixed records.

About the explosion, I have experience with fusion reactors. This was not a prime-reactor failure. Please be wise. I'm here tonight if you want to know more.

Jason Cruz

This was the mustached man he'd met at Heritage Hall last night. So he must also be attending the closed sessions. As for whether he had evidence about the blast . . .

Brock voxed him back and heard a single violin note. "Yeah-hello."

"Brock Rivers here. I just received—"

"That was fast. Didn't think my job application was *that* good."

"I haven't yet read your document. Today has been busy at headquarters."

"Yeah. I admit I was watching."

Watching, not attending?

"You staying at the Ark? We can meet tonight in the park outside."

12

BROCK TOLD ALICIA HE WAS STEPPING OUT. HE bypassed the hotel's levitator. Each step down in home gravity gave him solid comfort, but on the ground floor, his legs ached.

Over at the hotel kiosk, two staffers spoke under echoing, quiet splashes from the hotel's main fountain. Two thin glass doors released Brock to the warm night air that bathed his arms, bearing green musk from the nearby lakeside that resounded with droning insects and bullfrogs. Walkways shone with gold splashes from pedestal lamps. Over them loomed Ark Hotel's great wooden wall, reaching biblical height before ending at the convex roof. Far above this vast grounded "boat" lifted the dark and unclouded canopy of Earth.

"Mr. Rivers?" Cruz stood near a light pole whose sides were carved with lion motifs.

"Jason Cruz." Brock took his firm hand.

"Yeah. Listen, I'm . . . sorry about your grandfather. And for my behavior last night."

Brock had nearly forgotten. "You mean your restraint of that angry man?"

"He needed help. Should I've grabbed him? That's another matter." Cruz released his hand. "I meant my behavior to you. First I attacked you, then I groveled a bit."

"Then let's have no groveling tonight."

"Can do that. I guess I'm celebrity-conscious."

Cruz leaned as if to walk, but Brock stepped in front. "I presume you follow Jesus first?"

"Yeah. Since I was young. This is my first time visiting the CIRCLE prime preserve."

"I've now read your dossier. It said you're from New York, but which preserve?"

"Originally . . . New Zion."

This did not sound orthodox. "I've never heard of that preserve."

Cruz gave a nod. "They like it that way. Me, I came to think otherwise."

"Did you change denominations?" Brock asked.

"Any of them are better than my old place. Mr. Rivers, I was raised in a cult."

Truly? Some called CIRCLE a cult, but Brock knew better. Down in the water quivered one stripe of light, cast from windows at CIRCLE headquarters. Someone was working late. The sky was moonless, yet there in the southwest shone that faraway world where Brock's children waited for him.

"I'm sorry to hear that. Was this cult one of the classic models, or a new variety?"

"Couple decades old," Cruz said. "One founder. Spiritual sociopath. God's new apostle on Earth and all that. Trains the men, arranges the marriages. All grounded in the mountains, looking forward to death or the Second Coming, when we all turn into angels to fight Satan."

Clearly he saw through it now. "That's not the Resurrection I was taught," Brock said.

"Soul slavery is what it was. But has some good people. Helped me get out long ago."

"Where are you staying tonight?"

Cruz pointed back. "Got a small grackle grounded on Benning Street."

That couldn't be comfortable. "Not long ago, my family lived in a slightly larger quev."

"Right. You spent seven years on Mars?"

"So you've also read my background. I didn't see that level of detail in your file."

"I put in my career data," Cruz said. "Engineering. Com science. Pilot's license."

"Well, I may have skimmed. Your military background surprised me. You were born in one preserve, then moved to another before you joined planetary defense?"

"Yeah. Started learning life skills. So I know enough to talk about the blast cause."

At the walkway's end, that great cavern punctured Heritage Hall like a meteor's impact. Bones of wall and ceiling protruded from the crater's cragged edges. Light had fled the building, save for tiny red security viz lines shining around the space at waist level.

"Mr. Cruz, as soon as the Ministry departs, CIRCLE Security should investigate that, but I do have other questions." Brock knew he sounded overly formal, while Cruz spoke more casually. "You said my words encouraged you. Thank you, but the meeting was limited to CIRCLE leaders. Are you a deacon? Did someone give you remote access?"

"First, I want to know what you think about enemy conspiracies against Christians."

The perceived question hung before them like humidity, but in theory, the answer was simple. "I don't think *some* form of conspiracy is out of the question. Last night I saw Causians arriving on campus, and not merely sneaking among public officials, but uniformed and proud. I've worked alongside Causians on Mars, but they're more honest about the secular state."

Cruz lifted his chin toward the lakefront. "But you've already tangled with local civics."

"Only before we left Earth, when they forced us to file for interplanetary asylum."

"Heard about that. And about your son. Can't imagine the pain."

"We've built another life." Brock's own voice sounded dismissive, but for tonight, his hopes were his own—and growing more distant if the enemy would truly go this far.

Cruz sniffed. "Any preserve has issues, but CIRCLE campus is better than others."

"Do you mean compared to your own?"

Cruz rubbed his head. "Maybe it helps that CIRCLE was one of the first preserves. Your ancestors stayed neutral during the Last War. They had relationships. Now, my preserve? Yeah, it's a blasphemous cult. But that's no excuse for secular harassment. So maybe you see why I got mad at the Ministry the other night. That's also why I'm sure the explosion was planned."

"You do believe the Ministry would do that."

"Or their local overlords at CAUSE. Especially if they're spying on us."

This was a new accusation. "Please explain."

"You were right. I was able to watch the Epicenter meeting. With one poke I opened pinholes even wider. That operation system plays Accordion."

Not in years had Brock heard that name. "You can't be serious."

"Version 2101. Weak enough to let in spies."

Dr. Van Campen had once scoffed, *"If any man does not provide for his com system, and especially its upgrades, he has denied the faith and is worse than an unbeliever."*

"How much spying did *you* do, Jason?"

"A lot. Only heard the encouragement, but I'm not trying to flatter you."

"I'll tell our com department," Brock said. "They can switch to Bassoon or Viola 3."

"Telling them might only alert them."

"Alert *who*?"

"Whoever spied on us, then set off this attack to kill your grandfather and others."

Night breezes tugged at Brock's shirt. It felt securely theoretical to discuss this privately, yet if Cruz publicly shared this suspicion with any credibility, he would set off cultural explosions across CIRCLE and beyond—and worse, endanger the mission.

"Prime reactors don't overload like that," Cruz said. "It would've left no one alive."

That might depend on the reactor capacity, fuel quotient, and many other factors.

"It's up to you, of course." Cruz sounded nervous yet clear, not like some activist or gadfly. "If we could get into the Hall, I think I can prove it."

Brock couldn't ignore any promise of evidence. "I might know a way."

• • •

BROCK
10:38 PM EDT, FRIDAY, JUNE 22, 2125
CIRCLE PRESERVE, CINCINNATI

Imaginary alarms insisted that Brock was now trespassing into the basement of Heritage House. Just last night, Grandfather had been so full of enthusiasm while leading him and Alicia into this rich mustiness, never knowing this would be their last meeting. Just down that basement corridor stood the corner safe, hiding its gate to the shelter whose secret wealth could fund the Space Mission. Brock turned left toward the other entrance.

"Mr. Cruz, are you married?"

The other man's boots trod on wooden floorboards.

"Jason?"

"I heard. Where I'm from, the family gets complicated."

If they worked together, Brock would need to see his answer in writing. Still, this man had disclosed an Epicenter system weakness and behaved like a trustworthy brother.

"Never been in Heritage House before," Jason said.

Brock found the corner closet and unlatched the door, then tapped a side switch. Arc-shaped golden bands flickered on and raced forward to light another hallway.

Jason looked in. "Where's that go?"

"Underground, toward Heritage Hall."

Caleb Rivers must have built the war shelter at the same time as this passage. Someday, Brock would ask him about that habit unmentioned by biographers—digging out tunnels like any survivalist, while also fighting for his people's security in a new world.

Brock moved into the passage. "Our elders and historical committee probably know about this. I learned about it like any other student. Fortunately, CAUSE shouldn't know."

This corridor opened wide enough for them to walk abreast. Brock slightly bent his head. Jason's short dark hair scraped further beneath the repeated light bands. After a few meters, Brock pointed to the intersection with two other tunnels. "Those are dead ends."

"Guess from here they'd need to go far to join another basement."

"Aren't you new to this preserve? You seem to know the geography well."

A dormant lumen band cast Jason's head into shadow. "I'm a big CIRCLE supporter."

"That's helpful, but if you're seriously applying, I must know more about you."

"So you *would* consider me? To be part of the Space Mission? I'd give anything." Jason said this without hesitation.

Brock bent his head lower. "So would I."

The tunnel turned slightly upward, as predicted by the old building schematics. How would this passage intersect with Heritage Hall's basement? Would the way be blocked?

"Let's hope the Causians aren't scanning down here." Jason spoke Brock's thoughts.

"We'll find out. Here we are."

Tunnel lights ended, returning them to darkness. Brock's foot struck an object. Jason extended dual beams from his face clip, sweeping over unfinished ceilings and smoother walls, all seared by fire. Broken pieces littered a polished floor. A few meters away, the peeling floor panels vanished into blackened shreds.

Only the Lord could have preserved anyone still down here when the Hall went up.

Brock led them between scorched edges of the tunnel, where ashen remnants of a door had tumbled aside. Supporting pillars had been charred where they stood.

He pointed left. "The blast zone should be that way."

Jason's beams preceded them, lighting a surface filled with broken boards and chair pieces. Papers littered larger debris. One metallic glint might be someone's lost jewelry.

By now, city investigators would have removed all the human remains.

Brock stepped through another opening and walked onto thin concentric concrete ridges, like a pond whose ripples had turned to petrified gray sand. Here the ceiling ended in knots of cord and molten steel arteries. Brock braced his right hand against the edge of the charred, half-meter-thick wall. This could be Heritage Hall's power room.

"You fine?" Jason said.

Brock must think less as a grieving man and more of an engineer. "What do you see?"

"The blast goes up and out. Not strong enough to erode the load-bearing walls. At first the explosive force glances off the Hall ceiling and weakens the structure. Then fire cuts away at ceiling and the rest. Everything falls and gets shoved back by the eruption."

"If this is the power room, why are these walls still here? They're not load-bearing."

"Could depend on the reactor model."

Brock used his old personal access and paged through records. "Heritage Hall, auditorium and offices, runs a medium-structure unit with four-twenty SOL core."

"Can I see that?"

Brock instigated a twenty-minute expiration before sending it to Jason.

"Got them here. Ground floor, energy." Jason halted. "Nope. Not it. *It's not here.*"

"What do you mean?"

"Did you see the schematics? Not to mention the backup power cords?"

They lay on the floor, interwoven bundles of gray, red, and navy, running back . . .

"This way." Jason retreated from this ruined place and strode through the entrance, avoiding more debris. By now they may have passed under the Heritage Hall offices. Next the shorter man turned left between two columns, and Brock ducked a low beam.

In the center of this larger room—still linked to the rest of the building by grids of ligaments—sat a darkened cylinder-shaped machine. The prime reactor's metal plate was marked 420–SOL, its bulk adjoined by three auxiliary tanks. Each of those tanks gleamed in the light, without crack or blemish, in full working condition and untouched by the blast.

• • •

BROCK
6:56 AM EDT, SATURDAY, JUNE 23, 2125
CIRCLE PRESERVE, CINCINNATI

No matter Brock's change of position on the bed, or his quiet adjustments to the hotel room curtains to block out campus light, sleep evaded him, chased by unseen fires and uniformed officials speaking in soft voices. What a sick feeling, to be so grounded and useless for five hours. There was no point checking his com clip on the nightstand. Not even Templeton or Mashima might be up early to see Brock's message about Jason's evidence.

Dr. Van Campen may not need Brock's note to know about the vulnerability.

For all Brock knew, CIRCLE Security had already examined the basement to confirm the Heritage Hall reactor still existed. Many of the elders had science backgrounds. Some may have quietly concluded Grandfather and the victims had been killed.

But by whose design? CAUSE ignored old religions to cross orbits and settle worlds. But back on Earth its gentler servant, the Ministry, knocked politely at religious preserve gates to offer poisoned fruit. How on Earth would some evil actor expect Grandfather's declaration, then install some device to murder him? Only a few other people had known the Space Mission plans.

Last night, the Ministry knew Brock and Alicia had returned here. Their visit was allowed for one week on his visitor's visa, just as Earth residents could visit outer colonies. But if they stayed here longer, would local authorities or CAUSE itself do worse than re-banish him?

His homeworld could hold more dangers than Mars.

He couldn't afford sleep anyway. Soon he must dare himself to check the time—

Skriiiikkk. Ice raced over his sweating arms. He rolled to the nightstand, where his com clip repeated the alarm like a low-air alert. Alicia stirred. He brushed a flicker of viz and made the time appear: 7:00 am. One new note had arrived from Alexander Moore.

"Anything important?" Alicia murmured.

Alexander's note only reminded him of the meeting, and did not mention Brock's report. Like the elders, if he knew anything, he was waiting to speak about it.

"Nothing." Brock turned onto his back and rubbed at his throbbing forehead.

He must avoid temptations to speculate about secret enemies in the world, lest he fall into cultural snares that had trapped Christians for generations. Either way, he needn't tell her about this. Maybe he could protect her by withholding this news, or maybe . . .

Brock sighed and rubbed her shoulder. "Listen. Last night, a brother and I went to Heritage Hall. We found the prime reactor intact. Something else caused the blast."

Without sound, Alicia listened to his full explanation.

Then she sat back to process. "I suppose we've faced plenty worse up *there*."

"Whereas the Earthlings aren't used to this." He hadn't thought of it that way. "But would Grandfather have announced the mission if he had known this would happen?"

Alicia switched on the light. "I'd have to think he knew the risks, to him and to us."

"Theoretical risk," Brock said. "We expected quiet opposition, or else amusement about these old-time religious people who think they can compete on CAUSE's domain. Perhaps a challenge under the Accords, but easily answered by our legal department based on all the reasons he mentioned. None of us expected CAUSE or anyone to actually *kill* him."

Brock said this so easily. If nothing else, he wasn't suppressing that truth.

"There could be other explanations," she said. "Maybe the elders think so."

Brock's earspace chimed high. He slipped on his clip but saw no viz. "Rivers here."

"It's Alexander. Thought you'd want to know that Dr. Woodford heard from CAUSE."

13

BROCK
9 AM EDT, SATURDAY, JUNE 23, 2125
CIRCLE PRESERVE, CINCINNATI

STARSONG MUSIC FADED INTO SILENCE AS BROCK
and Alicia descended the ramp toward the center table. Members of
the deacon council had spared the two front-row seats from before.
More people filled the encircling upper rows, chatting cordially, some
with coffee and confections from the downstairs cafe. But here at the
table, all the elders held silent, as if they too heard the swells of Brock's
heartbeat pulsing, like a vox signal, behind his ears.

Brock exchanged gazes with Dr. Van Campen, who gave a quick
nod and turned away. At least he had replied earlier to Brock's note
with a simple, WE'RE INVESTIGATING THE BLAST.

His viz changed to 9:00 AM. Immediately, Dr. Woodford lifted to a
stand. He raised his hands, revealing white sleeves under the folds of
his crimson coat. "Good morning. As acting president, it falls to me
to bring you crucial news. In response to President Rivers, we have
received our first warning from the Ministry."

Now came the stirs and whispers, not among elders but 552 total
deacons tallied by viz, most of those members off-site, with 186 in
this room.

"The letter was brief and clear." Dr. Woodford did not temper this
with polite smiles. Nor did he cast the letter onto Epicenter viz. "In
short, the Ministry reminds us about the Accords that have secured
all believers' religious freedoms, within preserves, for over half a
century. If we stray from their righteous path, we might surrender these
privileges."

Brock and Alicia had seen the letter, forwarded by Dr. Woodford
via Alexander. Brock had read it three times, forcing each gently

threatening word to sink into his vision, just as he had done not two nights before while watching the death toll from Heritage Hall.

> To the leaders of Religious Preserve–Biblical Christianity–Ohio-1, greetings.
> Our domain has become aware of public remarks made by the president of your preserve's founding organization, CIRCLE President Jerome Rivers, about the time of 7:21 PM (EDT) on June 21. A transcript of the president's statement is enclosed. This evidence shows troubling rhetoric in which President Rivers promises "a new CIRCLE outreach" for "gospel missions" going "beyond our homeworld, to the moon, Port L5, Mars, Jovian space, to any world that needs this gospel."
> Per the terms of your preserve charter as organized under the One Humanity Accords, any further action toward a "mission" into non-preserve territories for religious propaganda purposes, either within global regions or extra-orbital, will be held in violation of global and interplanetary law as enforced by the Coalition for Advancement of United Space Exploration. Should your organization pursue this project beyond the bounds of merely personal rhetoric, you will risk a multitude of withdrawn privileges and criminal prosecutions, including but not limited to . . .

"The longest section describes the consequences." Dr. Woodford did allow a smile. "If we try a space mission, local authorities won't protect us from vandalism, assault, or worse from our neighbors. Anyone can come here and do whatever they like. And worse—"

He needn't say *worse*; the room had already erupted, with fearful eyes and outraged expressions blurred behind Brock's grayscale viz of the bulleted penalties.

"Worse, they will block CIRCLE residents from trading in the secular world. No existing or new commerce outside our preserve. Any other religious preserves that do business with us, Christian or otherwise, risk sharing in our punishment."

There it came, the rising anxiety, a magnification of Brock's own response earlier today.

"And to get us back in the good graces of the Ministry and their Causian master?" Woodford smiled, not nervously, but attempting to show confidence. "They would make us officially retract Jerome's statement, and reaffirm the Accords in a public confession. If they can accuse anyone of trying to share faith outside the preserve, even without words, they will. That means they can seize our property. Or throw us in prison."

At that, even elder Timothy Sheldon looked troubled. CIRCLE's legal department had replied with fierce objections based on the CAUSE Constitution Business Class provision. Next, CIRCLE would appeal this threat to every local and state office, going all the way to the hollowed-out federal institutions in Washington, DC, for all the good that would do.

"That's the summary," Woodford said. "I hope you all practice wisdom in how, or whether, you share this news with people you know. I expect it will get out. But CAUSE sent this letter to CIRCLE's elder council. It's meant for us. We will face the consequences."

Voices tangled in the upper rows. Someone called out, "We're all facing this!"

Their earnest fears settled against Brock's shoulders, driving him to his seat. This time, he had not endangered his people. Grandfather had done that, then left the burden on them.

Alicia nestled close, sinking even lower. He drew his arm tight around her shoulders.

Here the mission dream would end, if the Hall explosion had not already destroyed it.

Dr. Templeton swept up from the table. Long navy coattails brushed his knees as he took the platform. Without a word, he lifted high his broad hands, as would some prophet to still a raging sea—and like a miracle, this did calm the people.

"We do face this together." He lifted his voice, booming like a revivalist. "No one denies that! This week, we've been wounded as a body. No matter the cause of the Thursday night disaster, we're wondering if we're safe. Should we expect so much from our people, not only in our home preserve, but from all Christian families across the world?"

He needed no notes as he circled the platform. "This warning is honest. It reveals the truth we'd rather not face. CAUSE and its Ministry would persecute us no matter what we do. But can we afford to be so selfish? Jerome reminded us that CAUSE harms all humanity! When the settlers of Mars need bread and water, their rulers say *no*. And when the people of our world and other worlds need eternal life, what are they given? Stone-cold false promises."

The people remained silent, either in disbelief or genuine conviction.

"This should remind us about other concerns about this mission. Early estimates do show that funds for a ship and crew will cover at best three years. To support the mission, we need help. And not just from all Christian preserves. I believe we need help from others."

Dr. Templeton cast a viz globe of the Earth, tilted toward the western hemisphere.

"Before I began serving as elder, I led CIRCLE's comparative religion studies. I wrote *Unknown Gods*. I've visited many religious communities outside the Biblical Christian faith. They do not agree with us, but if CAUSE attacks one of us, they attack all of us." Dr. Templeton halted at the table's far side, opposite the vice president. "We need preserve alliances."

This sounded unsettling, but not half so much as the prospect of secular persecution.

"We need support from all other preserves, not simply to resist CAUSE, but so we can love our religious neighbors." Templeton cast his own bullet points into the air. "Questions?"

"Would you approach *all* preserves?" asked Father Dyer from Our Lord of the Cross.

Templeton nodded. "For this purpose alone, yes."

"For fringe groups too? The cults and apostates? Even the Human Nature preserves?"

After hesitating, Templeton said, "I'm not closed to that conversation."

People whispered and Brock resisted a scowl. Templeton was being honest, but would he truly work with such groups, even those who practiced open perversion?

A woman said, "Shouldn't we share the gospel *with* other religious people first?"

"Lord willing, let's do both. Imagine building relationships with our neighbors from other religions, even competing to share our beliefs beyond the Earth."

If that single quote escaped containment, Templeton could face a revolt.

"Harold, do you already know anyone who's interested?" Dr. Woodford said.

"I do. In fact, I've asked some friends to attend this meeting."

Heads turned and people whispered louder. If Dr. Templeton had already gone this far, how much further would he go? What kind of influence would other allies have?

"Good sir," Dr. Mashima said. "We reserve this place for CIRCLE members only."

"My guests can visit by com." Templeton turned to the com station, where Bryony raised her long arm. "Miss Sedgewood, do you have them in the queue?"

"They're waiting, doctor. If they're permitted . . ."

"Our bylaws show elders can invite guests, even non-members," Templeton said.

More people murmured, and one deacon blurted, "Even outsiders?"

"Well." Templeton smiled. "Let's call them our neighbors."

Brock could tell that skeptical deacon so many truths about *outsiders*. Grandfather might have said this, even if he privately encouraged Dr. Templeton to show humility.

Dr. Morrison rattled a page. "We gonna share this, Harold?"

Templeton apologized and relayed new text into midair. He listed the names of his guests: one Jewish rabbi and two Islamic scholars. Bryony Sedgewood began explaining how each man would attend the meeting.

A line shone in Brock's viz: CAN YOU SAY MORE ABOUT SPACE MISSION? -HAROLD.

More personal to his own people or to these others? At this point, did it matter?

Brock replied YES, then prayed for wisdom.

Flat viz flickered over one of Templeton's floating lists, revealing one man dressed in a light tan suit. His bright red puff-tie hung beneath a slender black beard.

Templeton waved. "Rabbi Leventhal, welcome to CIRCLE."

Rabbi Eliyahu Leventhal, 47, Orthodox Jew from Israel, held degrees in ancient languages and archaeology.

A second man arrived on another viz, also bearded, wearing a headscarf.

Templeton greeted him in Arabic. "Mr. Al-Hazmi will use a translator."

Imam Khalid Al-Hazmi, 35, American and Muslim, held degrees in theology and religion. He consulted with popular groups in American Islamic preserves.

Bryony signaled. "Dr. Templeton, guest three is phased only."

"Pardon?"

"I can't compress this stream for normal viz. We'll need the new module."

From one of the chandelier pockets emerged a gleaming sphere on nearly invisible fishline. With whispered whirs, this device probed down and halted two meters over the aisle. Viz emitted from the sphere, shifting into planes that drew taut into complex shapes.

An image solidified into a tall and trim man. Viz scribbled in his short dark hair and beard until he became a full person. His coal-gray coat swished with dust-hued edges, and his white collar folded down about his neck. The sensor tube protruded directly from the back of his head, making him look like a humanoid robot; this system might need calibration. Their guest's creased trousers hovered over the floor, and he wore no shoes.

Templeton stood before the ramp. "Dr. Aziz, welcome."

The new man surveyed the room. "I see your world as if I were actually among you."

The voice was refined and lightly accented, perhaps western European, with another tone Brock couldn't discern. His dossier said he was Dr. Mahmoud Aziz, 32, Saudi and Muslim.

"I am Dr. Aziz, of the Institute of Truth. Thank you for your invitation. I admire your Center. We join you in the hope of a world newly open to our faith. A space program run by religious preserves would answer our prayers. We stand ready to help any way we can."

"Thank you," Templeton said. "Rabbi Leventhal, let's start with you."

"I'm grateful, sir. I believe that if we have a spacecraft and crew . . ."

Alicia whispered, "That sounds like they assume partial ownership."

Brock fished in his pocket for the cufflinks. One dove's tiny silver wing had chipped. The other was mostly burned. Years ago, an elderly sister had given these to Grandfather. He had said, *"Maybe they can remind me to work with hands of peace."*

Onscreen, Leventhal said, "CAUSE claims to show the human spirit. But they ignore ancient traditions. Should we join the Space Mission, we can share this old wisdom with new friends at each port of call. We will host prayer and other rituals. In all the materialism of space and technology, we will give to our human family ancient pictures of sacred truth . . ."

When he finished, Templeton read a statement from Dr. Al-Hazmi. It sounded much like Leventhal's words, but Al-Hazmi specifically called the mission an *interfaith* outreach.

"And now, Dr. Aziz?"

That man would have more to say, and unlike the others, he had a larger presence.

Aziz lifted his arms. "There is only one god. We all believe that. He is named Allah. We do not all believe this. You do not accept Muhammad as god's messenger. I do not expect you to fulfill *sharia* law. Still, we are like you. CAUSE blames us for the actions of Muslims during the Last War. CAUSE forces us into quarantine as if from plague. For over seventy years, we have practiced Islam among ourselves. We cannot meet in public or build new mosques in cities. We cannot sound the call to prayer outside our preserves.

"If we have a ship, we can escape gravity. We can travel into Allah's heavens aboard ships to share moral teaching. We can build mosques in stations and on other planets."

His strong voice drifted; he gave no notice of these hundreds of silent stares.

Was it Brock's duty to rouse them?

"Thank you," Templeton said. "Now, representing CIRCLE, Brock Rivers."

Brock sprang from his chair and took the platform. "Yes, brother. All right. I was called to be mission overseer. Let us imagine a vast ship, a specially built starcraft. Its fusion core and plasma jet engines will propel its launch from Earth. Long-range drive will take this ship to orb stations, the moon, Mars, L5, then onward to Jovia and Saturnine."

He needed no notes or disclaimers.

"We won't be like those CAUSE ships with their practical grays and blacks, as if they want to hide in a vacuum. Instead, behold. Watch our starcraft approach the *Olympus* station dock or a terrestrial site. This ship dazzles your eyes. Onlookers might say, 'CIRCLE Space Mission? What is that?' Our people can show the meaning. We will host a small crew of our best com specialists, two pilots, and a staff of proven ministry leaders."

Al-Hazmi frowned, possibly awaiting translation.

Brock could skip discussing evangelism. That theme was clear enough. "This ship will keep open doors. We can represent many Biblical Christian denominations and, I suppose, many other religious traditions in a sense. No, those traditional religions do not agree on Jesus, but I suppose we agree on the need for loving our neighbors, helping them look beyond CAUSE to find meaning in the greater callings of . . ."

Someone coughed.

He was losing them. But forthright speech could cost him the mission and worse.

"Despite our differences, I can learn to work with . . . even as we . . ."

This was not right. He must speak plainly. Otherwise he would not be fair to them, true to himself, or honorable to the Lord.

"Hmm. I may have almost turned political there." Now he could find a natural laugh, just like Dr. Woodford. Brock turned from the other guests, facing the upper rows. "For seven years, my wife and I have fought to live on Mars. I've met those real people my grandfather referenced on Thursday. Let's not use them for pet social theories or tokens for our personal conflict with CAUSE. And they don't need *ancient traditions* or *moral teachings*. They need Jesus Christ."

If only he had time to learn more about Mara, Justine, Sayed, and those countless others.

"Amen," Templeton offered. "And hearing that, we—"

"Let us say our ship is partly funded by Muslims, Jews, other religions." Brock saw a new destination and set the course. "Let's say our ship carries them. As ministers? As missionaries? This can't work. One ship cannot serve two shipmasters."

Dr. Aziz fixed eyes on Brock. "You call this a ship of slaves and masters?"

"No, sir. But we all want to steer the ship toward *our* beliefs. How could we not?"

"Amen!" came several shouts, followed by quick applause.

Don't talk so fast. "On a ship like this, my first mission would be to convert my crew!"

That renewed his people's applause, which grew higher, louder . . .

"Mr. Rivers, we do not agree." That wave broke against Dr. Aziz. "Dr. Templeton, I was told you would permit equal discussion."

Templeton had made such promises to strangers?

The elder said, "Yes, and in the future, we are open—"

"The future, yes," Brock interjected. "Allies can help us resist CAUSE. So let's make alliances for *that* goal. We can compete to evangelize. But not on this ship for the same mission."

Applause returned, with more shouts of *amen*.

Dr. Aziz donned a smile. "Mr. Rivers, are you afraid to work with Muslims?"

That was not an approved Epicenter meeting tactic. "I've worked with people who don't believe in any god but themselves. They're the same people whose beliefs destroyed—"

"Do you love your CAUSE people more than other religious people?"

"Why do you ask me this?" Oh, for more time for Brock to plan his words. "I see God's common grace in all humanity. But that grace is still *common*. Jesus gives us saving grace."

"Mr. Rivers and Dr. Aziz, please!" Templeton stepped too close to Brock. "We share common cause against *the* Cause. What about possible alliances based on this shared creed? Could we minister on a single ship, together yet separately?"

Brock couldn't avoid this debate. "Sir, does anyone here want a *mission* ship with crew members arguing key doctrines among themselves? These are foundational issues, such as Muslims who believe the Bible was corrupted many centuries ago. Dr. Aziz, is that your belief?"

The man's image appeared paused, perhaps a signal interruption.

Then he lifted his arms and extended his palms. He opened his eyes. "I speak truth to you. I believe Allah demands submission. He will not tolerate partial truth. That is why I requested your hearing."

All the Epicenter fell quiet.

"CAUSE is the spirit of *al'Masih ad'Dajjal* that deceives the world. The end of ages draws near. Only some will submit to Allah. Even many Christians will join Muslims to oppose him. Do you believe Antichrist is coming? Will you fight his spirit?"

None of this was relevant. "We can discuss eschatology in some other—"

"Would you reject Allah's word? Would you reject the one who comes in his name and turn back to corruption? Your deeds fall on his scales. They have no weight. Allah's judgment is coming. The one Allah has appointed for salvation is nearer. I would take his warning to the stars themselves, and I would die for this purpose."

The man held conviction, Brock could grant him that. "For my part, I would live for a mission to glorify Jesus Christ. He has a name. He has a gospel. He lives."

"Hear! Hear!" people said.

"Our ship will go where people need light and truth and beauty. So I . . . don't envision a simple crew. I imagine a church." If only he could draw this picture in the air. "A ship that is also a church. A cathedral in space. With stained-glass windows to the stars. How I long . . ."

Under his fists, these wooden lectern edges felt ancient and strong, like these next words.

"How I have longed to reach new places, even on Mars. We could help baptize that desert. I can't promise floods of converts or cleansing revival. I won't promise to overthrow the preserve system on Earth. But if we are set free to do this, I know that I will live for this mission. I hope the Holy Spirit will bring us friends who will do the same, and not just for this mission. We will live *and die* for our Savior who gives us eternal life and family and . . ."

Applause was regathered, again rolling forward.

"These people outside my preserve? They aren't my family, but I want them to be! And *this matters* for people and planets we haven't imagined. My fellow Christians, we might live secure with our families in preserves. But we're cut off from other potential family in Christ! People like . . . Eliyahu and Khalid and Mahmoud, and Justine, Sayed, Mara, Shanon,

Michael, Elizabeth, Rachel, Perrona, Josef, Charline, Benjamin Reyes! *Deus vocat ultra orbis, vade ergo.* God calls us above the circle of Earth. Go therefore—"

Cresting applause buried Brock's words and the people's shouts of *Hear! Hear!*

Among the elders, no man stood, but five of them looked pleased.

Brock palmed his eyes, clearing his vision. Alicia stepped up to take his hand. She supported every word he had said? Even with tears in her eyes? He had passed through this moment. He'd said nothing about his own desire to escape Mars. In fact, until now, that thought had not occurred to him. With it came a great weariness.

Dr. Van Campen ushered Brock and Alicia to their seats, then sat beside them and whispered his thanks. Somewhere behind Van Campen, Templeton was gamely trying to recover the floor, until at last Dr. Woodford stood and began chiding him.

This might be a blessing. If any of these guests thought working with Christians would be easy—with or without a space outreach—soon they would see the mess. But without their financial support, could the Space Mission even be launched?

"Order, please," Dr. Mashima kept saying. "Order. Please."

Today they were cheering. Tomorrow they might recognize that Brock, based on his great uncompromised conviction, had overthrown the only practical solution for CIRCLE and other religious preserves to stand against CAUSE. For the second time in his life, his desire to serve the Lord might condemn him to exile. Why then did he feel no guilt?

• • •

BROCK
12 PM EDT, SATURDAY, JUNE 23, 2125
CIRCLE PRESERVE, CINCINNATI

When order returned, CIRCLE's elder council confirmed James Woodford as the new president, by 9 to 2. The deacon council ratified that decision, 499 to 53.

Finally, Dr. Woodford called for the elders' most important vote.

"Please think carefully about your choice, not from fear, but faithfulness," he said.

By a vote of 7 to 4, CIRCLE's elder council approved the Space Mission. Then, just as Grandfather had proposed, they ratified Brock's and Alicia's appointments. Deacon council support rose even higher, at 520 to 32.

That night in their hotel room, Brock lay awake, shuffling ideas on dimmed viz.

CIRCLE had officially launched the program. Most of its leaders had given their support. Now he would only need recruits, supplies, fundraising, time, protection . . .

Even if this worked, how on Earth was he supposed to build a starcraft?

• • •

BROCK
6:41 AM EDT, SATURDAY, JUNE 25, 2125
CIRCLE PRESERVE, CINCINNATI

Brock waited two days out of respect before he sent a diplomatic note to Dr. Woodford, saying he looked forward to working with CIRCLE's new president and the elders. But more importantly: *Please also see these enclosed records from Heritage Hall.*

The elders must know. It must be addressed as soon as possible, especially once local authorities cleared out.

On Tuesday, Alicia cleared funds and ordered 49 minutes for a live viz to Port Ares. All the children looked happy. Very soon, Brock would need to tell them what happened to Grandfather, that distant figure whom they had seen only on viz.

By the afternoon, hotel doors opened and closed, trash bags appeared in halls, and janitorial staff outnumbered room guests. Most lingering conference attendees were leaving the preserve. On top of all other tragedies, this cancelled anniversary celebration broke CIRCLE's record of uninterrupted June events dating back to the 2075 founding.

Neither Dr. Woodford nor any other elder had responded to Brock's note.

Once the city and its Ministry liaisons officially left campus, CIRCLE honored the life of Jerome Dwight Rivers at Sola Cathedral. Like the best Christian memorials Brock knew, including for his grandmother, this service encouraged full expressions of grief, yet always, *always* gilded with hope.

Seven years ago, soon after the Mars landing, Brock had used a public-access telescope to look back on Earth. Dim sunlight showed him a darkened homeworld. But today, while Dr. Van Campen and Dr. Woodford spoke about biblical promises, Brock could imagine Earth's eternal future. Someday this very world would become a perfect preserve, shining like a vast sapphire on black velvet, a pure circle filled with the Lord's glory that pierced clouds and reached outward to illuminate all other worlds across creation.

Others wept, but for today, Brock did not. Maybe he had already worked through the worst of his mourning before turning that energy toward early mission work.

For his eulogy, he introduced himself as Grandfather's grandson and as Space Mission overseer. With Alicia's help, he sang the last of Grandfather's song about the five *solas*. Unlike Jerome Rivers, Brock survived, and the people applauded.

Grandfather would not mind if they used his legacy to gain mission support.

● ● ●

BROCK
9:40 PM EDT, THURSDAY, JUNE 28, 2125
CIRCLE PRESERVE, CINCINNATI

Alicia turned over in bed. "When d'you plan on putting that away?"

"I thought I was being quiet." Brock cleared his viz. "The elders finally replied."

Now she was awake, her face washed in faded light. "Did they? Dr. Woodford?"

"Templeton and Dr. Mashima. They want to meet tomorrow to discuss the mission."

Elders had stayed busy shutting down the conference and organizing the memorial, but they may have waited too long. Brock and Alicia had already planned their return trip.

"Still nothing about Heritage Hall?"

"Not here, anyway." Brock gave a sigh. "If CAUSE or its Ministry were truly behind that, and if they can exploit com weaknesses, they may have simply erased evidence."

She glanced upward. "If we filed an extension . . ."

"No. The kids need us home. At least we were able to see Grandfather once more."

Even if they were drawing new salaries, could they plan a mission from so far away?

"There's another possibility, love." Alicia drew in her lips. "One of us could return home. And I think we know who should stay here. Probably not the mission specialist."

Separate? "Love, that doesn't seem fair."

"No, it's not." She smiled to herself. "Who would think, you'd be facing CAUSE threats here at home, while I gallivant to the sister planet where it's safe?"

Brock hadn't considered that, but she knew exactly how to win such arguments. Maybe it was their afternoon nap, or the humid winds blowing gently outside, but despite the grief and threats and every possible doom, the Lord might be readying some wondrous future.

• • •

BROCK
10:20 AM EDT, FRIDAY, JUNE 29, 2125
CIRCLE PRESERVE, CINCINNATI

One week ago, Dr. Van Campen had brought them, as if by forbidden magic, directly into the basement lab of the Harding School. On this day, Brock and Alicia crept alone beneath low-hanging panels that auto-illuminated and cast shadows off the shelves of old engineering equipment. They found CIRCLE's secret quantum vault poised in the furthest corner, humming like a beast. Its gateway glinted silver, and the side stat glowed violet. Dr. Van Campen had pre-activated this before leaving for another task.

Brock had studied the vaulting instructions, which seemed absurdly simple.

He leaned Alicia's luggage against the vault's curving glass wall, then linked with the vault stat that showed the last transmitting location on June 21, 2125: PORT ARES QUANTUM TRAVEL PLEX HUB 21, UNIT

318. Brock signaled the receiving CAUSE vault with his passport code and sent return-trip authorization and payment. Now they must wait to enter the distant queue, giving time for his stomach to feel heavier.

He'd left one task undone. "We didn't find gifts for the kids."

Alicia reached into her pocket and withdrew a clump of ordinary grass.

Lord willing, they would see how precious that was. "Next time, I could find my old Bible among Grandfather's things." Brock drew her close. "Vox me as soon as you reach home."

"I will."

The vault stat and Brock's earspace chirped together. Their place was confirmed.

Alicia gripped his hand. "Go therefore. Find a ship and build His mission."

Brock took her and kissed her, clinging to her scent, her confidence and beauty. If only the mission could help him forget this parting.

It began when Brock released the heavy door. She followed the vaulting guide by standing in the exact center circle. One meter away, Brock steadied his fingers while keying the final sequence check. One pad lit red. He pressed that and shut the door.

Alicia caught his eye. She smiled as if excited for this journey.

"I love you." Brock steadied his voice and lowered his fingers to the stat.

"Love you too, so much."

The stat light flared green, and his wife vanished into a whirlwind of tangled lightning.

14

FOR THE FIRST TIME, ALICIA HAD VAULTED FROM one alien planet to another, by herself. On this world, for as long as needed, she would act as a solo mom and missionary-in-waiting.

The vault walls changed color and pulled outward. Her first step sent her skidding into the front door. Martian gravity made her body appear overjoyed at returning. But this separation wouldn't last. One way or another, their family would reunite.

"Welcome back to Port Ares. Please carefully exit the vault."

Alicia lifted her much lighter valise and cleared the door. One human operator manned this section, but in the hall, few travelers waited their turn to vault away.

Her time showed 06:18 LMST. She had lost about four hours.

Lord Jesus, I need to nap. Later today, please gift my children with deep sleep. Amen.

Alicia easily found the levitator and stepped inside. She hovered a moment before lighter gravity drew her down within the transparent shaft. Neighboring tubes were empty, except for one slender woman whose drifting blonde hair shrouded her face. Alicia looked over, and their gazes matched. The other woman gave a friendly smile.

Alicia stepped onto the floor, ready to vox Brock.

"Excuse me." The other woman emerged. Her golden skirt hovered over slick tiles, revealing small white legs. "Can you help a fellow traveler?"

By now, Alicia was practically a Martian settler. "Is this your first time here?"

"As of today." She lifted her shoulders. "I'm Nathaira. Which way to the tram?"

"That's where I'm going."

"Could I join you? I figured you were native. How long've you lived here?"

Alicia might not enjoy a quiet trip to the grounded quev. "About seven years."

They were moving onto the walkway over Probe Point with its CAUSE cathedral.

"That long," the other said. "Imagine. What is your trade?"

So this woman would be a talker. "Music and general education."

"Really! What kinds?"

"Well, early childhood, middle grades, humanities, geography."

Nathaira seemed truly interested. At the dockside, tram doors pivoted apart, and Nathaira sat first, pressing tiny wrists into her skirt. "Did you come from Earth, too?"

Brock's grandfather himself had appointed Alicia as mission specialist. Any meeting could open a new mission, however small. After all, God's providence had led to Brock's encounter with Michael Starr and the salvation of a family.

Be guarded, yet kind. "Yes, I'm from Earth. My husband and I were visiting."

No one else boarded. The tram's dimmed lights flashed orange as the doors sealed. Voices gave announcements in many languages. Segmented walls drifted past, then opened to a red-shaded airlock; then, with a hum of spectra, the tram surged forward until all port walls and lights rushed away, replaced by chilled sky.

"So where are you from, Nathaira?"

"I'm also of Earth, from a London branch," she said.

"What company? Or group . . . or government?"

"Uncanny. I trained for this gravity, of course." Rusted light glinted off Nathaira's glittered eyelashes. "But this sense of lightness. It's almost a spiritual experience."

"Five-eighths gravity. Yes, it feels like flight, but without training, it rots the bones."

Her own children, after a week spent in the native well, could be rotting a little. They would need adjustment meds in small doses. Back at home, Alicia would drop gravity closer to Martian level, then slowly ease upward until they were acclimatized to Earth level.

"Now boarding, industrial port," came an announcement.

The tram halted. Alicia settled back into place. "Do you have a trade?"

"I do therapy, counseling, some education. I'm just out of apprenticeship."

Oh no. "You're with CAUSE?"

Spectra hummed faster as the tram lifted from its stop.

"I'm a Minister."

Nathaira must *not* see how much Alicia fought for calm. "I thought the Ministry oversees domestic preserves on CAUSE's behalf. Are the preserves now coming to Mars?"

"Not at all. Religious preserves will stay on Earth."

Brittle plastic felt hard on Alicia's back. Both doors had shut as the tram moved.

"Unlike some preserves, the Ministry believes in the dignity of one humanity."

This woman couldn't be over 25, but she spoke as if she were some grand guru. "What an interesting religion, Nathaira. Myself? I'm happy with my beliefs."

"Does your family or coworking unit feel the same?"

"Of course."

"So you are part of one family?"

The question must be rhetorical. She already knew this answer about Alicia.

"Now boarding," the tram declared. "Admin district."

"Of course." *Well! This is my stop. Hope you find your way.* She could say this, or else wait for her actual destination, before leaving this . . . emissary? Spy?

"What does your partner do? Do either of you have more family?"

No other passenger slipped into the tram before the doors re-sealed.

This was an interrogation, no matter the woman's kindly tone. "I have many brothers and sisters. Maybe even some on Mars. You never know."

"Mm. I do hope you are being treated well."

That was enough. "Nathaira, sometimes I wonder! Every day I stay home, cooking and cleaning. My husband barely lets me write songs."

No, she had said too much. Alicia lifted her valise onto the next seat and sighed. "I'm a Biblical Christian. We might look strange to you, but for us the most important things are about God and His Lordship and eternal salvation."

There, she had replied firm but graciously. And over here, this was still allowed. *We're not on your planet. Just wait until we return to Mars with a spaceship.*

The woman didn't blink. "I've studied your faith, so I know all of your ideas."

"Oh, *have* you. Nathaira, what are we really doing here?"

"Do you mistrust me because I'm a Minister?"

Alicia glanced at Brock's name on viz, and encountered a red null sign.

She tried text over Q-link. Null sign.

Had the woman done this? Wielded that kind of power, without hint of viz in her eyes?

Nathaira looked down the long tram car with those many empty seats beneath blackened glass. "Alicia, I know we make your people afraid. Please ask yourself. Did we approach you with a show of force? Did I meet you at the quantum vault, a public unit managed by CAUSE? Could we have intercepted your own vaulting sequence? We did not. There are no prison camps. We have no re-education facilities or secret labs. I am not some monster."

"Nathaira, I won't answer for whatever propaganda you've heard about my people."

This young Minister faced her. "How has Adam been?"

They knew his name. "He's . . . he is . . ."

"By now, he would be seven."

"Don't worry about my family. For all I know, we're the only Christians here."

"Do you evangelize to others?"

At any other time, Alicia could laugh. "I evangelized you a moment ago."

"It was hardly effective."

"That part isn't up to me."

Another stop brought the announcement, "Now boarding, vehicle grounding bay."

Alicia remained firmly in her seat. If she got up, Nathaira could follow her to the *Legacy*. Again, no one boarded, and the tram resumed. The next round trip may take another ten minutes.

Then why not use the time well? Alicia pointed to the closing doors. "Maybe you can educate me about your beliefs. If my husband and I start a Christian community on Mars, would the Ministry try to regulate that as a preserve, like they do on Earth?"

Nathaira leaned back as if sincerely pondering this.

Soon the agent voice announced this tram had returned to Port Ares Hub.

Nathaira sat forward. "Preserves have purpose. Without them, we lack perspective. We'd have no history of humanity. That is the life story of Earth. But this will not become the future of this planet or any others. I see on Mars a world of growth and change—the human body running, then flying, not crawling back into its crib or left for dead."

Her fine-sounding poetry couldn't compare. "My Lord brings the dead back to life."

"So you do plan to evangelize."

"Doesn't your religion intend the same? Look at that. We're *both* human." Alicia may have just copied one of their debate-the-secularist roleplay lines from college. With one deep breath, she might enjoy a reprieve.

The tram paused for Industrial Port, waited for no one to board, then resumed.

The young prodigy had no response. Alicia may be gaining control. "You watched the recent declaration by CIRCLE's president. Or you heard about CAUSE's reply."

Nathaira faced the front of the tram.

"That's why you've come all this way to give me this warning."

One stray light cast over the Minister's face.

"Now boarding. Admin district." The tram restarted and dipped lower, then coursed back upward. A moment later: "Now departing, Admin district."

The woman had not stirred. This was some rebellious gesture or else a power move.

Well, she could sit there forever. Alicia would sleep peacefully tonight while those Ministers stayed awake writing panicked memos about religious theocracy creeping onto Mars.

The tram slowed. "Now boarding, vehicle grounding bay."

All doors unsealed and opened. *Now.* Alicia stood and stepped out to land on the bay's smooth rust floor. She strode away with sure-sounding footfalls.

The now-distant tram voice called after, "Now departing, ground—"

She turned left toward sections 32 through 42. *Legacy* rested in Section 31, like Alicia's age, and in Row 12, like the disciples. She swung around the row's corner slot, occupied by a sandfly. Her shadow touched another shadow.

Nathaira was following her.

Chilled air caught Alicia's sleeves. "Well! Here is my pretend destination. Farewell."

Golden folds swished at Nathaira's knees. She advanced with that same balmy smile.

Alicia strode faster, and Nathaira mimicked every step.

Ministers supposedly carried no weapons, but could that thin skirt conceal one? She still didn't appear to be using viz. Their eyes met; Alicia glanced away. Why had she lost that tiny battle? *Jesus, help me.*

Large letters etched on the wall indicated section 30. Beyond it waited section 31.

Even if she voxed port authorities, what could she say? Who would respond to—

"Oh, Madam Rivers?" A man slipped out from between two quevs. He wore a single blue garment full of pockets. Tools shone at his waist, and a gray hat covered his short blond hair, but she recognized that smooth face—Michael Starr. "I'm here to retrieve you."

15

BROCK ATTEMPTED SEVEN TRANSMISSIONS OVER the last half hour, but Alicia did not reply, no matter how often he re-paced the floor of Ark Hotel's lobby. Was this a quantum vox problem? Such network interruptions across the orbits were often resolved within fifteen minutes.

At last his viz pulsed green. "Love, I'm here. Michael is with me."

With a prayer of thanks, Brock palmed the double doors and pushed into the foyer, like an airlock, but with stagnant air dripping with humidity. "What happened?"

Alicia explained her confrontation with a female Minister.

They had come to Mars. Those wretches had actually found her there and stalked her.

"Brock, can they trace coms or vault codes?"

He couldn't afford the luxury of hoping otherwise. "After those Ministers showed up undercover at Heritage Hall, I don't see why they wouldn't watch the vault system."

"But she didn't mention the other children, only Adam. Maybe they're still off-record."

Brock set his gaze, pushing through the hotel's final door into daylight's warm bath. To the west, bright skies broke through clouds to form clear lines of sunlight.

"For now, I'm leaving *Legacy* here," Alicia said. "We're taking Michael's vehicle."

"After the blocked signal, I asked him to find you. Did the Minister see him?"

"Yes, but he acted like a hired driver."

A man approached from Brock's left. Jason Cruz stopped when he saw Brock's viz.

Brock summarized Alicia's Causian encounter.

"You got community housing?" Jason said. "Any coordinates in CAUSE records?"

"We own Areopagus, and I'm sure it's still hidden. All the same, Licia, let's plan for you to stay with the Starrs. Access the skiff and check if anyone pinged the system."

"I will. But you should stay on mission. If *they* feel urgency, I guess we should too."

Brock stretched, pressing his hands against a bench's hot steel rail and lifting his shoulders into warm sunlight. "Jason and I will meet with the elders. Lord willing, we can forge ahead faster than the Causians. I want to find the best shipyards today."

• • •

BROCK
12 PM EDT, FRIDAY, JUNE 29, 2125
CIRCLE PRESERVE, CINCINNATI

Back in CIRCLE headquarters, Brock could have used the levitator, but preferred to honor the Lord's home gravity. At the highest level, another thick door with warm glass opened easily. He and Jason crossed onto a smooth stone-paneled floor, scattered with tables and chairs near the rooftop gardens of headquarters. Past that balcony wall, slender shadows glided over CIRCLE's green campus, cast down by dazzling solid white clouds.

Alexander Moore emerged from the canopied levitator doorway, followed by Dr. Eiichiro Mashima in his crisp gray suit, then Dr. Harold Templeton, who brushed off his navy coattails and waved to Brock. Apparently he would bear no grudge today.

Jason grunted. "That's the man who wanted to bring pagans into the mission. Yeah?"

Unless he straightened this bad posture, Brock might need to apologize to good men. "Dr. Templeton wants to support the mission. We need to respect him."

Jason stared placidly.

How to act first, as mission overseer or new friend? *Oh, just be genuine, only perfect.* That was Dad's phrase, at first said with sarcasm, then in later years, more sardonically.

Brock shook each elder's hand and thanked them for coming.

"I presume your wife returned safely to Mars?" Dr. Mashima said.

"She did, and yet . . ." Brock summarized Alicia's recent encounter and her safety.

Alexander held his chin tighter, while Dr. Templeton lowered his head for a nod. "So our rulers are not letting up."

Jason took his hand. "Jason Cruz. New crew member, I hope. And I agree."

That was well-spoken. "Dr. Woodford cannot join us."

"You can imagine his schedule," Dr. Mashima said.

Could he not prioritize this, if not for Christ's sake, then for Grandfather's?

Templeton beckoned to the table and they took their seats. "You should know that your grandfather asked me to get data on starcraft firms. At first the results were promising . . ."

He let the last syllable trail while Alexander pushed a stack of pages across the table, then fanned them apart. Page one showed a grid of manufacturer logos—Lightstream, Perloff, Quarx, Orbcourse, and Fleet. More pages held lines of names with addresses and codes.

Brock fingered a line of text, and the page shifted to one California dealer. Then all text descriptions and ship images blurred under a black-trimmed box: THIS ACT OF COMMERCE IS SUSPENDED, PER TEMPORARY EMBARGO. REFER TO MINISTRY OF ONE HUMANITY, FIRST MINISTER SALOME ROCHELLE, CAUSE DOMAIN OF PUBLIC AFFAIRS, PORT CINCINNATI.

Templeton lowered his head, soberly watching for Brock's response.

Brock could try switching back the page, but the legal warning would remain.

"That came up this morning," Alexander said.

Templeton nodded as if disclosing a deficit. "CAUSE would never rely on quiet notification alone. It seems our preserve can still trade with the secular world for things like food, water, medical supplies, technology. However . . ."

Brock shut his eyes and drew in long breath. "No spaceships."

"So we're locked out." Jason sat back in his chair. "First they hit the Hall, then this."

That silenced the table. Mashima kept a neutral face. Templeton bent his head as if merely hearing about a church member's hard situation. Alexander alone glanced aside.

Brock took the chance. "Has there been no further news?"

Templeton lifted his shoulders. "As we've told you, there is an investigation. And I'm sure CIRCLE Security knows you found the prime reactor, untouched, at the disaster site."

Jason kept silent, wisely so.

"Any suspicions about the blast cause?" Brock asked.

Mashima stepped in. "We have a few. But without specific proof . . ."

Public accusations of CAUSE would be pointless, and any risk would multiply tenfold even if their preserve could show clear evidence of the attack. At least this injustice brought some hint of reward—the truth that CAUSE saw them as a threat. And Brock, the man they had once caught in a child-citizenship trap, had returned home to challenge their gods.

If they had found Alicia by herself, they must know that Brock had stayed on Earth.

Alexander's voice slightly chipped as he asked, "What about other preserves?"

"Few of those invest much in starcraft construction," Mashima said.

Templeton offered another stack. "Worth noting this—we are likely blocked from markets that would have priced us out anyway. Here. This is frozen from earlier."

Brock perused the page that showed images of new ships in a Calcutta market, each with tiny touchable arrows that permitted closer views. He plied the page corners, but looking further back would do little good: 310 MILLION YUN, 350 MILLION, 380 MILLION. "To stay under that three-year budget, our ship can't exceed two hundred fifty million yun."

"We would need a smaller crew, and I doubt that's acceptable," Templeton said. "Instead of building or buying new, what about reconditioned ships?"

Brock had wondered about this. "It would raise costs later."

"It depends where you look." Dr. Mashima moved his chair closer, catching stray sunlight on his gold com clip. "After Jerome gave his speech, some friends with Navistar approached me. They are based in the Japanese refugee settlement south of the river."

Dad had once spoken at churches there about math and the gospel.

"They do not build ships, but they refurbish ships," Mashima said. "Even the large models. Japanese Christians work there, but Navistar is not a Christian company."

Brock turned another page. "All of this might bother some CIRCLE supporters."

One of those critics might be Jason, despite his silence now.

"In either case, we're seeking the impossible," Brock said. "A nonsecular firm, possibly within a religious preserve, that retails used starcrafts."

Templeton smiled. "That is not so impossible." He spoke as if he'd waited for this opportunity. "You may recall my quiet friend from the meeting, Dr. Al-Hazmi?"

Jason's fingers tightened across his page.

"Oh, I have faced the truth." Templeton laughed. "My original idea of preserve partnerships did not even warrant a vote. Still, he is a good man. His group partners with Egyptian and Saudi firms to buy old abandoned starcrafts that are often immobile. They relocate these ships for grounding in their own preserves, used as multifamily housing."

"They aren't spaceworthy?" Had Jason meant to sound so flippant?

"Not yet. But after refurbishment, maybe so."

"Can we contact him?" Alexander said.

"We might, if he still talks with us."

Brock held back a scowl. The other day in the Epicenter, not even the hardline elders had spoken rudely against those non-Christian guests or accused Templeton of an ambush.

"Mr. Cruz, can you search for *Marwan Khaldun*?"

Jason obliged, and his page flashed. "Arabic only."

Brock tagged the page and touched his clip, copying content to his viz. English words showed a generic welcome, followed by a black-on-white corporate logo, then tiny lines that Brock magnified: KHALDUN CONCERN, based in CAIRO, owned by MARWAN KHALDUN.

"They make supplies for L5 and Jovia." Jason flipped sheets. "Place looks bigger than a port. And it's all inside a religious preserve? What kind?"

"Traditional Islam," Alexander said.

Brock scrolled through questionably translated text. "I see no starcrafts."

"Nevertheless," Templeton said, "Dr. Al-Hazmi assured me Khaldun sells them."

"Wait." Jason jabbed the sheet. "Line item, page eleven."

Brock found the text. "Eight 'undisclosed large items' in inventory?"

"Range from one to two hundred million?" Jason said.

Those could be spaceships. "I see no visuals or schematics."

"One can only view that inventory . . ." Templeton cleared his throat. "With a visit."

Brock had recently traveled between planets. If this preserve had a quantum vault, they certainly had the means, and the assurance of vaulting directly from one preserve to another without public danger. Grandfather had left the 308 million yun to Brock's and Alicia's discretion for the Space Mission, assuming the council approved their expenses.

Alexander said, "Brock oversees the program. He would need to go."

"True enough, but I must confess . . ." A separate concern pursued his thoughts. The other men faced him. "CAUSE knows I've returned to Earth. I would not want to bring greater danger to my people, not even for a good mission."

"Yeah, meanwhile, they're tracking your wife," Jason said.

Alicia hadn't yet messaged Brock about reaching the Starrs' apartment.

"I appreciate your caution." Templeton leaned closer. "But listen to yourself from the other day. This mission is long overdue. Some would say it's seventy years too late."

Mashima cracked a smile. "Besides, we could all simply join you on Mars."

Brock couldn't even politely smile about that. "I wouldn't wish this on any of you."

"In any case, are you willing to go?" Templeton said.

"I believe so." And he was. "We haven't spoken of crew quarters or mission staff . . ."

"I could do a hiring inquiry, even today." Alexander's voice trembled, yet he sat still, as if restraining his own eagerness. After all his mixed history with CIRCLE, he had kept his zeal, now tempered with some wisdom. Would he himself apply to the mission?

"Or we could ask our mission specialist to do that," Brock said.

Jason showed a recast page. "Got a map of southeast Cairo with the preserve." He magnified between blue areas for the Nile River and Red Sea—familiar shapes, like print Bible pages showing Paul's missionary journeys. "Closest vault is in a small plex a few klicks from the preserve. It's not public. After vaulting in, we'd need to walk a ways."

For a preserve-to-preserve journey, they needed no civic passports. Alexander and Dr. Mashima watched Brock.

"That's why I keep training on the stairs." Brock stood. "Alexander, make sure Alicia can get the staff records. Dr. Mashima, I want to hear more about Navistar. Jason, how about you join me? As soon as tomorrow, we can vault into Egypt."

• • •

ALICIA
09:13 LMST, EIN. 19, 44 (SYNDIC)
PORT ARES

Alicia must not envy the Starrs' apartment or its prime location in the Lightstream corporate housing. She could distract herself with gratitude. In these empty halls, lit by diamond-shaped panels, no young Minister with falsely gentle words would chase her.

"Welcome back to Port Starr." Michael opened his door and entered first, proceeding to a decorative wall shelf, where he removed his hat and clip. Light activated in the shallow foyer, while he fixed his three belt tools—*clink, clink, clink*—onto very specific hooks.

His tiny foyer opened to a spacious living area, lined by sofas that joined by a corner recliner. The room's opposite corner was rounded, with gentle scalloped edges containing the family firewell, where hovering viz showed ocean waves tumbling against a cliff overrun by vivid grass. Two side doors opened to wide bedrooms.

It looked like a migration ad: *Move to Mars! Stake your claim on humanity's last desert frontier. Find your destiny in space. Free public transport. Bonus: secular Cause to worship.*

Despite low gravity, she resisted an urge to cling to the floor. "Where are my kids?"

"They sleep. They stayed up late. In native gravity, their abilities are remarkable."

Yes, and she needed to train those out of them. Had the children been responsible with their powers? Michael may not care. Elizabeth might be amused. Either way, Alicia must dare to ask more of them. "Brock wonders if we can stay a few days longer."

"Oh. I will check with Elizabeth. Wait. Are you hungry?"

He moved to the kitchen, where he retrieved a plate of pale wafers with some center orange substance, maybe hummus or some other hyper-organic treat. "Thank you."

"Also, I am checking our surveillance. No one should watch us without my knowing. I do not know the Ministry well. But in my old preserve, anyway, Ministers did not bother Secular Conservatives. They only harassed our neighbors who were actually religious."

What stories he could tell, if she could get him to share. "What about our home?"

"You need my secure link to check the skiff. Today I am assigned to test code for new security measures at the water mines." His gaze drifted to the wall. "So the Ministers are here . . ."

Her viz pulsed for an incoming Q-vox. "Where can I take this call?"

Michael pointed to a side door.

She stepped into the main bedroom, where lights revealed red-carpeted floor with cream-toned walls and two small corner firewells. Embedded shelves arched over the doorway to a bathroom. From there came the sound of running water, likely from Elizabeth, home from the public clinic and enjoying a full, fresh shower. Their wide bed with a polished wooden headboard had been perfectly made, with no unfolded laundry.

All this, while also managing three guest children? "Brock, I'm here."

"Jason and I just finished meeting. Dr. Templeton is finding us some living space, and we've already set our next action. If you're free, I have first assignments."

Alicia tried to ignore the floral-scented moisture drifting from the bathroom door, as if she had returned to Earth. He told her about their planned trip to Egypt and early hopes for Space Mission recruits, probably starting with Jason Cruz.

"So he's our first hire?" Alicia said.

"I checked Jason's dossier. He taught four years in basic engineering at Freedom Hills College, in a small Christian preserve in Virginia. Before then, he spent four years with Strategic Orbital Armed Reserve."

"Based on what you've said, I have a good sense about him."

"Excellent. Of course, he won't be the first recruit. You would be."

He was being kind, giving her the chance to rethink all this, just in case.

Alicia placed both hands on the bedroom window. Green shrubbery lined its outside edges, not viz but real, part of the building's vertical foliage layers that faced the suburb district's enormous covered park. Artificial skies lifted into multiple peaks, like the corners of a tent; CAUSE planners had covered blocks of the city with these membranes. Michael and Elizabeth could walk outside into a facsimile of Earth, complete with bred plants and simulated streams, and the best Martian markets of hydroponically grown fruits and vegetables.

Even in a radiated wasteland, their Creator allowed sinful humans to make good things. How much more would the Lord permit good gifts to them, His children, even after He had sent them into this struggle? Restoration with their people. A home in the stars. Training their family, regaining the call she had felt years before she knew Brock . . .

"I will be," Alicia said, "*if* we add a greenhouse to the ship requirements. We can't be like those early CAUSE ships, all ugly and brutalist. We have to show the beauty of God."

"Condition noted. So, even after what happened, you want the mission?"

"Yes. More than ever. And if Jesus wants this, He will make it happen."

16

BROCK
8:30 PM EEST, SATURDAY, JUNE 30, 2125
CAIRO

WHIRLING SNOW ENTANGLED BROCK'S RIGID LIMBS
and trapped him in a maelstrom. Patches of gray, like metal, flashed
between whipcord energies. This vaulting sequence was taking too
long. Would he even reach the receiving quantum vault?

Maybe the old fears were true. This violation of nature's law would
tear him apart.

Roaring became shudders, and the tornado spiraled away, letting
him fall against a center flange. A synth voice spoke in another tongue
before segments appeared and a door opened, letting him stumble into
home gravity over a dull crete floor.

This was a vault plex, yes, but absurdly smaller than the Harding
basement, with cramped gray walls and ceiling. Two windows and one
open door revealed murky skies. No one was here. "Jason?"

"Yeah, outside."

Jason stood beside the door, under the glow of a large bulb. Barren,
hot air carried rusted, industrial scents and made Brock's jacket retract
its sleeves. Hard-packed ground reached far past a chain-link fence and
intercepted a ridge of globe-lit structures, which lifted like foothills,
not more than two stories high. He had not left Earth, but this place
was alien.

"Should've known this was a pirate Q-plex," Jason said.

Viz twitched in complaint. Something interfered with his com
access. *"Pirate?"*

"Unsanctioned. Not locally regulated."

Martian settlers called those *leapeasies*. "Isn't that good?"

"At least we're here. But our yun's gone to some dark market. You got the way?"

Brock started forward, each step kicking up dust. They rounded the shack's corner and entered a large space encircled by the decaying fence. To their right, old crawlers lay mostly in shadow, like the corpses of insects. To the left, pieces of another fence mixed with vehicle parts and girders. Nothing moved here, not even rodents or stray wind.

Beyond that fence, a flat horizon ended in clumps like hillsides, too round to be iconic pyramids, too uneven to be buildings, and too shallow to be mountains.

Cursory research told how much of eastern Egypt was abandoned 50 years ago, after the Last War's lingering disputes between African insurgents and the Russian-Chinese alliance. In the 2070s, the burgeoning CAUSE tried to release airborne hordes of radiation-neutralizing specs, yet few people had retaken this country. Just as in ancient times, only Cairo and other Nile-bordering areas hosted a few large settlements.

"Got no com," Jason said. "This preserve *does* exist, yes?"

Brock blinked again, now summoning a green arrow. They were following Harold Templeton's map. He fetched their local contact with Khaldun Concern.

A man answered with thin-voiced, unknown syllables.

"Brock Rivers here. I'm seeking Nabil Sadat."

"That is me. I'm told you are coming to see the ships. You know the way?"

They approached another fence, where two small buildings formed an open gate. New and dry gusts cuffed at Brock's eyes. "We do have a map. However—"

"Good. When you arrive, vox me again. I will arrange your landing."

"Our *land*—?"

The signal ended.

Brock re-sighted the code. "Jason, this man expected us to arrive by air—"

"Hold." Jason snapped up his hand. "Men on foot."

There they were, four figures, shambling several paces behind them, half in shadow, half in stray lights that revealed their loose-fitting clothes. Male voices drifted into stilled air.

These could be late workers, out for whatever recreation they could find on a Saturday night. Brock mustn't be prejudiced. Conversely, he couldn't afford to be naïve. Despite all CAUSE's promises, natural oxygen and peaceful technocracies did not sanctify people.

Orange viz wrapped Jason's eyes. Quietly he said, "Just in case, I have two glazers."

Six years ago on Mars, other freelancers had insisted Brock carry protection. He had reluctantly bought his own glazer and stored it in his quev, yet never used it. Missionaries should not carry weapons. But he had not come to this land as a missionary.

What if that Ministry woman had been armed? Shouldn't he encourage Alicia to defend herself? They why not consider the same action against unknown figures?

Jason clutched his right pocket and pulled out a crumpled object.

Harsh light stung Brock's eyelids. It came from a moving vehicle, a crawler easing over the ground beside the vault building; then the beams swung about, cleaved in half by a tall metal shard stuck into the ground. Cast inside the long and pointed shadow, Jason unfolded his hand, wearing a slender crimson glove.

Pfsh. Air punched the ground next to Brock, gushing out sand and steam.

That was a shot. The group had fired upon them. A projectile weapon? "Get down."

That metal refuse formed a barrier. Brock dove behind this, crouching his body onto hard land. He clutched his head between trembling hands. No, his body dare not betray him, not after he had already survived the Hall explosion just days ago!

Jason fired two silver-tinted bolts that punched earth between the attackers. They hurled back more bolts, stinging the wind with steam trails, blasting into the debris pile.

He thrust the second glazer at Brock. "Sir, get this on."

The glove came to life, rubber-like, smoothing itself while capturing his fingers.

"Two hostiles on your left, one right, two ahead. Clench your fist three times to join the glazer with your com clip. They're trying to box us in." Jason fell back and clawed at his own temple. "Father, help. Not this, not now."

Were neither of them prepared? "Cruz—"

"It's real. Should have known. Not just a pirate Q-plex."

Viz splashed Brock's eyes with his own orange grid. "Is this lethal?"

"Can be, if you aim it wrong."

Lord save us. "How do you activate this one?"

Jason raised his hand. "Focus target. I've set both glazers for people, else they won't shoot. Lock on, aim for center mass. Two fingers out. Punch the air, once for each knuckle shot, like you're jabbing. I'm sorry. Didn't know I'd bring you into this."

"What are these people?"

"CAUSE hirelings? Or thieves? Not just pirates. The Q-plex was a lobster trap."

That meant the trappers would rob them or hold them for ransom— or worse, these locals had been told to expect the arrival of outsiders.

"I'm watching bodies. Drop your glove to clear viz. Try to get back a map."

Orange lines vanished when Brock eyed for more. He got a red warning: NO SIGNAL. "Either they're jamming us or this area has terrible com range."

Jason swore.

"I think our path took us that way." Brock gestured toward those outer foothills.

More bolts etched over the sky; one hit the fence's top edge and erupted in sparks.

"Sir, can you shoot?"

Brock's right hand trembled. He clamped his left fingers onto his gloved right wrist. This wasn't right or fair. He did not even know his enemy, yet had no other option. "Yes."

He stared into tangles of debris. Four men tried to get closer.

Lifting his right fist, Brock returned glazer viz that turned shadows into orange shapes with edges trailing fire. Objects in those figures' hands caught scattered light. Behind them, that crawler advanced and opened its sides, releasing two more men. One carried a spear-like object whose tip held a spark like a bubble.

Two fingers out, and punch the air. His glove heated and fired, with little kickback, casting one bolt. It stung one man's leg and threw him against the crawler.

He needed to use this as warning, not to wound or worse!

That spearman raised his weapon and blasted a wild scribble of lightning, carving streaks in the air. Brock recoiled and blinked away gashes in his vision. He opened his eyes—the spear fell with that attacker. Jason's shot had pierced his arm.

Brock lifted his hand to bring more advancing fiery shapes, eight or ten. Were they holding back? Their crawler halted, unmanned but throwing light that painted a faint grid through the fence ten meters away. There—was that a gap through the crumpled metal? He tagged Jason's shoulder and pointed that way, to the west.

Jason stood and edged backward, training his hand against onlooking men. Brock moved to join him, searching the ground for obstacles and throwing shadows into starkly lit land. At the fence gap, Jason crouched inside. Brock followed but kept eyes on the men. They advanced quicker, one carrying the spear, with shouts and heavy footfalls. This decrepit fence wouldn't block weapons fire. Did these men want them dead or alive?

More debris was strewn over bare earth, an open and vulnerable space, yet Jason turned and charged forward, shouting for Brock to follow. They might lose themselves in this mess. Brock lowered his hand, clearing the orange grid.

They veered into garbage piles that quickly became small hills, blocking his view of the distant shack with the single quantum vault. What a strange place to install such costly technology. Whose government ruled this zone? Had they vaulted to some territory uncontrolled by civil society or religious preserves?

Crawler engines roared.

Refuse piles blocked their way, leaving few trails. So those structures Brock had seen earlier were not hills but foothill-sized mounds of garbage.

The attackers might give chase into this wasteland that they surely knew better.

At the end of one trail, Jason stopped at a dark opening in the side of the refuse hill. Back into Brock's mind leaped a phrase from older Martian legends. *Every cave hides alien tombs.*

Bolts arced up into the night like signal flares.

Jason went in first, tunneling into the pile. This was no accidental structure any more than the walls of debris held aloft by girders and sheets, or that cold yellow heat from a lamp hanging over the floor, which was filled with blankets and mattresses. And people.

Two women tumbled into a corner, legs kicking inside their skirts. Over there lay an old man, a young man, and another child. High voices shrieked—

And each human shape turned into fire behind Brock's orange targeting viz.

Were they enemies or innocents? Why were they here?

Viz showed no weapons, but metal glinted nearby. Jason kept his glove raised.

"Ah . . . allah-dee who . . . !" Jason was trying to speak the language, but he couldn't use a translator; his nose was bare. He must have lost his clip, yet viz clearly projected from the bridge of his nose. "We won't hurt you."

Green figures painted Arabic letters into midair over his head.

Both women trembled, but the men didn't move. They might not be able to read.

Jason's com clip must have been decorative—a cover for the truth that his com clip was embedded in his skin—subcut, likely from his time in military service.

As if from Jason's own head, a vox agent translated better Arabic.

The older woman shook her head. "Who is chasing us?" Jason tried.

Something flashed behind, and Brock turned against a new shining tool held by a hooded figure. He lifted that weapon toward Brock's head.

One hand thrust aside that gun. "Don't move, or die." Jason's agent translated.

The man moved. Jason clamped down the man's left shoulder, fingers lit red, flesh burned, and the man weakened, dropping his weapon. Jason lowered him to the floor. He moved so efficiently, leaving Brock to watch.

"Why do you attack us?" Jason shouted.

That man returned a long answer, which the agent translated, "This is our land."

"We know! We came here by accident. Now we're leaving."

The man shut his eyes and traced a circle in the air. "We must slay unbelievers."

"Who are you? What faction?"

"Mah-dee."

"What's that?"

"*Mah-dee*!" The man added more, which the agent translated: "He will come."

"And you will tell us a back way out."

A tear crept against the older man's eye. Then a younger man spoke up.

Jason waited for another translation. "There. Let's go."

They crawled through a tighter channel between debris walls until they met thick plastic shreds that covered a rough entrance. From here a tight trail clung, like a ledge, beside this vast pile of old machine parts and other waste. Below all this yawned a chasm formed by the same refuse. What had been done to this place? Brock could move, but not far from the whimpers of children and women. The trail led past openings and doors, stuck into the mound like holes in an anthill. From these crevices spilled pools of light.

"Those people . . . Jason, I think they live here."

"Not our problem." Green viz sparked in Jason's eyes. "Just got enough signal for satellite. It shows we're approaching the border."

"I can try voxing Sadat."

"The Khaldun man? After they baited us here?"

"We don't know that was him." Brock sighted for vox, and now it went through.

"Ah, Mr. Rivers, yes? Which craft is yours?"

"Mr. Sadat, we did not fly in. We vaulted into a bad Q-plex, and we've been attacked."

"What *plex*? Where are you?"

Coordinates shone at Brock's upper right viz. "Outside, in the garbage . . ."

"Send me your place. I'll tell you the nearest Khaldun gate and send guards."

Jason might object to this, but Brock relayed their location. They climbed over shallower debris near the crest of these garbage-formed foothills. More piles rose higher, their corners jagged against the black sky with its dim undercast of artificial light.

"You are close. I will send a map. I will see you in ten minutes."

Brock relayed these instructions to Jason, just as the skies flashed new lightning. A crevasse sunk to their left, and a long slope flanked their right. "Up there." Brock fought his own numbed arms to grab chunks of steel. Thank the Lord for his strength conditioning that let him ascend, pulling hard against gravity. Plastic sheets tore and spilled out fetid garbage.

Those people lived in squalor, and Brock could do nothing about it.

Another bolt singed the sky. Men ran up the slope, cast under viz shapes.

Jason and Brock clambered over the waste hill's edge onto a vast, flattened terrain of crete or encrusted soil. This forced them to flee under open sky that cracked with violent flashes. Beyond this span of earth—there, a solid ridge of broad walls, like a castle keep, containing more distant structures that sparkled crimson and blue-violet. Before this tall barrier lay a moat under ghostly light, and over this, one surface lowered like a drawbridge.

Somewhere in the sky an object gurgled like a caged monster. Brock dared to look backward. Many attackers retreated, but a few advanced, all on foot and rear-guarded by one crawler that sped forward. Rotating machinery swiveled and turned down to the land, a cannon, its great mouth ready with unspooling fire.

17

BROCK
9:15 PM EEST, SATURDAY, JUNE 30, 2125
CAIRO

KROOM. A TONGUE OF GREEN FIRE SLAMMED DOWN from the heavens, exploding in lava that tore into the earth. Brock fought to stay upright. Sweat and hot smoke stung his eyes. His right fist shuddered, punching shot after shot into the chaotic inferno that blotted out these assailants.

Lord help me, Lord help me. Where was Jason?

From the blackness came the enemy crawler—which leaped across a new fireball, hurled up over the hard land. Night became day, ablaze in roiling flames. Wreckage fell like hailstones. Suddenly he was leaning back against some surface. The drawbridge? It had fallen far enough, and Jason was scrambling onto it. Brock shoved boots against land and lifted higher, until his shoulders caught the thick metal edge. Up and over he went, under an airborne river of smoke fed by distant *booms*. Down he slid on metal until his back struck hard on the bridge's other side.

Surrounding faces peered down at him. Their collars were tight, the rest of their clothing looser and of many colors, shining more vivid against every light-stabbed crevice.

Distant impacts crumpled any words these men said.

They held weapons.

Brock fought to reclaim a stand. Yes, there was Jason, secure on this side, crouched between these men. Brock lifted his limp hand—someone gripped him and thrust down.

"You are here! Safe! Welcome to Khaldun Concern." Folds of a light-brown shirt fell over the speaker's denim jeans, and thin white fabric encased his head like a turban. His broad arms lifted in powerful gesture toward the guard towers that flanked the re-ascending bridge.

That voice sounded right. "You are Khaldun?"

"What! No. I am Nabil Sadat." His dark eyes flared, and he palmed his belt. Viz over his waist showed another face. Sadat shouted down to that man, then flipped a solid visor over his eyes. *"Ahlan wa sahlan,* Mr. Rivers. Our enemies are retreating. They are your enemies too?"

"Your enemies attack outsiders?" Brock said.

"Not often. It is surprising. Maybe they are celebrating an old revolution. Hardliners have many factions and weapons. Some go back to the Last War."

Jason was approaching breathing hard. "They had an active vault."

Cannon fire ceased and let the night slip closer to silence. Yet distant noise carried over that great wall, like machinery, perhaps even the sounds of women, wailing in grief. Maybe they had found their men, all those men, choosing for whatever reason to assail a guarded preserve.

Firelight coated Sadat's neck and hair. "Do you know about *Islam*?"

"Yeah," Jason said. "Heard of it someplace."

Was this not the man's own religion?

"The word means *submission,*" Sadat said. "Followers obey one god. Some are peaceful. Others have fought us for many years. As for Marwan Khaldun, if you trade in war, we will not do business. That is why some call us *apostate*. You and us? Let us be apostates together."

Had CAUSE somehow contacted these factions? But only a few people had known Brock planned this trip. He had not mentioned this in the Epicenter or near any listening systems.

Sadat turned down to his viz and spoke in Arabic. Moments later, he intercepted a small four-wheeled vehicle that whisked to a stop, bearing a wide front bench and two single seats perched in the back. "That means you qualify for Khaldun's apostate friends discount. Medical treatment is free. Lodging is free. Especially given the purpose of your trip."

• • •

BROCK
10:30 PM EEST, SATURDAY, JUNE 30, 2125
KHALDUN PRESERVE, CAIRO

Every surface in Brock's guest room reflected golden light. Walls of gilded swirls shone down over polished cherry footboards, and steel fixtures chained to high ceiling hooks resembled downcast minarets. Thick beige-and green-patterned curtains obscured this room's corner sink and shower. In the center, a great double bed offered six pillows and a plush green comforter. After such an evening, he might even sleep out of schedule. And if he struggled to rest, this bedside table held a cup and tray of items, including capsules labeled LAG-AIDE* NATURAL.

Under this bizarre silence, his ears yet rang from the past hour's explosions.

Q-link, vox Alicia.

She replied quickly. "I saw your note. But you're all right now? In the preserve?"

"I am. Some kind of militant factions came after us. I'm sure . . . some of them died."

Alicia hesitated. "I found a better map, but too late. You vaulted into a place called the *hard line*. Like someone used a thick brush to draw preserve borders, leaving space between."

Wasn't it Templeton who provided those vault coordinates? All those theological degrees and books about Christians reaching their neighbors, yet the elder had not confirmed the vault plex's neighborhood. Had these people simply been defending their home? "People *live* here."

"We knew those waste places still existed," Alicia said.

The comforter sank underneath him. "And now I have seen them."

"It sounds like early Mars."

"Mars is a frontier planet. This is long since post-frontier . . . post-civilization." Brock pressed his fist to the wall. "And now here I stay in luxury. I landed among suffering people and did arguable violence. Then other people defended my life while I fled away."

This confession did nothing to change that possibility.

"Brock, imagine me holding you. My arms around you."

This sense of calm was more unearned luxury.

"You fought to live," Alicia said. "But you're not fleeing from evil. You are working to make a secure place for your family, and your people, so you can share this security with others."

Thank the Lord for her strength, even after she must have prayed with tears for his life.

Brock opened his mouth for air, lest he recall that taste of burning.

• • •

BROCK
10:55 PM EEST, SATURDAY, JUNE 30, 2125
KHALDUN PRESERVE, CAIRO

Glass doors parted for him so promptly, revealing a small terrace that adjoined every room on this floor, facing away from the Khaldun border. Rusted light shone from low buildings that resembled a port terminal, each light's twin reflecting back from land that gleamed like a frozen surface. Faint shadows might be vans or crawlers, all shut down. To the north shone the brightest structure. Earlier tonight, Sadat had introduced this as Marwan Khaldun's palace, a vast complex of twirling towers, each cast in crystalline white like a solid-formed diamond. Networks of canals, Sadat boasted, surrounded the great home to feed greenhouses and gardens.

"The man got his own New Jerusalem." That was Jason, waiting on an outdoor couch, his elbow propped on its cushioned arm. He lifted one boot to pour out clumps of dust.

"You look well, soldier."

"Aye. It's performance."

Brock edged into the other seat that felt ridiculously soft like the bed. He removed his own boots, wincing as dry winds played with his sleeves.

"All those human lives . . ." Brock whispered. "Each reflecting the *imago Dei.*"

"Yeah. Never surrender that truth." Jason looked away. "Not even when you need to strike that reflection. Don't justify it. *Oh, we use glazers. Only shoot to wound.* If you killed a man, you'd remove his pain. If you glaze a man, he might die anyway, or else suffer forever."

"I agree, but, Jason—"

"Did you think I'd sit here quiet about what happened? Or defend my actions?"

Quiet airs stirred out there in the night, with no echoes from the battle. Jason was either confessing or stating the truth as he saw it, and either way, Brock should ask more. "Of course not. But if you hadn't acted, we would probably be dead now."

"It's been years since my training."

Something out there hissed and whined, perhaps a generator or vehicle.

"October ninth, 2113." Jason leaned back to face the sky. "I arrived at Fort Drum in New York. That day I enlisted at Strategic Orbital Armed Reserve station 68. Four years and one week later—October sixteenth, 2117—I was discharged from SOAR."

He did not say whether he meant to leave. "Did you see battle?"

"Kind of. My first two years of training were Earth-based. They have huge firewells. Give you weapons, put you in the middle of synthetic land. Then they fill the place with your enemies. It's all artificial. Bipedal robots wrapped by human ghosts. But it's solid. They replay scenarios from the Last War and older battles. They hide no details. If you get hit, your embeds paralyze you. Then ghost *you* as a dead body. Others see you strewn on the ground. Trainers can show severed limbs, hiding the real men by viz of debris. Even worse? The women who suffer. I *lost* a lot of friends. Over and over, just like reality."

None of these training methods were public. "So tonight you fought your first . . ."

"Yeah. First real battle, not a simulation."

Despite that experience, no wonder Jason had nearly broken under the stress.

"And how does this mock-violence fit with SOAR's overseer, our peaceful CAUSE?"

"Easy. They talk up man's violent past. *Let's not forget this history and fall back into barbarism.* Most of the officers know better. All the 'historical reenactment' hokum is real training, in case we do get another war, on Earth, or in space."

CAUSE-endorsed fiction and political pundits did explore this risk. Such fears would always haunt humanity.

Brock must voice another dangerous thought. "There's a chance, however slight, that by our daring to oppose the preserve system, we could provoke new conflicts."

"Yeah. That would make the old *Last* War label all lies and propaganda, wouldn't it?"

"Rather than risk those conflicts, why wouldn't CAUSE arrange this attack on us here?"

Jason pressed his knuckle to the bridge of his nose. "Could be. But for one problem. People around here hate the Cause even more than they hate strangers."

Brock and the elders had discussed their trip in secret. He and Jason had used privately owned and even dubious quantum vaults. Not even Alicia had known their exact destination. For all its power, CAUSE was not omniscient or omnipotent.

"With or without CAUSE, humans choose violence," Jason said. "Next war's inevitable."

Desert winds tugged at Brock's damp hair, just as a melodic tone swept over the darkened skies, resembling a human voice. "That doesn't sound like an alert."

With a grunt, Jason stood. "Just another portent of death. See you in the morning."

Brock retrieved his boots and shut the door, sealing himself back in his guest room where fans blew gently from the ceiling. He removed his shirt and used the bathroom, washing his face and arms. Moments later, he slid under the bedcovers.

What was this other sound, like the whispers of a man? Brock pressed his ear to the wall. On the other side, some unseen tenant spoke in Arabic, like a mantra. Of course. That earlier tone was a message broadcast across the preserve from an outdoor system, sounding the *adhan*, Islam's call to prayer.

All words aside, the sound was almost beautiful.

18

BROCK
7:30 AM EEST, SUNDAY, JULY 1, 2125
KHALDUN PRESERVE, CAIRO

BROCK AWAKENED TO AN AUTO-SUMMONS, LIKE A
concierge agent, directing him to a meal center. He and Jason arrived
among the bustling Khaldun Concern laborers, all of whom wore
green-and-beige uniforms; others, likely the managerial class, looked
less formally attired.

Sadat stepped into the queue before Brock, then removed a lid from
the buffet. "This is *shakshouka*. Egg and tomatoes. Or try this omelet
or these waffles."

Brock fought his aching limbs, and they followed Sadat around busy
tables, closer to the tarmac. No reverse-toned sunrise of Mars could
compare to this rose-warm light filling half the sky. This morning,
Brock could pray for small signs of renewal, even resurrection.

"Our third shift begins at eight." Sadat smoothed his beige shirt,
beckoning Brock and Jason to take an empty table. "Over eight hundred
staffers, many senior level."

Even these bland eggs bore more flavor than Martian meals. "What
kind of work?"

"In manufacturing, we forge life support tubules. We make pieces
for small reactors made by other companies. In the humanities, we have
classes for new engineers. That was Mr. Khaldun's special interest. His
first wife founded a newer wing to teach Islamic history."

Jason tried a forkful of waffle. "First wife?"

"Yes. She was Zakiyyah, but she died seven years ago. His second
runs the school."

Brock needn't share their own preserve origin, but he could speak
like Grandfather. "I don't share your religion, but know more about

it than you might think. So your men work in manufacturing, while women tend to humanitarian studies?"

"Generally, yes. But none of us build the ships you will enjoy seeing today."

Brock finished more *shakshouka*. "To be clear, today we're only looking."

Their host caught him in a stare, as if Brock had misspoken. "Mr. Rivers, I am certain we have the ship class and price you want."

Brock had not meant to bargain, only to speak truth. "We don't yet have access to funds."

"That is too bad. Especially now that your quantum vault is guarded by enemies."

Brock waited, but after that statement, Sadat barely twitched one eyebrow.

To return home, they would need to risk CAUSE exposure with a Q-plex in Port Amman, or else find other options. "So you have no quantum vaults yourself."

"We have not, out of respect for Mr. Khaldun."

Jason grunted. "I once worked on a nearby SOAR base. Some recruits came from Muslim preserves. They wanted vaulting exemptions. Some think it's against Allah's law."

"How did that work for those recruits?"

"SOAR forced them to do it or else return to the preserves."

"Old traditions do linger. Our preserve began in 2073. Mr. Khaldun's father, Saleem, had strong beliefs. He made this land into an Egyptian Islam preserve. But what has more power than religion? Business." Sadat grinned. "This is the beauty behind *submission*. To a god? Perhaps. But submission to humanity? That is more like our religion."

"This sounds like the Cause," Brock said.

"It is different. The Cause fears tradition. My people and I embrace it . . ."

Their host looked away. Plates and cutlery clattered, and one nearby man stood up, provoking others to follow, including Sadat himself. Someone had begun a chant with prolonged notes like last night's signal, perhaps another religious call.

"Excuse me." Sadat gave a bow as other men gathered behind him.

This was another *adhan*, but Brock had not heard the earliest call to the *Fajr* prayer before dawn. The chant continued over vox, echoing outside and from nearby emitters.

Sadat whispered, "Sometimes we run late."

Brock stood with them by instinct . . . then looked back and saw Jason still sitting. Well, now Brock couldn't take back this stance. He would not participate in worship, only show due respect. The others' chant lifted with beautiful yet blunted syllables. In a moment, the guiding sound had concluded, but left men around them facing the same direction, likely to the east.

Brock would not look that way, but he could silently pray to Jesus.

The men began: *"Allahu akbar."*

Sadat spoke this loudly with his chin set forward. *Allah is the greatest.*

They continued, and Brock eyed for translation viz. THERE EXISTS NO GOD BUT ALLAH. I RECOGNIZE THAT MUHAMMAD IS ALLAH'S PROPHET. MOVE QUICKLY TO PRAYER. MOVE QUICKLY TO SUCCESS. PRAYER IS SUPERIOR TO SLEEP. ALLAH IS THE GREATEST. THERE IS NO GOD BUT ALLAH.

Rather, Lord, there is none like you. I won't forget that, especially in such places.

When the prayer ended, men took their seats. "Thank you for waiting," Sadat said.

Brock nodded. "I'm glad to watch how you practice your religion."

Jason grunted and retrieved his empty plate. "We heading to the shipyard?"

"Yes . . ." Sadat did not mention Jason's clear disagreement. "I will guide you."

• • •

BROCK
9:05 AM EEST, SUNDAY, JULY 1, 2125
KHALDUN PRESERVE, CAIRO

Inside his front bubble, Sadat put the van into autodrive while he excused himself for a vox—and Jason turned toward Brock. "Why'd you stand during the prayer?"

Brock had already prepared his answer. "I felt that was the wisest choice."

"Yeah. Guess I wanted to see some pro evangelism happening."

Brock *had* studied several old "witnessing" guides as recently as months ago. "Perhaps I could have, but today we've only come to look at ships. Meanwhile, I think we can observe up close how other people practice their religion . . ."

The van's curtain rolled aside, and Sadat called back, "Here is the yard."

A long sea of beige crete-covered earth ended beside rows of vivid foliage, lifting into swells like a green ocean. Over there shone a sparkling cataract, two meters high. How had Khaldun built all this within a desert preserve, and at what tremendous cost?

Sadat slowed the van onto a silver path between towering palms, whose thick branches reached out to catch the vehicle, yet bent aside for easy passage.

There, peering just through the dangling vines, shone the metal of a starcraft.

"Gentlemen, please suspend your coms. Khaldun inventory is confidential."

Sadat asked politely and had not blocked their signals. Brock sighted the glyph to take his clip off-grid. He would try to memorize the details.

• • •

BROCK
11:38 AM EEST, SUNDAY, JULY 1, 2125
KHALDUN PRESERVE, CAIRO

Sadat showed them a starcraft called *Light-Catcher* in English. That ship could ground itself like a tripod, meeting Alicia's hope that their ship would not be limited to starway docking. But their host admitted the engines needed replacements, making the ship a non-option. That honesty was admirable. They did not even go inside.

Starcraft two, named *Green Lands* with color to match, was too small.

On the ground, Sadat presented schematics for *Fasel el Samaa*, or

Sky Divider. This third option was beautiful, with a smooth ocean-hued hull, upturned lines, and wide canopies. But . . .

"She needs an overhaul of life support," their host said.

Brock had sent him their ship needs—room for a minimum crew of thirty, cabins for ten small or medium families, high-yield com facilities, spaces for teaching and minimal recreation, and a cost under 250 million yun. So why did each of these ships not begin to comply?

The next two ships were too small, more like yachts, hardly worthy of a passing glance.

Sadat then announced the final ship, *Human Journey,* capable of carrying over 100 passengers while boasting vast storage, two galleys, fifty cabins, two shuttle docks, and a vast command deck. The final cost for craft and delivery? About 200 million yun.

"And after repairs . . ." Sadat grinned. "She may even prove spaceworthy."

On deck six, their host brought them aft, where they stared into an enormous wound in the hull left by some great impact. Structure work alone would cost another 150 million yun.

Jason quipped that this ship's *journey* was all but finished, and their host took the hint.

When they broke for lunch, Brock retreated to compile his notes. Not one of these ships had potential. He had been foolish to hope for some secret breakthrough this soon.

19

BROCK
3:14 PM EEST, SUNDAY, JULY 1, 2125
KHALDUN PRESERVE, CAIRO

A SILVERY GLASS FOOTPATH REFLECTED NATURAL
light and drew narrower, letting tall ferns encroach from both sides.
Somewhere behind those branches, a channel of water ran alongside
the trail. Sadat said this intricate system circulated over 170,000 gallons
each hour, forming separate men's and women's bathing pools closer to
Mr. Khaldun's palace.

Brock slapped his shoulder, where some evil species craved to
sample his DNA. He and Jason had applied a repellant in vain. For all
the faults of Mars, that planet had no mosquitoes.

Between palm trunks rose a surface of smooth, gleaming metal.

The path opened to a wide crete platform. Here rested the next ship,
a navy spheroid about one-third the width of Brock's home. Its five
layers of horizontal oblong segments might help absorb the structure's
own weight on the ground. Heat rippled over its polished hull.

Sadat must know that this craft was also too small for their needs.

But a great navy pillar, lined with swirling silver textures, lifted high
from the craft's segmented crown. Not forty feet away rested an identical
segmented craft, bearing up a pillar that arced inward to approach its twin.

Brock stepped forward, underneath the tall curving column and its
shadow, until a broader shadow fell over him. When he looked higher,
he saw the original shape.

A much greater structure loomed many stories overhead, clad
in similar sculpted navy metal—a spheroid whose widest center
diameter might span over 150 feet. Ah, so these grounded, smaller
twin structures were not individual ships, but dual foundations resting
on the land. From these two supporting feet, the two swirling pillars

arched higher and drew inward to join the great ship's body on port and starboard sides.

What a magnificent machine. Now he must learn of its flaws.

"Gentlemen, I am pleased to introduce our best of the lot. This ship you see offers three central levels, command deck, split living deck, and labor deck. There are backup operation stations in the labor deck and lower bases. As you want, this ship has flexible docking. Distinct gravity spectra in both bases lets you land on any solid celestial body."

That would be the day, when any missionary ship could approach an asteroid or planet.

Sadat passed under the greatest shadow. "She has new systems for motive power and coms and life support. She has traveled fewer than one AU, never beyond Earth orbit. In fact, she was Mr. Khaldun's personal ship. By coming astern, you will see the aft bay and refueling ports. Standard pulse engines can operate in the domestic 'sphere, with plasma propulsion beyond orbit. This starcraft is spaceworthy. She is called *Caelestis*."

Brock approached the segmented foundation and touched smooth metal. Heat swelled on his fingers. Were those tiny seams? During high-speed travel, these apertures would open to deflect debris with graviton pulses.

"Gentlemen, would you like to go inside?"

Jason advanced to the hatch, but glanced back.

Even after those last ships, Brock need not act reserved. "I would, yes."

Sadat tagged his belt, then spoke to another. "There. I have granted you authority. Now I think I must deal with work duty, so I will be delayed. Many minutes."

"Something urgent?" Jason said.

Sadat grinned. "I want you to see the craft by yourselves."

Their host departed, heading for the thicket of palm trees.

Jason opened the door, which pivoted inward. "Future captain should go first."

Only if the Lord was gracious . . . and yet, what disappointment awaited inside?

He climbed into the hot and musty chamber. Lumen threads flared across the eight-foot-high ceiling of this tiny space. Small screens, none activated, gripped the interior walls.

Fans activated and poured down air, attempting to cool the workstation. He looked aft, where an archway opened into a transparent vertical shaft. "Levitator, activate?" Gravity did not change. He found a control stat with a sunlight glyph. Soft indigo lights responded, revealing a tall curving cylinder that rose into the starboard pillar.

Jason said, "Try the emergency measures."

Brock tagged a ladder glyph. With echoing *clicks*, horizontal rungs obtruded from the levitator sides. He grasped warm metal and ascended first, resisting his leg pains. Soon the slope eased its angle as the ship's pillar arched inward.

Tools. Take video.

By now the illuminated shaft slanted about 80 degrees. There was the opening.

He climbed out and stood in a broad corridor, illuminated by domes set into a ceiling about two feet overhead. Rough metal flooring appeared several shades grayer than the walls. All this area gently hummed like a single musical note, discernably louder from the right side bulkhead—likely closer to the core reactor. This was the labor deck.

They moved down a long hall that opened into curved walls with side hatches. Multilevel workstations formed a center ring for backup control. Some screens were active, showing water recycling and power levels. Brock relayed one sheet to his clip and received an eyeful of Arabic. Both fuel tanks were half-full, secured like stomachs just below this lowest deck. Given full reservoirs and normal power use, the ship could traverse the Earth-Mars orbit within weeks without a Hohmann transfer.

"*Caelestis*, I'm Brock Rivers. I request vessel specs."

"Yes, sir," replied a liquid-voiced agent.

A viz model of the ship emerged in midair. Brock asked to see fuel lines and engine locations. As expected, the prime plasma thruster appeared at stern, just beneath the cargo bay, while the twin bases housed aft- and fore-facing pulse thrusters. *Caelestis* could use all these in conjunction to rotate the ship with zero-turn radius.

She might truly have flight power.

Jason returned from a side hall. "Reactor purring. No issues on surface diagnostic."

"So let's seek our doom uptube, or else learn she costs four hundred million." Brock turned. Where was the way up? Oh, of course. In the very center of the backup stations—and likely of the ship itself—that cylindrical bulkhead was actually a levitator that lifted straight into the ceiling. Two flat sheets beside the shaft entrance blinked their invitations.

Jason stepped in first, and his sleeves drifted with his ascent. So the zero-G worked?

Brock followed him. Sweat released from his arms, small drops, quickly attracted to tiny filter bands in the levitator glass. As he drifted up, the labor deck descended, replaced by a meter-thick white glowing surface between ship levels. Here was the next floor.

Brock found twin door handles and slipped back into gravity.

Oh, Lord, help me avoid coveting my neighbor's spaceship.

Past an alcove of beige-patterned titles, plush crimson carpet swirling with interlocking gold arcs covered most of the living deck. Ceiling tiles held perhaps 18 feet high, shining with inset illumination that warmly washed every curving wall, many of which were lined with paintings of nature scenes. Khaldun's people had left a few sectional seats and tables, while indented spaces revealed more furniture that had been removed.

Between flanking forward walls, one twenty-foot hardwood circle and overhead inset dome disclosed a viz firewell that could be viewed by all passengers here. Past that costly feature was the deck's forward hull. Was this made of actual gold-tinted glass? It revealed the Khaldun palace of minarets that lifted from greenery and shone its own gold.

"Incredible," Brock whispered aloud.

"Yeah," Jason confirmed. "That window cover the whole . . . ?"

Brock approached. This glass spanned at least fifty feet, past openings to his right and left. Each opening led to ascending paths, two ramps, that sloped to the upper floor.

How many people could live in this place? "I've never seen a transparent hull this wide, not even in CAUSE ships."

"Must be crawling with synthient materials," Jason said.

Someday that land would be replaced by a black field of stars, ready for harvest.

Brock skimmed his hand over the starboard ramp's inner silver handrail. He fetched the ship model copied from downtube. "This says the ship's hull is triple-reinforced with synthient specs, even more than the glass. They haven't needed self-repair, at least not on record . . ."

"We going to the top level?"

"In a moment," Brock said.

This map showed the cargo bay astern, with room for shipments. As for living quarters, the ship held two levels of aft-facing cabins between this deck and the labor deck. Beside another entrance with stairs, Brock found a short ramp that sloped down into another hallway, like that of a luxury hotel, lined with shining wooden rails and four cabin doors on the left side.

He tried the first door. "*Caelestis,* can you open this?"

"I am sorry," the agent said. "Please repeat the command."

"Open. This door?"

Natural dark wood grain flowed and spiraled into knots. A latch whirred but did not click; evidently the ship wasn't sure whether to grant entrance. This system needed work.

Stats showed eight upper-level cabins of larger sizes, and 22 smaller lower-level cabins. They could put single adults in the large cabins, all on the upper level, leaving many rooms to spare. Two cabins were so large they spanned both levels. Would this door lead to one?

Brock turned the handle and pushed. With a faint musical tone, the door swung in.

"Oh, Alicia, if only you could see this."

This cabin opened to a small foyer, lined with doors for a closet and a private office. Straight ahead he found a small living room with its own outside window. Between these rooms, a switchback stairway led down to a split-level kitchen, then on the cabin's lower level, a parallel hallway. Two smaller bedrooms, *with a private bathroom*, were perfect for the children. One last door opened to the largest bedroom, with its own closets and bath, and another transparent hull spanning from waist-high to the ceiling.

Out there the Khaldun gardens lined the horizon. Someday this window could reveal a field of stars. It could showcase the outer discs of Olympus Station or cragged lunar mountains.

As for the smaller cabins, each of them appeared to occupy a single level, but with sufficient room for one person, or a couple, to enjoy private living space and kitchenette plus two bedrooms and a shared bathroom.

If only Alicia could be here . . . and if only his dreams were not launching too quickly.

Brock found Jason waiting at the main levitator, which lifted them to the command deck. Two sets of dual-level rooms at starboard and port were divided by halls from the rear cargo bay bulkheads. As for the bridge, the place for the captain—there it was, just ahead of him, an arcing staircase flanked by terraced ridges. This opened to the highbridge, shaped as three-quarters of a circle, its solid gray surface bearing rearrangeable sheets, glyph columns, and viz arrays.

Like a prow, this highbridge swept over the living deck. Any captain standing here could command an epic view through a taller broad glass canopy, divided by support beams from flanking glass hulls. He could steer the ship by the central control yoke that was sculpted almost like the wheel of a sailing ship. Brock might even convey viz onto the canopy glass itself.

Two curving wings, the lowbridge stations, flanked the highbridge, accessed by separate ramps. Support crew would work down there, run coms, manage supplies . . .

"May need some updates." Jason eyed viz diagnostics. "Still looking fine."

"How's telemetry with the labor deck?"

"Total interface. Fuel, reactor, all lines, life systems, skin specs, rear bay, firewells."

Jason swept a model into the highbridge. This viz panned about the ship, rendered in navy metal and encircled by horizontal silver bands above and below gold-tinted glass.

"Firewells *plural*," Jason said. "Most cabins have one. *Caelestis* is showing off."

Brock's earspace pulsed. "Gentlemen? Permission to come aboard."

That was strange to say. "Sir, this is still your ship. We're up on the command deck."

"He asked permission." Jason looked over. "You see what he's doing."

"You mean, he wants to make us feel we—"

"Already bought the ship."

"You think so?" Brock said. "That is some confidence."

"Or foolishness, to think we can't see his . . ."

Sadat stepped out of the central levitator. "So. When do we launch?"

"You're jesting," Jason said.

"Oh, but you see the possibility." Sadat inspected one garden bed and gave a smile. "This bridge can be secure. Levitators have gates. So can the living deck and ramps. Your infirmary and forgery need new tools. But the galley was recently upgraded. You will find the culinary systems—"

"Mr. Sadat." Brock lifted his hand. "I want no more details, until I learn one truth."

"The cost of her." Sadat lifted his voice to echo across the deck. He meandered to port and strode down the ramp, admiring the canopy view. "*Caelestis* was built in 2100. The builder is Lightstream. Mr. Khaldun bought the ship that same year. He and his family took one jaunt into upper Earth orbit each month. But space travel is expensive. After his first wife died, he began to see this as waste. How could Allah be pleased by this? Khaldun grounded the ship. He and his new family would forego opulence and build his company to help others."

Perhaps this was salesmanship, but it was working.

Sadat slowly ascended the ramp. "Man should stay on Earth. That is Mr. Khaldun's belief. Perhaps unbelief had caused Allah to take his wife, on this very ship. Now I think differently. Allah did not take Mr. Khaldun's first wife. The world took her. Neither of these will take any more of his family, because he will use the sale to build our preserve. That is why he set the cost at two hundred ten million yun."

That low. Truly that low! Brock tried to keep a neutral expression.

Jason, however, gasped aloud. "Does that include—"

"It includes taxes. About six million for Egypt. Six point six million for CAUSE."

"This has high potential." Brock spoke quickly. "We need time to consider . . ."

"Ah, gentlemen. I already know *Caelestis* is your favorite. So let us test her."

"What do you mean?"

"Mr. Rivers, I would not expect you to purchase her without a true test flight."

20

BROCK
6 PM EEST, SUNDAY, JULY 1, 2125
KHALDUN PRESERVE, CAIRO

BROCK FLUNG TANGLES OF VIZ AWAY FROM THE
command console. Far below the glass canopy, Khaldun's oasis spread
like a garden paradise. Sadat relaxed in a port-side lowbridge chair, his
face engulfed in viz. He hadn't spoken since Brock had shared his pilot
certification.

In the Lord's providence, two years ago, Brock had cleared time to
make that trip to Port Ares and earn that credit. Now, for his first time,
he would command a real starcraft.

Jason returned to the highbridge. "Done with core reactor tests.
Runs quiet. We're ready when you say, Captain."

Brock waved his hands, making the console erupt into glowing specs
that rushed like fire to form active sheets and larger beveled glyphs.
Each symbol matched his instincts and memory.

"You good for this?"

All at once this was terrifying and thrilling. "Yes, but pray anyway."

Jason shut his eyes, taking that seriously.

Jesus, give me courage.

Brock widened a single nav sheet to display ten square klicks. No
other ships appeared. Khaldun had no official port control. A third
step? Flight guidance.

"Starting synth-gravity." Humming began, but without floor
vibration. One-quarter of the forward console lit dim orange while the
surface grew out a viz control dial. Brock found vertical polarity and
dialed this upward by one-meter increments.

Trees scarcely moved. *Caelestis*'s altimeter showed six meters. She had wrapped herself in zero-G field and beautifully countered this with interior spectra.

"Jason, I felt no gravity switch."

"Yeah, inside a point-oh-three percent variance."

Three times better than the minimum? Increments changed to ten, not one. Brock edged upward, making the ocean of trees pan lower. *Caelestis* had begun its flight.

"Cleared the gardens, Captain."

The control yoke's handles enlivened and contoured to his fingers. Brock pressed left, turning the world to starboard and rotating their horizon.

He gripped harder and pulled.

Green land fell away, and blue skies expanded. Their pitch hit +30 degrees, altimeter shifting from dozens to hundreds. Khaldun's preserve shrank into a map of itself.

At this ascent rate, they could clear Earth's atmosphere in minutes.

Carefully he released the yoke, letting *Caelestis* drift into a halt. The ship's bow pitched back to zero, halting the altimeter at two hundred meters. Nav showed they had glided nearly half a klick south of their launch point.

"We're still within Khaldun space," Brock said. "How high can we go?"

"Khaldun airspace extends three hundred meters," Sadat answered from lowbridge.

Brock adjusted the yoke. Pulse engines surged and the ship leaped forth. Speedometers showed 50, 80, 100 kph, yet grav cushions arrested any interior sense of momentum. One man's arms could command such technological power.

"Yee-haw." Jason braced his hands on the console and grinned.

Brock could fly this ship across the pyramids, the ancient lands of the Exodus, perhaps even the Red Sea the Lord had once divided for His people.

He held altitude at 210 meters, but added speed. *Caelestis* hurtled over the world at 100 kph. Soon she cleared the preserve, where all below lands blended into distant gray and brown surfaces edged with silver lines. That sunlight-gilded ribbon must be the Nile River.

Could he try any tricks, only to test the ship's power?

He veered to port, swapping land with sky. Grav cushions flared yellow, but gave no warning and held everyone's feet to the floor. "Mr. Sadat, can we see the Mediterranean?"

"If you keep going." He didn't sound excited or bothered, only a neutral observer.

With no cautions of competing vehicles, Brock aimed north. In moments their new horizon showed darker blankets of waters spread beneath a clouded sky.

"Just cleared shoreline," Jason said.

This was the same Mediterranean Sea that the Apostle Paul had crossed three times on his missionary journeys. What would Paul have thought if he had known that 2,100 years later, future disciples would hurtle a ship high over the waters . . . and now go faster, and *faster*?

Caelestis traveled subsonic, following the north African coast.

He needn't grip so tightly. Autodrive could now assist. Brock released the yoke, and *Caelestis* kept soaring.

Lord of all heavens, if you're appointing me as her captain, please give me wisdom.

They would need to conduct tests, which could last for weeks, all essential before making such an absurd decision as—

"Gentlemen." Sadat stepped up to the highbridge. "Where are you from?"

Jason glanced at Brock, then said, "North America. Cincinnati, United States."

Didn't their host know their origin and intent for a ship? If not, an honest answer might ground their chances. But for this straightforward man, a dishonest answer certainly would. "We come from a Biblical Christian preserve there. It's led by a group called the Center for International Renewal of Christian Life and Education."

Sadat let out a smile.

Templeton or his contact must have told him. "Did you already know this?"

"Yes. And your hopes for missionary work."

Brock might learn to trust him. Did he dare do more? But if ever in his life he tried anything like this, this time with the support of his people, why not now?

"So you don't mind Christians flying your starcraft," Jason said.

"Mr. Cruz, I sell to anyone except CAUSE—"

"Jason. Please take the bridge." The time was now. He had laid in his course. None could stop him, and he did not want to be stopped. If this was pride, let the Lord rebuke him, and within the next few seconds.

Brock led their host down to the port lowbridge. "Mr. Sadat, I want this ship."

The lowbridge alcove needed upgrades. What did all those inactive consoles do? Thin-carpeted floor showed a few indents from missing furniture, needing replacement.

Sadat gave a mild bow. "Very good."

He sounded confident, as if he had predicted this choice. Brock turned to the glass barrier that held back speeding skies. "Of course, this purchase is conditional. I want . . . our team . . . to provide a full inspection." *I have a team?* Once people saw this ship, he would.

"Khaldun Concern can work with your financiers on interest rates."

"We shouldn't need that. My people can offer the full price in gold."

21

INSTINCT ALONE TOLD JASON THAT HIS FUTURE captain had just bought the ship.

Why else would Brock have pulled Sadat off the highbridge to confer? Jason knew a few celebrity leaders, good and bad, most Christian, some otherwise. All of them practiced caution to a fault. But maybe exile on the red planet had truly changed Brock Rivers.

Jason was no big leader. Last week he'd taken great risk traveling to the CIRCLE conference. He'd even drawn from his savings, down to 1,400 yun. All worthwhile. God had put him there in time to hear CIRCLE's president announce a real missionary outreach. Some enemy had killed him—either CAUSE or some proxy CIRCLE had yet to expose. Either way, Jason had taken another risk and dared to attempt his providential meeting with Brock.

Now the president's grandson had put him in charge. On the highbridge of a great starcraft. Spectra made their course smooth as an angel's. Jason had visited larger ships, but never flown past low orbit or earned his way into command. *Caelestis* was grand and elegant.

One could almost forget about last night.

Really, he should have expected trouble in any land ravaged by war and neglect. But four years of Reserve training wouldn't help Jason hold onto his holiness. If he'd sinned last night, he would ask God's forgiveness, then do better.

After the violence you've done, He won't listen.

After you left your family in that sick preserve, He will leave you too.

That was a lie. They'd defended their lives, just as Jason had defended himself in New Zion. Today's action had also protected Brock and maybe helped guard this preserve.

Had he attacked innocents? Men fighting to provide for their people who lived in that squalor? No. They were organized. And they'd jammed his and Brock's coms, just like the Ministry woman had done to Brock's wife on Mars. Maybe they'd trained with SOAR like Jason. Or with a private militia force. Egypt had a few of those, ceremonial relics from the Last War. Local governments tolerated them. Anyone born here learned violence. Sin was stitched into this people's DNA, going all the way back to—

More lies. God had forgiven him, and he could be a missionary to serve this dark world.

Jason must preach that to himself until he felt it again.

Sunlight held steady, even as *Caelestis* flung herself through the atmosphere. Sadat left the lowbridge and moved for the main levitator. Brock joined Jason on the highbridge, found autodrive, and entered coordinates for a new destination.

"Well," Brock said. "I've arranged pre-purchase of this ship."

"Yeah?"

"Yes. I am surprised myself. As overseer, I'll get used to quick decisions. You can help."

Help run coms? Serve as ship's regent?

"I need training." Brock relaxed his shoulders. "I believe I'm called to missions. But I must also be captain, with some measure of authority. If you're hired, I need your counsel."

Yeah, Jason could do that, to an extent. "One reminder, then. Don't say this to the crew."

Brock faced the oncoming clouds. "Agreed, yet I also believe in *servant* leadership."

"Lead like Jesus, yeah. Except the Lord would never be wrong."

"Agreed again," Brock said. "If you serve under me, I want necessary pushback."

The man sounded overjoyed with the possibility, but he showed discipline and very little ego, even while guiding a spaceship that could help save his family.

"I would if I had to," Jason said. "But you're a good man, Brock. That's been my view since I heard about your exile. That's why I slipped into the Epicenter to hear you. You were grounded. Didn't go posturing. I think I needed to see that from a CIRCLE man."

Sunlight crested Jason's fingers. Far below, the Mediterranean shone murky blue.

Brock nodded. "Thank you. I do wish my grandfather could see this."

"I'm guessing our enemies didn't want CIRCLE to keep him, or find this opportunity."

That sober look left Brock's face. Rightfully so. Sure, this looked like victory. But they were flying into greater dangers. If CAUSE had somehow attacked Heritage Hall, leaving behind little to no clear evidence, they would be even less happy about CIRCLE's new mission ship.

"Best we not discuss the news in public," Jason said.

"Of course not, even if we had no other threat. First I'll inform the elders, who will approve any final purchase." Brock turned back to the bridge. "I've set arrival for eight."

"Where can we land?" Jason might know the answer.

"Let's try the Japanese settlement, specifically, the company Dr. Mashima knows. Lord willing, they'll not discover they're the only project bidder." Brock smoothed his jacket and stepped beside the yoke that held itself steady. "Oh, Lord help me, what have I done?"

They were doing the impossible. Surely God would bless it.

"Can you work with Sadat? Arrange his return trip? Consider it diplomacy practice."

How unlike Jason. But now necessary. "I'll train for that."

"One more thing. Yes, I need you as regent or whatever your role. For my part, I also need a brother. And I haven't had earnest camaraderie with a mature Christian in years."

Jason grinned and lifted his hand. "This here's called a brotherly handshake."

"Signifying spiritual affection between the godly? Ah, yes, I recall the catechism."

• • •

JASON
7:14 PM EEST, SUNDAY, JULY 1, 2125
MEDITERRANEAN SEA

Sadat was nowhere on living deck. That made Jason's nerves tighten. Couldn't the ship track people? *"Caelestis*, apart from a man on highbridge, find a third passenger."

The ship agent declared a syntax error.

Jason fetched a map and headed for the largest cabin to starboard. One shiny wooden door stood open, letting him enter the large cabin. Past the stairs, Khaldun's people had left one gray sectional sofa that faced the room-spanning window. Tangles of cloud outraced the sky.

Sadat lifted his head over the sofa. "Welcome to my quarters."

"So you're reserving the VIP cabin."

"This one was mine. I stayed here during the orbital flights."

Sharing old memories to add purchase value, even now? "Good times, I hope. We should reach Cincinnati before night. Might take days to finish the buy. Then we'll fly you back."

"Or I can use my personal quantum vault, the one Mr. Khaldun never knew about."

Yeah, the man really admitted that. "I can forget I heard you."

Sadat leaned back into the sofa. "Answer me this. When you arrived, why did you not identify your preserve? Why not mention you wanted the ship for missionary work?"

Diplomacy, Brock had said. Jason lifted one leg onto the sofa's backrest, and Sadat didn't object. "Maybe we get used to silence. I spent four years with the Reserve and never admitted I was Biblical Christian. When they learned I was, they threw me out."

"Whereas I want to build trust between preserves."

"Good goal. Glad to hear it. Others don't want that."

"Including the hardliners who attacked you?"

"Or worse," Jason said. "Our people live near the CAUSE capital of the American Midwest. And they're determined to keep it that way. So . . . keep quiet about the ship?"

"Until you purchase the vessel? Yes. Then until after you launch? Of course."

"CIRCLE would thank you."

"I look forward to meeting your people. If you like, I will pray Allah's protection over this ship and its crew, more than he protected its last passengers."

He'd said his wife had taken ill aboard. No, that was the unseen Mr. Khaldun's wife.

Sadat stood and strode between two artificial plants guarding the window. "When I began enjoying rides on this ship, I would picture myself inside a mountain cabin. The outside is a hostile blizzard. But inside the shelter, we have heat and food and family."

He made snow sound luxuriant. "Sounds nice. Still. You need outside wood for heat."

"Not if you prepare wisely. Mr. Cruz, I believe preserves are great blessings. Inside the preserve, you are free. You can work and rest. Have a family. Live in peace."

"All fine enough, for those so gifted." Jason could have said that better.

"I am not gifted. I began life with nothing. Then I found favor with Mr. Khaldun."

"Even for Muslims, isn't that your gift from Allah?"

"Not for bad Muslims. That is why I may pass this ship to you." Sadat tapped his belt. "Why try a religious mission? Does your preserve want to be vulnerable?"

Jason could say the Great Commission was Christ's last command to His disciples, and all that. "Some of our people may not like the mission idea either." Not just New Zion's leader. If only he could see Jason now.

"Then why oppose your people? Is it really worth it, to evangelize others who hate you? Would you open my comfortable cabin door and let in the blizzard to destroy you?"

Safe aboard now, Jason could easily feel bold, ready to resist any Causian cold fronts.

"My old preserve could've used an icy blast," he said. "That also lets in the daylight."

Sadat moved closer to the window. "Will families live aboard?"

"Probably. Brock and his wife could move in there. Most Christians have children."

"Not your family?"

Yeah, no thanks to that topic. "I had family. Not now."

"I am sorry."

"Thanks." Now they could talk simpler stuff, like Christian evangelism.

"I don't mean preserves are perfect," Sadat said. "Even for those wealthy enough to afford a spaceship, you may find bad habits. Like forgetting to see the beauty on Earth."

"Yeah. But you got to look for beauty in that bad winter storm, don't you?"

Sadat tapped on glass. "Perhaps, but why open *my* cabin door to the evils? You can use windows like this. They filter out radiation and let in whatever light you allow."

Where was he going with this imagery? "Maybe. I haven't done much space travel yet, but I've seen in low Earth orbit. The windows aren't worth much. They show a black void with pinholes of light. Pictures only make space *look* gorgeous. Putting nebulae in every sky, painting rings around every planet. All of it's lies and color-correction."

Sadat smiled. "Then make your own good things."

He touched a window stat and changed the glass. Light danced over the surface and congealed into blue-white strands that rushed from left to right. Stars with four points glided further beyond, only slightly dimmer than the real-life visible sky and clouds.

But this beauty was fleeting.

22

BROCK
7 AM EDT, MONDAY, JULY 2, 2125
SOUTH CINCINNATI

COOL AIR STIRRED DOWN FROM THE HIGH CEILING
as home gravity pressed Brock's bare feet onto thin cabin carpet. He
reached for the cabin's window stat, which shifted viz and slide-vanished
the artificial curtain. Several meters beyond the glass loomed the gray
crete walls lined with the footbridges and frames of the ship's new
lodging: Japanese Refugee–Resettlement District–Ohio–3, Navistar
Manufacturing Hub, Reformation Hangar Bay 1.

Golden viz pulsed with audible starsong flourishes in his ears; he
had let his earlier wakeup call continue playing, summoning him back
to work. The time was 7:00 AM.

Monday awaited, his first day of Space Mission labor.

Last night, Sadat had helped him land the starcraft. Getting
clearance from Navistar, to say nothing of storage even within the
older retrofitted hangar, had been an act of providence. In exchange for
hosting *Caelestis*, Navistar would get first rights to refurbish the ship.

Sadat had taken a strangely hospitable role, dashing about ship
stores to find fresh linens with pillows and guest kits. Meanwhile, the
three most active council elders, Templeton, Mashima, and Dr. Van
Campen, had only praised Brock for his seemingly impulsive choice.
Van Campen even suggested the Lord was active in the timing and ship
availability.

Brock sighted his newest glyph, the tiny *yun* symbol blended with a
little rocket. It fetched an image that might govern his life over the next
weeks—a circular chart.

Just last week, the Space Mission had begun with 308 million yun,
a massive sum.

If this purchase succeeded, CIRCLE would pay ¥210 million plus fees. This would leave less than ¥98 million. He could scarcely estimate the cost of reformation, which was likely over ¥40 million. By the time she was ready to fly, they might have less than ¥50 million for food, fuel, tools, books, education for children . . .

Brock fetched the newest com release sent by Alexander Moore.

> CIRCLE joyously announces early recruitment for the new Space Mission outreach. Overseer Brock Rivers seeks out dedicated believers in Jesus who have: (1) long training in ministry and/or scientific disciplines, (2) sincere hearts for missions beyond preserves, and (3) experience with space travel and/or engagement with CAUSE and other nonbelievers. May our good Lord bring unity among His people as we seek to support this outreach to glorify Him by shining gospel light to the nations.

If the people of CIRCLE—not just their leaders—truly wanted the Space Mission, they would need to pledge their support. Brock himself would need to stay careful about his public appearances. After all, this release revealed to any enemy eyes that he had remained on Earth and was still forging the mission.

Now he might truly see whether the Lord fought for them.

After updating Alicia, Brock exited the cabin hall and took the stairs from the living deck to the commons. Jason had found a table on the upper tier, meant for ship's crew, yet both commons levels needed more tables and chairs. What about décor? Brock should make a list.

Near the upper-level galley, the fancy coffee dispenser worked well. Other nozzles could provide water and juice straight from galley supplies.

Jason offered a packaged breakfast and early schedules. "The director with Navistar, Sumisawa, is assembling work crews. First shift arrives at nine for structure check. At nine thirty, we meet with Navistar staff, get to know them, with interpreters on hand."

His nose was still bare, after losing his false com clip the other day.

"We can find you a new decorative clip," Brock said.

"Yeah. I know you saw that. Until I get one, I'll use pages. By the way, did they tell you they plan to *remove* the support pillars? Yeah, it's a tight fit in the hangar. But can they do that?"

"I saw this, and their reasoning makes sense, to strengthen the ship's foundation." Brock took Jason's sheet that showed the process. "Both arching pillars are formed of older nano-woven composite metals that could be weakened by age. At port and starboard joints, they will destabilize the bonds at the molecular level, loosen them, then detach. After testing, they reform both pillars, stronger than before. It's quite a concept from both technical and spiritual vantages."

Jason gave a nod. This poetic view of ship engineering might be Brock's gift to keep.

The coffee dispenser tagged Brock's viz, and its espresso brew smelled amazing.

He answered a new vox. "Alexander! I just read your superb release. Any response yet?"

"A few. First, I have a Heritage Hall update."

Brock removed his full cup, very carefully. "One moment." Holding tight onto the lid, he took the steps back to living deck, then crossed open gates to enter the ship's cargo bay. Gray shadows fell over him, cast between hangar lumen threads beyond ship windows. "Go ahead."

"Security knows the prime reactor survived. They are doing the investigation."

"What have they found?"

"Don't know yet. Dr. Woodford has not addressed it. I expect he may not want CAUSE to know our suspicions. What can we do anyway?"

The point was fair but frustrating. "Tighten security, especially around reactors."

"Maxwell Adams already did that. If the enemy attacks again, it won't be that way."

That was likely true. First they dispatched their little priestess to intimidate Alicia. Next they might wait for Brock to make one mistake, miss some ship filing deadline, then legally besiege him. Back to Mars he would go, leaving his people worse than he found them.

Rather, this time was different. He was not raging against the laws—whether his people's or the world's—but working with godly leaders, pursuing wisdom and peaceful resistance.

Brock found a wall stat and pressed the largest key. Quiet whirrs pitched down into deeper hums, then both cargo bay gates obeyed, each layer withdrawing into the sides of the ship as three divided triangular segments. Brock added a viz note: ENSURE CARGO BAY SECURITY. Navistar should check the horizontal veil that could separate bay storage, on the floor, from the separate airlock portion above the veil.

"Alexander, where can I find replies to the Space Mission release?"

"Ahhh . . ." His friend's voice cracked. "You sure that you want them?"

"Why wouldn't I?"

"They're not the most edifying."

· · ·

ALICIA
07:19 LMST, EIN. 22, 44 (SYNDIC)
PORT ARES

Alicia needed no medical degree to diagnose new cabin fevers plaguing the Starr apartment. Early this morning, Adam was best behaved as normal, retreating from boredom into any book he could find. Emma, however, had left most of her toys back home, and her feelings about that had reached ordinance-defying volumes. Daniel, usually the louder one, played like a little gentleman with three-year-old Rachel, rolling toy vehicles across the sofa.

Retreating to the bathroom, Alicia retrieved Brock's newest message. He apologized and included several disclaimers, but had relayed recent responses to the mission call.

By the time she was washing her hands, she wanted to saline-blast her eyes.

Someone screamed from the living room.

Alicia rushed back and found Daniel . . . rocketing down from ceiling to sofa? He struck headfirst and flipped over to land on his rear, then shrieked and readied for another jump.

"No sir, no *sir*, no bouncing on furniture!"

He howled when she scooped him up. Rachel Starr lifted her head from behind the sofa, all blonde curls and pouty lips, jealous she couldn't jump like her friend. Heaven forbid the kids had behaved like this while Alicia was gone.

She found no damage to Daniel or Rachel or the sofa.

"My sister in Christ!" Elizabeth swung about the kitchen counter, letting her fine blonde hair and tiny skirt settle in low gravity. She held up a roll of tape with several heavy rice bags. "I have solutions. Here, Daniel, hold still a moment."

"Noooooooooo!"

"Daniel, it's fine. Aunt Elizabeth is being silly."

With a sigh, Elizabeth released the bags and tape, which fell slowly to the floor. "Or else this—outdoors. Michael! Come out of your viz pit for an hour?"

After a moment he called, "Be right there."

Elizabeth returned her items to the kitchen. "Alicia, want to keep a secret? Michael is updating his resume. And he's doing remedial theology homework."

That last part was wonderful, but why the former? "I thought he loved his job."

"I'll let him share more. You'd be lucky to have him. I mean, blessed."

When Michael entered, Elizabeth drew arms around his waist and kissed him.

Even before they found Jesus, they'd found this love. It made her miss Brock even more.

At the front door, Michael retrieved a small pin that he fixed to the back of Rachel's pink shirt. "Oh, I have extra pins for your children, Alicia."

"Locators?"

"Indeed. It is precautionary. Still, I doubt *they* know our location."

Michael's employer owned this section of the suburbs' vast and pressurized park, in partnership with CAUSE. They or any visiting Ministers could be out there waiting.

Elizabeth tagged each pin to Alicia's com clip, then pressed them into Alicia's palm.

Only a precaution. Alicia distracted each child and stuck the pins under their shirts.

Michael led his family down the hall, then downtube. They entered the apartment complex's quietly lavish anteroom, which could become an airlock in case of emergency. Thick glass doors opened to let them pass—and blasted cool air from the doorframe, making Alicia gasp. All four children whooped as they exited. "Everyone, stay close!"

Her viz pulsed. Another message. Another critic's ugly note she could ignore.

A small girl ran past, chasing an insect that buzzed against a palm tree's branch, then dove toward a pond whose murky waters hosted schools of bright-orange fish. From that small oasis, tiny aqueducts followed this narrow path of native cobblestones through imported foliage, reaching toward a wider walkway of rusted crete.

That girl found her parents, a handsome dark-haired couple in blue CAUSE uniforms.

Alicia turned and breathed calmly.

She walked atop wrong gravity, under wrong light, trapped in a wrong kind of place. Webbed ceilings lifted high over the tallest treetops, hiding this world's dark atmosphere between grids of white glows, which hung like ropes between stretched polymer barriers. Natural daylight would not reach Port Ares for another hour.

From the opposite way walked a mother, pushing a wheeled stroller. Two more young children ran beside Alicia and eagerly swiped at low-hanging vines.

What? Her son held up a branch limb, fresh and green. "Daniel, that's not yours, drop it!"

Great, he must have torn it off with his last jump. Any more of that and she would owe the Upstream Corporation or CAUSE itself ¥5,000 for a genetically modified palm. "You must not steal. Jesus says so. So if you can't touch without stealing, don't touch at all."

Daniel protested while Alicia tossed his branch into the thicket.

No other parents within eyeshot had seen.

Behind her, Michael and Elizabeth walked together, like a perfect human image, letting Rachel wander ahead. Their own daughter might not recognize the true wonders of this garden, built by the same CAUSE that divided people into preserves.

Elizabeth approached and touched Alicia's elbow. "You all right?"

This gracious spirit had started their friendship, after she'd helped with Emma's birth. "Well . . . CIRCLE released news about Space Mission response."

"And?"

The children were examining a pond fish with Rachel and her dad. Alicia had a moment to fetch the first note she'd seen, and she read it aloud: "'I watched the President Rivers speech. He could have offered love and grace. Instead he presented guilt and shame. I forgave him. Especially when these were his last words on this Earth. Now CIRCLE is falling into the same trap. Why cancel the landmark fiftieth year conference and redirect everything to this program? God commands us to live quietly and in peace (1 Thess. 4:11). I feel like CIRCLE wants to recruit my children and send them to the heathens.'"

Elizabeth took a park bench and crossed her legs. "Well, that's not too bad. Is it?"

She might hope that such critics, while keeping any donations to themselves, also kept to her people's fringes. "The next message has a larger print size . . ."

> I received the notice. I will NOT support a Space Mission. YAHWEH says, "Come out from among them, my people, and be ye separate." We spent fifty years healing from those who longed to "influence the world." We are one. We are protected from the god of this world. How does this COMPROMISE help anyone?

Elizabeth tapped her own forehead. "They're all like this?"

"Well, here's a positive one: 'President Rivers has called us back to gospel truth. This is being speedily and rightfully put into action. I welcome this mission. *Soli Deo gloria.*' That's from Dr. Van Campen, one of the elders. So he doesn't count."

Little had changed in twelve years. Late into their nights at college, Alicia and Brock had lamented their people's flaws, often joined by their little party's members like Joshua, Annette, and Alexander, with occasional appearances by Dr. Van Campen. If only one of those old friends could be here now, not just to hear this foolishness but to bear the burdens.

A new burden showed up while her viz was open. She couldn't

help but read the text that bristled with many errors, starting with capitalizations.

> Rest in peace Jerome Rivers but the fruit of Brock Rivers has fallen far from the Tree of Righteousness of his Grandfather. It proves that all Great Men of God can fall to corruption. CIRCLE will go astray before his bones are cold! Why put this program in the hands of an exiled reprobate whose own Sin of Obsession with The World resulted in being put out of the Congregation? God Will Not Be Mocked.

If this page were physical, she could tear it in half and use it to litter this place.

"That one claims to be a Christian high school teacher, but his writing is . . ." Alicia sighed. *"God will not be mocked?* Who says that? Real mockers. Anyway, God does get mocked, and only He knows why, over and over, He tolerates this nonsense instead of correcting—"

She wanted to add her own falsetto mockery, but suppressed tears wouldn't let her.

Why now? For seven years, she had not confronted her anger at this. Now after this folly from their own people, did she really want to go home to that mess?

Elizabeth's strong arms enfolded her.

23

BROCK
2:10 PM EDT, MONDAY, JULY 2, 2125
SOUTH CINCINNATI

NEVER ON MARS DID THE EARLY SUMMER
afternoon sun shine this bright. It forced Brock to use eyeshade, drawing
a coat of shadowy viz over his face as he awaited Navistar's team.

"Alexander, why have you been letting Alicia read all those nasty
responses?"

"Didn't you want to be transparent?" came the reply.

"Of course, but since yesterday, I think our critics have grown
worse." During their last vox, Alicia had loudly dismissed these as
fringe scoffers, or else spiritual family members acting on their fears.
But he hadn't needed a better com signal to discern her own anxieties.

"It's just our people." Alexander made a derisive noise. "Again."

Yet they were still holy saints in the eyes of Christ. Brock must
avoid weakness but show humility, and not just for the sake of mission
support. CIRCLE accounting would handle those details. What they
couldn't do was defend the mission or publicly answer criticisms. "Can
we filter for positive replies?"

"Alicia asked me to relay everything."

If she were here, Brock would caution and praise her all at once.

A new note appeared from Director Sumisawa. She promised the
crew would finish *Caelestis*'s first inspection by noon. That task alone
would cost several thousand yun.

"Hold, Alexander."

Navistar's vast tarmac of smooth crete spread before him, slate-gray
and matte, yet magnifying the light. Beyond that surface, here they
came—an approaching vehicle convoy.

Right on time.

Brock strode to meet them, extending his own shadow that reached back to the hangar's twenty-level-high wall. With a groan, the hangar gate began folding like accordion bellows. Navistar's approaching vehicles shifted into a single column to enter the hangar. Flatbed cars carried scanning drones, solvent canisters, and spec forges. One fuel truck was blanketed by red warning symbols. Other crafts bore troops of Navistar technicians. That last flatbed carried one tall and broad-shouldered man, standing, his hairy arm wrapped around a vertical bar—definitely American, with a wide, ruddy face and shoulder-length brown hair. He saw Brock and hollered.

Brock offered a return wave. Would that his own enthusiasm remain this high.

"Alexander, I'm sure we have *some* edifying responses you can relay to Alicia?"

"That's a challenge with this job," Alexander said. "You should have seen the mail after your grandfather's keynote. Most came from outside Christian preserves. Before the funeral, we saw two claims of 'responsibility' for the Heritage Hall blast. Mr. Adams investigated and closed both cases. Five people from fringe preserves threatened CIRCLE elders with fiery judgment."

"Naturally."

"And of course, your grandfather went straight to Hell. James Woodford will follow him. Harold Templeton will go to the *lowest* level, and as for Dr. Van Campen, he is the Antichrist."

On some days, Van Campen might confess that tendency.

Alexander paused. "Mr. Adams did keep one credible threat. Someone scrambled his viz to tell us that when the true savior returns, he will enslave CIRCLE to serve the caliphate."

That one was new, from another wild religious preserve that badly needed Jesus.

"Come on, we can do better," Brock said. "What do we hear from happier neighbors?"

"Oh, let's see. Better than the silence from most of the Christianity-in-name-only preserves? Mostly skepticism or curiosity. I did see strong support from Brazilian Evangelicals. And the African Orthodox? They're behind us all the way."

"And what about mission applications?" Brock asked.

"None yet. But they'll come. In fact, later today, I'm applying myself."

. . .

BROCK
3:17 PM EDT, MONDAY, JULY 2, 2125
SOUTH CINCINNATI

In the starcraft cargo bay, Brock hauled another box out of Jason's grackle-class vehicle when Dr. Van Campen arrived. The elder stood tall, lit by the ship's erratic ceiling bands, and gazed across the bay, up to the ridge of interior windows that glimpsed the command deck and higher footbridge. His voice echoed: "*Mag . . . nificent.*"

Perhaps someday, Brock could bring his parents aboard this ship. And in the eternal future, Grandfather himself might share this joy, exchanging so many stories.

Van Campen broke his reverie and joined with the unloading. "So, these levitators . . ."

"Bring supplies up to the top-floor storage." Jason stepped past and tagged a wall stat, receiving a buzz. "Or they will, if we restore polarity. This is galley side. Brock?"

"If the levitators need repair, let's manually carry supplies through the living deck."

"Where then do you want your boxes?" Dr. Mashima said.

"I will take them. They're Grandfather's mementoes, so I'd like them to be first aboard."

Brock grunted and pulled up two boxes, then started for the staircase to the living deck's inner gate. He refused to adjust the gravity; today he would earn this oxygen. *Record vox.* "Sort these items—galley inspection and upgrades, estimated food costs for one year, estimated forge machinery and materials. Cost comparison—carrying supplies versus vaulting them aboard. Procedure—method of assigning crew cabins."

Could they add a gym in the few spare rooms on living deck, near the infirmary? Brock caught fresh oxygen, moving through the levitator alcove to the main lounge.

Van Campen signaled Brock. "Your friend has no com clip. By chance is he subcut?"

Brock could tell him about Jason's embed. "He is."

"I like this crew already."

Four professional and expensive Navistar technicians worked in the lounge. Three more techs paced down the hall toward the cabins, armed with macro-sized tools, likely to test utility lines for all thirty cabins. They may need to bump Sadat out of his refuge in the VIP space.

Brock set down his boxes, while Dr. Van Campen gazed over the vast empty lounge.

"Mr. Rivers?" Here came Director Sumisawa. At half a meter shorter than Brock, she had twice his girth and a broad smile that shone beneath black hair and pale viz. "Our team works on the forge and the old quantum vault. Next we will assign firewell upgrades. What are your firewells used for? Entertainment? Communication? Cartography?"

"Can we discuss it this afternoon, perhaps at four?"

"Brock," Alexander said over the active vox. "I just learned that at that time, Dr. Woodford may have an opening. He would prefer meeting in person on campus."

Brock had been avoiding the preserve, asking Jason to use his grackle for shipments between here and CIRCLE campus. "I don't know if I can make that appointment or if I should even risk being seen."

"I had to beg. Dr. Woodford cleared the time himself."

Why must they spend so much effort simply to meet with CIRCLE's new president?

24

BROCK TOOK THE GRACKLE, WHOSE REAR FLOOR WAS STREWN with tools and an old red blanket. Piloting the small craft proved a challenge, thanks to this narrow, stiff bench that lacked one armrest and made him miss even his decrepit *Legacy* grounded back on Mars. Jason's vehicle, however, would more easily fit on the lot behind CIRCLE headquarters. Any summer students or other passersby wouldn't question a strange vehicle there.

A new note arrived from Alicia, telling him Alexander's job application had arrived.

She added, DO THE ELDERS KNOW HE'S CONSIDERING A JOB CHANGE?

Alexander had no space travel experience, but his heart beat to the rhythm of missions. Clearly he had recovered from his college struggles. The Lord must have spent ten years fire-blasting him until he was refined and finally restored to CIRCLE. But now that Grandfather had passed, Alexander likely wasn't content to work under a new president.

Brock added a fourth task list: *crew*. He placed Alexander's name at the top.

He took another drink of espresso. Even lukewarm, the brew wasn't so bad when the drink cost nothing and glorious summertime filled the campus. Bleached glows clung to every tree and window, pooling their reflections on silver walkways and forming one great reflected sun in the center of Lake Heritage beside Ark Hotel. So far, everything looked normal, with no lime-green vehicles or invading Ministers to question him.

Brock turned the grackle to port and brought headquarters into view.

A group of about 50 people milled near the portico. What gathering was this? Some of the people carried objects on rods.

The grackle extended two legs and settled on the landing pad.

Brock's short walk was enough to make him sweat. Ninety-three-degree heat had not deterred these people. From up close, he could see they carried no cameras, only hand-drawn signs with Bible verses like 1 THESS. 5:22, 2 COR. 6:14, and 1 PETER 2:9.

One woman stood on a small platform, wearing the violet robes of a United Free Methodist deaconess. *"Avoid every form of evil! What fellowship can light have with darkness?"*

Beside her, an older man wore the all-black vestments of Antioch Assemblies, a truly brave choice in the summer heat. He quoted, *"You are a chosen generation, a royal priesthood."*

People were saying amen.

An older man took the deaconess's place and blared louder: "We all know what's brought us here, an area of grave concern . . ."

Brock might pass them without anyone looking his way.

". . . spent my life warning about the prince of the air . . ."

Brock knew that face. On the night of the explosion, Jason had physically restrained that man. Secure scans revealed he was MICAH McCARTHY JR. with PRE-PARED MINISTRIES.

"Now CIRCLE wants to go into Satan's kingdom? That place *the devil* rules over? Where you can be destroyed by the bone loss of perdition or the radiation of iniquity? So will those who breathe evil air be destroyed! CAUSE is the pit of Hell."

Brock's chest twisted, as if burning from the old beverage. So the Space Mission critics had gone beyond letters and videos.

This was his home, his gravity, a place of winters and summers he had enjoyed for years. But like seasonal allergens, his people's foolishness had lurked here, unchanged, waiting to trouble him. If he had ever presumed his seven-year exile had given him resistance, he was just as foolish as they.

"We must lead the kingdom, not become like the world," Micah McCarthy Jr. said.

"Amen!" one woman cried. Others cheered and lifted their hands.

People moved aside to let Brock pass. Quietly he made for the headquarters portico. Polished silver marble pillars with copper trim gleamed hot, supporting the triangular structure's wider upper levels and outer-rim porches. Inside the second golden *C* of *CIRCLE*, one dark blot stuck out. An insect colony had constructed its nest up there.

"Earth is the Lord's," several repeated. "Earth is the Lord's."

And the fullness thereof, from Psalm 24. Many other Psalms spread the praise beyond Earth's borders, because the Creator had fashioned all the universe. Logically, if the Lord owns the Earth, why should His people stay in preserves? Still, as certain as that glaring sun, public debates would not help here.

"Here are the plain facts." The next speaker's voice chased Brock across the growing distance. "God's people live on Earth. We cannot breathe in a vacuum!"

• • •

BROCK
4 PM EDT, MONDAY, JULY 2, 2125
CIRCLE PRESERVE, CINCINNATI

Dr. James Woodford had changed very little of his new seventh-floor corner office. The bookshelves, once happily installed by Grandfather, now stood empty, their contents moved into storage or else aboard *Caelestis,* while other walls had been cleared of the former president's tapestries. The new president had kept only the potted plants, bureau, and original desk that followed the curved outer window overlooking CIRCLE's campus.

Woodford gestured toward a chair, yet Brock kept standing. "Still settling in, doctor?"

Dr. Woodford brushed at his shirt pockets. "It's hard. Your grandfather was president for over thirty-five years. I began my first CIRCLE position two years into his first term."

Brock had read his bio. "Then you taught church history at the Dallas branch."

"Until 2122, when they made me vice-president. I'm still settling into *that.*"

Dr. Woodford did resemble the part. Unlike Grandfather, he wore no jacket, but he did wear a crimson puff tie. Grandfather often joked that he only dressed more formally to please supporters who expected this of him, but in truth, he enjoyed the look.

"I regret I've taken so long to meet," Woodford said. "Mr. Moore said this was sudden."

"You've had a harder time clearing your schedule." Still, Brock might let him feel some pressure. "We needed to meet. But you know about the pending starcraft purchase."

Woodford relaxed in his chair, letting his shirt's beige fabric crumple against his backrest. "Of course, and about that, I am thrilled. Impressed. Two weeks since Jerome's declaration, you have done the most . . . Mr. Rivers, won't you sit with me?"

"I think we should move to the rooftop."

The president leaned closer and lifted his gray brows.

Brock must speak plainly. "Sir, we could have eavesdroppers."

"Ah, yes. Dr. Templeton mentioned the risk. Even outside the Epicenter?"

"This whole building runs on a weak operating system."

Dr. Woodford stood and opened a tiny refrigerator to retrieve four water bottles. He followed Brock gingerly, as if fearful of making the floors creak. They moved down the hall, past several elder offices, heading to the stairwell. Woodford gave a soft laugh.

"I know this feels strange," Brock said.

"It does. But our techs will inspect the system."

Grandfather often showed similar vulnerability, but without appearing so sensitive.

"About the starcraft," Woodford said. "I *am* excited. I don't want you to think I am not. That's why I want to clarify potential problems."

So he wouldn't start by requesting updates. "All right."

Woodford gripped the stairwell's handrail. "You have your task, to oversee this mission. I have my task, too, as president of this ministry on Earth."

"And soon to reach above the Earth."

Woodford took the lead and opened the door.

"By the way, walking over here, I saw our happy supporters below," Brock said.

"Ah, yes. They began at noon. Campus rule allows them six hours to demonstrate."

Brock may have spoken too tritely, especially if Dr. Woodford lacked a sense of humor.

The president led him to covered tables and took a new chair. Brock sat opposite him. "I prefer a cautious approach," Woodford said, "especially after these threats from CAUSE."

"They've said more?" Brock asked. Alexander had not relayed any news.

"Of course not. That would be too honest." Woodford lifted his eyes, as if perusing invisible viz notes. "Dr. Sheldon has started the appeal process. This gives us thirty days to make our case. After that, presuming we fail, CAUSE becomes free to punish us."

Only 30 days. Brock had presumed a short timetable, but this limit was . . .

"Is there any chance of finishing the work before then?"

Completing reformations and then launching? With what crew, mission destination, or purpose? "I'm not sure. Certainly not if we fail to plan well, and then risk bringing unseen consequences onto us when we cross into Causian territory. I presumed Grandfather's claim of legal defense would cover the work, giving us enough time . . ."

"That's presuming their law would be fair." Woodford spoke wryly, meaning no insult.

Brock could find a smile. "Believe it or not, some conditions are better on Mars."

"Would you want to bring the ship there?"

One month. Brock would need to find some other way, or else, count on miracles. "I . . . thought about it. But those plans come after the repairs and recruitment."

Slowly the president nodded. "Speaking of which, Harold mentioned you've not yet sent him your proposed schedule for the elders to approve. As long as the mission exists, it must stay under the supervision of CIRCLE's elders."

What did that mean? "Sir, I would *never* do ministry outside your oversight."

"I'm glad of that. I only want to clarify—"

"If you have private suspicions, let's discuss them." Brock leaned over the glass table. "This is my home and my people. You are my brother and now the president."

Woodford tapped on the table with four fingers. "Thank you."

This should be reassuring. This man was a long-trusted leader, not some spiritual authoritarian. "I'm eager to avoid any hint of dispute between us."

The president gave a smile.

"But I've felt we've been on opposing sides since the Epicenter debate."

"I wouldn't characterize it that way, Brock. Like some other elders, I did doubt the wisdom of starting a missions outreach by Jerome's original timetable. And as for your role, well, when you left for Mars, I did hear the rumors." Woodford shifted in his seat. "People spread so many negative ideas about that man Brock Rivers, the one acting like a rebel."

And had Woodford ever believed those rumors?

"I despise gossip. That sin can divide the Church as much as heresy."

Brock relaxed. "They were only rumors. I want to earn your trust."

"I feel the same about you." Woodford offered Brock one of the cold waters, then unscrewed the cap for his own bottle and raised this in mimicry of a formal toast. This might be the extent of his humor. "I also despise the gossip in those replies to yesterday's com release."

"They're not so shocking. Most of those come from remote or smaller preserves. They may have poor teaching about missions or no teaching at all."

"But today's protestors are very local." Woodford focused on the clouded sky. "We've also received letters from several churches. They say that if we seriously continue the Space Mission, endangering our security, they may pull funding from CIRCLE."

Of course they would do this. "None of these churches pay for the mission."

"But you can understand their fear."

What did he hope Brock would say? "We need to show them biblical confidence. Do we want their later support? Perhaps. But we've faced worse challenges. The Chicago CIRCLE branch nearly split over some controversy, and people blamed my grandfather back then for being too loving *and* too truthful. How is this instance any different?"

Woodford renewed his smile. "Because this time, we speak about opposing CAUSE and the preserve system. For the first time in fifty years, we risk attracting the secular world's hatred to our families, and schools, and thousands of Biblical Christian preserves."

Lord, give me gracious language. "It's that risk for us, versus a greater community."

Dr. Woodford took more water and waited.

"I mean the community of our founders. Not just my great-grandfather, but all the others who gathered their resources and moved to this area in the late sixties. At the height of the Last War—after the worst persecutions and bad Christian responses to that—Caleb Rivers and his allies anticipated the preserve system. They sold their businesses and started CIRCLE. You know that, but you may not know this next part of our history."

Brock was about to share the secret. Why shouldn't he?

The president waited, his eyes calm and incurious.

"After the war ended, when the One Humanity Accords began establishing preserves and restricting missions, our founders took money from their sold property and redirected savings from existing missions. Today that's over three hundred eight million yun."

The president lowered his water bottle.

"They converted this to gold bars, now located in a shelter hidden under Heritage House. They planted these like a seed, so that future generations could turn this into profits of ten- or a hundred- or even a thousand-fold. They longed for a future harvest of souls. That's what I have to say. We should heed our ancestors' wisdom."

Woodford was older than Brock, yet he had patiently listened. He lifted one finger. "That's a good message. I mean this. It helps me understand you."

"I share only the truth."

"And I can hear it. We might use this truth to answer the worst criticism."

"I would say more myself," Brock admitted, "if I were able."

"No. I agree with Harold and Colin. Your place is on the ship, especially when CAUSE knows you've stayed near the preserve. On that note, relating to hard conversations . . . it's time I spoke with you about our investigation at Heritage Hall."

Brock had hoped for this. "You must know the prime reactor didn't explode."

The last word lingered between them, with all latent conclusions.

Dr. Woodford leaned forward, his brown eyes wide and tender, like a counselor. "I'm told that night we lost some Hall records. CIRCLE Security found enough to match campus operation data, which went temporarily offline after the blast. But in summary, even Maxwell Adams is ready to conclude the investigation. We've identified a bad portable reactor."

Hot air and birdsong drifted around them. "A backup system."

Woodford parted his hands and drew back. "Millions of people tried to watch your grandfather's keynote. Base archives show the Heritage Hall prime reactor was being overtaxed. In this situation, campus operation takes the prime reactor offline. Then, to power the building, they would install a temporary replacement."

This couldn't be right. There had to be some process breakdown, some loophole.

"Maintenance staff took the prime reactor offline at 1:00 PM. They installed the port reactor with power extensions running to the building's opposite side. We have the names of the men who did this. Maxwell reviewed their records and vetted the staff."

Was this a disappointment or relief? Had Brock secretly hoped for some enemy to blame?

"So no evidence would show, say, a conspiracy by Causian Ministers," Brock said.

"We all wondered about this, even if we said nothing. But no, there's no sign of that."

That was it, then. And this summery world would go on rotating.

Brock could say this. "I'd like to see CIRCLE Security's final report."

"When it's ready, I will send this. But I ask that you not—"

"Contact them? Write bad letters?" That did sound patronizing. "Dr. Woodford—"

"I know this is difficult. But consider how this looks. When we're left vulnerable like this, do we want to grant the Causians *more* reasons to invade campus? What if the authorities decide to claim that all our reactors, or port reactors, are at risk of overloading?"

The reasoning was sound. "But one port reactor *did* overload."

"Maxwell believes so. Dr. Van Campen's team at the Harding School had selected that product. The port reactor was forged by a Christian-owned company, Xolo."

The name wasn't familiar. "Did that model have history of failure?"

"Dr. Van Campen would know. Either way, the timing was terrible. As if Satan himself hated your grandfather speaking truth and sent his fallen angels to destabilize the reactor. This is why, that night, I lashed out at those Ministers. You corrected me then, and you were right."

So Grandfather had died for no reason other than the seemingly random yet sovereign will of the Lord. For any more explanation, Brock must wait until Grandfather was resurrected at Jesus's return, and in that eternal future, the answer might not matter.

Here in this world, Grandfather should have overseen the Space Mission. He would have confronted CAUSE and responded well to these saints who protested the outreach.

The good Lord may have given CIRCLE a spaceship, yet taken away their best leader.

25

NAVISTAR'S CASCADING PAPERWORK KEPT BROCK awake long past midnight.

At 5:11 AM, he stumbled to the galley for a larger mug of espresso, then deposited his stack of pages atop a commons corner table. This place would become his workstation, prioritizing urgent tasks over unpacking Grandfather's boxes.

Reaching into his pocket, he jingled the tiny dove-shaped cufflinks.

They had twenty-nine days left to refurbish the ship and launch. Assuming no miracles or manmade evasions, they must do this by Tuesday, July 31. Brock could insist Navistar finish the reformation project within three weeks. Meanwhile, they could escalate the search for crew members. Could they finalize the ship and crew as soon as July 21, exactly one month after Grandfather's declaration?

Halfway through his espresso, Brock received Alicia's data from the Martian skiff, along with a note from . . . Benjamin Reyes, back on Mars. GOT NEW OPENING. REPLY SOON.

Not weeks ago, Brock would have been desperate for any word back from him. Today he had the honor of simply postponing that action and moving to the next note, from Dr. Woodford himself, asking if he and other elders could finally visit the ship later today.

• • •

Brock risked another ride back to CIRCLE to retrieve Alexander and three important passengers. Outside the hangar gate, however, he requested that Jason let him disembark.

"Just some brief personal business," Brock told him.

Brock slipped outside into the heat, leaving Jason to lift the warbling grackle into the hangar. Through a man-sized door, Brock found the hangar's elevated supply room, unstaffed this early, but offering a row of equipment for use in zero-G . . . including those hoverpacks.

Those professional Navistar techs would think nothing of this, but he had long hoped for the chance to try one of these.

The largest unit fit snugly onto his back, and he let the straps auto-adjust. From the pack's side pockets, he retrieved two orange control gloves and waited for them to adjust to his hands. When the pack's glyph blinked onto viz, Brock accepted control.

Past that other door, a small landing topped the stairs that led down to the hangar floor. Beyond those stairs lifted the starcraft *Caelestis*, now looking quite different. As planned, both vast pillars had been temporarily removed. This left the spherical main structure, now mounted atop a load-bearing pedestal and braced by flanking appendages like cranes.

Cooled air carried scents from clean exhausts and solvents, echoing shouts and clatters. Down near both separated pillars, floating technicians probed the foundations' splayed components, fine-testing all systems. Higher above, *Caelestis*'s glass canopies were temporarily shielded by ridges of panels, and her surface gleamed happily with the collective light from thousands of white lumen threads set in the hangar walls. Brock needn't change the ship's original navy color, like the deepest oceans of Earth. But he might alter the silver trim to gold.

What would this feel like, to approach this reforming vessel like a tiny ship himself?

Poised at the supply room landing, Brock pushed his hand through the doorway. What a bizarre sensation, his fingers floating while his upper arm and body were drawn to the floor. He stood half-inside natural gravity and half-inside the hangar's internal synthetic gravity.

He stepped over the threshold, over the landing, fully into the zero-G. His legs drifted.

All those professional techs, with their workstations and apprentice drones, wore hoverpacks. But none used them like Brock was about to attempt.

In this moment, he could temporarily shed all weight of responsibility.

Reyes note, reply. This redirected to a mailbox. The time was midnight in Port Ares.

"Mr. Reyes. I no longer work as an indie contractor. Thank you for your time."

Send vox. Now and possibly forever, that old life had passed away.

Brock clung to the wall handle and crouched to the floor. He took one deep breath, then shoved the surface, letting go, launching higher into weightlessness.

Gray hangar walls, shining with light, pivoted as his body slowly turned.

For now, he had freedom.

He summoned hoverpack control and activated directional sight. *Fffffssssstt*—his pack burst with airpower, stabilizing his descent. Thrusting jets were kept safely distant from his back. Each strap about his chest and hips tightened, adjusting to redistribute force.

He sighted *personal library, music, Alicia, "Lorica."*

Synthetic pulses filled his earspace. Alicia's composition swelled into echoic chorale, sweeping like golden comet trails, summoning him higher.

Jets drove him up through chilled air, his arms lifted, his legs trailing beneath him.

What a vision! The starcraft's great main sphere held true and solid. Against this side, Navistar had affixed a scaffold on which human workers examined the hull. Upon the vessel's bow, human technicians' apprentice drones swept in circles across the temporarily shielded enormous gold-tinted glass canopy, orbiting a fixed point as if imitating a miniature solar system.

Caelestis was a fine name, but should they change it?

From up here near the cargo bay, none of the visiting elders could see him.

Brock used air jets to pivot. Now he tightened his fingers . . . and the world lapsed into spin . . . ceiling became floor, all walls reversed, returned to normal, inverted.

Enough with dignity. Time to soar.

Brock let out a *whoop!* His echo returned from the hangar and echoed again.

There, he had done it. He clenched fists to halt his motion. Soon his vision would right itself. All those techs may have heard him, possibly assuming he had lost control of his hoverpack or himself. They used their packs as tools, not toys. But why not both at once?

Alicia's music dipped to a slow wash of strings, accompanying Brock to swing about the port side, across the now-removed pillar's ringed intersection with the main hull. He veered aft. In the bay's lower left corner, he grasped the edge and swung about, stuck one foot to the floor, then his other foot, and wavered back into gravity.

Two clenches of his fists powered down the hoverpack. He faded her music to silence.

Over at the grounded grackle, Alexander was helping Dr. Morrison step down.

Jason intercepted the elder and shook his hand. "Sirs, our bay has plenty of room for storage and workspace in side chambers. All can be sealed for airlock." He may become a fine diplomat, but not by lifting and lightening his voice as if addressing a classroom. "Another team will inspect the interior. Might install a new airlock veil . . ."

Alexander left them and approached Brock. "You were right. The ship is incredible."

"God has been good."

"All the time," Alexander said, without hint of scoffing.

Together they moved for the stairs, but had to wait for Dr. Morrison to go first, very slowly. New boxes were stacked in the living deck, while replacement wall-trim pieces lined the alcove walls. In the forward space, Navistar techs stood on ladders; these workers had split open an interior wall, like brain surgery, to withdraw tangles of nerves.

Dr. Templeton watched. "What are they doing there?"

"Upgrades—lots," Jason said. "That's a viz firewell, over twenty years old."

Dr. Woodford said, "We might use this to share gospel presentations."

Jason chuckled, a bit rudely.

Where could the ship go first? Olympus Station, Atlantis Station, Port L5, Tranquility Base? Could they dock with merchant ships? Where would they meet people? Who among them could best find common ground with strangers? Would outsiders even care? If guests did come aboard ship, what would Brock's team do? Share dinner and drinks, or host basic Bible studies? Follow some expert's old script for witnessing?

"Captain, want to take over?" Jason said.

Brock led the elders to the living deck's forward opening between both side ramps. "Brothers, imagine a field of stars beyond this canopy. If our ship is like, well, a cathedral . . . this is the ambulatory. See those spaces under the ramps, between these walls and the outer glass? I envision small, comfortable chapels in those areas. On this lounge side, budget-depending of course, Alicia wants to add embedded bookshelves."

"Does need more furniture." Dr. Morrison used his gold-tipped cane to ground himself like a tripod. "Y'know, my church works with a company. Indianapolis, I think. Does chairs and tables. Reclaimed stuff. Been in that family for generations. Good family."

"That's possible," Brock said. "We want to show our best, like the Temple of old."

Dr. Morrison knitted his white brows. "Better to work with spiritual family."

Alexander kept a staid face. In the past he might have blurted, *No one asked you.*

Could they build great bookshelves of rich wood, spanning floor to ceiling? Could they add stone fireplaces with real chimneys?

Dr. Woodford asked to see the command deck, and Brock led them up the port ramp. There at the highbridge, a dozen more Navistar staffers dissected the gleaming console. Open cabinets dangled out nerves with sacs and other components.

"We're doing a *little* work here." This was the project's most expensive line item, nearly two million yun. "We want to be able to carry bridge extensions anywhere aboard."

There was Sadat, leaning on the port lowbridge balcony, eating a sandwich. So their quietest guest had emerged to see his shadow.

Sadat exchanged handshakes. "Men, I am glad to see your investment in my old friend."

Templeton said, "I hope God can use this work to bless your people."

Drifting viz gave Jason a distraction, while Sadat returned a polite smile.

Then one of the men tagged Brock's shoulder. With a troubled look, Dr. Woodford beckoned for Brock and Alexander to join him on the starboard ramp.

Dr. Woodford murmured, "CAUSE just went public."

With that, Brock's earlier flight of fancy was ended.

"They published the same letter as before, with new features. This time our Minister friend, Ms. Rochelle, did a dramatic reading. They added the July thirtieth deadline for appeals. If we persist in the mission, they say, they'll start penalties. Travel bans and trade bans . . ."

For all Brock's and Alicia's tribulations, they'd had only one child to protect, and the option of leaving the planet. Like an escaping scapegoat, that exile had guarded their people.

Alexander stepped in. "The Ministry appended twelve words to the public version of their warning: *'Any unlawful guests must depart your preserve or else risk criminal charges.'*"

One could scarcely imagine who those unlawful guests might be. And just as with his sanctuary clearance seven years ago, Brock felt the absurd impulse to laugh at these words.

After a moment, Woodford said, "Now all our people have heard this doom."

"Campus protestors probably know," Alexander said. "Bryony tells me they're moving closer to headquarters. Even starting to harass employees and block the doors."

"Wait," Woodford said. "Some of *our* people cannot enter the building?"

"Bryony says it's bad and getting worse."

"Then we need more than a com update," Woodford said. "Maybe if I speak to them . . ."

Alexander shook his head. "You're the president. Don't get drawn to their level."

Grandfather would have addressed this movement firmly and in person.

"With respect, sir." Brock took a breath. "I think you should confront this."

Woodford shut his eyes. "You may be right. My absence could've let this grow."

He may not have meant it, but those words stung like conviction. Grandfather would also have not taken refuge on a spaceship, hiding from CAUSE or his own people.

Brock prayed quickly, then released the words. "But you shouldn't do this alone."

26

BROCK
12:10 PM EDT, TUESDAY, JULY 3, 2125
CIRCLE PRESERVE, CINCINNATI

IN ONE DAY, THE PROTEST OF CIRCLE HAD MULTIPLIED
threefold. Now over a hundred fifty protestors crowded the campus.
Some leaders unfolded larger platforms, such as the Micah McCarthy
Jr. Pre-Pared faction near the headquarters portico. Another legion of
followers sat on the grass and listened to some unfamiliar preacher
expound on his stage.

Brock's heart quickened, and not from his brisk approach with
Dr. Woodford.

How many more would arrive? Another hundred? A thousand?
Would they all be Christians, or would any CAUSE Ministers take this
chance to lurk among them? At this point, either burden, if allowed to
grow, could permanently ground the mission.

On the flight over, he'd found one encouraging thought: Woodford
had not criticized him or challenged the mission. CIRCLE's president
had allowed Brock's help.

Woodford murmured, "This far shall ye come, and no further."

"Sir," Brock said, "do you want me to—"

"I recommend you don't." Alexander held firm. "Not unless
absolutely necessary."

If only the Holy Spirit could interrupt and give Brock special
words to say.

Some people linked arms to block the headquarters entrance,
leaving CIRCLE staffers to wait quietly inside a shadowed alcove.
Nearby, more protestors erected an orange camping tent.

Woodford hurried forward. "Excuse me. Let's take that down,
please!"

". . . made of fabrics the Hebrews were not allowed to use." The mellowed, mature voice of the unfamiliar preacher climbed over these many people, who heard and nodded. "Was there some problem with those fabrics? No. Would wearing the fabrics corrupt the people? Yes."

Brock would want to listen and engage, except for the louder argument closer to him.

Against the president, a woman shouted: "We have a right to speak! Who are you?"

"Ma'am, ma'am." Dr. Woodford was in earnest. "I *am* CIRCLE's new president."

Her lip curled like a toddler's. "We have rights."

"Rights to say what you believe, yes, of course. But not a right to camp on campus."

Brock had to smile, but she wouldn't, and this task was clearly not Woodford's forte.

"CAUSE will not bring paradise." From his platform, the preacher sounded wise and appeared much wiser, thanks to that trimmed, full beard like an ancient church father. "To enter that world is to become like that world, adopting their beliefs and their cultures . . ."

Alexander tensed. "None of us wants to do that."

". . . but still, the unbelievers of CAUSE have no right," the preacher continued, "to oppose the Church's mission of sharing the gospel!"

That stopped the crowd, and Brock eyed the preacher with greater surprise.

"Our Lord's Great Commission has always been our purpose. Let no earthly authority stand against this preaching of His word. His kingdom will never pass away!"

The preacher's voice drifted under a rowdier noise, caused by Woodford, who had retreated from the tentmaker lady and now advanced to the human barricade. They replied to his pleas by waving flags with handmade emblems, shouting slogans, lifting their hands.

Brock stopped before colliding with a protestor—who wasn't really there. Faint viz linked that woman and her ghostly friends to a vertical projection rod within their group.

"Earth is the Lord's," murmured their leader. "Earth is the Lord's."

But the actual Lord, in His providence, was allowing several CIRCLE

Security officers to approach. Brock recognized their leader. "Constable Longoria?"

They shook hands, and Longoria lifted heavy lips under a gray mustache. "Been years since I seen you." He clipped his words but sounded good-natured enough. "Or was it at your granddad's memorial? Anyway. Guess it's you who caused all this ruckus."

"We're not responsible for banned structures and ghost viz."

"My office was told the president authorized this."

"Untrue. There's the president himself. Ask him. That group near the door—"

"So we heard conflicting orders," Longoria said. "Remove them? Don't remove them?"

Brock didn't oversee this. "Please speak with Dr. Woodford."

"Mm-hmm. Just hope you see what's happening, brother."

Brock began to follow the officers, then lowered his shoulders. Air was draining from his lungs, and warm earth and grass sank under his boots. He mustn't give into this feeling.

With a few choice words from a golden tongue, Grandfather could have fixed this mess.

If nothing else, Brock should know his political enemies. *Toolbox, viz utilities, face ID.* Shaded boxes appeared over every discernible human, tracking with their eyes. A few boxes vanished as people turned or raised arms to cheer for the bearded preacher.

"God bless the missionaries of old," the preacher said. "They once faced persecution abroad and temptation to compromise. Christ must keep their feet beautiful and not stained!"

On whose side was this man? Brock caught his face and compared him with CIRCLE dossiers: JOSIAH BUSCHE, SHEPHERD OF THE HILLS CHURCH, NASHVILLE. He was a senior pastor, author of a New Testament commentary series, and father of five.

Voices squabbled, and people cleared to reveal Woodford, raising his long-sleeved hands. "Please! I ask for your peace and attention—"

"No, you listen!" a woman shouted. "Talk to my children. Look them in the eye."

"Your *mission* will bring CAUSE down upon us. Ruin families and businesses!"

They were BETH-ANN TURNER, 38, and DEIRDRE WHYTE, 45.

"You don't understand!" said MELANIE KRAHN, 61, FOUNDER OF HOMEKEEPERS.

"You saw what they did to Jerome Rivers!"

"Earth is the Lord's." One dark-haired and sharp-chinned man laughed at Woodford. "You think we should abandon our homes? You think we need a *ship* instead?"

They already had their homes. Brock had only the spaceship.

"What's this liable to cost anyway?"

Woodford glanced backward, and Brock shook his head. Even if Brock revealed the funding source today, this wouldn't assuage their fears. Anyway, he mustn't let them anywhere near the mission, or especially the ship—his own family's potential refuge.

"Excuse me," called the bearded preacher.

Wise leaders must respect their people, Brock knew. Also, good men serve Jesus by sharing only as much truth as needed, minimizing offense from people who aren't ready to listen. So what would these fearful students, parents, and pastors say about *that* excuse?

"Excuse me!" the preacher tried again.

Protesters fell quiet.

"Some of you are troubling that elder. He deserves your respect. Sir, if you would?"

Woodford moved close and took the preacher's hand to ascend the platform. Dr. Josiah Busche stepped away from the president, not rudely, but to respect his place.

"*Shhhhh.*" The preacher silenced his audience, and the effect spread outward.

"Thank you, everyone. I am James Woodford, CIRCLE's new president."

"No, what's he doing?" Alexander whispered. "We didn't plan this. Pull him down."

Woodford continued, "I know everyone here has concerns about the Space Mission . . ."

Alexander fetched viz. "We need notes. He needs a script. We must—"

"Hold," Brock told him. They should watch how the new president responded.

Woodford held his floor. "But we have already seen God working in this outreach. We as elders approved Jerome Rivers's vision, and we oversee the mission progress."

"Those people are *apostate*!" someone shouted.

They meant Brock and Alicia.

Woodford glared down over the crowd. "There are rumors and gossip among us. *Let no corrupting talk come out of your mouths.*"

Beside him, the bearded preacher nodded.

Micah McCarthy Jr. stalked over from his platform, waving his arms. *"Put away from among yourselves that wicked person!"*

Brock lowered his head and tried to breathe. Jesus died to save His people. He would always love this future-perfect bride. Not for a single instant should Brock speak in vengeance, act in anger, or sin against them.

Dr. Busche gave something to Woodford, like a small pen. Woodford held the device near his face. "CIRCLE will—"

Emitters shrieked back at him, making Brock and others wince.

Dr. Woodford held the mic away from his face. "As soon as we can, CIRCLE will share more truth about the Space Mission. Please keep open minds and hearts."

They responded with open mouths. Homekeepers shouted slogans. Deaconesses booed. Antioch Assemblies members chorused quotes. McCarthy shouted about fornication and city gates with Amorites.

What if they recognized Brock? Would they mob him or do worse?

"Brother . . ." Alexander was scarcely audible. "Getting too bright out here."

"What do you . . ."

"Too much sunshine." He pointed to Brock's nose.

Brock summoned his eyeshade, maximum level, and viz wrapped his face in shadow. He retreated, away from Alexander, the stage, and all these foolish messengers sent to torment him. Across the way, campus officers were collapsing the illegal orange tent, but awaited further orders from Dr. Woodford or anyone who could actually lead. Only a fierce thunderstorm could wash away this crowd, or perhaps Earth itself could open and—

"Oh! I'm sorry."

Brock had nearly backed into someone. "No, it's my fault."

The woman faced him with dark eyes and opened a beautiful

smile. Her delicate dress shone with crimson-gold patterns of waves and diamonds. "Oh. I'd think that anybody with sense would flee that foolishness." Her accent sounded American, with hints of other inflections. Shaking her head of dark ringlets, she outright laughed.

"Thank you . . ." Who was this woman? Her skin only gleamed, while he was sweating from summer heat. She looked nothing like the Minister in Port Ares, yet could she be another CAUSE Minister who had bypassed preserve security?

"It's funny," she said. "Christians need help rioting. This one's just sad."

She sounded sympathetic, but he couldn't rest in that. "I'm glad that you—"

"You should see how they riot in really bad preserves."

Viz paired her face with no data on record. Brock withdrew his eyeshade.

She offered a firm grip. "I'm Julia Peters. Jesus wanted us to meet today."

"Oh, did He?"

"I know He did, because I have a word from Him for you."

He dared not react with skepticism. "I hope this comes with Scripture citation."

"Is that how it is?" Julia Peters laughed again. "My word isn't from *the* Word. It's from a great preacher *about* the Word. When you see people attacking a caged lion, how will you defend him? Arguments? Lectures? Appeal to reason?"

She waited.

"Well, tell me."

"Answer? Open the cage. Let out the lion. He'll defend himself."

Julia lifted Brock's arm and pressed sheets into his palm. "That's from the Reverend Charles Spurgeon. And this here's from my husband and me. We want to join your Space Mission. That's all. Thanks for your time."

She full-on embraced him, then whirled to head down the walkway.

This woman was an ally, and he had nearly rejected her. These pages showed Julia Cynthia Peters and Lawrence Monroe Peters, members of Ezekiel's Tabernacle in Kansas, "Gift of Ministry" holders, and certified biblical counselors.

By today's end, Brock might benefit from biblical counseling. But by some gift of godly presence, Julia Peters had already helped him find rest and encouragement.

• • •

JASON
1 PM EDT, TUESDAY, JULY 3, 2125
SOUTH CINCINNATI

Unless God said otherwise, Jason would never again host CIRCLE elders on the ship.

What did these men even like? Food. That seemed to be the only subject they took lightly and kept using for their small-talk joking. He couldn't laugh. "How about we go see the galley?"

The older men followed him easily enough. He led them down the aft starboard hallway, keeping distant from the black curtains Navistar had installed to cover the old quantum vault. Behind those curtains, Navistar workers buzzed with some tool.

"Here's the galley. Plenty of room to feed people. Lots of storage up those stairs."

The oldest elder, Morrison, kept smiling but shook his head.

"We have hot and cold running water. The original culinators work fine."

Morrison tapped on one device. "Why you need 'em? You'll have women aboard."

A few elders chuckled.

Jason still didn't. "Classic. I myself, being a man, make a great clam chowder."

Templeton studied one of the culinator's triple arms with its slender, ten-fingered hand. "Mr. Cruz, what do space travelers enjoy eating?"

"When I was with SOAR in low Earth orbit, we had packaged meals. But upper classes can get decent galley fare just like home kitchens. We aim for that level."

"How come?" Morrison said.

"Because you, ah, shouldn't need human riches to get appetizers for God's feast." That sounded good, but Brock could have said it better. Soon he'd return to rescue Jason from playing tour guide, right?

"Sounds like a waste if you ask me."

Keep that ministry smile, soldier. "But no waste of your personal donation, sir."

"We can always show God's love with good food," Templeton said.

Of course the men laughed. Jason could thank Templeton for that one.

"Lotsa theory." Morrison waved his hand. "Lots of ideas starting with *if we just.* Like, *if we just* feed people the right food, and *if we just* say things right—"

"Feed whom the right food, I'm sorry?" Dr. Van Campen said.

"Outsiders, nonbelievers. They don't *eat* right. Don't listen right."

Jason might expect that from the protestors Brock had mentioned. But among the elders? Would he be right to show this elder off the deck? "Over here is—"

"With respect, my good elder, that's wrong."

This came from a new and resonant voice, booming from the galley steps. A big man in wide-legged gray pants and a loose white shirt descended the steps, three at a time.

He landed hard. "Hey, I'm Derek. Consider this story. It is the twentieth century. The Sawi tribe of Indonesia are jungle dwellers. Headhunters too. They befriend neighbors from other tribes, then kill him, roast his body, and eat him. Guess those people don't *eat right* either."

That bulging voice slapped against the walls. His arm patch read NAVISTAR * D. SOREN. "In 1962, the Sawi tribe get new neighbors— Don and Carol with their baby boy. Gospel missionaries. When the Sawi tribe heard the gospel story, they praise Judas Iscariot as the *hero* because he betrayed his friend Jesus so artfully. So they don't listen right either.

"Don and Carol ask, 'How in the wicked world do we teach this kind of people?'

"Then the villages start battling each other. Don and Carol beg for peace. So one chief fulfills an ancient tradition. Chief One gives his young child to another village chief. Chief Two adopts the boy as his own. It's the peace child. A living redemption symbol."

All that sounded historical, but Jason might check the details.

"Now the missionaries have a new way to share. And the Sawi tribe might listen better. Maybe eat better. Now, we can listen, too, if we got bigger ears than mouths." Derek gave a broad grin and pointed at Jason. "I've an update for you. Up here?"

He bounded back up the steps, somehow dodging the doorframe.

Jason followed, turning left to pass under the black curtains. Back here, the Navistar techs had divided the old quantum vault exactly in half, leaving the back portion standing. Metal-rimmed thick parts leaned on the wall like great museum cases.

"I thought to stay mute in here," Derek said. "Then I thought—eh! I can take the hit."

What was he talking about? Clearly someone had taught him missionary stories. Jason stopped before bumping the man's treaded boots. "What's the update?"

The tech offered his hand, sweaty, with huge fingers. "Derek Soren."

"You're a Navistar contractor?"

"For three years." Derek pivoted to the vault. "I'm revamping pieces now. My team pulled out the flanging and sold it for salvage. That yun goes to the ship's account. The new set should be here tomorrow. Anything is better than that last dinosaur."

"So, this should be ready for a test vault . . . what time tomorrow?"

"I'll tell you *noon*, then try to finish by ten."

"Fine, that's good." Jason had to ask more. "So you speak . . . Christianese?"

"What now?"

"Your missionary story down there."

"Sure, but that's new to me. *Christianese*." Derek tapped his chest. "Me, I'm from Florida. After I heard the Jerome speech, and then this assignment, I wondered if that mystery project might be a CIRCLE spaceship. So I got myself transferred here."

No other tech had shown curiosity about the ship's purpose. "You are a Christian?"

"Sure. Before that I was Causian. Bought the whole myth. Jesus is a better king."

Very rare to meet a former CAUSE adherent. "What do you do?"

"Astrophysics degree. Which is why I'm with Navistar fixing Q-vaults for a living. Hey, you have a moment to hear about my old 'savior' of multiverse theory?"

"Yeah . . . not now, I guess. So the Cause truly had you."

Derek shrugged. "Grew up in secular worlds. Thanks to this brilliant mind and body, I worked with the strangest men and women. I did about everything *against* God's Law. Never met a commandment I didn't break. Then, as in the book of Romans, chapter one, I invented new ways of doing evil. After I came to the light, I got powerful stories. God's given me much. So I'll give to others. Whether it's repairs or the evangelisms, whatever."

Jason tried to follow all that. "You . . . want to work for the Space Mission?"

"*Space Mission*." Derek spoke as if testing the name. "Sure, maybe? Depends on whether the mission can work with me. I'm hard to work with. Ask my brother." Derek grabbed a sandwich and swallowed one bite. "It's one idea to fight the CAUSE that's persecuting you. Us. It's another idea to share gospel with CAUSE itself."

Derek paused, then dragged his finger squeaking across the vault glass. "They only do what they know." Now he struggled to form words. "Like I once did."

Someone approached from beyond the curtain. "Excuse me, Soren."

Jason peered out to see Navistar Director Sumisawa, who cleared her viz and faced him. "Sir, we finished our initial probes. I think that within two weeks, your ship can fly."

27

BROCK
1:30 PM EDT, TUESDAY, JULY 3, 2125
CIRCLE PRESERVE, CINCINNATI

THE CIRCLE INN HAD NOT CHANGED AT ALL, WITH its elevated rows of wooden booths where for over thirty-five years students had met for conversation or dates. Brock's favorite corner table was close to the main counter, lined with colorful bottles before tall mirrors. That so-called "pub" area performed the traditional pub functions, at least for Christians who either compromised with sin or else found liberty in Christ, depending on your side.

Brock met with Alexander and found no protestors had pursued them inside. The postgrad student who fetched their appetizers didn't mention the outside mess.

"I think we can rest." Brock leaned back on the hard cushion.

Alexander poked at his cheese stick. "Just hope I don't revert to my old self."

"Ah, trust me, I struggle with that same temptation." Brock could share this more honestly. "A young man, acting like the old man, bitter against his own people."

"I doubt you felt the same. I was in a *bad* place before your grandfather intervened."

"You make me envy the time you spent with him," Brock said.

"Don't mean to. In truth it feels strange knowing him at all, after growing up with his study Bible. All the other good books. Then I met you, and then him."

"And you learned we are seriously flawed."

"*Those* people seem worse. Feels like seeing into the Church's darkest soul again."

Alexander had grown enough to sort rightful criticism from reckless idealism, so Brock needn't mention specifics. "I think it's natural to feel 'awakened' when you're young. For my part, I let those mission biographies go to my head. Their authors wouldn't approve."

"Remember the William Carey one?" Alexander said. "I read it three times."

Brock had read Alexander's many articles about that book; in fact, his writing had drawn them together. Before long, Alicia and others had joined their discussions. Dr. Van Campen himself had graced their "Inn-group" meetings to out-rant them all.

"I keep asking myself . . ." Alexander's last syllable broke, like a younger man growing into his new voice. Once another student had laughed at this habit and provoked Alexander to anger. This time, he laughed at himself. "These people rejecting the Space Mission, don't they prove what we thought about our people back then? But we aren't rebuking them."

"No. Dr. Woodford needed to intervene."

"I hear you. And I do support that leadership."

Their waiter arrived with two chili bowls. Brock ordered a refill on thin black coffee.

In this depth, he might help Alexander while reminding himself. "We aren't weakening. We're being prudent. Wise men tell the truth, but not always the whole truth."

"But if we don't give *the truth* to people now, then when?"

Brock glanced toward heavy oak rafters. "At this time, I'm not sure."

The chili sauce was savory, but didn't blend well with black coffee.

"I did want to work in com relations," Alexander said. "After my church problems, doing this seemed the best way to make amends." He meant whatever happened with Sola Cathedral before he withdrew from CIRCLE.

This topic could be sensitive. "You never told me about your exact *church problems*."

"I guess you should know the details."

Brock nodded. "Of course, for anyone hoping to join the Space Mission."

"Mm. Didn't want to hide anything. Your grandfather encouraged me not to. But back then, I misjudged everyone. I thought your grandfather only wanted to protect his powerful church friends. They'd kicked me out, and he said nothing against them."

Had the problems been so bad that leaders forced Alexander to leave CIRCLE? "I thought the elders never advanced you through a formal discipline process."

"Well, they would have, if I hadn't left first."

Even at Sola Cathedral, spiritual home to four generations of the Rivers family?

Alexander glanced aside, toward the bottles lining glass cases. "They tolerated my articles, at first. Until the elders learned I was leaving CIRCLE's theology program."

"But you preferred engineering."

"It wasn't enough. Dr. Templeton warned me. He said my Moore Truth writings were borderline slanderous against our people. Even if I disagreed with my people, he said, I could still catch more flies with honey. And so on. I told him that must mean our *people* are like repulsive insects, enmeshed in the sweet stuff until the spiders arrive."

Brock groaned aloud, pressing his palm to his forehead.

"I thought myself clever. They felt I was unrepentant and arrogant."

If he had written such rhetoric and repeated this to elders, Brock may not blame them. "Admittedly, in our debates, you wrongly challenged people's sincerity," Brock said. "But when you left the church and then CIRCLE, I thought that was your choice."

"I thought it was my choice too. Now I'm not sure."

All this had passed ten years ago, but some pains never left a man. Brock had not witnessed the elders' criticism or Alexander's response. But for love's sake, couldn't they have considered Alexander's insular family background and passion for the lost world?

"After that, you and I never met like we once did," Alexander said.

Church discipline did not shun people, but simply instructed Christians to treat them as if they were unbelievers who need tough love. This was the apostle Paul's ideal.

"I did note the shift," Brock said.

"You didn't want to probe. That may've been best. Later, after I'd left, I heard you and Alicia had to escape Earth. I thought: *CIRCLE rejected me, and now they're casting out Brock.* Not long after, your grandfather reached out. He didn't apologize for Dr. Templeton or the other elders. Just met me like a mentor. I guess it worked."

Brock had read Alexander's dossier. It showed that in 2120, five years after Alexander had left Sola, he'd re-enrolled at CIRCLE. In 2123, he graduated and joined the president's office. Earlier this year he became chief of com relations. He never tried to restart his own ministry platform, though he did join another church in a neighboring Christian preserve. During the last five years, those elders had reported him faithful.

"That's why I need the Space Mission." Alexander clenched his fist on the table. "I know I still have temptations. But with your grandfather gone, I think God wants me with this mission. We can redeem the *preserve* concept. But this time, let's do it right. Leave all the protestors behind. Really follow Jesus and grow His kingdom."

Brock should engage him on this topic—but his vox chirped. He excused himself. Still, the good camaraderie helped fuel his own engines.

Van Campen reported the small cargo quantum vault had arrived at Harding School of Engineering. After lunch, Brock would retrieve that device. It would help him preserve the secret of Heritage House, yet move some of its treasure to a different steward.

• • •

BROCK
9:23 AM EDT, WEDNESDAY, JULY 4, 2125
SOUTH CINCINNATI

Today, on the command deck lowbridge, Brock would arrange the most significant purchase of his lifetime. Jason and Sadat would witness this, and both men would likely see through Brock's use of deep fatigue to cover his excitement.

Brock took the document and leaned forward for optical scans. With his stylus he signed his first name under the printed CAPTAIN BROCK STANFORD RIVERS.

Sadat went next. "*Caelestis*, I am Nabil Sadat. Connect the ship with Khaldun preserve. Authorize for transfer of deed to Center for International Renewal of Christian Life and Education. New regent is Jason Joshua Cruz. New captain is Brock Stanford Rivers."

The page did not flash, only held each signature—a fixed record, for good and ill.

Sadat shifted his backpack, now filled with keepsakes from below. "Please care for her."

Clearly he felt no need for a stoic posture.

"I absolutely will." Brock led them off the lowbridge to the starboard hall adjacent the galley. There he pulled aside the black curtain, revealing the ship's newly refurbished quantum vault, with sealed door and new silver flange, ready for action.

He sighted for standby, clearing his signal. Any moment now . . .

Lightning stabbed the vault, swirling into energy floods that poured from the flange to the floor, roaring about a new object appearing in shared space. That simple box held the ship's assessed worth in solid gold bars, vaulted directly from the Heritage House shelter where Brock had installed a smaller cargo vault earlier today.

Jason whistled. "Happy independence."

Today marked 349 years of celebrating July 4th. Praise the Lord for those old ideals.

Sadat opened the small vault door to inspect his gains—210 million yun, by Brock's thrice-checked measurement. Moments later, Sadat nodded.

As of now, by global laws, this ship belonged to CIRCLE. Sadat had not changed his mind, and no one had interrupted. The gold had arrived as planned, nearly 70 percent of the total Caleb Rivers and other founders had bequeathed the organization.

From here, its people must decide whether to support the mission.

Sadat dialed in the code for his own secret vault and activated another sequence. In seconds, the vault drew spaces together, and the gold vanished.

"Brock, thank you for hosting me, to enjoy the ship a few more days."

"Mr. Sadat, I'm grateful for your honesty and graciousness."

"Also, Mr. Cruz." Sadat took his hand. "I have appreciated our talks. We do not share a religion, but I'm honored to have fought beside another soldier."

Jason gave a nod. "Yeah, thank you. Still need Jesus."

"Aha. I respect you, but not your religion."

This time Brock served as operator, letting Sadat enter the new quantum vault. Brock confirmed the Khaldun preserve's receiving vault was emptied of gold bars, perhaps removed by Sadat's confidential ally. He auto-skipped the vault safety lecture.

Sadat vanished. Seconds later, he notified Brock: MA'A EL SALAMA, MR. RIVERS.

· · ·

BROCK
12 PM EDT, WEDNESDAY, JULY 4, 2125
SOUTH CINCINNATI

Brock awakened to the sound of starsong, under a new ceiling washed in light. He had exercised one prerogative—moving into the captain's cabin, his family's future home.

This starcraft belonged here, not to *him*, but to his people and all of Christian history.

And today, the Navistar techs had promised the restoration of her support pillars.

He faded the sound and checked the time, exactly noon, after his thirty-minute nap. Last night he had found some sleep despite his late espresso. But now his neck and shoulders cramped, a due punishment for his too-early awakening at 4:30 AM.

In the far corner drifted blue viz like mist, able to provide work or recreation.

Brock stepped into the viz. He accessed CIRCLE's base and pointed to campus feeds that showed more protestors. Today's patriotic occasions had not discouraged them. In truth, their number might have redoubled to three hundred, though without banned tents and technologies.

What about that front platform? Could he talk with that fairer man, Pastor Busche? Brock would not reveal the new starcraft or invite anyone to see this ship. Instead, he could make good arguments. He would persuade people about the need for missions, regardless of the cost, while reassuring them that Christians had every right to do this even under CAUSE.

Anyway, the people needed firm reminders about the dangers of fear, didn't they?

And if they confronted Brock with the *apostate* label, he would rebuke them sharply. Or he would remind them about great missionaries like William Carey, Hudson Taylor, Amy Carmichael, Eric Liddell, or the usual heroes. If they ignored these, he could cite his own family's legacy. *If they act foolishly, answer them according to their folly!* Or else he could . . .

• • •

BROCK
3:13 PM EDT, WEDNESDAY, JULY 4, 2125
CIRCLE PRESERVE, CINCINNATI

People stared until they drew toward silence.

Brock walked directly into the crowd, heart pounding. Their gazes lingered, and their voices quieted into whispers: "That's Brock Rivers."

He would not hide.

He brought no president or security escort—only two brothers, Alexander and Jason.

"Brock. The president's son."

"He's doing the Space Mission."

"Oh, the Causians won't like this."

Others repeated his name. They opened a path for him. When he made eye contact with Dr. Josiah Busche atop that platform, the other stood and watched curiously. Some of the people sounded impressed. Micah McCarthy Jr. retreated a pace.

Brock stopped before the platform. "Dr. Busche, may I say a few words?"

The older preacher stepped forward, then agreed.

Brock's soles struck on wooden boards—and the noise erupted. People raised their signs. Micah McCarthy Jr. raised his fists, but his followers out-shouted him. Homekeepers checked their children and waved their banners. College of Health staffers hung at the edge. Some people lifted a new chant: "Let's stay home! Let's stay home!"

Amen. And also, go therefore.

He did not touch this pulpit or place sheets on it. He wouldn't ask for silence, only wait.

Their shouts faded, and he found his opening.

By heart Brock quoted, *"Jesus came and said to them, 'All authority in Heaven and on Earth has been given to Me. Go therefore and make disciples of all nations, baptizing them in the name of the Father and of the Son and of the Holy Spirit, teaching them to observe all that I have commanded you. And behold, I am with you always, to the end of the age.'"*

Gentle splashes echoed from the Waters of Life fountain. He also knew that verse.

"'I am the Alpha and the Omega, the first and the last, the beginning and the end.' Blessed are those who wash their robes, so that they may have the right to the tree of life and that they may enter the city by the gates."

Saints would enter the city, like passing through an airlock into a perfect preserve.

"The Spirit and the Bride say, 'Come.' And let the one who hears say, 'Come.' And let the one who is thirsty come; let the one who desires take the water of life without price."

Alpha. Omega. Those words seemed to give silent echo.

God was sovereign. Jesus Christ was working. And let the Holy Spirit reflect for His people these words from the very end of Scripture.

The people stirred and murmured. Brock departed the platform.

28

THEY WERE ONLY MEN. JUST TWELVE POWERFUL and immensely Christian elders who could, in theory, fire Jason from the mission. So he'd spent days preparing for this night.

Two weeks ago, Brock had ratified the ship purchase. In that time they had spent fourteen early mornings and late evenings meeting people, holding interviews, and doing far too much paperwork with CIRCLE and Navistar. Jason was ready for this. Right?

Carved oak doors whispered shut behind him. The red-carpeted slope led into a hallowed space between rows of encircling chairs. At the center, the council awaited.

The floor absorbed Jason's and Brock's footsteps.

Brock had shown courage. The protests had dispersed, an odd change that Brock credited to that one pastor in the middle of it. CAUSE and its Ministry had kept silent. Dr. Sheldon even said CIRCLE was making some progress with the mission appeal process.

Father, help us all.

This was Jason's first time entering the Epicenter for real. Back when he'd learned of deeper Christian faith beyond his old preserve, he'd heard of this place. Now the leaders would hear from him. Hopefully they'd be the only ones. CIRCLE claimed that techs had patched the pinholes. But they'd not mentioned any plans to replace the whole system.

"Good evening, Jason!" Which man was he? Oh, Dr. Woodford, the new president.

Jason laid his sheet on their pulpit and shook his hand. Woodford reintroduced Dr. Hendricks, the white-haired and usually silent vice president, whom Jason had met aboard the ship on that tour-guiding day.

"Alicia Rivers," called Dr. Woodford. "You have joined us from Mars?"

Over the room-wide vox, Brock's wife replied, "I have."

"Then, Brock, let us begin."

"First, our ship's regent will lead us," Brock said.

Dr. Woodford extended a welcoming arm.

Jason couldn't return that gesture because his own arm might be stupidly shaking. "Thanks. I'm Jason. Cruz. Biblical Christian since age nine. Last month, I left my position as assistant engineering professor at Freedom Hills College. That's in Virginia. Now I'm with the mission. Under the captain's lead, we are nearly done reforming a starcraft. Here."

He tagged his sheet's ready glyph. Over the dais, viz sparkled to life—the ship with its hull in freshened royal blue, with new golden trims glowing aside her twin arching pillars, back in place. Onto the bow faded the custom Space Mission emblem created by CIRCLE designers.

Then it all collapsed. Color poured down like mud and dissolved into nothing.

It wasn't his fault. What a silicate system!

Dr. Templeton departed to go check on that.

Fine. Jason wasn't using notes anyway. "Using your imaginations, you can see the progress. We'd like more time for interior work. But the minimal changes are done enough. It's on track for the test launch—three days from now, July twenty first."

He wouldn't be preaching anytime soon, but good enough.

Dr. Templeton called from the back workstation, "Try it now."

Viz reappeared, and the ship shone again.

"Brothers, this is the starcraft *Caelestis*. But we have one last change."

Jason touched the last glyph in sequence: AΩ. On the ship's bow appeared the same symbol, between the two gilded words forming the starcraft's new name, ALPHA OMEGA.

"If the Lord wills," Brock interjected, "*Alpha Omega* will serve Him for many years."

Elders murmured amens. They liked this part.

"Tell us about the crew," Dr. Woodford said.

"That's next," Jason said. *Stop talking so fast.* "This ship will test launch with seven initial crew members: Brock Rivers, Alicia Rivers,

Jason Cruz, Alexander Moore, Julia Peters, Lawrence Peters, and Tameria Lightheart."

"Some of you men will also join the launch," Brock said.

One elder said, "Don't we need more than seven for a mission?"

"We expect six members will join full-time, and we're considering more." Brock meant that Starr family from Mars. His family was staying with them, and Alicia was using their com. "Miss Lightheart won't join the crew full-time. Alicia will say more."

That was an interesting find. You never knew who you'd find lurking in a library.

Brock went on about Lawrence and Julia. Their interview was also *interesting*. They'd spent years living near a Human Nature preserve. Very different from older religions. Naturally, Brock didn't name that place or mention the people's debauchery.

• • •

ALICIA
02:32 LMST, GOD. 11, 44 (SYNDIC)
PORT ARES

Alicia listened for Brock's cue. This static and distant image of the Epicenter hardly helped her imagine being there, and she needed to speak quietly. Michael and Elizabeth, and certainly the children, had already been asleep for hours.

"Alicia is my wife, and now mission specialist as well as quartermaster," Brock was saying. "On launch day, she plans to return to Earth to serve a key role. Alicia?"

Brock was growing well into his position, and so would she.

She stood, trying to picture the council table. "Thank you, love. With both of these jobs, I manage the ship's inventory. Meanwhile, working with Alexander, I will oversee the ship's coms back home, especially future fundraising."

Jesus, please equip me for all that.

No one replied, or else the signal was interrupted.

"Mm," one man finally said.

Either they wanted more or they were skeptical. Some needed to reckon with her position. She would not be any elder or pastor, but also not limited to solely domestic jobs.

"Alicia?" That was Dr. Sheldon. "How will you support your family?"

There it was, and she was ready. "We follow Scripture. Godly husbands and wives both care for their homes, churches, and jobs. This spaceship will be like all three of these."

"Up there," Jason added, "Alicia's already managed a small Martian colony."

She could have led with that. "Exactly, Mr. Cruz." *Don't let them upend you. Just give them truth, like a servant-leader.* "Brock first wanted me to be mission archivist. But that's a lot of hats to wear. Then I got a note from Tameria Lightheart in the School of Education—"

"And you knew Tameria during your student years?" Brock said.

Love, don't trip me when I'm on a run. "Actually, we had never met. It's strange that we didn't. But after I read her message, and interviewed her, I wish I had."

• • •

BROCK
7:42 PM EDT, WEDNESDAY, JULY 18, 2125
CIRCLE PRESERVE, CINCINNATI

Brock might need to put this in writing: *Do not interrupt the ship's quartermaster.*

"In the old days," Alicia said, "missionaries would bring back photos to show in their churches. They helped present the work and gain support. For that reason, during our test launch, Tameria will record everything for the CIRCLE Library."

"That's good," Woodford said. "People need to see."

But in truth, Brock had disagreed with the president on this point. Brock had argued that if CIRCLE promoted the mission too early, they would antagonize CAUSE and invite harsher criticism from unfriendly preserves. Still, Woodford insisted CIRCLE must promote the mission before any final launch. To compromise, Brock had offered to share brief and pre-scripted viz.

"That brings us to the test launch," Woodford said.

Brock cast his summary over the ship's image. "We are set for launch this Saturday at 3:00 PM. On the main deck, we'll record my conversation with Alexander for public release."

Some elders stayed quiet, but if those protests returned, they might speak up.

"Brothers." Brock should be clear. "I don't want this mission because of Jerome Rivers's dream, or to follow our ancestors, or to chastise our own people. I want this because Christ's call to missions has resonated in our people's hearts. For decades—"

"Ahhhh, Mr. Rivers," came a bodiless voice. "You should not deceive yourself."

All light vanished. Men shouted. Brock blinked to regain tiny lights in the dark, cast by viz from several elders' clips.

Alpha Omega's replica dissolved into specs and fell into nothing.

29

WOODFORD CALMLY ASKED, "CAN ANYONE BACK there check power?"

Light returned, but from dim glows that spun higher, then became clouded snow that congealed into a blanket . . . then a human outline of clothed arms, legs, and a faceless head. One higher limb lifted, resembling an arm. "Elders of CIRCLE, do not be afraid."

The speaker lifted his pitch, then dropped low, as if imitating a music artist.

"Who's this now?" This time Woodford shouted, "Cut that com!"

"Mr. President, I prefer you not."

Brock's viz flashed red null signs. The intruder had blocked new signals. Clearly those CIRCLE techs had *not* properly secured any of the system.

The figure's arm pulled light behind him like comet tails. Down at the floor, the leg edges overlapped as if caught under a robe, flickering until the ghost touched its feet onto carpet. Whoever made this apparition was using a complex effect generator.

The shape took one long pace, its head staring without eyes, toward the elder table.

White specs danced against Brock's elbow, then reattached to the ghost.

From back at the workstation, Jason called, "Can't shut this off."

"Where is this coming from?" Woodford said.

The shape paused, two meters from the president. "Why not ask me yourselves?"

"We do not know you. We did not invite you."

"But I am a longtime admirer." Two extensions like arms folded together over the shape's chest. "And I admire your work on the new *Alpha Omega*. I have come to warn you about your mission, which will lead to your doom."

Brock stepped closer to the shape. "Who are you to say—"

Woodford held up one hand, warning him away. "Sir. Are you with the Ministry?"

"I am not," the visitor said flatly. "I do not speak for the Cause."

He might come from a protesting preserve.

"Then for whom do you speak?" Woodford said.

"I speak for myself. You might say I come to 'speak the truth in love.'"

"By making false prophecies?"

"I need no divination to reveal your sin." Slowly the ghost turned, as if rotating on a platform, without moving its feet. "Brock, James, Gregory, Timothy, Harold, Charles, Calvin, Eiichiro, Darien, Samuel, Maxwell. Also, Jason, and Alicia, and Colin and Patrick, who have just left the room. Your lies will bring judgment."

So this scrambled human knew biblical texts and language.

Brock needed to say it. "No brother would accuse his family like this."

"You assume I come from your people?"

"That's enough!" Woodford said.

"Here is the truth of you, Brock Stanford Rivers. You believe the Space Mission will honor your Savior. But this is a device to honor yourself. You make your family and home into idols, and to worship these idols, you would sacrifice anything to *preserve* them."

Two shallow pits on the head fixed down, as if to trap Brock on this floor.

"And for Jason Joshua Cruz, you claim to follow God. But you want vengeance on people you hate. You cannot fight like a man. So you imagine your enemies are like the people who oppose the Space Mission."

Jason stood in place, locked down like a stone figure.

"Alicia Beth Rivers? I hope you hear me."

It wouldn't dare. "Alicia, mute your vox."

"Alicia, your religion talks about a woman's silence. They cannot teach men. In fact, they must submit and find salvation through child-bearing. You have borne three children. Can you also bear this burden of saving your family?"

Three children. Not even the Minister on Mars had known that.

Woodford stepped beside Brock. "Is there anything else?"

"Well spoken, doctor. You doubt the Space Mission. You know what happens when Christians seek power. What happened in history when *brothers* who look different from you owned the churches? What did they do to your ancestors?"

Woodford stared back to the ghost. Only he could rebuke this.

"Did your so-called Savior ignore the cries of His own—"

"Shame on you! *Shame*." Woodford stormed forward and stopped half a meter from the coalescing specs. "You don't know my history or my people or my Lord."

"Here is another truth—"

"Can anyone cast out this devil?"

Brock had never heard Woodford so enraged.

Samuel Morrison stayed in his chair. Maxwell Adams leaned back, his long legs shoved far under the table. Charles Montague's face was a mask of restraint.

Up at the workstation, Jason swiped through his own viz. "Sir, can't do it."

"Unplug something!" Woodford pounded up the aisle. "Cut into the console."

"Mr. President, that would risk losing all your Epicenter archives," called the ghost.

Brock shouted, "That is a bluff."

Perhaps it wasn't. System issues aside, how did this enemy know all these secrets? Anyone could lose a staring contest if the opponent had no face.

"Be still and listen. You believe you can break your own skin, leave yourselves, and enter the world. This only brings poison into a body. I am that poison. Or am I? Maybe I come from elsewhere. One of you may have left open a wound. Am I invader or antibody?"

A protestor could have infiltrated the building, or a rogue deacon could have planted a virus. This specter may have truly followed CIRCLE for many years.

"Brock, if you launch the *Alpha Omega*, here is your truth. First, the launch will fail. Second, you will suffer the wrath of CAUSE, losing more support for your mission. And third, if by some divine mercy you learn to seek the truth, you may learn that you must join with people of the truth. Only they can help you."

Nothing showed on the face. It had no wings, no false halo crowning this angel of light.

Jason dashed down the ramp. "What do you mean? You'll attack the ship?"

"My ancestors would have. Some say this is our *heritage*." Chills undulated from the shape. "Gentlemen. I am not your enemy. I show you mercy. Consider this truth. I will return."

Somehow this being had drawn, as if from Brock's darkest dreams, almost every fear.

"As for you, Brock and Alicia Rivers, hear me. Yes. I know about them."

The shadowed head collapsed into shoulders. All four limbs unspooled into specs. As the ghost vanished, the silver skull that possessed its head withdrew on its cord to fasten back inside the projection chandelier. Normal lights flared back over the Epicenter.

CAUSE could not read Brock's thoughts or wage such personal warfare as this.

No, the elders wouldn't believe what it said. Even after his exile, they knew him better, and the ghost had also slandered them. Before the Lord, his conscience should be clear.

Brock ordered *local systems* and *access*. "Jason, detach your personal com. In fact, power it down." He used spare sheets to find a log of recent Epicenter coms. One active line showed at the top: Q-LINK * MARS CORE * UPSTREAM UNIT, followed by the Starrs' apartment code.

The ghost had left no records.

Brock ordered security scans, then sent Alicia's com to his ears. "Love, you there?"

"I heard everything. Was that an open vox? I could ask Michael to check systems."

She'd heard every threat to the ship, their people, and Brock's own children. Who else would know this? "Don't tell Michael, in case he . . ."

Brock must not suspect him. They knew the Starr family. Alicia and the children had stayed with them for weeks. Still, Michael did work with secular corporations aligned with CAUSE. Even if he were sincere, had CAUSE hijacked his system to do this?

Maxwell sat there, as if in stunned silence. Woodford whispered to Templeton. Two other elders were arguing, while others bowed their heads and prayed.

Brock interrupted. "Gentlemen, I suggest we relocate."

Woodford agreed, but several elders asked why.

"Because our guest was spying for much longer than this."

• • •

BROCK
10 PM EDT, WEDNESDAY, JULY 18, 2125
CIRCLE PRESERVE, CINCINNATI

Ark Hotel's open atrium echoed with running water from the center fountain, closer to Brock's position, cycling through its patterns. At this hour, any guests still awake would be unaware of the emergency meeting below them. Dr. Woodford brought the whole council over here and requested last-minute space. A lone desk attendant had discreetly summoned one of the small rooms near the hotel gym.

That ghost knew about Brock's three children. How far did the compromise reach? Brock must presume trust in the Starrs. "Licia, can you ask Michael to join?"

She sent him an alert and waited a moment. "All right, Brock, he's here."

Brock explained the incident. "Can you inspect an institutional system, originally installed in 2101 and playing Accordion?"

"Ah-um." Until now, Michael had kept silent. "Oh-*one*? Accordion?"

"I can't speak further."

"Your people never upgraded to Bassoon? Pull it all out. Switch to Viola Three."

That small room door opened between two potted plants under the second-floor balcony. Jason emerged and did not look happy. "Captain, the elders can't agree about the launch. All in favor to keep us on blocks—Hendricks, Sheldon, Keller, Montague, Morrison, and Adams. Leaning their way is . . . Dr. Lombar-ish. In favor of launch is

Templeton, your engineering professor, the Presbyterian elder, plus Dr. Mashima and President Woodford."

At least the Lord was working some good through James Woodford.

"Hendricks said he agreed—this invader spoke like he'd attacked us already."

Based on what? "The ghost made no such claim."

"Brock, he implied it," Alicia said, "after Jason asked if they would attack the ship."

Jason moved closer. "He said the word *heritage*. With emphasis."

Somehow that ghost had learned about their three children. How? Undoubtedly the ghost knew about last month's Heritage Hall disaster. Like the other hateful critics, he may want to sound prophetic, endowed with secret knowledge. "He could be lying."

Jason swore and looked away.

Brock lifted a hand. "Please mind your language. Hotel guests are still awake."

"Love, our Q-link has been open a while," Alicia said. "We can't go over budget."

She was trapped a world away, yet might be more secure than staying in this place.

"I'll pray hard," she said. "Michael will stay in touch. Godspeed, love."

"Godspeed." Brock cut the vox.

Jason stepped closer. "Anyone who found the pinholes could infect the Epicenter. I doubt it's the Causians. They don't need to be secret. Why would they do this?"

Ceramic fountain tiles pressed cool under Brock's palm. "He spoke biblical phrases."

"Yeah. Religious-talk. Could be from a bad preserve. Holding a grudge against us?"

"Quite a special preserve, with com-savvy residents and a manipulative leader."

"False prophets," Jason murmured. *"Performing great signs and wonders."*

He opened the meeting room door just as Templeton exclaimed, "Doing whatever he can to prevent us from launching the ship on time as planned."

Brock closed the door and checked for locks, but found none.

"You think this was a man?" said Vice President Hendricks.

"I don't know what else."

"That was an agent." Maxwell Adams harrumphed. "Some CAUSE algorithm. But if he's a man, how many allies? Is he givin' us official CAUSE diktat or some shadow play? What about our brothers attacked in Egypt last month? Who else do we sacrifice for this mission?"

Brock could interrupt and say the Cairo attack was unrelated—

"I'm with Mr. Adams." Dr. Hendrick's meeker voice somehow cleared all the others. "We have much controversy. Now we have direct threats. A launch is not worth it."

"With respect!" Brock called. "As the overseer, I'm responsible for this crew."

Adams pointed back. "No one questions that. But it's my job to keep them alive." The man was head of CIRCLE Security, so of course he would feel this way. "By the by." Adams pointed to Brock's com clip. "You gonna turn that off?"

He wanted to keep the Epicenter infection from spreading. "I can."

"That's unnecessary," Templeton said. "As if we don't trust that repairs—"

"I certainly don't!" Morrison tapped the table with a shaking hand. "We got to this point last month 'cause we let nonbelievers blink into the Epicenter. We talked about flying off and sharing a spaceship with them. Now that, *good* sir, that was unwise."

"Mr. President." Templeton kept his composure. "I invited our guests, because I still believe we cannot resist the preserve system alone, and because I try to live at peace with all. Meanwhile, our critics risk ignoring our Lord who told us to beware of enemy opposition. Did we hope to obey Him without facing these threats?"

Jason moved to the table. "Do you think this is from the Ministry?"

"Mr. Cruz, I don't know who's done this."

"Try a guess?" Jason grunted. "We saw violence in Egypt as if someone knew to expect us. Days earlier, the last president announced the Space Mission, then got killed by an explosion that didn't even touch the prime reactor, which was conveniently offline."

Maxwell Adams murmured something about there being no evidence.

"If rumors leaked that Heritage Hall was sabotaged, what happens to our preserves?" Templeton asked. "To our critics? To people who reject the Space Mission? Think of those who dismiss CIRCLE just because we have applied science departments. What if our people accept the rumor of an *attack* that was *engineered*? Who would fall under suspicion? Dr. Van Campen? Dr. Mashima? Darien? Perhaps even Captain Rivers and Mr. Cruz?"

Woodford had not mentioned those effects, and Brock had not considered them.

"No weapon that is fashioned against you shall succeed," Templeton said. "No matter who attacks us, we need to stay in full accord and trust in His protection."

Several elders murmured amens, but others held their tongues.

• • •

BROCK
10:48 PM EDT, WEDNESDAY, JULY 18, 2125
CIRCLE PRESERVE, CINCINNATI

Brock let the hotel anteroom's door ease to a close. Late winds had already driven the evening rains across this tiled floor. Back on Mars, these sensations would be a miracle.

"You seriously bought that pile from Templeton?" Jason said.

Brock shut his eyes against incoming mist. "He spoke some truth."

"He spoke clichés. That ghost did better with the Bible talk."

"No, listen to me. Do we want the elders to postpone the test flight?"

"Of course not." Jason's back hit the wall. "But they shut down the Epicenter for more *repairs*? Naïve. Plus we have the incredible shrinking vice president, Dr. Whatsit."

"Seven elders approved. We still have three days to test launch. What else do you want?"

Jason drew back as if remembering his lines. "With respect, I think we should post guard for the ship. Change that launch date. And don't publicize any of it. Not before, and not on that day. Not until we know just who's been watching us and why."

"Disagreed. Any sign of fearful retreat is a betrayal of the mission and our people. I can't care about what some fringe interloper claims when our own people need answers!"

Let God arise and His enemies be scattered.

Fatigue pulled Brock toward the floor, but he must stay disciplined. "We can talk later. We don't need news escaping that I've been seen here. I'm heading back to the ship."

"I'm staying a bit. Want to speak more with Maxwell Adams. Take the grackle."

"Keep your own grackle." Who was overseer again? Brock unclenched his fists. "I'm sorry. I can use a shuttle. And if Maxwell has better security ideas, I'll gladly hear them."

They parted, and Brock headed back to the grounding pad. Warm rains drenched his hair and dripped into his eyes, lit by campus lampposts whose golden lights pooled against shrouded skies. His boots whimpered as he sloshed over the walkway. Lord willing, he could climb into his cabin bed just before midnight, then seize at least four hours of fitful sleep before he awakened at 5:00 AM. He could not complain. Was this not the life he had wanted?

30

AT LONG LAST, BROCK BEHELD THE ELECTRIC snowstorm that whirled Alicia back into existence, standing in the same secret Harding basement vault they had used last month. When the door opened, she tried to stumble across the floor. He caught her just in time.

How warm and wonderful she felt, certainly less strong than before, and yet so perfect. For one earthly month they had been apart, and they embraced as long-separated lovers.

Brock did not release her hand until they reached the first floor hallway.

Alicia tried to laugh. "Elizabeth's nasty muscle supplements aren't helping much."

"I take it you were not—"

"Not detained for religious intervention, no."

They stepped from the Harding School of Engineering back into a humid Midwestern summer. Cloud blankets drifted over the shadowed grasses and walkways of campus. Alicia stared at the wealth of sky she must have been missing for all this time.

Lord, please let this be our final separation.

Rain and lack of Saturday classes had limited today's campus traffic. No passerby would see Alicia leaving this building after she had never entered it.

She held to Brock's arm. "Sorry you're stuck with an invalid wife."

"Oh, make it up to me tonight. I've booked the upgraded cabin."

Alicia winked at him, then put on a serious face. "No more enemy interference?"

"None that we know. CAUSE and its Ministry are quiet. So is our prophet of doom."

. . .

BROCK
12:45 PM EDT, SATURDAY, JULY 21, 2125
CIRCLE PRESERVE, CINCINNATI

Heritage Hall's destroyed portion was bordered by CIRCLE Security's new golden tape, which retraced the original exterior, reaching between pillars of shredded wall to divide grass from the hollowed shell. Debris littered the blackened red carpet inside. Officers had built a metal fence around the central crater that was ringed by ligaments of wood floor.

Between the Hall courtyard and pathways to Heritage House, mourners had created a new memorial. Flowers mingled with posters, photos, and handmade cards.

> Jerome Rivers, 2043–2125
> 80+ years in the Faith.
> Long live our President behind the Gates of Heaven.

A child's crayon handwriting spelled out, *Rest in Jeus, MR Revers.*
Alicia tugged his sleeve. "You all right?"
"Ah . . . I am exhausted. But that's against ship regulations."
"We didn't need to come here first."
"I did need this. Now that CIRCLE Security finished the investigation, I need the closure."
"They never learned the port reactor's problem?" Alicia said.
"Supposedly there was no more to be learned because the port reactor is destroyed. Security checked similar reactor models, but found no problems."
"So the port reactor installation may have gone badly."
"Those techs were pressed for time. I suppose we can learn from their mistakes." His clock showed nearly 1:00 PM. "We have two hours. Let's go to the ship."

• • •

BROCK
1:29 PM EDT, SATURDAY, JULY 21, 2125
SOUTH CINCINNATI

Brock did not apologize to Alicia for the state of Jason's grackle. This was nothing compared to the wonder she would soon behold. The craft, at least, brought them quickly to the resettlement preserve, and rushing toward the hangar, he found himself lifting the grackle too fast. He pulled back to stabilizing altitude, then banked the vehicle toward the hangar gate, open wide to receive them. And there, poised between the hangar's walls that held access ramps and gridwork, waited the *Alpha Omega*, fully restored, complete with her arching support pillars.

Alicia could not take her eyes from every shining, gold-trimmed navy surface. Her excitement alone would give him enough momentum for today's test launch.

Brock landed beside the Navistar shuttle and gave his tin to her. "Captain needs a refill?"

"Oh, I think Captain can fetch his own coffee."

With a laugh, Brock opened doors and leaped out. "Regent Cruz?"

"Welcome aboard." As expected, Jason showed no hint of attitude from their dispute after the council meeting three days ago. "Navistar techs are finishing up. Now we wait for Dr. Woodford with the CIRCLE party, plus the Peters couple and Miss Tameria Lightheart."

Brock moved to the craft's port side to help Alicia. "Can you walk all right?"

"Yes. Let's get you ready. Do you have a suit jacket for the post-launch media?"

"It's down in the cabin." Last night, Brock had spent one very tiring hour practicing his interview with Alexander. "Jason, update me about ETAs. I want to show Alicia the ship."

"Yes, sir."

They had spoken about speech protocols, but Jason sounded like a different person.

• • •

ALICIA
1:50 PM EDT, SATURDAY, JULY 21, 2125
SOUTH CINCINNATI

Alicia couldn't stop wincing from gravity pangs. These would *not* hold her back. After all, Brock had fought through much worse to reach a moment like this.

She managed to follow him down this short ramp and passage while he murmured, "Task list B3. Autoguide for cargo bay, dispenser in captain's cabin. Add to list A2, plumbing design, hydroponic systems for living deck inner room, perhaps near infirmary . . ."

He opened a broad door and led her into a cabin of slate-blue walls with silver trim.

Within minutes, Alicia had toured both levels, with open foyer, storage, office, dining, and living areas above, and three bedrooms below, divided by the center split-level with a small but complete kitchen. This upper floor alone was bigger than their Martian skiff. Here they would have a *real* home, and she could step outside this into a world of godly purpose.

From their new walk-in closet, Brock withdrew his navy jacket, now well-pressed and without dust. Two tiny objects tumbled out of it. Resisting a groan, Alicia instinctively bent to retrieve these—his grandfather's silver dove cufflinks.

"You're still nervous," she said.

Brock inspected himself in the jacket. "The elders believe some unknown visitor planted a virus in the Epicenter system." He returned to the stairs, ascending more slowly. "Jason and some elders also think Dr. Templeton accidentally let in the infiltrator. After last Thursday, and Templeton's criticism, I don't expect he'll join today's launch."

"That's too bad. I know he believes in the mission. Can't they make peace for one day?"

Brock kissed her on the wrist, then her lips. "We'll let the Lord handle that."

They returned to the ship's cooler cargo bay, where a new shuttle had crowded inside. Opening doors revealed that five elders and the president had arrived.

Alicia had spent time memorizing them. She lifted her shoulders and approached to shake hands. "Dr. Woodford. Dr. Van Campen! Dr. Mashima and Dr. Sheldon, welcome. Mr. Adams, we appreciate your joining us. And oh, Dr. Morrison." For him, she gave the strongest handshake of all. "How are you? How is Rosario?"

Dr. Morrison said his wife of fifty-three years was in good health. They had become great-grandparents twice over since Brock and Alicia had left Earth in 2118.

A blue dot shone on her viz. *Alpha Omega* itself wanted to greet her. *Well, new ship, what have you to share?*

"Welcome, you all," Jason said. "This test flight begins in one hour. Captain and crew are expected on command deck by 2:45. Most of you will stay on the living deck . . ."

Newfound viz showed Alicia COMMAND DECK, LIVING DECK, LABOR DECK (RESTRICTED).

"Director Sumisawa?" Brock was listening to vox. "Yes . . . Soren, the Navistar tech? No. We haven't used the quantum vault since Mr. Sadat returned home."

One iris scan let Alicia access all COMMAND DECK STATS (LIMITED) plus the SCHEDULES, MANIFEST, SYSTEM, INVENTORY, and ERROR LOGS. Something real moved beyond her viz. Far below on the hangar floor, a pale violet vehicle emerged from the smaller gate and pivoted its needle nose into ascent. This might carry the woman Alicia was eager to meet.

Brock ordered vox off. "Navistar says their tech found strange data from . . ." He lowered his voice. "The new vault. It is active, but it's scarcely been used."

"So *their* technician monitors the vault from offsite?" Alicia said.

"Apparently so. Jason told me he said he's a believer."

At the ship's gate, that new violet craft arrived, then landed in the final bay space. Its single front door lifted like an eyelid, letting the occupant slowly climb onto her vehicle's lower ledge. She landed on the floor and wobbled, murmuring to vox or herself.

This was her—short with sandy hair and a round face. "Tameria? I'm Alicia."

Tameria Lightheart found a smile and opened her arms. "Do you . . . do hugs?"

"Absolutely."

As expected, this woman earnestly embraced her, as if they were close family. Only then did Tameria step back and lift her gaze. "This is . . . greater than I thought?" She sounded like she had missed something. "It has a two-level cargo bay. Multiple airlock partitions?"

She had done her research. "That's right."

Tameria's knee-length skirt spun about loose violet-patterned trousers. She opened the side door of her shuttle. "I could set up my things in here. They won't be in your way."

With that nervousness, she sounded like she felt they wanted her to fly the ship.

"I prefer you on living deck." Alicia took two of the four tiny cameras, then showed their guest up the stairs and past the central levitator's anteroom.

Tameria leaned on the doorway. "Praise God that you have this."

She kept speaking about them in the second person, like she had during their last-minute interview the other day. "Sister," Alicia said, "the mission belongs to all of us."

With a polite smile, Tameria gestured across the deck. "Where can I set up?"

At the forward firewell, Alicia found controls to make the ceiling dome cast down glimmering specs, which quickly assembled a waist-high wall encircling a complex centerpiece. Artists had rendered this wonderfully, down to the intricate stone patterns. Now the center sculpture burst into animation. Audible splashes matched the flow of liquid.

Tameria leaned over the facsimile. "The Waters of Life fountain?"

"Alexander's idea. We should film Brock's announcement down here. Our main visual will show him speaking, as if he's really on campus. Then we'll draw back to show our surprise, that he's truly standing aboard the new ship."

If they timed this right, people would see the forward canopy just in time for a slow ascent. People could watch *Alpha Omega* break out of rainclouds into the sun-emblazoned sky. Lord willing, every Christian in every preserve would be inspired by this day when their people dared to resist CAUSE and begin this mission above Earth.

"Hope I'm what you need." Tameria fixed one camera in midair. "How'm I doing?"

Alicia tried to laugh. "Only if we get a grand piano in here for you to play sometime."

"I can't. Not here."

"What if I promise to show you the command deck?"

"Oh . . . maybe." Tameria placed two more aerial cameras. Her platform shoes padded on the floor until she stopped beside the forward window. She looked upon the flat hangar wall, which gleamed like metallic gray eggshell, speckled with white lumen threads.

She might be taken with some new idea, or else simply distracted.

"Walls of the world. Giving way." Tameria's murmurs drifted backward. "Look again, and see the starlight. Far light. Mars light. Like silver jewels? No. That's too much. Try . . . pinpricks in the world-cloak. Or . . . bizarre light. Note the alienation."

She turned back to Alicia and shrugged. "Oh. I do this sometimes."

Alicia could be kind. "You should see me when I'm composing."

"You're a musician?"

"When I can, and I'd love to do more."

"Would be like music to see space out there. Oh, but not *space*! That's a bad word, if you take the medieval vantage. Not a space of death. That place is filled with life. Or else it could be. Maybe after His return. Maybe then we'll have true æther."

In a moment, Alicia might follow that stream of thought.

"Hallo!" A deep shout echoed in their deck, then the speaker bustled onto the floor—a large fellow whose ruddy brown hair jostled past his neck. His Navistar jacket held tight over his shoulders. "Ladies. Afternoon. I seek Regent Jason Cruz or Captain Brock Rivers."

Alicia said, "They're in the big bay—"

"Came from there."

"Or uptube on the command deck. We launch in half an hour."

• • •

BROCK
2:40 PM EDT, SATURDAY, JULY 21, 2125
SOUTH CINCINNATI

After that big Navistar tech found him, Brock might not recover his hand with intact cartilage. "Yes, thank you, Mr. Soren. Pleased to meet you."

The man let go and pointed back to the highbridge steps. "Saw you had a problem."

Did he expect praise for saying this before six elders? "We can talk down there."

"Sure, I just need to know how recently a human used that vault."

From meters away, Dr. Morrison's white eyes flared under his spectacles.

Get behind me. "Soren, we've used no such machine for human beings. Run any diagnostics you like in the starboard stern. We launch in twenty."

Soren plodded off, leaving the command deck spectators in silence.

Dr. Morrison broke it. "He don't mean one of *those things* is aboard."

"Doctor," Woodford said, "for the last thirty years, any ship has cargo vaults."

"Not any ship to serve the Lord Jesus, I should say . . . !"

Brock had a ship to prepare. He voxed Jason. "What's the update?"

"Alexander just returned with the Peters couple."

And with eighteen minutes to spare. "Send them to command deck."

"Yes, sir. We waiting on Dr. Templeton?"

"We are not. Let's just say he wants to avoid work on the old Sabbath."

Brock headed aft to find Derek Soren exchanging bows with Director Sumisawa.

"Captain," the big man said. "Can I stay aboard?"

"We already have three techs here," Sumisawa said.

Soren was gazing over the ship as if seeing it anew.

Loudmouth and all, the man was a professing believer, and reportedly skilled. "He can, only to check the vault. Mr. Soren, please keep discreet about this. Yes?"

"Ey. Can do. Vault's working. I just caught a few irregularities, and—"

"Thank you. Report to me after launch." Brock headed to the galley to refill his coffee.

He returned to command deck just as light pulsed atop the main levitator gate. Alexander slipped onto the deck and turned to help Julia

Peters, clad in a copper-and-black blouse with skirt, and Lawrence Peters, whose broad shoulders and green coat were stained with rain.

Brock shook Lawrence's hand and drew into Julia's tight hug. "Welcome aboard."

Julia also held Brock's left wrist between her hands, jingling bracelets. "Mr. Rivers, based on your pictures, I didn't quite get the meaning of the *name*. Isn't that it there, in the bridge shape? Like the great Greek letter *omega* with two arms."

"And here might be the *alpha* portion." Lawrence's mellow voice echoed as he beckoned to the port-side lowbridge wing, the left curve of the capital letter *A*.

"Indeed. Perhaps a sign." Brock might truly believe this. "We have ten minutes to launch. I want you watching the operations and anything else that strikes you as new. After this, we can discuss whether the Space Mission is right for you."

They had clear desire for missionary work, though no experience with space travel. That standard might be unreasonable; so far, only he, Alicia, and Jason had met this.

Alexander swept personal viz onto the *omega* console. "Captain, at three o'clock, we record the launch. I've placed two cameras outside, one in the hangar, one on the landing pad." He flicked away an alert. "Forecast has more rain coming."

"I assume water-resistant cameras?"

"They are. At 3:15, our conversation. Test question: Why hope to do missions in space? Why not minister to our own people on Earth?"

The question evaded CAUSE threats and focused only on theology.

Brock felt prepared, especially after his refill. "Our Lord Jesus told us to go into all the world. We don't obey Him by merely teaching one another. Yes, home is a great blessing. But our neighbors need Jesus. If our 'Caesar' restricts that work here, we will go elsewhere."

"Inspiring stuff. And we have eight minutes."

"Then take your station at starboard lowbridge. Of course, you've overviewed the—"

"Fastidiously, Captain."

Jason exited the main levitator and ushered more elders onto command deck. Lawrence and Julia would stay on port lowbridge with Alexander. Alicia was downtube, likely welcoming the newcomer, Tameria, whom Brock could better meet this afternoon.

Minutes later, he retook the highbridge. All viz lit with high-priority options.

Living deck, show cargo bay. Open gates shone before his eyes and sharpened into three dimensions. No people were in the way; no vehicles protruded where they ought not.

His clock showed 2:58 PM. Brock sighted the bay-close glyph, and all three door points began drawing inward as the highbridge floor vibrated a low hum. Signaling with his finger, Brock summoned Jason to the highbridge. "Confirm clearance."

Jason crossed back to speak with Director Sumisawa one last time.

Alicia emerged from the levitator, walking fast as if readjusted to gravity. She saw him, gave a wide smile, then took her place on the starboard lowbridge with the elders.

"We have clearance," Jason said. "Reactor is powered. Prelaunch done."

"This starboard lowbridge station manages external coms," Alicia told the elders. "The port lowbridge station monitors internal stats. Only at the center highbridge does the captain guide the ship, using autodrive and manual control."

"Testing nav firewell." Brock sighted the globe glyph. Like magic fire, imagery burst from new microscopic arrays in the console's upper edges and over the great vertical glass canopy. Flaming particles streamed up to him and coalesced into a replica of the ship's true surroundings—a mirror of the reformation hangar, with lights, high girders, and two tiny doors flanking the enormous gateway.

"Our new highbridge firewell," Alicia went on, "lets our crew stand in place of the ship itself. Systems can plot courses and avoid midair or ground collisions."

The time was exactly 3:00 PM.

Brock sighted *crew vox.* "This is Captain Brock Rivers. We are launching. We will ascend three kilometers into public airspace, then another two hundred kilometers beyond the level of low Earth orbit. After a brief tour, we return to the settlement by four o'clock."

His hands were steady. Everyone seemed ready for this.

"Director Sumisawa, release the hangar moorings and open the gates."

"Moorings released, gates opening," she said, over vox and from his left.

The vast interior stayed in place—the hangar's actual wall beyond *Alpha Omega*'s glass canopy, and the mirrored tiny ceiling and mirrored walls rising to his sides. Of course every part of this starcraft's great body was fulfilling its purpose. *Take heart, Captain.*

"Clear course," Jason said.

They could have easily fetched autodrive, but Brock had practiced for this.

Gravity spectra control lit, and he dialed up ten meters. The hangar ceiling and floor dipped lower. He saw the hangar's viz-mirrored back wall, barely visible, projected over the real-life hangar's back wall.

Brock nudged his yoke. The ship moved forward while suppressing all inertia. In three seconds, *Alpha Omega* passed under clouded daylight. Before the ship stretched their vacant landing pad, nearly four times the hangar size.

"The ship will start by lifting straight upward," Alicia went on. "Synthetic gravity spectra powers the ascent and provides speeds up to Mach 1. Then our gravity is nullified while pulse engines take over. During any spaceflight, our three plasma propulsion engines would provide more powerful thrust, fueled by the fusion reactor."

During any spaceflight. Oh, what a dream, possibly coming true within months.

Jason stepped closer. "Captain, got a climate factor. Storm cell in five or ten."

"Well, if our hull can deflect space dust, it can handle raindrops."

"And better than my first vehicle's wiper blades," Jason said. "Just telling you."

Brock drew the ship fully onto the pad, whose miniature replica now covered his surrounding viz mirror. He released the yoke. *Alpha Omega* halted, awaiting further orders.

This was the moment.

Rainclouds loomed beyond Navistar factories, the settlement's taller central port monolith, and this vast tabletop of the landing pad. Brock shut his eyes, making all vanish.

Lord Jesus, for all my doubts, past and future, and all my recent sins, I repent. You have given me this mission. I'm so unworthy. Help me lead my people. Let these good guests see our commitment to serve with excellence for Your kingdom.

"Captain." Jason spoke on shipwide vox. "We're ready for ascent."

Brock reopened his eyes and returned to the highbridge.

He followed the scripted prayer. "Lord God, Creator. We pledge this ship and our mission to You and Your glory." Softly he sang aloud, "*Soli Deo gloria.*"

He turned the spectra dial. *Alpha Omega* leaped ten, twenty, fifty, seventy meters skyward. Brock pitched at zero degrees. No need for weather compensation. Soon this vessel would rise higher than all the winds.

He released the dial. Yoke material realigned with his hands. Pitch: +40 DEGREES.

Clouds filled the window and drew aside their shrinking homeworld.

"Whoa!" exclaimed an elder from lowbridge.

"All clear," Jason reported.

He could breathe. "*Alpha Omega* crew and guests, we have successfully launched—"

"*Whoop!*" That shout echoed astern, possibly from that technician, Soren.

From down in the port lowbridge, Alexander looked up, watching Brock.

Follow the script. "We rejoice for this opportunity. Exactly one month since my grandfather, President Jerome Rivers, announced the Space Mission, we can fulfill—"

Red light speared Brock's viz, and alarms erupted.

31

BROCK
3:16 PM EDT, SATURDAY, JULY 21, 2125
SOUTH CINCINNATI

THESE ALARMS COULD NOT BE RIGHT; THEY MUST be negligible, a false reading.

Alpha Omega's flight path and ascent had not changed. Brock's scanboard was clear. No projectile streaked over the forward canopy, energy was stable, gravity spectra and thrust were holding, and the hull was intact.

"This alert says life support's failing?" came Jason's voice.

Brock leaned over the board and found a CLEAR button. This silenced the blare, but too late. Everyone in both lowbridges faced the highbridge, barely restraining their questions.

Any genuine failure would prompt the ship's one-hour backup—

New alarms screamed. Scarlet haze filled another board. "Jason, this says we have failures in synthetic gravity *and* port and starboard thrusters?"

"We aren't even running those, Captain."

Brock palmed the board, but it refused further details. He could still raise the ship. *Alpha Omega* was brushing against clouds with no tangible problem.

"Captain, got no bad readings from life systems."

Brock sent a note to Alicia: *False alarms?* She read this and took to vox: "*Alpha Omega* crew and guests, you may hear alerts, but we believe these are false alarms."

Oh Lord, please be true.

Alexander called, "Brock. Something is wrong. Several consoles just exploded."

"Exploded?" He had really just said that? "Like some kind of pyro—"

Down on the starboard lowbridge, Alexander glanced about in confusion. His mouth had not moved, and yet Brock had just heard his voice.

This was false, just like the alarms.

Brock sighted for signal trace.

NO VOX WITH ALEXANDER MOORE IS ACTIVE.

"Regent, I just heard a faked Alexander voice report damage."

They had put imposters on his spaceship? Brock slowed their ascent until the vessel stopped at 1.2 kilometers above Earth. Now he truly voxed Alexander and called his name. "Run a check and see if any system—"

Boom. The floor swept under Brock's legs. He clawed through the air before red carpet rammed his shoulders and back. He grabbed for the console and hoisted himself back up. *Alpha Omega* groaned, battered by some real and serious problem. Something was happening down below. Whom to call first? That woman downtube, what was her name? *Vox Tameria.* "This is the captain. Are you on living deck? Do you see anything strange?"

"That big thump under the floor?"

"Stand by." Brock returned to his yoke, but *Alpha Omega* clung faithfully to the sky. "Regent! Find a partner and check on labor deck."

Jason ran for the levitator, followed close behind by Soren.

• • •

JASON
3:21 PM EDT, SATURDAY, JULY 21, 2125
SOUTH CINCINNATI

The metallic scent in Jason's nostrils stung hotter. It was turning into something worse—visible gray wisps trailed up the levitator shaft. He grabbed another handle and shoved himself further down into the smoke. Fine. Some alarms were telling the truth.

Drifting overhead, Derek Soren banged something and yelled, *"Filth and scourge!"*

They had so many people aboard, including women and elders. If this was CAUSE, they hadn't stopped at one sabotage. This strike could be worse.

Smoke thickened. What else waited down there?

Jason slipped on his glazer. He'd kept only one, leaving the spares in his grackle.

First, another need—this stuff was pricking his throat, even through his collar pulled over his mouth. Hanging onto the levitator's last handle, he tried to wave off the smoke. He landed so hard on the labor deck that his forehead struck the levitator arch, and his vision spun.

Soren landed next and caught him. "Cruz, you good? You good?"

"Yeah—fine—" Just outside the tube, one cabinet had lost its door, exposing two hooks without oxygen masks. "Captain, we got bad smoke on labor deck. Not life support. Could be dissolved spec hordes from the reactor subsystem. Seal the levitators."

"I heard you."

Wait, Brock had mentioned a fake voice. Was this really him? "Sir . . . can you tell me my grackle's name?"

"You didn't give her a name!"

Good. And emergency barrier stems obtruded in the levitator shaft.

Soren dropped to the floor, under the smoke. "Regent, that stuff rises."

Jason bent for clearer oxygen, over tiles that buzzed like insects. He crawled toward labor deck's workstation.

"Labor deck," Soren boomed out, "start the ventilation fans!"

Of course *Alpha Omega* didn't respond, because Soren wasn't linked with the core.

Jason repeated the command. Station displays swiveled to meet him and lit green. Life support, synth grav, core reaction, stellarator fields, fine. All refuted the alerts.

He scrambled down the hall. Gray smoke from the ship's hissing interior filled this place, dragged in tangles across white rays streaming from lumen lines. Walls gave way to machine tubes, conduits, valves, access ports, spec repair lines. Against one station, a red light flashed.

Jason clambered beneath the main duct leading to manual dials and filter sockets. His own viz didn't change. Was this structure the main screen?

"Life support's powered down," Soren said.

"The ship has a one-hour support buffer," Jason replied.

"You sure?"

"Captain, do you hear me?" Silence. "Captain?"

The ship heaved and drove Jason forward against the life-support console. Soren vanished through smoke, leaving Jason behind. He might be escaping the sabotage he'd helped arrange. Or else he was heading for the levitator to tell the captain.

That hissing continued from down the hall. Maybe the core reactor. Another noise joined it, like an energy pulse. Gravity spectra? Why was Brock lifting the ship?

• • •

BROCK
3:25 PM EDT, SATURDAY, JULY 21, 2125
SOUTH CINCINNATI

Alpha Omega had cleared 1.3 kilometers. "Jason, we're ascending, but why—"

"Good. Now I will start clearing out this smoke."

Hold. That voice was too calm. Brock should curse his own foolishness in listening to this. "Regent Cruz, *why* did you just tell me to increase our altitude?"

"It is necessary."

"Well, what is the name of your grackle?"

"It . . . does not have a name."

So that test was no longer useful. "What is the grackle serial number?"

Brock didn't know this either, but he had silenced the false Jason. Brock released gravity control, then gripped the dial and spun down, shedding altitude. He ordered another signal trace. NO VOX WITH JASON CRUZ IS ACTIVE.

The big man, Soren, swept up onto highbridge, breathing evenly. "Captain, we should re-seal both locks on the main levitator. I had to get them to unlock 'em. Regent Cruz is—"

"Licia, find the emergency measures board, with red lining, over there."

"Prime life support's down, so we can't go up," Soren said. "Can we end the flight?"

"Mr. Soren, we officially ended flight two minutes ago." Brock turned down grav control and set the ship for auto-descent.

Alicia re-cast her voice shipwide: "We are returning to land. Stay in place."

"Thank you, love. Over there is the navboard. Please retrace our route to Navistar. Soren, you're not crew, so leave the highbridge. Alexander!"

He arrived, breathing hard under sweaty blond hair.

"Vox the Navistar tower. Tell them we have an emergency. Alicia's at nav, so you're now the ship's voice. No need for polish; we seriously don't know the problem. But we've kept gravity and thrust, and we're heading back."

Alexander vanished behind viz.

"Captain, I found our course," Alicia said.

Brock secured the yoke and displaced her, pulling the navboard closer to highbridge center. "Thank you. Alexander has your old job. I can't reach Jason. Go downtube, but not to labor deck. Inform the other elders and Navistar staff. Alexander?"

"I'm here. Brock, I can't reach Navistar, and the fuel's wasting."

Brock confirmed—they had perhaps twenty flight minutes left. He held all their lives in his hands. Where else could he land the ship? Port Cincinnati, the heart of local CAUSE? Even if *Alpha Omega* survived that landing, CAUSE would seize her!

The deck lurched, but Brock clung to the console. Violent groans rippled through the ship. Beyond the window the world quaked, throwing Brock to the floor, where he skidded to the highbridge's other side. His feet slapped into the console and he cried out.

Again the world overturned. *Alpha Omega* fought to stabilize internal spectra.

Where was Alicia? He tried to reorient his own spinning vision. She and Woodford hovered within the levitator, unaffected.

But now the bridge alarms had silenced, as if the ship were denying her own pain.

• • •

JASON
3:30 PM EDT, SATURDAY, JULY 21, 2125
SOUTH CINCINNATI

New bruises pricked under Jason's arm, but he'd kept his bones together. He climbed off the floor whose gravity had turned against him. Medics would have come for him—if this were a SOAR training exercise. "Jesus, help me."

Smoke thickened near the floor. He yanked off his jacket and tied one sleeve around his face. This wasn't the spec horde from earlier. Maybe this was tank coating, darker stuff.

Almost like it came straight from—

Jason rounded the corner and stared at the bulkhead.

Roiling black smoke blocked all lamp light, except for a red trail that burned like lava and etched down the charcoal-metal wall. Over that mortal wound hung two great intersecting scars, one horizontal gash, the other vertical and twice as long.

• • •

ALICIA
3:32 PM EDT, SATURDAY, JULY 21, 2125
SOUTH CINCINNATI

Alicia landed on the levitator tube's new floor formed by emergency seal. Gravity reclaimed her. She clutched the doorway, wavered on the shifting deck. Further ahead, past the firewell with splashing viz fountain, couches and chairs had slid across the floor.

Dr. Woodford landed behind her and stumbled forward.

Tameria and many others pressed near the glass canopy, which shuddered over the city's distant field of towers. Dr. Mashima knelt beside a reclining Dr. Morrison.

"We're returning to Navistar," she said, "so please pray."

Dr. Woodford kept silent.

"What is that smell?" Dr. Keller said.

Labor deck was sealed off. Was the metallic odor related to the clanking sound near the levitator? Alicia approached the main shaft. That noise grow louder and more rhythmic. Brock had told her to avoid labor deck, but wasn't Jason down there?

Alicia tagged the small levitator stat. Barrier stems parted. Odor rolled over her face.

One meter down, Jason clung to the tube ladders. "Ma'am . . .

vox . . . captain." Jason gasped for clean air. "Fuel tank. Compromised. I am *trying*."

"Is the smoke harmful?"

"Not sure. I conveyed prime life support. Evacuating smoke to the cargo bay."

If he couldn't reach the highbridge, something was jamming their coms. They needed another way. "Dr. Mashima or Dr. Woodford? Please go up to command deck. Then please repeat only *real, audible* shouts from me or Jason downtube."

Both men headed that way. Alicia stepped in. "I'm coming down."

"You're not, ma'am."

Do not even. "So you expect to shout from the labor deck all the way up to me?"

"Fine." Jason thrust a small yellow thing into her hand. "Fifteen-minute filter."

She fastened on the mask and descended after him. Despite the fading smoke, stenches like strong ozone clung to her face. Jason led her deeper down the corridor. Here the floor was covered by glowing lava for maybe ten square meters, issuing new geysers of steam. This must be the ship's very fuel supply, toxic to human touch.

That new gash on the wall—its heat burned in her throat, and the meaning in her mind.

Jason murmured through his own mask, "I'll have to neutralize. Hit our own fuel with a coagulant. Keeps it from damaging the floor." At a wall, Jason pulled down a screen like a periscope. "If this system will even listen. Silicate!" He jabbed the screen. "Take the command! Ugh! *Hate. These. Things!*"

Alicia fell back, but he wasn't raging at her.

Jason shoved the screen and tore at a bramble of cords. With some tool he banged a pipe and opened a lid. He tugged at a handle beneath.

Serpents hissed under the walls, and the ceiling burst into floods of gray foam.

"Thousands of yun," he said to himself. "Wasted."

She turned back to the levitator to call, "Tell the bridge we are neutralizing the fuel!"

Even from here, that splintery lava shape carved on the bulkhead—that *cross*—shone within the gray flood, throwing scorched light down the dark corridor.

Dr. Mashima called to them, "The captain asks, how much fuel is left?"

Alicia repeated the message.

"Estimate nine percent," Jason said.

They had launched with thirty percent because Brock had not wanted a full load.

"We could waste most or *all* the starboard tank!" Jason called. "When do we land?"

Alicia repeated his question, and they waited in clanging, hissing darkness.

Dr. Mashima shouted, "Brock is finding a place to land."

She shoved back her filter mask and repeated this to Jason. Then her ears clicked. Brock's voice echoed: *"Alpha Omega.* I am sorry. I cannot find a place to set down. This ship will lose power. I regret that your lives must end. Pray to your gods."

• • •

BROCK
3:50 PM EDT, SATURDAY, JULY 21, 2125
CINCINNATI

Lord God almighty, help me protect Your people.

But gravity's Creator was upholding the law Brock needed to defy, and every system resisted his control. Clouded skies poured rain torrents that peacefully danced off the canopy's invisible field. Out in the city, slate towers lifted like jagged knives.

"Sumisawa to the bridge. Sumisawa to the bridge!"

One tank had ruptured; another could soon follow. If Jason had truly neutralized escaping fuel, these specs wouldn't stop until they had ruined the potency of every fuel molecule that touched another. Without a halt, the spec horde would proceed into the very reactor lines and stop the reaction cold—assuming no other system suddenly failed. Then, unless emergency power held, *Alpha Omega* would drop as if felled by arrows.

Sumisawa stumbled onto the highbridge.

"Without navigation, how can we return to Navistar?" Brock said.

"If this ship has total failure," she said, "I wouldn't trust my maps."

"Clarify?"

"These are not flaws in your ship. This is strategic and systemwide—"

"I know this."

"—and it's affected every linked com, including yours and mine."

Jason's voice said, "Captain. The second tank is ruptured. I also see anomalies in the gravity spectra. I estimate the ship will fall within two minutes."

What other lies would this synthetic haunt tell Brock after reading his thoughts and activating more fears? Even if they reached Port Cincinnati, more than forty klicks south of here, they might not find a landing pad in time. What if that second tank truly ruptured?

If only Brock could revert to maritime navigation.

Could he? Through the bridge mirror's duplicate horizon, at about one o'clock, rose the nexus of Cincinnati. He telescoped viz into those stair-stepping green-and-navy structures, dressed in spiraling light rail lines. Uglier round pillars of faux-brick-and-copper rose near the Triad Towers. None of these landmarks provided orientation.

There. In the center stood the tallest building, the great silver monolith. Its logo held two letters like fingers and three letters like another hand, connecting in the middle with a starburst: IN*SUR. That logo faced south. So this direction was north.

Home was northwest.

"Alexander, vox CIRCLE and request landing space!" Brock leaned on his yoke and *Alpha Omega* leaped that direction. Did he have time to amend the flight plan?

"I'm sorry, but my com is jammed."

"Jammed with Port? What about CIRCLE?"

Slowly the downtown district approached. Brock added speed but stayed under half supersonic. At this altitude, they might avoid most trade streams.

"Captain, I can reach CIRCLE. But what *landing space*? I can't think of one."

"Find a vehicle lot. Have that cleared, especially of people."

By now any ships with conflicting flight paths should have pinged this ship, so either no one was flying in the way or their signals were blocked. *Alpha Omega* swept through the rainstorm, bypassing all of downtown, gliding against its own groans and shifting gravities. One minute passed. Then another. She reported no more false or true failures. Cincinnati's landmarks fell away into lower buildings and flatter streets, while train lines slipped underground like worms. Public parks covered grounding bays.

Now to risk descent. He eased the ship down, down, until those streets and structures added details and speed. *Alpha Omega* heaved as if rolling over air pockets.

Another jolt. The entire command deck lifted and dropped, throwing Brock to the air and slamming him back to his feet. A woman screamed. What about the living deck with loose furniture? One impact could kill someone, but he must focus on landing.

Alexander lifted his hand. "There we are."

Curated land drifted below the horizon, bringing that familiar forest of apartments. Next came the sparser trees south of campus near the Ark Hotel.

Brock threw on speed, pulling *Alpha Omega* into brutal shudders.

Another alarm pointed to the energy board, which showed decaying core power loss because of wasted fuel. Backups snapped offline. Did this mean anything?

"Hello, this is Moore. Yes!" Alexander listened. "Gilead Apartments? Where?"

Of course any landing site would lie further east. And of course these would be *those* apartments, closer to the preserve border, as if the Lord himself were showing Brock a penalty.

Ahead port, almost 60 degrees.

CIRCLE's campus fled about and reappeared in micro on the bridge mirror. The ship passed into preserve territory. Anything that happened now would fall under CIRCLE jurisdiction, so anyone lost aboard would die near his homeland.

Falsified or real, the ship's energy reading dropped from seven to three percent. The altitude hovered near 240 meters. There sprawled those layers of L-shaped duplexes surrounding three rows of apartment structures. To the east lay that enormous half-paved lot, the place where some developer had long ago promised to build more housing.

With no autodrive and no tower assist, the ship held two percent power.

Apartments beside the water tower rushed up toward them.

Ninety meters. Forty-two meters. Power level flashed zero.

Alpha Omega lurched, striking land. Brock's hands tore from the yoke. Someone behind him shoved his body back to the console. He scrambled for the console's edge to pull for the gravity dial and spin it all the way down to zero.

Taper descent. Taper descent! Lord, help me!

One greater lurch made bulkheads groan and strain. G-forces tugged his hair and arms. From somewhere outside, objects smashed and tore, as if the ship were plowing directly into the apartment complex, destroying vehicles, homes, even people.

Energy boards flashed red. *power 0%, power 0%,* as if oblivious to the reserve energy that powered lights, independent systems, and these very boards. The altimeter showed zero.

Alexander slumped with arm bent over the console, blood trickling from an open gash.

Brock called his name.

He looked up. "Are we down?"

Brock cast shipwide vox, also drawing reserve power. "This is Brock Rivers, the real one. We've touched down in our own preserve. If you are injured, please reply. If you're not, stay off the vox. Security should reach us soon."

Somehow he had managed to speak clearly.

"Captain . . . Jason here. I could be injured."

Surely no imposter could mock those emotions. "What's our status?"

"Single starboard tank, still ruptured. Otherwise no change."

Rain and new-heated mists rose beyond the canopy. "What about other systems?"

"I think the life support lied to us. No change there either. I vented into the bay."

"Good . . . good, thank you. Open the bay doors and let's vent the rest."

"This is Dr. Mashima. Dr. Morrison has struck his head, but he is conscious."

"Julia Peters!" Brock called, and she looked up with disheveled black hair. "Living deck is now the ship's recovery center. Go downtube. Alicia, your status?"

"I think I'm well."

"Then organize human recovery. Dr. Morrison goes first, Alexander next."

Alexander climbed up the console and hunched with a grimace. "We have many inbound coms. One's from CIRCLE Security. Two more from private security firms. Behind them we have an auto-summons from . . ." His eyes reappeared. "Yeah, it's CAUSE."

Brock uttered a silent curse. "We're in a preserve. Not their business."

"We were flying damaged in public airspace."

"You take Security. I can respond to the civics." What could Brock tell them? That CIRCLE had suffered a *second* mass disaster that required rescue, one month after the last crisis? "I'll need Dr. Woodford and Dr. Sheldon, if they can speak—"

"Brock Rivers, it's time *we* spoke. I send you greetings."

The new voice was cold and thin, smothering all other sounds. The last syllable fell strangely, but the voice sounded lucid and naturally accented, without distortion.

"I am glad you have saved your people. Now my people offer you help."

32

BROCK
4:13 PM EDT, SATURDAY, JULY 21, 2125
CIRCLE PRESERVE, CINCINNATI

THOSE WORDS, WITH THEIR PATRONIZING SENSE
of conviction, sounded exactly like a Minister, a messenger of CAUSE
sent to torment him. "Unknown voxer, identify."

"Captain Brock." The voice offered kindness, like a parent. "Have
you been hurt?"

No one else looked up, so Brock alone was hearing this voice. "I'm
standing . . ."

"Praise to god. What about Alicia, down on living deck?"

Out there on the canopy's other side, hordes of rain pelted directly
on glass, drowning the chirps of console alarms and the fainter groans
of the ship settling. Bridge stats showed their position was stable, but
he needed to check ground damage.

The voice wanted a reaction. "Voxer, identify yourself."

"Was anyone else hurt? How about your elders? President James
Woodford?"

Of course it knew them by name.

"Jason Cruz? Lawrence Peters? Alexander Moore?"

The voice also knew their crew manifest.

Jason stumbled back to the highbridge. "Captain, the Causians—"

"Hold! *Unknown voxer*, identify yourself, or get out of my head."

"Captain," Jason said. "CAUSE has the crash report. So do the local
authorities."

"So the Port already knows that we . . ." Too late, Brock had repeated
this aloud.

"Yeah." Jason pulled viz to confirm. "They'll be here fast. City might
beat them."

Three new voxes waited from Dr. Van Campen, Alicia, and James Woodford.

"Captain Brock, let us ignore all of those," said the voice.

Each of the tiny scrolls cleared away of its own accord.

This enemy had taken over his spaceship, tried to destroy her, and invaded his personal com. Brock stepped closer to the canopy, watching trails stream down the glass that no longer repelled the rain. "Tell me why I should listen to you."

"Because I know who attacked your ship, and I can help."

Don't ask his name. He wants to be asked. "Are you the Epicenter invader? Well, I'd like to know how you did this, but I need you to wait. I'll vox back. Goodbye, ghost."

This was probably a futile dare.

"Captain, that is nonsense. Do not follow your elders. They don't know your enemy. That's why they decided not to stop the test launch after you were threatened."

"*Your* threats, the other day."

"We met long before that meeting. Today I do not mask myself."

The man wanted Brock to guess his identity, and indeed, Brock could replay that same voice from weeks ago. Of their surprise guests Templeton had brought into the CIRCLE meeting, only one of those men had spoken like this. Even more recently, Brock had heard that cadence. "Are you *Aziz*?"

"You have said it."

There it was, then. Dr. Mahmoud Aziz, the third Epicenter guest, had attacked the ship. Why do any of this, only to offer *help* now? "So you're an enemy to CIRCLE."

"So says a man whose people have long persecuted mine as their enemy."

Jason dashed to the levitator entrance and lifted a sheet of his handwriting: *James fine. Drs. Mash, Sheldon bruised. Dr. Mor, maybe worse. Crew stable. Ships incoming. No ID.*

Brock took his sheet and pen, scribbled *Aziz*, then pointed to his own right ear.

"Captain, I offer truth. Your true enemy is CAUSE. Let us say they did this to you."

The man spoke as calmly as if they were enjoying drinks and preparing for debate.

Brock returned to highbridge, whose scanboard showed incoming objects. Out in the dreary skies, three bright blue crafts like tiny birds swept over the land. They bore gold trim and faded triangle emblems. They weren't local authorities, but CIRCLE Security.

"So, Aziz, after you hurt my people, you want me to . . . who do you think you are?"

Red and orange lights flashed into the rain. The vehicle came from the city.

"Captain, I am sent to unify the people of god to defeat our shared enemy. If you also act as my enemy, you will be weighed and found weightless. So says the *Mahdi*."

Another voice cut in: "—essel captain, you must respond. We are CAUSE."

So now they spoke with human voices, and expected immediate answers. This was almost worse than the ship failure. *Lord of hosts, help us all.* "Good afternoon, CAUSE. I regret the delay. We are a private preserve vessel. Please give me your name and domain."

"*Caelestis*, we identified. I am Epsilon Zavier Safran with Domain of Public Affairs."

What was next? His people needed medical care. Brock could let Maxwell Adams and Dr. Sheldon disentangle the legal mess, like they had sorted the Heritage Hall disaster.

"Provide your name with your ship's classification and flight logs."

Aziz had referred to the *Mahdi*. Was this someone local? Had he accessed *Alpha Omega* by working with Navistar, or exploited the old pinholes in the Epicenter?

"Provide your manifest and any injuries, then submit to physical inspection."

Not in a thousand years. "Epsilon, this ship landed in the protection of RP-BC-Oh-1."

"Irrelevant. We recorded your sudden course change in public airspace."

"Domain—domain policy allows business starcraft to amend flight plans." Brock fought to recall the requirements for domestic travel. "We can amend flight plans within domains or one hundred klicks, if we file within thirty minutes of flight deviation."

"*Before* the ship has landed."

"This includes emergency landings! Vox my preserve security and talk to them."

"Captain, provide *your* name and details, now."

Either this epsilon was bluffing, or Brock was. "We protest. Talk to my preserve."

Brock cut that vox, but the other line was equally silent.

This wasn't news he wanted to share, but he turned to Alexander. "We need a com release. Meet with Security. We will not lie. Nor should we reveal everything. This was a starcraft making an emergency landing. Jason! If we vented anything, we need files from Domain of Industry and the Ministry to verify discharge of gaseous fumes in a preserve."

"Yes, sir."

"I agree, Captain. This is another truth." The voice returned, apparently content to wait in Brock's earspace. "Once you release a poison, it will infect the whole world."

That was no grandiose poetry. The enemy might really believe this.

"Join me in one of those empty rooms, alone."

Brock signaled for Jason to take the station. He departed the highbridge and ascended port-side stairs to enter the lightless corridor. "What do you want?"

"This attention from CAUSE is your first doom. More will come."

For what group did this man speak? "I'm listening."

"Instead of this wasted Space Mission in secret, which will bring only these dooms, I instruct you to submit all your desires, resources, and talents to the truth."

He said this like a proper name. "You enforce *the truth* with evil actions?"

"Brock, you cannot fight me with doctrines and ethics. In this world, your decisions have consequences. If you do not submit, surrendering your ship and more to a partnership between us, your true enemy will take your ship. Then they will take your preserve. None of us wants this. But if you do not obey, we will take these things first and by force. We will take your ship, your people, and your family, starting with your wife."

Brock pinched his clip and detached it from his nose, then stopped himself from hurling away the device. Only fools would destroy good things.

"Hello! Aziz? *Mahdi*?" Brock must *not* call him that. "Don't you dare threaten—"

The vox was cut.

Brock descended the steps. Dr. Woodford should hear this first.

Alexander met him. "We just released info to com. I wrote one 'graph, very succinct."

"Thank you. Watch for replies and get any available staff to react."

"Captain." Jason approached him next. "What are you—"

"Aziz just spoke to my personal com. That's our ghost from the Epicenter. He all but claimed responsibility for this and clarified his threats. It's now clear he can fulfill them."

"Father help us."

"Please return to labor deck," Brock said. "Probe every system you can."

"Hey, CAUSE is knocking at the door." This was Soren, ambling over from the levitator.

Brock recalled his first name. "You are Derek, yes? They said you're a believer."

The big man knotted his dark brows. "Yeah. Else I wouldn't be here."

"Then go help Jason on labor deck. It's unstable there, so set regular check-ins."

"Captain," came Alicia's voice. "CIRCLE Security needs cargo bay access."

"Good. I need to talk with them. Jason, are we—"

"The bay's vented. All that paperwork's on standby."

"Thank you. Alicia? Meet with Alexander. Help create our message for the elders. No other news leaves this ship. We are a private vessel from Navistar. That's all."

She agreed from downtube. He needn't fear for her safety. For now, their saboteur had done his work and vanished, but left the starcraft vulnerable. What next? *Almighty one, blind this enemy.* First they must find the infection point, and one council elder was best for the job. "Dr. Van Campen, can you contact campus for an anon relay? I want to make a secure quantum vox to Port Ares on Mars."

"I'll do that," Van Campen said.

Jason said, "Can we run damage assessment? I've got no ground data. And I can't climb down the ship's starboard pillar if it's crashed into someone's living room."

Unless they shouted across the decks, they were forced to rely on coms.

Brock gave Jason clearance, then dropped into the levitator, wincing against the airborne stench rising from labor deck. Beyond the tube's glass, near the living deck viz fountain, Alicia and James Woodford knelt beside fallen elder Samuel Morrison. Despite his irritability, the council's senior member had volunteered first for this flight. He had even dressed for this as if for church. Now he was suffering on the ship Brock had chosen.

• • •

ALICIA
4:28 PM EDT, SATURDAY, JULY 21, 2125
CIRCLE PRESERVE, CINCINNATI

Alicia watched elder Maxwell Adams limping as he led four CIRCLE Security officers onto living deck. Two men brought a stretcher to carry out Dr. Morrison. Sometime soon, Alicia should reach out to his wife, Rosario. They had been married over fifty years.

Standing near the fountain, Tameria Lightheart tightly held her second camera.

This should be obvious. "Let's hold that footage for now."

Tameria turned away.

Lawrence and Julia sat nearby, atop one dislodged sofa. "We beseech thee, Lord," Lawrence said. "Send your angels to safeguard the ship."

Alexander conferred with the president. "We will face questions tomorrow."

"Then I will make the statement today," Dr. Woodford said.

"Brock urges caution. Let's wait an hour, especially if we have any deaths."

Dr. Woodford bent his head. "Maxwell, can we return to campus by shuttle?"

"No sir. Can't spare a driver. All my crews are fixin' on the impact site."

"I would drive," Alexander said, "but I'm only certified for ground operation."

All other crew should stay here, especially if CAUSE was advancing, and if their crash had hurt anyone on the ground. Alicia was quev-certified, which also qualified her to pilot shuttles. "Brock? We need Dr. Woodford back at headquarters. I can take him there."

"You don't mind flying through rain?"

She tried to laugh. "It's some relief, seeing water from the skies."

"My love . . . I'm so sorry."

"Why? How is this your fault?"

"I am captain. It's in the fine print." Brock sighed. "Make the trip, but stay with others, and return soon. Our ghost has threatened you and thinks he's the Mahdi."

Mahdi. That was an old title from her comparative religions class. *The guided one.*

In the cargo bay she found two hovering CIRCLE Security crafts, trailing water into puddles that would need later cleaning. She folded her arms tight, barely guarding herself from gusts through the open gates. Alexander joined her, and they led the elders into the CIRCLE shuttle. There she activated engines and comforting heat. Using autodrive, she cleared the bay and swept this vehicle against pouring rain.

Never had she flown so high off the ground. Lights flashed far below. Two more vehicles from the city emergency service had grounded near the ship's impact. Structures looked intact, not crushed underneath that giant starboard base but *behind* it. But the port base did rest atop many smaller vehicles. One small power center had turned into steaming bones against the base's mangled metal.

How could they hope to fix this?

Stray winds shook the craft and jolted Alicia before synth grav compensated. At this height, she couldn't easily follow roads. "Alexander, I need a route to campus."

He climbed beside her to survey the terrain, then pointed toward ten o'clock.

Her ears tingled. Someone was voxing her, source unknown. "Yes?"

"Licia? This is a secure channel." Brock sounded uncertain. "I want to change plans."

"How so?"

"Please don't repeat this to anyone. I don't want to sound fearful. After you drop them off at headquarters, I want you to go to the Ark Hotel."

What about the false voices? "First, tell me where your parents live."

"Of course. They are Stanford and Olivia Rivers. They left CIRCLE just before you and I were exiled. Now, for all we know, they're still teaching in Russia."

Only he would know that.

"Let's keep confirming like this," Brock said. "Vox me when you get there."

• • •

JASON
5:05 PM EDT, SATURDAY, JULY 21, 2125
CIRCLE PRESERVE, CINCINNATI

Jason bent his legs against the floor and pivoted out of the levitator. His vision stirred. Not good. But that odor may be *only* odor. And it might never leave these walls. His boots sloshed through gray foam stuck to the floor, like soapsuds mixed with filth.

"Soren?"

Down the hall, the big man climbed waist-deep inside the ship reactor buffers.

"Soren? I told you to stay out of here!"

The man's large hands gripped a girder. He yanked himself out to a stand. "Thought you'd be down sooner. Did I go too far with—"

"Mind the ship's authority structure. You're a guest."

"Hey, regent?" His dull voice drifted into echoes. "Do you think I bombed the ship?"

What kind of answer did he expect?

"I'm Christian, man," Soren insisted. "I have the evangelism gift. Like Apollos, I think. And maybe God's put me here. That's all I want to do. Help any way I can. Like when I saw the quantum vault reading, that's all, I thought you needed help."

A real saboteur might not talk so much. "Fine. Tell me about the vault."

"That strange reading? It looked like a pre-link before any active vaulting sequence."

"Could it be used to send quiet signals on board?" Jason said.

"It might."

"Get on that. Remote-link to the vault."

Soren coughed. "Tarnation. Stench is horrible."

"It's byproduct from the fuel tank. The enemy had to weaken the outer epidermis, dissolving it like a parasite. Some hidden spec agent could do that. It quick-releases from a central source, rounds up the materials, paints itself on the bulkhead."

"So that's intentional."

Of course it was. As if the giant cross carved on the wall wasn't blatant enough.

• • •

BROCK
5:32 PM EDT, SATURDAY, JULY 21, 2125
CIRCLE PRESERVE, CINCINNATI

Brock messaged Dr. Woodford and the council about these new threats. Newly placed cameras from CIRCLE Security revealed the extent of the ship's devastation.

"We landed on nine grounded crafts. Looks like they weren't occupied." Maxwell Adams pressed his fingers into his beard. "The worst is the damage to the apartment complex power center. All the apartments have utility failures. We've announced the outage."

If even one person had stayed in that parking lot or been caught in his vehicle . . . "Tell me about casualties."

"We're still knocking on doors and checking debris strikes."

A structural diagnostic revealed the ship's own damage. *Alpha Omega* leaned three degrees to starboard. He could imagine one or both bases mangled by their landing's blunt force. More of the hull might be split open, without hope of auto-repairing skin or muscle. If only he had brought down the ship more carefully.

He wrote a note to Director Sumisawa: CAN WE MOVE BACK TO NAVISTAR?

Maxwell continued, "CAUSE is still climbin' our backs. They want all the ship info."

"The investigation's pending. No info, no manifest. This is not a business craft."

"Dr. Sheldon says for purposes of *this* incident, we need to be." Maxwell's voice cut the air, sharpened with blame.

This man needed to act more like a council elder. "Talk with Alexander and the president," Brock said. "I'm not working com relations now, and I won't apologize to CAUSE for events I cannot control."

"Speakin' directly, *Captain*." Maxwell rose to full height, despite being shorter than Brock. "I am upholding preserve security, and I won't polish your profile either."

He left the bridge.

Still, the man was doing his job, after Brock's defective ship had nearly killed him.

He voxed Van Campen for a com update.

"Brock, I found the anon relay. Your code is for Mr. Starr on Mars, yes?"

"Yes, put it through." Brock waited for the tone before explaining the situation. "Michael, I don't know if the enemy can do anything up there. But please be careful around your apartment. Otherwise . . . you could leave Port Ares and wait in my desert skiff."

For a moment, Michael breathed quietly. "Who did this?"

CAUSE might have nothing to do with it. What advantage would CAUSE have by sending a subversive Minister or some other official styling himself after an Islamic militant?

"Could be some other preserve," Brock said. "I don't want to endanger you."

As for Alicia, she had left ten minutes ago and should be back by now. *Vox Alicia*.

• • •

JASON
5:39 PM EDT, SATURDAY, JULY 21, 2125
CIRCLE PRESERVE, CINCINNATI

Crash. Derek Soren flipped a chunk of hull debris across the labor deck floor. "We can't get too far here, regent. Any chance we can power down the backup core?"

"Probably nil," Jason said. "What power can we use then?"

"Well, CAUSE ships have five backups. Port reactors. They'd be stationed in other segments of the ship, each linked to systems that work solo if a prime reactor fails."

Port reactors. Like the one moved underneath Heritage Hall before its explosion.

Against the corner hung one wide cabinet door. Jason switched its handle to open it. Inside waited not just one port reactor, but three. Lurking in darkness, they resembled giant grenades, capped with pentagons of buffer nodules-in-miniature.

Jason crept inside, ducking the low ceiling. None of these would link with his com. He shone his outward beams on the closest reactor's tiny metal plate.

These were Xolo models, XI10-F, all of them. The same type that overloaded and killed Jerome Rivers.

But these devices looked different. Each nodule held an extra protrusion, like a tumor. That didn't match his memory of the other data. But wait, he *had* seen that very shape, only seconds ago, at the corner of his eye.

Jason clambered back into the corridor, under the glow of that cross scorched onto the fuel tank wall. Back in the corner lay that debris piece Soren had just tossed away. A little growth stuck from its side, like a fish's hijacking parasite.

Jason picked up the piece and requested a service link. One signal was active.

It had no product code. No spec downstream. This was a home-brewed device.

• • •

ALICIA
5:50 PM EDT, SATURDAY, JULY 21, 2125
CIRCLE PRESERVE, CINCINNATI

The young hotel clerk handed a sheet to Alicia. "Same account as before, yes?"

Alicia held back her shivering under loosened wet hair.

"Ma'am, are you all right?"

She had just stumbled through humid rains all the way from headquarters, where she had left Alexander and the elders. No hotel staff had reacted to Alicia's name on their account. If they did, and they had heard about the accident . . .

"I heard a ship actually crashed near campus." The older hotel manager's chair squeaked as he turned to face his colleagues. "It might even fall on some apartments."

The clerk turned toward that group. "What on Earth?"

"It's more persecution. First we get it from the Ministry, now from the whole CAUSE."

Another clerk said, "That Space Mission is attracting the enemy."

"We need to pray," the manager said.

But he neither prayed nor identified Alicia to ask her about the crash. Still, he had the right idea. So she also prayed, all the way up the levitator and hall, until she shut the hotel room door. Clouded light from the window shone on two blue-quilted beds. She had a closet, shower, sink, toilet room, and the faded wall mural of parading animals.

Her vox chimed. "Yes, Brock?"

"Please, let's not speak aloud."

"We can't even talk in my room?" Alicia said.

"So you have already gone there. What room is it?"

"I thought the hotel was secure."

"What room is it?"

The voice sounded like him. Just like any false teacher could seem authentic. Alicia drew shut the window drapes. "I need you to confirm it's you."

"I can repeat our children's names."

"No. Please tell me what you took in your pocket, after Grandfather died."

"I have the two cufflinks that are shaped like doves."

Only he would know that too. But could he really speak *this* calmly? "Who is this?"

"What is your room number?"

The true Brock wouldn't ignore her like that. "Shut up! Who is this?"

Her vox chimed. Was the other channel cut? "Hello!"

"Licia? Where are you?"

Him again. "So we weren't already talking."

This new Brock hesitated. "Not at all."

"Did you even ask me to go to the Ark Hotel?"

"*Ark Hotel!* I told you to return here after you dropped them off."

How far back did that deception go? "Prove it's you."

"We have three children, not one. No, that's not enough. Prove it's you first!"

"I'm wearing the magenta blouse with pointed sleeves."

"And . . . what else?"

"Your favorite. Black." They wouldn't enjoy *that* tonight. "Now you."

"At age five, you first visited that butterfly garden, and a monarch landed on—"

This was him. "I'm sorry! The other voice sounded like you. He even verified."

Brock breathed hard as if running. "I want you out of there."

"Love, there's nowhere else to go, I can't—"

"Then stay in that room. If you can, trip the fire alarm."

"Do you want me to double-lock the door?"

"Those locks are useless, but try anyway. Add any barriers you can."

Alicia flipped the deadbolt and clipped on the chained hook. "Jesus, help me." She wrenched the first bed away from the wall, then slid herself behind that headboard to shove until the legs dug dark trenches into beige carpet. Earthen gravity resisted her.

From out in the hallway, someone shouted.

Another indistinct shout. Then more. All male voices. Something crashed. A girl screamed. The back of her neck tingled. "I'm hearing problems downtube."

"What level?"

"Third floor. Room three-oh-seven." This channel had better be secure.

"I'm on the way."

Things were breaking out there. Could she use anything for defense? The shower rod? The curtain rod? Alicia hurled her chest and knees against the headboard. Finally she wedged the bed against the door.

Footsteps pounded down the hall like an army. They might know her location. They had heard her conversation and they were coming.

Bang! Her door resounded. A man yelled strange words and struck again.

Something snapped, and the door was breached.

33

BROCK
6 PM EDT, SATURDAY, JULY 21, 2125
CIRCLE PRESERVE, CINCINNATI

BROCK WINCED AGAINST THE COLD RAIN THAT BLASTED HIS FACE from beyond *Alpha Omega*'s cargo bay. His vox echoed a great pounding over there. "Licia, what's happening?"

"They're trying to break—"

The vox cut. Brock flung open the grackle's pilot door. As he climbed inside, Maxwell Adams advanced down the bay steps, arms lifted. "*Captain* Rivers, why are you leaving?"

"Alicia's at the Ark Hotel, and the enemy's upon her." This was real, at this moment, in his homeland. "If you have any officers left on campus, send them now."

Brock drove the vehicle off the bay floor and plummeted sidelong into the wind.

• • •

JASON
6:10 PM EDT, SATURDAY, JULY 21, 2125
CIRCLE PRESERVE, CINCINNATI

"Captain's still not answering me," Jason said. Or someone was jamming them again.

Derek Soren was hunched inside a tighter tunnel, where he'd yanked out a wall-mounted workstation sheet. Now he deftly snipped arterial bonds on the alien device, cutting it from the port reactor.

"You stopped any receivers on it?" Jason said.

"Didn't just flip switches, neither. I crushed them."

Jason found his embed's hidden option and powered it down. "String it up."

Soren knelt, sinking his knees into filthy suds. He stuck the device on one leg and put the sheet on his other. With a wand, he bonded tiny threads between them. His white sheet flickered. "Naw. Gremlin's resisting. Doesn't want to talk with anything else."

Black symbols twitched on the sheet. No English, no Arabic, just snarled-up code. This thing wasn't legitimate. "Pathogens," Jason said. "Protecting core functions."

"That stuff's outside my field."

"Mine too. But that friend of Brock's . . ." Jason reactivated com to find Van Campen's supposedly secure anon relay. He voxed Michael Starr.

Seconds later, a gentler voice replied, "Is this Brock?"

Jason shortened his intro and emphasized his role as ship's regent. "We're dealing with some unknown device in *Alpha Omega*'s energy core. Can I send you the data?"

"I would need to be there. Right now we're all heading out to Brock's home."

"You have his kids with you?"

"Yes, and we—" A woman spoke over Michael. "I'm glad you reached out," Michael said.

"Is that unusual up there?"

"Not often past twenty-three-hundred."

Don't be naïve. "Does the scow have a registry?"

"Not that I can see. This is a rented sandfly with limited scanning."

It couldn't be CAUSE. This enemy had recruits a whole orbit away. That meant serious risk. But they may have already proven they could raise up radicals from desert wasteland. And a newly converted com tech and his wife—she was a nurse, right?—couldn't guard against that. "Michael, I heard Alicia left Brock's quev grounded in Port Ares, yeah?"

"Yes."

"Send me that location. Soren, this way."

Jason thrust himself into the main levitator to glide up past living deck, then took to the command deck. In the galley, he found three dense sandwiches and stuffed them into his left pocket. "You're deputized." He shoved pages into Soren's broad hands. "Give these to

Maxwell Adams. Follow him for security and work crash recovery with Van Campen."

"I'm not with the Space Mission, man."

"Want to prove you can be? The enemy's coming for the captain's family."

Soren's strangely blue eyes went wide.

Jason made for the quantum vault. "If you can, send me to Port Ares."

"As in Mars? Just like that? From here?"

"Yeah, best if easternmost side of the port." This was demented. He'd only visited Mars in the battle simulations. But he had a passport. And if his SOAR record, honorable discharge and all, didn't impress them, they could detain him for illegal immigration.

Soren dialed several codes. "Vault's open. You'll need a fund source for vaulting."

"How much?"

"Twelve hundred yun."

Really. That exact amount? Jason sighted his yun, found his prime account, and sent to Derek the total of his life savings—¥1,236.

The big man saw the sum and glanced back to Jason.

Alpha Omega's quantum vault slipped open. Jason stepped inside the palpitating glass heart of this beast. His glazer was folded tight inside his right belt pocket. That shouldn't trip any Martian sensors. Years ago he had disabled the register function.

"Receiving port's ready," Soren said.

Jason took a breath and prepared for this mad science.

• • •

BROCK
6:21 PM EDT, SATURDAY, JULY 21, 2125
CIRCLE PRESERVE, CINCINNATI

Sheets of rain suddenly cleared to reveal the pillars of headquarters. Brock dipped the grackle toward steam that rose in columns from a new impact site.

Two CIRCLE Security vans rushed toward the blackened scar. More wreckage was strewn across the lawn like meteorite fragments. That couldn't be Alicia, not if she were trapped in the hotel . . . unless that transmission was also a lie.

Room 307. Which way? Room 330 was on the north side, 320s and lower to the east.

She wasn't answering vox.

Ark Hotel loomed beside the wind-tousled surface of Lake Heritage. Third level? There, that second row! One light inside one window switched on and off like a ship's alert. Brock pivoted, pointing the grackle's bow straight toward the ground. Visible far beyond the glass panes, Alicia pressed against a bed she had wedged against her hotel room door, yanking her hand from the room's light stat. Brock leveled off and the world righted.

He struck the grackle's horn. Alicia whirled and saw him.

No other way. Brock drove forward until the vehicle struck hard. Alerts shrieked while glass shattered and metal framing crumpled. He dropped a few centimeters and horribly scraped against the hotel's outer wall. When he released the grackle's center hatch, the panel slid up until winds drove rain onto his back. "Licia!"

She headed his way. The bed jolted against the door. Was that *electricity* sparking against the doorjamb? One red bolt flew inside.

"Licia, *down!*"

She dropped to the carpet. Brock crouched under liquid torrents and groped under the pilot chair. His fingers closed around two of Jason's glazer gloves.

Just like Egypt.

He donned one glove and clenched his fist three times, making orange viz wrap his targets—then he stood and fired lightning at the room door, carving a black scar at chest level. Another blast. Another. How many enemies?

Not like Egypt. They were threatening her and invading his homeland.

Alicia reappeared, wrapped in orange viz—*do not fire!* He approved the signature, turning her green. She lowered a chair to the window and swiped across, breaking away loose glass. *Crunch.* Her door struck the bed. From the gap emerged men's arms with guns.

Brock shot the mattress, blasting the fabric into flames. "Licia, now!"

He reached with his non-gloved hand. She pulled and stepped onto the window's edge, then leaped forth, wet hair slapping his face as she fell into the passenger chair.

New people invaded the room with strange headgear like bronze-colored masks. They fired blasts, puncturing furniture and shattering more glass. Brock cast back his own red bolts. "Close center hatch!" The grackle didn't hear him. "Close—"

The grackle whirred; Alicia had found the control.

She threw the craft back from the window and any firing range. He toppled back into the pilot seat. "You all right?"

"I—I don't—who—" She pointed to a screen. "Below."

Hailstones pelted their vehicle's underside. Men dashed out of the hotel's entrance. Their upturned weapons flashed, shuddering the grackle with each impact.

Brock swore, trying to lurch away. *Vox CIRCLE Security.* "Armed men at Ark—"

"Gone, spectra's gone!" she cried. "What are they doing?"

They dropped nose-first. Metal crunched, but the grackle's crash field pinned Brock to his seat. Glass burst apart as the vehicle groaned and turned over. His hand clung to Alicia's arm. She was fixed to her chair, now suspended over him.

New sirens wailed. Wet turf and glass beads struck him, and he choked.

Gravity pulled from the port side. Brock felt no fire or serious injury. Alicia stirred. But that shattered window would expose them to the enemy. Movement came from before the Ark Hotel entrance. There a new gliding craft shone pale green—a Ministry vehicle, surrounded by humans who were obviously not Ministers.

• • •

JASON
23:57 LMST, GOD. 15, 44 (SYNDIC)
PORT ARES

Jason had passed into new gravity for a new world. Unlike the training floors in Martian mode, the real planet's attraction, only three-eighths of Earthen gravity, would follow him everywhere.

The port officer's interrogation lasted five minutes. He stated his purpose: visiting friends. This was true. Thanks to his honorable discharge, Port Ares accepted this without asking about preserve residency. They only tagged his embed. If he wasn't on record leaving orb within forty-eight hours, they would track down a runaway.

These vast corridors and atriums might resemble any earthside Causian port.

Jason asked Michael, now on standard wave, I'M HERE. THAT SCOW STILL CHASING YOU?

The train's window showed no red soil under pink skies, only total blackness draped over this alien world. Jason's viz clock shifted digits to 0:00 LMST SHARP, a Martian midnight.

At the correct stop, he departed. With gravity-boosted steps, he moved further into this huge and probably underground vehicle lot. Automated viz guided him to Brock's quev. The marble-blue creature had smooth lines with rear-opening, stingray-shaped wings.

Michael's long-distance overrides opened the doors. *Legacy* let Jason power it on. He activated spectra that returned Earthen gravity. Brock had kept this level nearly every day.

The quev heaved itself up, then set autodrive for Brock's home by way of the airlocked exit. Window viz showed low winds. Climate looked mild. Less than a minus-hundred degrees Fahrenheit chilled the frozen skies surrounding Mars' capital city.

For seven years Brock had fought for life on Mars. His children would not die here.

Past the outer gates, *Legacy* shone feebly against the multihued, glowing complex of central Port Ares. Human civilization obscured alien sights until Jason cleared an outer road, which a hovering map labeled ALAIMO COURSEWAY. Before long, frigid desert floor scampered beneath *Legacy*'s flood lamps. Generations ago, men and women had stepped out of primitive capsules into this frozen hell, but now Jason had simply flung himself here from Earth. The quev's heat fans worked overtime. Nerves scraped at his ribcage.

Jason reopened vox. "Michael, I'm here. Where's that scow?"

"I think our strange vehicle has fallen back. We just reached Brock's home."

These people wouldn't be armed. Two adults, four children in an old skiff? Hardly defensible. "Do you have a secure room? Storm pod? Airlock?"

"The bay's nearly pressurized. We can look for one."

"Mr. Starr, do not let anyone inside. Not even if he's the premier himself."

It couldn't be CAUSE. That man Aziz had made his threats. He may have allies up here. Could he use that old lobster-trap vault to send his followers from Cairo to Mars?

As soon as Jason left Port Ares limits, Martian law would let *Legacy* exceed 200 kph. Technically she could exceed threefold supersonic. Whether this old quev could reach that speed was another question. Few would listen, but spying satellites might see.

"Jason, the scow is approaching."

"They're passing by," said his wife.

No, they weren't.

"It approaches the bay," Michael said.

"Both of you, get somewhere safe. Cram into the old power closet if you need to. Those walls should be reinforced unless Brock removed them." They'd better pray the skiff's inner chamber was still airlocked. Otherwise the enemy wouldn't need to get suited. To kill anyone inside, they need only smash into the skiff.

A green circle lit. *Legacy* cleared the Port Ares zone and faced southeast. At this speed, Jason would arrive in six elongated hours.

He threw the quev to 1,235 kph. That pulled his ETA under 25 minutes. May the Lord blind any spies, and may internal grav spectra not fail and pin him gasping to the seat.

"Jason!" Michael called. "The other ship just struck the bay gate."

• • •

BROCK
6:40 PM EDT, SATURDAY, JULY 21, 2125
CIRCLE PRESERVE, CINCINNATI

A new vehicle fell from the sky, gleaming blue amidst gray rain streaks. From above Brock a man's voice blared, "CIRCLE Security! Drop to the ground and surrender."

Rain cleared to show the occupant, black-mustached Constable Sergio Longoria.

The green Ministry van turned, but Longoria's ship pivoted to face it. Green wingtips radiated like unnatural fire that narrowed into streams and slashed against Longoria's craft, blasting out debris. Slowly the CIRCLE vehicle sank, folding nose and glass down into churning soil.

Aziz was attacking the whole campus.

Alicia crawled out from the fallen grackle and Brock scrambled after her into chaotic swirls of rain and heat. They slammed through the hotel's outer and inner doors, heading deeper inside. He sighted for secure campus airways. *CIRCLE base, public affairs, Security.*

"They're after the Rivers couple. Longoria is down. Third division, status?"

"Arriving at the hotel," came another voice. "Confirmed ship down. Is this Ministry?"

"Director coming with backup. Not the Ministry. Ministers are *not* on campus."

Could these imposters still access Brock's com? By listening to the secure campus lines, had he just given the enemy free links to CIRCLE Security?

Something rattled overhead, but not gunfire. Rain drilled the hotel's vast skylight that held the pterodactyl with eagles and other flying beasts. No weapon or enemy peered over any of the surrounding balconies. Then first-level doors flew open to expose masked men— Brock threw lightning, one invader returned fire, and Brock thrust Alicia toward the hotel desk. Behind it lay several bodies, three of them stained with blood.

Brock shut his eyes, long enough to burn rage into action.

At the hotel doors, he fired a fusillade at a masked man and dropped the enemy. Beyond those doors, streaks of light traded back and forth; CIRCLE Security must have engaged the firefight, filling the hotel with screams. He'd brought the battle into this place, endangering innocent families. What about his own children? These enemies had invaded a sovereign preserve, and could easily reach Mars.

VOX FROM ALEXANDER. "Brock, I'm coming. Got a shuttle. You're in the hotel?"

"Yes! Avoid the east side." Two other men splashed into the

anteroom, and Brock rained bolts toward the glass. Hold, was this truly him? "Alexander, please verify!"

"It's me. That night at the campus café, at two o'clock? You and I 'saved' the faith."

"Then I'm heading for the hotel's west side. Take the service entrance."

• • •

JASON
01:22 LMST, GOD. 15, 44 (SYNDIC)
ARES VALLES

Scanboards showed Jason no ships in earshot. Little traffic favored overnight routes east of Port Ares. Beneath the quev searchlights, desert floor flowed like stony waters.

"We're inside the old core room," Michael said. "Brock did shield the reactor."

"And the scow?"

The wife said, "It's quit hammering the doors. Now it's pushed against the skiff."

"They're trying to cut inside," Michael said. "I will try to seal us in."

Protection, of course. Jason needed that. *Legacy* could fly itself, so he made himself release the yoke, shedding speed to approach 200 kph. Back in the cargo hold, he opened cabinets and searched until he found a crumpled gray atmoskin, patched and dusty. It had no spec bonds, only microzips. And the battery would last barely 30 minutes? Fine.

Jason stepped into the legs and slipped into the arms. He tightened them. Fastened gloves to the sleeves. Then pushed his head inside the solid neck rim. Synthetic lungs fixed over his chest and linked with his viz, granting five hours of life.

Rockier terrain made the quev pull higher, casting white beams to the dark land. Spectra throttled down and speed dropped even lower. He was nearly there.

Jason took manual control and killed exterior lamps. *Legacy* settled closer to the Martian surface and tracked itself up a long slope that bore signs of a path. Upon the hillcrest, a dark and rounded shape blocked the stars with its own light.

"Mike, I'm here."

There was the rear bay. That small barge-like scow hovered nearby, pressing its blocky rear against the gates. They had ruptured the bay gate.

Normal quevs had no weapons. He could use one natural force against them.

Jason drove *Legacy* up the path, meters from the enemy. He grabbed height and lifted directly over the scow—and let down. He dropped outside grav past zero, then dialed beneath Earthen gravity, enough to stick a probe to an asteroid. *Legacy* groaned with the impact. By now the enemy should be trapped underneath. "Mike!"

"Yes. That's crushing the scow. It's detaching from the skiff."

More shudders. If the enemy had already pressurized, atmosphere would escape the gate gash. Jason pulled *Legacy* off the crumpled scow and grounded directly beside it.

His glazer glove fit over his atmoskin glove.

He'd have to do worse than supposed "nonlethal" hits.

It began in his shoulders, that cold crackle of energy, coursing down into his chest and legs. He took breaths, shut his eyes, opened them, fought to regulate focus.

This was little different from the lunar simulations with even less atmosphere than Mars.

Outside temp: -80 CENTIGRADE. *Father, keep me over twenty-two.*

He shut himself in the quev's tiny airlock partition, whose air would drain in seconds.

"Jason, we hear noises at the door. Yahweh help us. They're nearly inside."

Dropping from the quev, Jason stepped onto the dust of Mars. Hard land pressed underfoot. Any fast step would throw him into a spring. Jason found a stride, leaped high, and landed atop the scow's buckled roof. Unnatural torrents shoved at him, cast from the gate's vertical rift, but only whispered puffs reached his ears. No one walked outside. If he had punctured the scow's hull, its driver could be dead.

Jason skidded down the scow ridges until he fell through the skiff's shredded gate, yanked back into Earthen gravity. Walls flashed red, but any alarms were smothered by silent whirlwinds rushing around the bay that held one grounded sandfly. Around that vehicle waited all Brock's cabinets and benches with organized parts—

Two men in skins. They lit orange. Jason fired two bolts and dropped both figures.

Up two steps, both inner airlock doors spread open. The enemy was inside.

Jason landed in a hallway among spinning papers caught by fiercer winds. One hostile advanced and swung a large arm. Jason dodged and struck the other's ribs, punched a bolt into his side. Two more men rushed him—too slow, they moved too slow—were they weighed down by gravity or Martian natives? Jason hurtled among them and shoved one man against the wall. Something cracked. He threw his arm around one man's neck and pulled. Another appeared. He raised a weapon and fired—at a wall stat. It vanished in smoke.

One step launched Jason to the ceiling. So they'd killed the skiff's internal spectra, raising gravity to Martian norm. Back on the floor, three men advanced.

• • •

BROCK
7 PM EDT, SATURDAY, JULY 21, 2125
CIRCLE PRESERVE, CINCINNATI

Brock and Alicia rushed back into driving rain. Muddled skies drenched the grass and a hedge of trees, the lake's edge to the left, and pads for supply vans to the right. Alexander still wasn't here.

Hostiles advanced and cast light streaks, so far without hitting—

His shoulder opened in lava. Then dulled heat shoved his back.

A bolt had thrown him against the hotel service door. Grass padded both legs. Hornets stung his left arm, and his throat tightened; he couldn't even scream. No blood came out? So this wasn't a hard weapon. Freezing tingles meant they had glazed him.

Men came running, three of them. They wore imposter Ministry green, with those bizarre masks, and ignored Brock.

One hostile came for Alicia. She struck at his head and kicked his leg, but a third man restrained both her arms. Brock cast bolts that only stabbed at the land. Dirt and grass clutched his side and his burning arm, while mud blinded his eyes.

Behind the enemies opened a green metal door, leading into the false Ministry craft.

They were taking her. Aziz was taking her.

They threw her into the craft and shut the door. Brock fought for air and screamed after them. Synth grav rippled, lifting their vehicle until it cleared the grass and lakeside.

Earspace crackled, "Brock, where are you?"

Paralysis ebbed, letting him move. "Alexander, I'm near the exit. They took her."

A tiny CIRCLE shuttle landed in gusts of new spray, then whisked apart its left side. Brock limped forward until he could pull the door's edge with gloved hand, fighting pains to climb inside. "That green vehicle. Enemies in masks. They have her."

Alexander throttled up into rain that swirled about the shuttle windows. He flicked on viz. "CIRCLE Security, the enemy is moving to headquarters."

Brock crouched in the passenger space, bracing his forehead on glass. His left arm tingled against numbness. Outside, there it was, a pale green craft, gliding like a serpent's head, over the grass between headquarters and the Harding School building. "That way."

"Enemy vehicle on the move to Harding," one officer confirmed on vox.

Brock pointed. "Ground us here!"

His friend drew down to land thirty meters from the enemy. Brock threw open the door, re-blasting his face with cold rain. Over by the school ran green-clad knots of men. *Where is she?* The group divided; one faction headed for the school entrance, while another swerved onto the grass behind stately trees, breaking for headquarters.

Two CIRCLE Security crafts dropped before them with sirens wailing.

Enemies fired on the crafts, striking their open doors. Brock dared to look back. Here came the new cause of their aggression. President James Woodford, clad in his dripping brown suit with bright red puff tie, ran toward the scene.

Why hadn't the man stayed away? They mustn't hurt him.

CIRCLE officers leaned from their shuttles and filled the air with bolts. One enemy projectile scorched past them all, dipped to the earth, and pierced Woodford in the chest.

Alexander shouted Woodford's name and ran toward him.

Alicia? She was not inside there, not dragged by that group!

Brock made for Harding School, where the enemies had vanished behind dignified doors. He nearly fell upon the walkway's slippery stairs. He charged for the doors where two green-clad hostiles stood like guardsmen, and his red lightning felled them.

Where were the rest going? He should have known moments ago.

Brock dashed through halls, around the corner, between classroom doors, past rows of paintings that showed famous engineers, and now into the corridor to the basement. Another hostile lifted his hand. Brock's glove burst wild, and he plowed into the assault. Screams echoed—that man tumbled down the stairwell, one arm snapped and smeared the steps with blood. Brock cleared the body and rounded the bend.

Metal speared his right temple and smelled of burnt iron.

His arm curled around itself. Both legs locked together. No muscle control. Nothing.

They had glazed him again, now much worse.

Hard stairs took him, over and over, their edges beating his back and legs. Brock fought for vision and tried to shout her name. And there she was, trapped inside the old quantum vault that now hung from the ceiling. His precious butterfly. Upside-down men stood beside her, their legs clinging onto floor like bats. Thunder rippled. Lightning tore the machine until it filled with physics-defying fiery clouds that corroded away their images.

They vanished, just above Brock's outstretched fingers trapped by the air.

CIRCLE's vault throbbed. Glowing glass walls swelled and then burst into fire.

34

THREE HOSTILES TANGLED BELOW JASON. HE SHOVED the ceiling and pounced onto one man's head, slamming him to the floor, then struck the face of a second figure, sweeping him away, clearing space for a third. One knee to the stomach made that man collapse. Jason slapped away his weapon, which bounced off the wall.

They'd switched the home to native gravity but given him the advantage?

No one else? Only those three. That left two in the bay, maybe one more in the scow Jason had crushed. Now for the airlock door. Jason kicked away loose books and pulled the inner door's two handles against roaring wind. *Clank.* The door shut and sealed with a hiss.

At last the windstorm stilled. Only one body on the floor barely moved. This could be it. For now. "Mike. I secured. The area."

"Did you seal the airlock?"

"Yeah. Your enemy broke through the gate."

"This shelter wasn't quite airtight. Breathing . . . difficult." Michael broke off to shush a child. "I'm linked to the home. Air has reached sixty percent."

The child cried even louder. They would have four kids in there.

Jason said, "Stay in there until we're fully pressurized."

Now for one terrible task..

He stood over the fallen men and lifted his glove to light them in orange. *Not mine. Not mine. Not mine.* He cast out two bolts. Four. Six. Three sets of two into each man's chest.

In theory, this was nonlethal, if they hadn't already died from physical trauma. If only his glazer *were* lethal. Then he could rightly punish them for attacking innocents.

Yeah, somebody's just-war theory might allow that. But he could not.

Jason turned over each man. Behind tinted shields, their dead-like faces locked in grimaces, the nervous system response to glazers. One bearded man. Two clean-shaven. Based on their gravity conditioning, they'd probably not come from Earth. Someone had been busy with religious recruitment on Mars. CAUSE would be thrilled to learn that.

From one bedroom, Jason retrieved a quilt, which he laid atop those men.

Down the hall, he found the shelter door and dragged it open. Michael stood in the dark, his disheveled blond hair mixed with faded viz, his frame much shorter than Jason expected. "Thank you. We never could have . . ."

Jason withdrew his face shield and knelt in the tiny space. Near the enclosed reactor crouched a lighter-haired woman in short sleeves and skirt, surrounded by children. The older boy, one girl, and younger boy were clearly Brock's and Alicia's. That smaller blond girl must be the Starrs' child. She looked younger than Jason's daughter would be.

More hostiles could be coming.

Michael gave the children's names, then asked what was next.

"Secure the skiff," Jason said. "Check for any leaks."

He would handle the enemy bodies, whether glazed or dead.

Jason reset his shield and cleared the airlock. The depressurized bay held two fallen enemies. The first was dead. Jason's headshot had sent him reeling, and the fall must have broken his neck. The second hostile was also dead, likely after suffering a torn atmoskin.

Jason shut his eyes, but he could not close theirs.

Despite their crimes, They were six *imagoes Dei*. Bearers of God's image.

The bay gate was broken. Later he would need to join Brock's quev directly with the airlock.

Back in the skiff, Michael had activated lights. The kids crouched on the floor, gathering things. Mrs. Starr warned them away from the hallway with its carnage.

Jason withdrew his face shield and found Michael in the skiff's common area, checking a window screen. He spoke more clearly behind thick viz. "The rest of the dwelling is intact," Michael said. "Adam and Emma? I see some of the larger books in the living room. Let's not forget those."

"What are they doing?" Jason said.

"They are cleaning the home—"

"That's considerate, but we need to go."

Michael stared up. "Where would you take them?"

And with what money, Cruz? Jason dropped his arms. "Yeah. Everything I had—used it to get here. But we can use Brock's quev or your craft."

"That sandfly is a rental."

This couple had risked their lives to preserve Brock's children.

"If this enemy group has members on Mars, your religious preserve may be safest," Michael said. "We can take Brock's quev. We should go to Earth."

He was serious. "Flying for weeks across orbits?" Jason said.

"Of course not. We can use a vault."

"Big enough for a whole quev?"

"I know how and will cover it." Michael checked the hall. "What about these men?"

"I'll clear them out. We'll use the rental to send them to Port Ares."

"With glazed bodies inside?"

Or worse. "Set it on course, shine a beacon, let the Causians sort it out."

Mrs. Starr moved closer, holding the girl. "With our name on the manifest."

"Well." Michael looked nervous. "I can clean that record."

Jason took a turn staring at him.

"We'll go with you, Mr. Cruz. Beth, this was our choice anyway. Is this not?"

Michael's wife shut her eyes. "I did not think . . . so soon."

Purging the sandfly data might safeguard his good name. Still, if CAUSE ever caught Michael, his secular career was over.

Jason secured his suit and dragged the two bodies through Brock's emergency airlock into the sandfly. He opened the skiff's punctured outer gate and trekked onto soil. Inside the enemy's scow, he found a third body, one more killed by vacuum exposure.

The Lord might grieve, but Jason saw no other way.

Over several minutes, he performed the grim task of stacking every fallen enemy into the sandfly. Inside the craft, he set auto-return for the owner's facility in Port Ares. Back in the skiff, Jason asked how they would vault to Earth in a quev.

"It is legally questionable," Michael said. "I think I can find a freight vault."

Elizabeth said, "And the ban against vaulters under age six?"

Michael didn't reply.

Brock's and Alicia's children found their things. Elizabeth packed every clothing item and the few toys she found. The older boy, Adam, rushed past Jason, taking one item from his and his sister's rooms. He stopped in the hallway, struck with a thought, then looked up to Jason. "Do they have more kids' books on Earth?"

They'd been living like this for seven years. "Yeah. Lots of them."

"Just the sheets? Or *real* books?"

"All real. They make 'em from trees."

The girl, Emma, took this opening. "We going to see Mom and Dad?"

"Yeah." With barely a wince, Jason lowered to a crouch. "They'll be glad to see you."

This couldn't be legal. Having emigrated here to escape the law, now they were doing the reverse. Could Jason hide the kids on the ship or somewhere at CIRCLE? The lawyers would have a fit. Either way, they might not return here for a long time.

He found Emma's eyes, then Adam's. "Hey, all those stray books? Let's find boxes for them. In low gravity, let's see how much you can lift. Your dad would be glad for the help."

Emma caught on fast. "Clothes and toys too?"

"Oh yeah. As much as we can carry."

"And that—that big crate in the cargo bay?"

Jason waited for more.

"It's got . . . special stuff," Adam said. "I think our dad was waiting to unpack it."

• • •

BROCK
9:41 PM EDT, SATURDAY, JULY 21, 2125
CIRCLE PRESERVE, CINCINNATI

Let me go. Brock's own voice repeated these words, but it would accomplish nothing. Instead he should turn his thoughts to commands, of course, like a real captain would do.

He needed to go somewhere, to return to the ship that was falling. "Let me . . ."

"Mr. Rivers, we're here." Another woman from out in the dark said this. "Lie still."

". . . Go."

"We can't go. We're waiting for the surgical bay. We'll take care of you." The voice faded into whispers.

His thought scraped at lucidity. What had he fallen against and how was he hurt? "My wife. Captain. Me." That voice sounded terrible. "Com clip."

"We have your clip, sir. Whom do you need to contact?"

"Jase . . . Cru . . . Jashun Cruz . . ."

The listener hesitated. "I'm sorry, your clip is not working."

"All of campus is locked down," said a distant man.

The woman muttered back.

"They've blocked all non-vital coms. Groundlines only, till they find the attackers."

"Lord rest his soul."

"Not yet. I heard from Wing D. They say President Woodford's holding on."

Three bolts. The first had struck Brock's left shoulder. Two more had entered his neck and thigh and paralyzed his system. These caretakers may give him nerve regen. Setting broken bones would take longer. He would be paralyzed. No ship or crew. No Alicia.

Enemies had invaded his home. He and his perfect mission had cleared the way.

"Wing C is ready."

"Brock," said the woman. "You hear me? We're sedating you for surgery."

After they finished, he could try to fight this evil. For that he needed information. All his desperation or rational responses should wait until he learned more about the devil who had attacked him—the devil who had finally given Brock his name.

Alicia was gone. His beautiful butterfly. They had trapped her in a vault and stolen her.

• • •

JASON
03:03 LMST, GOD. 15, 44 (SYNDIC)
PORT ARES

Legacy brought Jason, the Starrs, and Brock's children back to Port Ares, then 50 kilometers to the west. Spectra hummed in the walls, powering the quev at 300 kph and 80 meters across shallow ridges and flat sand. The children found fitful sleep atop piles of their own clothing.

An agent signaled the quev, requesting clearance.

Michael vanished behind viz to reply. "Did you see my script?"

"Yeah." And it was quite the fiction, requesting a transfer from Cibus Industries back to Earth, a shipment of defective *livestock*. One real human had confirmed this. And here was Jason, approving deception, because otherwise these children could die.

"I can take quev control," Michael said.

Over the next minutes, Michael lowered *Legacy* to align with an invisible queue, drawing them closer to the Cibus facility. He navigated between rows of sprawling one-level structures, nestled like large garden boxes among rusted rocks. They passed through an airlock into a taller complex. Somewhere behind those walls lay dozens of stalls filled with animals, mostly live cattle, awaiting slaughter. They'd be made into premium meals for wealthy Martian corporatists and, presumably, CAUSE officials.

Legacy glided through a ridged corridor. During active hours, Michael said, Cibus Industries locked the herds into tight gravity, then moved the animals in vertical racks.

At the end waited the vault, lifting like a silo, maybe ten times the quev's height. Gates pivoted like inverted wings into this massive structure. Crimson rims flashed. Michael nudged forward. Curving walls folded the quev into deeper red shadows.

"You got a reception point?" Jason said.

"It is a matching freight vault in Port Des Moines." Michael released the yoke. *Legacy* turned itself toward the vault's middle, leaving equal space to all sides. "It is not a leapeasy, but it seems least regulated. They shouldn't easily discern animal life from children."

What a strange world. "I've never vaulted while inside a quev before."

"Nor have I."

Elizabeth Starr sat awake, listening, but staring out the window.

Legacy obtruded landing pads and settled itself. Spectra powered off, replaced by the vault's louder thrum, audible through pressurized space. Jason leaned under the quev's front window to gaze up the tall shaft. Quadruple flanges lined the walls, already prickling with energy. So fast? No time to worry.

Thunder boiled. Tornadic lightning burst out. Quev windows and hull shook and rattled as if ready to fly apart. Elizabeth groaned. Michael shut his eyes.

Jason fell to his knees. This time the energy wouldn't touch him, only deafen.

Someone cried out.

Sorcerous tangles flashed against two small faces that wailed in terror. Jason grabbed Adam and Daniel, while Elizabeth took the girls, just as the maelstrom burst.

• • •

JASON
10:30 PM EDT, SATURDAY, JULY 21, 2125
IOWA

When the quantum storm finally ended to reveal the silo vault, it took minutes for the others to settle the children. Even the oldest, Adam, twitched with silent sobs.

They were on Earth, over new gravity and under new lights. At one glance the sky matched that alien canopy of the red planet. But these skies shone warmer, dusted with friendlier stars. What a journey. Jason could enjoy what little beauty he saw tonight.

Autodrive reported their new course, a fifty-minute arc spanning from

Des Moines to Cincinnati. Jason remembered to vox Derek Soren. "Hey. I'm back. Won't say where yet."

"Finally. I never linked with ship's core. I'm doing it manually, man."

"Where is the captain? How's the ship?"

"Unknown about the captain. Ship is intact. CAUSE is pesky, but local civics set a watch. Ah, yeah. Consternation! You wouldn't know that your people went on alert. There's been campus violence. No mention on public com. Then CIRCLE banned all its com traffic."

Jason silenced a curse. "So how are you speaking to me?"

"Well see, I'm not with your people. Not yet."

Jason sighted for CIRCLE's public channels. Sure enough, he found no access. That felt almost as strange as vaulting to Mars—cut off, as if that preserve had never existed. "Soren . . . Derek . . . I need a place to stay. Maybe get some lodging for refugees that's better than the captain's 2099 Lacewing-class quev. We got attacked up there."

"Yeah, man. Use my place at Navistar in the settlement."

CIRCLE should move *Alpha Omega* out of public sight and back into repairs. Could they spare ship guardsmen among all these crises? Jason combed for any public info. A few other Biblical Christian preserves in the Midwest reported sending officers to help with the *invasion* of campus. No other news had hit civic channels, only marginal notes about a business ship that made an emergency landing inside a religious preserve.

With half an hour to Cincinnati, Jason wouldn't have long for last-minute sleep.

• • •

JASON
7:17 AM EDT, SUNDAY, JULY 22, 2125
SOUTH CINCINNATI

Jason forced himself awake and groaned. That flat bunk may have ruined his back overnight. The time was 7:17 AM and someone was calling from another room.

"Good morning, brother. This is Derek. Navistar sent over this page and it's time-sensitive."

Not enough rest. That was the game. Especially not with all hell threatening to tear loose. Either way, Jason needn't spend more time in

Derek's flat, which *was* flat, and formed of glass-thin walls. The bunk compartment gave only centimeters of clearance under tiny windows that reflected daylight from an outdoor crete surface. Even *Legacy* had afforded more space than these submarine-like bulkheads that scraped at his elbows.

Derek's big self blocked the doorframe. "You want breakfast?"

Jason slid down from the bunk, ducking, lest he re-bash his skull on the low ceiling. Derek's page was a starcraft recovery and transport requisition, approved by Cincinnati civics, waiting for approval by a ship's regent. Looked fine enough, so Jason signed. CIRCLE Security had taken responsibility for the crash, along with damage to Gilead Apartments and nine vehicles in the landing lot. Also a power center. *Alpha Omega* had destroyed a whole power center.

Some of those debits might hit the Space Mission fund or clear it completely.

A slightly larger common space connected a tight galley and corner restroom. In the booths of an eating nook, Derek sat across from Michael.

"Too much man in here," Derek said. "Later I can open the whole side to air out."

Enveloped in viz, Michael raised and lowered his hand.

"Mike's deep in the details." Derek drew up a coffee mug. "I gave him that bad device we found on the *Alpha Omega*. Also some meds for his gravity adjustment. Oh. I detached a replicate device from one of the port reactors we found on the ship. So both fuel chamber and port reactors had the same device. Strange, no?"

"Do we know what this thing does?" Jason said.

"The function is simple," Michael said inside his viz. "It is an *auditor*. Listens for voice prints."

"Like what?"

Derek spoke for him. "Still need to learn. I think Mike spent all night compiling an index of pathogen fighters." He set down two shallow bowls, filled with brown flakes that popped and sizzled as if the dish were hot iron. "Don't eat this if you want coffee too."

Somewhere out there, had Brock and Alicia survived the night?

"We can't reach the president or the council." Derek's timbre vibrated the bowl metal. "Feels like the campus burned down. Did the enemy win? Can we fix anything?"

35

LIGHT CRACKED INTO BROCK'S STONY EYELIDS AND pried them open. His hospital room door also opened. Two tall men entered, their shapes resolving into Colin Van Campen and Harold Templeton, but somehow, in this place, they looked small and more elderly.

"Well," Van Campen started. "Looks like we're getting some nerves restored." He meant the nearby pedestal, whose tiny wires fed into Brock's arm.

Templeton went next. "I've cancelled my duties at Sola Cathedral today, so I can do whatever I can to oversee the campus, and—"

"Oversee," Brock repeated. "What about Dr. Woodford?"

They glanced to each other.

"Intensive care," Templeton said. "The trespassers hit him hard. And I must tell you . . . Dr. Hendricks has passed. He was behind James and was struck by a bolt."

May the Lord have mercy. "What about the vault?"

"They destroyed it."

Yes, Brock had seen that moment, just as blinding as that night Grandfather died. Twice this enemy had come to his homeland to destroy. "Where did they come from?"

"We don't know." Van Campen rested his hand on Brock's pedestal. "After one group vaulted out, the strange green craft took off. Local police haven't followed up. The vehicle wasn't registered. For all we know, it has long since left the state or country."

Aziz had either planned this or else spied his chance to invade the preserve after *Alpha Omega*'s crash landing. Did they intend to kill CIRCLE's next president?

Instead, they had taken her away. He couldn't deny it. Alicia wasn't waiting here on campus or somewhere on Mars. Right now he could recite the terrible words and feel nothing: *Our enemy captured my wife, and they may have killed her.* This was his willful suppression of the truth, or else his treatments' side effects were restricting his emotions.

"And the ship?"

"We've . . . begun recovery," Templeton said. "What's strange is that we can't find Jason Cruz. He left the ship, telling a Navistar tech this was an emergency."

Please, we can't lose anyone else. Where on Earth could Jason have gone?

• • •

JASON
8:04 AM EDT, SUNDAY, JULY 22, 2125
CIRCLE PRESERVE, CINCINNATI

Skies hung low and dark, but they withheld rain as Jason swept Brock's quev down into *Alpha Omega*'s open cargo bay. After the disaster, this powerful vessel yet stood, less like a regal machine and more like an invading monster.

For today, Jason knew his duty.

He opened the quev door to intercept Director Sumisawa. "Mr. Cruz? We're ready to move the ship on port reactor power."

"I hope you checked the port reactor for unknown tech."

"Our reactor is another model. It has no sign of the auditor Mr. Soren warned about."

Good for Derek, and for her.

Jason led Sumisawa up the stairs, then up the levitator.

Alpha Omega's command deck was a crime scene. But the highbridge looked glossy and innocent; Brock's design and Navistar's techs had seen to that. Jason needn't feel disgusted. If anything, he should hate the enemy for attacking this kindly ship.

"Director, I'm acting captain. Please help me return the ship to Navistar."

"Yes, sir. Please note that . . . we have another challenge." She faltered. "The ship's flight record, for all of yesterday's test launch, has been erased."

Jason stared back, silently repeating those last syllables.

"I am sorry. We need to recover all visible and audible logs from every deck."

More skullduggery. Without records, he had less hope of tracing the sabotage, much less the fake voices and alerts. What if they let Michael Starr in here? See what he could do?

• • •

BROCK
8:07 AM EDT, SUNDAY, JULY 22, 2125
CIRCLE PRESERVE, CINCINNATI

Brock lifted himself from the hospital bed. "Has the enemy leader voxed again?"

"All the campus is under embargo," Dr. Van Campen replied.

"That won't help. He broke into my personal com."

Templeton halted before finally asking, "Who?"

Of course they did not know; how could they have learned?

Someone at Navistar could have easily rigged the ship on behalf of a saboteur. What about that earlier business removing the support pillars, possibly compromising the propulsion systems? Or else, dare he think it, someone within CIRCLE itself was corrupt, perhaps as highly placed as the elder council. Dr. Hendricks was in the clear. But could Brock begin to accept someone so high in leadership, even some distant figure, could be in league with the enemy?

By now he was already negotiating a dark course of suspicion.

Dr. Van Campen ran the Harding School of Engineering. For years he had gently critiqued CIRCLE even while he served. No one else here knew much about quantum travel, certainly not enough to rig a vault for self-destruction.

Dr. Templeton had invited Aziz, and wasn't he first to suggest Brock and Jason travel to Cairo? He was the only elder who avoided the ship's launch.

"Our ghost is Aziz," Brock said. "He used his earlier access to infiltrate CIRCLE."

Templeton stared, not angered, but genuinely shocked.

This made sense. Templeton wanted success for the Space Mission. But in his zeal, he had given the enemy an entry point. Aziz himself had warned about this days ago.

"Harold," Van Campen said. "You couldn't have known."

The other tried his best expression of the wise counselor, but emotions tugged at his face. "Are you certain? You heard his voice? Did he claim—"

"Given all the mimicry, we can't know whose voice to trust," Dr. Van Campen said.

"No," Brock said. "It was Aziz. And yes, he said he is responsible." His head was clearing, but his chest muscles felt taut and weak. How could CIRCLE prevent further attack without shutting down its entire com network? The problem had gone too far. They had failed to protect themselves, and he had failed to protect them.

Van Campen remained standing, but Templeton sank into a chair, emptied of any more counsels to share. Never before had the elder appeared so vulnerable.

And now this man was their acting president.

The door scuffed. Someone else entered the room, a woman with dark curls. She handed Van Campen a device like an old wireless phone receiver. He held it to his ear and listened to a report; Brock heard only the words *Navistar* and *move the ship*. Van Campen beckoned to Templeton, and the two men retreated into the hall.

A light flashed atop the shelf that held Brock's shoes and crumpled jacket. Despite the campus embargo, his com clip was blinking.

Brock summoned any traces of strength and accepted the vox.

"I am sorry to invade your com," came a quietly familiar reply.

If this was the enemy, why would he apologize and wear another guise? "Michael?"

"Yes. If you doubt this is me, I can tell you about our first meeting. It was in Port Ares, near the premier's mansion. I made passing reference to us being like hired hands for Solomon's temple, and you asked whether—"

"I remember." Brock could calm himself. "How are you reaching me?"

"Because I just found the weakness in your com clip, and I used this to override your control, one last time. Now I inject some antidotes for enemy pathogens. Whoever invaded your com is smart. But for these last hours, they were not spying on you."

CIRCLE's people on Earth couldn't match Michael on Mars. Still, how would Brock or anyone be able to contact Aziz? "Do you see any logs from previous interference?"

"I'm cordoning those into secure archives," Michael said.

"Can you do the same repairs for others?"

"Yes. In fact, I am here already, on planet Earth, along with your friend Mr. Soren."

Brock needed to sit still in light of those words. Why had they come all this way?

"And here is Mr. Cruz. I've signaled him to join this vox. Jason?"

"Yeah, hello?"

This was Michael, somehow able to repair Jason's com. "Jason, where are you?"

"Back at the ship, returning her to Navistar. And *you*, Captain?"

Brock let down his shoulders, then turned on the mattress and made himself stand. Glistening wires followed his wrist, and the smooth floor held up his bare feet, giving him some solidity in this reeling world. "I'm recovering at Samaritan General."

"Alicia with you?"

Brock shared everything. Assuming his com was fixed, only allies would hear this.

Jason swore, repeatedly.

"Hey, Captain. This is Derek Soren. To clarify, Michael is here with me on the Navistar property. We have your wife and daughter too. Oh, and your children."

Air chilled Brock's bare skin. "Michael, how did you—"

"Was me, actually," Jason said. "I vaulted to Mars just in case. Took your quev. Knew you wouldn't mind. Went to your place, fought off insurgents. We came back in your quev."

Each sentence landed solid like this floor, as if to restore home gravity. How had they made such sacrifice? His children were safe, then, not captured or killed? But he couldn't yet rest in that truth. For all he knew, this enemy would outright kill Alicia as some show of power, rather than contact CIRCLE with demands.

There was something else, a truth Jason needed to know. "You took my quev."

"Yeah. No damage or anything—"

"Jason, I am sorry, but your grackle *was* damaged. I'm sure we can reimburse you."

All of his nerves tingled with remnant specs, the world's synthetic copy of a miracle.

"Ah." That sounded like Jason's bitter laugh. "Where I'm going, I won't need it."

He must mean Heaven, because the Space Mission was surely grounded forever.

"Captain," Jason said. "About that name you said *yesterday, Mahdi?*"

Brock practiced walking, then pulled a curtain and removed his hospital gown. He found his original clothes, from yesterday, all washed and folded, yet torn from the attack. "Aziz calls himself the Mahdi. In many Islamic teachings, that is a prophesied figure from long before the Last War. Muhammad's original followers referred to the Mahdi. They expect this military leader to fight Antichrist and bring in the caliphate."

"The global religious empire," Jason said.

If this Mahdi truly hoped to unite all deists against CAUSE, what wouldn't he do?

"Brock, we are coming to the hospital," Michael said. "We found a suspicious device on the ship's labor deck. Now we need records from yesterday on your ship."

Jason grunted. "Yeah, about that . . . Navistar says the saboteur erased the logs."

"I want to see the starcraft myself," Michael said.

"Michael, how long will you and Elizabeth stay here?" Brock asked.

"As long as I am needed."

"Then I want Mr. Starr cleared for ship security work. Also, we may have backup—"

"Captain, please hold while I am steering." Jason went silent, but

Brock watched a new sighted note appear on viz: SHH. THE ENEMY MIGHT STILL LISTEN FROM SHIP.

Brock replied, MISS LIGHTHEART RECORDED LAUNCH FOR ARCHIVES. SHE MAY HAVE COPY.

WHERE CAN I FIND HER? Jason asked.

TODAY IS SUNDAY, SO SHE MIGHT BE IN CHURCH. WE HAVE AN ADDRESS FOR HER MOTHER.

Julia and Lawrence Peters entered Brock's room, then halted, likely surprised to see him standing upright and dressed for returning to life. Lawrence's eyes were dark with fatigue. Had either of them slept since the crash? They had volunteered for this, only to be ensnared.

"I am so sorry," Brock told them, "for yesterday."

"Captain." Lawrence set a food tray on the bed. "That was not your fault. Not a bit."

"Satan is obviously hard at work here," Julia said.

"Then we need to pray," Lawrence said. "Immediately."

Brock had met these people mere weeks ago. Now they moved to embrace him. Julia nearly wept aloud. "Father, we bind your enemy in Jesus's name. We call on your promise that no weapon against us shall prosper, and give Your angels charge over us."

Lord, bless them. But they should never know his recent thoughts about the mission.

Lawrence stood behind him, half a head taller, pressing firm hands to his shoulders. "Confuse the enemy," Lawrence murmured. "Like you confused the Philistines."

Someone else knocked. With quiet thanks, Brock removed himself from them to open the door. Derek Soren, tangled hair over facial stubble and big shoulders, stood almost comically taller than the man beside him—Michael Starr, not far away in some Martian shelter, but truly here on Earth.

For him, Brock could provide a more natural embrace. "Thank you for coming."

"I am glad. You are better?" Michael withdrew and held up a strange egg-shaped item. "This is an *auditor*. Jason found it on the ship. It's a simple device that listens for an exact voice or sound pattern within a short range and responds with a specific reaction."

Brock could follow most of that, perhaps more than Lawrence and

Julia, who stood back to await any further need. "You found *this* thing on the fuel tank?"

"Naw," Derek said. "That was another damaged device. It had some juice left. But when we ran tests, it threw up pathogens and died. Jason thinks this one injected unstable ingredients into the fuel tank and triggered the warnings or an actual rupture. Then I found a duplicate device on one of the port reactors. Someone stowed those on the ship."

Brock needed to follow this. "Port reactors on the ship also had this foreign device."

"Aye, they're identical," Derek said. "If we'd left this thing fixed to the port reactor, and someone had bonded that port reactor with the ship for backup energy to replace the missing fuel tank, we might've had a worse disaster."

The device listened for voices within a short range. Any saboteur could not have sent a signal from outside the ship—meaning he had stayed aboard or else had a partner.

• • •

JASON
9:42 AM EDT, SUNDAY, JULY 22, 2125
CIRCLE PRESERVE, CINCINNATI

Wind tugged at Jason's sleeves like a tiny storm as he approached the Hyatt Library on campus. To his surprise, the outside door politely opened itself, and he passed from humid haze into the small anteroom. Past this simply adorned space, the bookshelves rose twice as tall as that cramped excuse for a library back at Freedom Hills.

He walked down the aisle to find a ridge of desks in the back. Silver glows shone from under them, as if they were hovering crafts. This was the only light inside, save for the dim viz over the face of that woman there, the one who'd been aboard yesterday. Silver-red specs glinted off her large triangle-and-cross-shaped earrings. She was working alone.

"Ma'am?"

Tameria Lightheart lifted her eyes. "Oh. Can I help you?"

"I'm Jason Cruz. We met yesterday, on that assignment. I'm ship's regent."

"I remember. I'm glad you're doing well." She tried a short laugh. "After all that."

"Yeah. Your mom said you'd probably be here. As opposed to . . ."

"Being in church today?" She fixed him with a look. "Believe me, this is more restful."

Great, so they'd traumatized this woman along with all the elders. "I'm sorry all that happened. We're investigating any causes. Your first time on a ship, ma'am?"

Tameria leafed through pages. "No. I mean yes. I don't really want to talk about this."

"But we might need your help."

Her earrings jingled. "I hope the captain's well. And his wife. I heard she—"

"You heard right, ma'am. Please listen. During the launch, you were on living deck. You were recording viz and other records of the flight, including any talk over vox."

Slowly she touched the golden tab on her nose.

"Do you have it with you?"

"Thought I might organize the records during lunch. No sense in that now, I guess."

Should he tell her? "After the launch problems, you have the only record."

"I didn't get data from the ship. Only viz from cameras and vox from the captain."

"That's all we need. Can we play that back somewhere?"

Tameria thought about it, then let down her shoulders as if giving in. She led him into one of the study rooms. "Did I leave open the library front door?"

"You did. Thanks." Jason reached to close the study door. "But this is confidentia—"

"Leave *that* open. Otherwise it wouldn't be proper. I'll just find the audio." Tameria summoned new specs to float before her eyes. She listened to something, then quietly laughed. "Pardon me. I'm skipping my introduction. Probably not very helpful to you."

• • •

BROCK
10 AM EDT, SUNDAY, JULY 22, 2125
CIRCLE PRESERVE, CINCINNATI

Two nurses refused to let Brock leave the hospital, so he asked to see the doctor, a solid-built and compassionate Samaritan man who proved willing to listen.

"My children are on the way home, from Mars," Brock said. "For the first time."

The doctor relented. But this meant that very soon, Brock must find a way to protect his family on Earth—and to tell his own children why their mother wasn't here.

Out in the corridor, he struggled to walk. Lawrence held his arm. Heat and moisture soaked through Brock's undershirt and stained his hair. Whether by medical treatment, his protein-rich breakfast, or his own ability, he was regaining physical strength.

In the hospital garage, Derek's shuttle fit every person, thanks to dual seat rows lining the cabin. Derek lifted the craft into the air while Jason voxed in.

"Captain, I found Tameria. She has the data we need."

"Does this include anything spoken over shipwide com?"

"Yeah. I ran it up to the first announcement, near fifteen hundred timestamp."

They would need to relive it all. "Derek, take my vox and relay it to the shuttle."

Sound ambiance filled the spacious cab.

"Jason, play it back," Brock said.

His own voice cut in: *"—tain Brock Rivers. We are launching. We will ascend three kilometers into public airspace, then another two hundred kilometers . . ."*

What had he been thinking yesterday? So foolishly had he ignored legitimate fears and impressed himself with visions of moving his whole family aboard this fantastic home to do the Lord's work. For those moments, he had glimpsed a door into Heaven.

"Moorings released, gates opening," Director Sumisawa answered the captain.

Moments later, Alicia recited her notes about the launch. Brock and Jason bantered a little and talked about the weather. No one else talked, except for Director Sumisawa, who gave remarks expected of a test flight. Had she been the one to utter some secret cue?

Jason's voice said, *"Captain. We're ready for ascent."*

"Lord God, Creator," the past Brock replied, sounding so devoted, *"we pledge this ship and our mission to You and Your glory."* Then his voice sang, *"Soli Deo gloria."*

A shrill whine cut in, piercing like needles.

"Jason, something's wrong with the vox."

"Yeah, that's not on my end!"

Brock stood and turned about, but the shrieking didn't change. Derek scrambled out from the shuttle cabin and shoved past Julia. He threw aside a plastic bin and fell to peer under a bench, then climbed back up and checked the ceiling.

Brock opened a cabinet to a storage bay. Something inside glowed.

Derek grunted. "Oh, scourge. That's the port reactor device. The auditor. Get down!"

The whining swelled into a *pop*. Debris pelted into the passenger space, ricocheting from rounded walls. Brock flinched and clutched his right arm; the skin stung from an impact, but showed no blood. No one else appeared hurt.

Derek crawled back into the bay and drew out the object. It looked like half of a gray clamshell, ripped open to reveal a tiny wedge of circuitry.

Over vox Jason shouted, "What happened?"

"That device detonated." And like a tiny bomb, even if attached to nothing.

"Did we set it off? Did we say a key phrase?"

No one else had talked! Unless . . . "Jason, my own recording was speaking the words."

"Or singing them," Julia said. *"Soli Deo—"* She stopped herself, touching her mouth.

"Well, now it's destroyed itself," Derek said. "We should be clear."

Claws pricked against Brock's chest.

"What's that for, man?" Derek asked. "Like a Latin phrase? *For God's glory alone?"*

Grandfather used to sing this. Brock's repeated phrase may have triggered this auditor's evil twin, the one stuck to the fuel tank, and caused the ship's cascade failure.

"But how could anyone know you'd say that?" Jason said.

If the enemy knew Brock, they might predict his behavior to some extent, yet no one could be so exact. At that time, Brock was speaking his heart, not following the script.

He dropped his head to his hands, now sure of the answer.

"Captain?"

Brock summoned viz and sighted for records, the ones he'd used just yesterday. He found the phrase and read the text three times to make certain.

He was ready to say it. "In truth, the phrase was scripted, but I said the words earlier than expected. We planned for me to start the interview with that song, quote Grandfather, and tie this launch back to the Heritage Hall accident and his final words on Earth."

Here was each line of Brock's written words: *SOLI DEO GLORIA*. JEROME RIVERS, CIRCLE'S PREVIOUS PRESIDENT AND MY GRANDFATHER, SANG THOSE WORDS IN PRAISE OF JESUS.

Grandfather had sung these words, and was himself killed by a port reactor.

"Who wrote this script?" Jason said.

"I'll get the file attributes."

"Tameria?" Jason went on. "Can you get public campus records from June twenty-one? Who *exactly* filed that request for a port reactor in Heritage Hall that evening?"

Brock accessed the attributes. He read the name, but he could not say this aloud.

Maybe some coincidence could explain all this.

Jason murmured, then said, "The reactor was ordered by Harold Templeton."

In Brock's vision hovered the same name, final author of the test launch script.

36

BROCK
10:30 AM EDT, SUNDAY, JULY 22, 2125
CIRCLE PRESERVE, CINCINNATI

BROCK LEANED FORWARD TO PRESS HIS ELBOWS TO
his knees. Gravity's weight dug his palms against his eyelids, driving
distorted shapes into the blackness.

Dr. Harold Templeton was a scholar in the best standing, grandfather
of five, respected church elder, and faithful husband. Never had he been
accused of the smallest scandal. Dare they believe this man planted
bombs and colluded with the enemy?

Jason spoke on vox, "Michael, can you delve into the Epicenter and
fix it for real?"

No one here was reacting to the name, but few of these people
knew the man.

Well, Brock could protect them from something. Despite the
embargo, he sent a note to Maxwell Adams, saying his com was
recovered and recommending Michael for full Epicenter access. A
complete records check would help resolve many problems.

Jason promised to copy Tameria's records and rejoin them. He
didn't sound pleased. But he had doubted Templeton from the start;
now he might feel vindicated.

Grandfather had been killed by the first sabotage, the explosion
caused by a port reactor Templeton had moved into Heritage Hall.
Templeton then seized for power. He openly colluded with strangers.
He supported Brock's and Jason's search for a starcraft, then gave
CIRCLE's enemy the code for the lobster-trap quantum vault near Cairo.

Brock might be reacting from trauma. He must stay rational,
accusing no one.

But every time, Templeton had protected himself. In the Hall,

Templeton had avoided the blast path—but to be fair, on that night, Grandfather had urged every council elder with Brock and Alicia to leave the platform. Unlike other elders, Templeton had avoided *Alpha Omega*'s crash. Now the vice president was dead and Dr. Woodford injured.

How could any man hide his double-mindedness for this long? Why would he betray his people? Speculations would strain credulity. So would theories about how Templeton had arranged all his trickery. On his own, he could not have infiltrated coms, much less programmed a secret device to listen for a voice to sabotage Heritage Hall or the ship.

"We come to the settlement," Michael said from the cabin.

Below the shuttle lay the residential section of Navistar, bound by shallow buildings that were pockmarked by tiny doors. Columns of glass caught needles of sunlight.

Brock's children had come to Earth. They waited below. In moments he would see them.

Derek grounded the shuttle and opened its doors. Brock dropped himself to the land. Weak but walking fast, he made his way across the courtyard. Derek hustled ahead of him, then opened a door into a hall like an airlock. Sculpted stone walls led them to an oasis where natural green ferns and faux white pillars surrounded a koi pond.

There they were, safely distant from the water, all three, enjoying a sandbox.

They saw him, and they shouted. Damp mulch cushioned Brock's knees, and he lifted his arms. They surrounded him, little arms clinging to his shoulders and face. Emma's hair spilled over his neck. Adam asked questions. Daniel asked for a drink.

They stood tall and strong in this gravity, looking so healthy! Of course they would. He and Alicia had trained them for years to survive on Earth—training for this terrible moment. She had worked so hard, and now she was suffering. She did not deserve that! Neither did the children, their innocent heritage, now dragged into this war.

Brock couldn't keep from weeping, even where everyone could see.

"Where's Mommy?" Adam said.

Never had Brock dreamed he would say these words. "Adam. Daniel. Emma. Listen carefully. We believe Jesus loves us, don't we? Even when it hurts, we must know that."

This was what any mature Christian should believe.

Adam and Emma tried to agree. Daniel stared elsewhere.

"Mommy isn't here. Some bad men took her. Those bad men don't like that I've been working on a space mission to serve Jesus. So now I am working to find Mommy."

Emma began to cry. Adam stood in shock.

He could save her. He could still fix this and guard them from any more evil.

Templeton must have allies, probably engineers, smart beyond their wisdom. They may not even know the greater scheme. All of this—CIRCLE, the Space Mission, the very idea of missionary work—was false. Only the enemy held power. How tiresome to find yet another group of false brothers secretly brought in. Always these germs infected the Body, forcing a terrible choice: You were doomed to be their victim, or else, the next perpetrator.

He needn't accept that choice. The only way forward was retreat.

"As soon as I find Mommy, and finish things on Earth, we will go home."

"Back home in the sky?" Emma whispered around her fingers.

"Yes. Back there."

"Brock." Michael cleared viz, standing beside an ornamental willow. "I have isolated pathogens in the Epicenter. And . . . please, I think we still need the Space Mission."

With a fierce expression, Jason pulled Michael away.

• • •

JASON
11 AM EDT, SUNDAY, JULY 22, 2125
SOUTH CINCINNATI

Jason guided him behind the trickling fountain. "Don't talk about *ministry* now."

"What do you mean?" Michael stared as if seriously aghast at the very idea. "Brock wants to abandon the mission. Everything he wanted."

"Fine, but shut it. He's in grief. He has every right."

"I know. I also believe we can find where they took Alicia."

"And what if you can't? The enemy never attacks you up front. He's more crafty. He hates good families, so he terrorizes them. Always the innocent."

"Well." Viz rewrapped Michael's face. "I did find the Epicenter problems."

Maybe this was how he coped, but it was good news. "So who did it?"

"I don't yet know. I'm finding cutouts for infiltrators and timestamps dating to May. This would let them track any adjoined com unit, including yours."

"So the enemy used Brock as a carrier to the ship." He could have been exposed last month. That probably meant Templeton had planned this even longer, and that the elder himself could also be exposed. "By chance can you track one of the elder coms now?"

"Well. I'm curing the track function. It already 'forgot' Brock's com and yours."

Any allies of Templeton may detect these repairs. In fact, he may have used the com embargo to cover his activities. "Use that pinhole," Jason said. "Look for *Harold Templeton*."

Blue viz lines swept Michael's eyes. "I don't see his unit on campus."

"He's elsewhere?"

"Wait. Here he is. The tracker pulls from twin receivers on the ship."

Jason stared at that viz. "Templeton's at the hangar? Here at Navistar?"

"Yes. Now I see those receivers on *Alpha Omega*. They also need to be purged."

The elder must have learned they had found his secret auditor device. He knew Brock's family had escaped to Earth and that Michael was uprooting his secrets.

"Mike. Keep fighting behind the veil. I'll need to borrow a shuttle from Derek."

• • •

BROCK
11:20 AM EDT, SUNDAY, JULY 22, 2125
SOUTH CINCINNATI

Brock's children had come to this hostile world of bad news, alien light cycles, and drastic time difference. He had tried to train them for this gravity, yes, but nothing could have prepared them for this terrible news. "Derek . . . can we get them some food?"

"Hey, so they eat too." Derek dropped into a kneel and fixed his eyes on Daniel. "I thought Martian kids only had Martian food. Didn't you like my special cereal?"

Daniel muttered, "No."

That big man had a way. He would have been perfect for the mission. So would Michael. Surely he hadn't traveled all this way, hoping to join the outreach. Now after Michael had defended the mission, he was gone, likely somewhere inside the Navistar complex.

Brock promised his children he would return soon, then entered the building and followed signs for a com center. One of three standing firewells was active, and its fiery viz closed around Brock, spinning to form floating sheets against a dark wall of specs. In the center, his friend was perched on a stool. "Michael? Listen, I do appreciate—"

"Do you want to give up the Space Mission?" Michael turned toward him.

Brock steadied his voice. "That choice is not mine."

"Doing that would contradict all you believe."

He was so new to a world full of Christians. "If I were a single male missionary, it might. But for these monsters . . . I cannot imagine what they might do."

"I will find them. We can recover Alicia."

"That won't last, Michael. The enemy is here, in my homeland. Pretending we can drive him out? That is *a delusion*. Listen to me. When you and I first began speaking about the gospel, I thought I was being so careful in how I described our people, never showing you some perfect image of my home. Well, I was a fool. Things are worse . . . so much worse."

"You told me Yahweh sometimes asks us to suffer. I don't understand."

Brock must teach Michael and make him understand. "I still believe this. But all my other ideas, conditioning my family and myself, waiting for some perfect time of returning to Earth? That was my will, not the Lord's. If he wants missionaries so badly, he can make that clear to *them*. Find someone who isn't so weak and sick of this whole mess."

"I am listening. But you are a missionary. You led us toward Christ. Rachel, Elizabeth, and me. And the Lord has preserved your children." Michael searched the air, as if scanning for words outside his viz. "Let me speak from outside the sheltered preser—"

"What are you talking about? I've learned from my sheltering! Seven years ago, I made a bad choice. Then I tried to act like the faithful exile, working for the invaders and earning their trust. We built new lives. We served our city and tried to raise a family. After all that, I return home to find . . . *what*? A ruined city. A preserve that uses all the free air inside. Once I believed the preserve system was the Lord's gift. I was wrong. Preserves are His judgment. So let them be judged. As for me and my house, it's time to escape.

"Yes, Michael, help me find Alicia, then do whatever you want. But I am taking my family out of here. Back on Mars, we can start our own church, even a preserve, a *true* preserve for true saints who truly know Jesus, love the poor, share the gospel, and prove their faith, and any hypocritical devils like Harold Templeton can go straight back to—"

Those last words chafed in his throat. He had spoken *his truth*, in this moment, but all of it brought back another conversation from years ago.

Brock had sounded like Alexander.

37

JASON FASTENED ON A HOVERPACK AND SPRANG OFF THE staircase, quietly maneuvering himself toward the ship. *Alpha Omega* filled the hangar, her navy blue hull gleaming under every light. But the ship leaned to starboard, favoring her wounded base.

The ship's cargo bay was wide open.

Jason slowed and slipped back into the bay's darkened floor. Gravity reclaimed him and he killed hoverpack power. He crept to the stairs. No vehicles or techs waited for him. The ship could be listening. For extra precaution, so would he. *Tools, vox record.*

Through open gates, he climbed the stairs into the darkened living deck. He donned his glazer glove, which lit the space in faint orange, showing no darker forms.

Someone's voice drifted from the levitator.

Pulling himself inside the tube, he ascended to command deck. His head cleared the floor. Upon the highbridge stood a column of shimmering viz.

"Mr. Aziz? I've come to talk." That older man with the fluffy gray hair and long tan jacket stood before the viz.

Templeton? Yes, this was the elder.

Jason let his foot sink to the deck. "I don't think your friend's listening."

Templeton turned, clasping empty hands at stomach level. "Mr. Cruz?"

"Dr. Templeton." Jason kept his gloved hand at chest level. "I want to know why."

"Why am I here, trying to call him?"

"And why the Heritage Hall blast. Why the power plays. Attacks over in Cairo. The Epicenter ghost. Exploiting the CIRCLE coms. The ship sabotage. Why abduct Brock's wife?"

Templeton stared back. "I never wanted this to happen."

"*No*, sir. I want the motive. What's it worth for you to collude with the enemy?"

"You think that I—"

"When did they get you? What did they promise?"

"I am not . . . ! Jason, Dr. Aziz contacted *me*. He called himself *al-Mahdi*. He promised the safe recovery of Alicia Rivers. That's why I'm here to speak with him."

"Just stop. We have the records, and it's over."

Templeton's face locked tight. "Where is Brock?"

"Not your business."

"No, brother, this is not appropriate."

"I am *not* your brother. That doesn't work on me anymore." Jason lifted his hand. With one signal he could send painful energies through his glove fingers.

Templeton recoiled, his pretense done. He bent his head with shut eyes quivering. "Would you really attack me, Jason? What then? Do I strike back? I couldn't. But for all I know, you're the man in league with the enemy, and it's my job to stop you."

Jason's hands shook. *Don't you dare let another religious leader lie to you.*

"Let's act in good faith, please." Templeton lifted both hands, like the pious stance of a worshiper. "I *am* your brother, and we are on the same side."

Earspace buzzed. Viz flashed an urgent message.

• • •

BROCK
12 PM EDT, SUNDAY, JULY 22, 2125
SOUTH CINCINNATI

Brock's hoverpack journey had provided little respite. Now he fought to ignore the full-body tension that smothered his aching elbow and other remnant pains, returned by the ship's synthetic gravity. He clutched *Alpha Omega*'s aft gate frame and stepped from the bay stairway onto living deck. All traces of hangar lights receded behind him, leaving only the human shape on infrared viz. This showed in dark crimson. What a color choice.

He moved forward and tugged the central levitator frame.

From labor deck, a human shape drifted up toward him, blond hair floating.

"There you are." Brock's casual tone came too easily.

Alexander stepped out of the levitator. "Brock? You've already left Samaritan."

"I did, though I'm still recovering. Still, I've found some answers."

No viz crowned Alexander's stolid face. "You knew I was here?"

After two terrible conversations today . . . this one may be the worst. "A good friend has been repairing the Epicenter system. He isolated the hidden source relay. After that, we only needed to find the human intercessor."

Alexander didn't break eye contact or change his expression. "I see."

He did not retreat. Instead he slowly walked past the living deck alcove. Brock followed him into the lounge, still littered with sofas and chairs, where the firewell's life-size viz mimicked the campus Waters of Life fountain.

"What would you think if I surrendered the mission?" Brock sounded so formal, as if proposing a debate topic. "Or if I no longer wanted to pursue a missionary calling?"

Alexander gazed up to the firewell dome. "Interesting. That may be the only choice."

That was true enough, so Brock leaned forward.

"After a single day of violence, CIRCLE chose to retreat," Alexander said. "I have prayed. I hoped we would grow stronger. But I don't think it's God's will."

How very spiritual. "Is that why you found another god?"

Alexander locked like a statue. Virtual waters cycled through splashes of cataracts.

"We checked the file history. Dr. Templeton did not clear that version of my launch script. You did. You added the words *soli Deo gloria* for me to say. You planted that auditor to listen for my words, then damage the ship's fuel tank. You corrupted the ship's com. Weeks ago, you invaded the Epicenter system, secretly letting Aziz slip in to spy on us. We think you used a similar auditor device to overload the port reactor under Heritage Hall."

Brock's coat pocket still held the two tiny mementos. Long had he wondered how these dove-shaped cufflinks had survived the explosion. Before the blast, someone must have taken them. Grandfather may have asked this of his young protégé. After the blast, the man had released them into zero-G near Brock, as if inventing some legend.

Alexander let down his shoulders and sighed. He even allowed a laugh. "Yeah. You're right. I'm the traitor."

"You are the traitor," Brock repeated.

"Mm. Spy, saboteur, apostate. Whatever you want to say."

Brock's arms held rigid. "And yet . . . you are proud?"

"We might save Alicia. But no one can save this preserve. Not even Jesus Christ."

The man said this with serious conviction, and Brock could not respond.

Alexander lifted his hand into the sculpted basin, trailing specs that hastened to reassemble into stone and liquid. In seconds the faux stone Bible re-formed to cycle the waters.

Brock could ask one question. "What have they done with my wife?"

"I can tell you she is alive. I'm sure you'll hear from them later."

As if Brock would believe a traitor? "Tell me where."

"I can't tell you because I don't know. We never meant to capture her. Once the ship crashed in the preserve, well, the occasion seemed right. We had men standing—"

"*Your men*? They wounded me and Dr. Woodford. They killed Dr. Hendricks!"

"You know, these viz modelers capture this fountain just right. Even down to the little coins in the basin. Why do people do this? Throw coins into a shallow well?"

Brock might clench Grandfather's cufflinks into dust.

"They go nowhere. They stay at the bottom of the pit. They're not even well-spent." Alexander cracked a laugh. "*Well-spent*, mmm. And the water just stirs in place. Over and over. Maybe that's how you keep out algae, but does it help anyone downstream? And this *edifice*, it's even worse. A shallow projection of a shallow world."

Jason was uptube on command deck. He'd gone to confront Templeton.

"So, for the record, you reject your Lord and your people," Brock said. "You wander toward some other god in another land. He'll let you take vengeance on your old people while feeling so much more holy from a distance. Is that your new salvation, *Alexander*?"

The man stared at the fountain.

"How long have you been working with our enemies? Give me the truth."

Spisss—Alexander slapped the virtual wall into spec fragments. "You don't know any truth. Back then, maybe you tried. I'll admit your grandfather was trying. I saw him up close. But that's not enough. He didn't genuinely care for *the truth* about these arrogant, hypocritical, privileged people who use religion for their own power."

"That is from Satan. It is no excuse for a man to betray good people!"

Red light specked in Alexander's eyes. He had summoned his viz.

No, you don't. Brock sighted voxes to CIRCLE SECURITY, JASON, and MAXWELL ADAMS, but null signs crowded his viz. His com was repaired, so Alexander must have a jammer.

Alexander brushed a hand through his hair and pointed up like a lecturer. "Did they really hurt you? People sent you nasty letters. That's all?" He burst out a laugh. "All for *your* mission, of course. Just another jewel in *your* crown on the shelf beside your parents' heavenly awards and your grandfather's riches and the sacred Scripture."

"That's enough—"

Alexander leaped, shoving Brock into a blinding mass of stones and waters. The deck floor had departed—and also the ship's gravity? Brock flung away panicked spec hordes and swung about, crashed back-first against the ceiling, then rebounded. Alexander's boots were just clearing the alcove. He was fleeing toward *Alpha Omega*'s cargo bay.

Viz, hoverpack controls, sight nav, go. His pack burst to life and impelled him across the floor, through the alcove, through the aft gate. There he halted. Synthetic gravity had failed. Down the stairs floated Alexander, pulling another hoverpack from a wall hook.

Where would he go? Would he summon his allies to storm this place?

The bay groaned, its walls flashing amber light, then all three curved triangular gates drew inward. Alexander veered in midair. His leg struck one of the segments just as it joined and sealed, ending the light flashes.

Someone stood at the command deck window. Jason had closed the gates.

"Ah"—Alexander shouted down—"the great Rivers family heritage!"

Brock grasped an aft gate handle to stabilize himself. Alexander floated high above, near the bay gates, viz masking his face. Small fissures reappeared. The three gates split apart, then shuddered and re-sealed. Alexander must be fighting to counter Jason's orders.

"Such a great Christian kingdom you have! The perfect wife and family. Oh, but not any holier, really, because your story has the *drama* that's better than perfection. Original sin, then exile into the world, then heroic return. Other people? Never had that freedom. Never that privilege. Still they stupidly follow the old God, singing the dirges, slaving away."

Either he was going on like this as a tactic, or he genuinely could not stop himself. "Alexander, what are you *talking* about?"

The ship's gates shuddered to open, then reversed.

"I found a better master. A better god! No more cheap grace from cheap people. No more hypocrites. I follow the Mahdi. He will unite the righteous to stand against evil."

What other truth would he reveal? Floating freely at the aft gate, Brock could only watch. "Your 'better god' can't remake reality or override these gates."

Alexander must not be carrying a weapon; otherwise he would have used it. His slender form hovered near the gates, face coated by silver viz like tinsel. "Why should I leave? I'm still in control. I . . . you see, I rigged the ship again. Worse than before. This time we'll all go down with the ship. Unless you open the bay gates. Open them now."

His voice broke, exposing his conviction as pretense. Brock shoved away the steps.

"I'll do it. One command. All I need." Alexander pointed to his viz. "Open the gates!"

Brock took control of his course.

"One word." Alexander's voice turned shrill. "I can do it with one word! Stay *back!*"

Brock fired hoverpack jets to stabilize himself. Someone moved inside the bay levitator, a man in a full suit. Harold Templeton clutched the tube's opening and halted in zero-G. He hurled an object.

Brock caught hold of Jason's glazer.

Alexander whirled toward him. "Open these gates!"

After slipping on the glove, Brock clenched his fist three times to turn his own viz orange. He lifted his hand, locked his three fingers, and pitched lightning.

Alexander hurled away from the gates, clawing upward but freely tumbling.

Brock fired again, and again, flinging each bolt wide. One struck the roof and bounced off. He had the opening and all control, while his enemy had no weapon. Brock rushed higher and fired again—

That bolt perforated Alexander's leg, and he cried out.

Brock blasted airjets until he body-slammed Alexander and pinned him to the ceiling. Brock evaded the flailing arms, then sank his fist through that coat of viz. Blood unspooled from Alexander's mouth like red ribbons in the air.

He was down.

Brock pinched off his viz-casting clip and tossed it away. Naked, glistening eyes stared back, and the face trembled without words.

"*Why* did you do all this? Where is your master? *Where did he take my wife?*"

Alexander cursed God and told Brock to die.

Brock lifted trembling fingers and pointed the glazer, his fingertips smoldering with sparks beneath Alexander's eyes.

Alexander turned his face away, pulling blood into longer airborne trails. His eyes ground shut and lips curled wide. "Don't. Please . . . don't kill me."

Brock lowered his glove. He clenched his fist three times and averted the power.

"I know I failed. Again." His eyes cast to the sloping walls and the great door that denied him escape. "Please don't. I failed you, Allah most merciful."

Brock withdrew. He lowered the glazer and removed its power.

Alexander was already destroying himself.

38

BROCK
6:37 PM EDT, SUNDAY, JULY 22, 2125
CIRCLE PRESERVE, CINCINNATI

SCRUNCH. THIS FELT WRONG, TRYING TO KICK IN THE DOOR OF A CIRCLE staffer apartment, as if Brock was attempting some vengeful act on the now-imprisoned former tenant. Jason's uncertain shove, however, had barely moved the door. He tried again, aiming his boot for the lock. *Snap.* The handle bent, and they pushed inside.

If anyone else here objected, Brock had approval from acting president Templeton.

Their outcast viz beamed into Alexander's apartment. Brock tagged one wall stat, making brighter light whisk into the space, filling the common area, which opened to the kitchen and the bedroom with adjoined bathroom.

"For CIRCLE Security, when you arrive," Brock narrated. "This is Alexander Moore's dwelling. No one else is living here. So far, I see no clear signs of evidence . . ."

The crash, attacks on elders, and all evils the enemy had brought to the preserve yesterday still occupied campus officials beyond their ability. Templeton wanted rapid answers. This record would capture these seemingly normal sights for cruel posterity.

Thin curtains hid tiny windows and three hardback chairs lined one wall. Those bookcases must have become standard since Brock's own turn in these apartments, or Alexander had added his own. The books sat in alphabetical order, starting with *Apologetics* and *Apostasy,* then the Bibles: a King James Version, a newer translation, and a CIRCLE Study Bible. Next came books on salvation theology, cults, major monotheistic religions.

Another bookcase showed stranger contents. One gaudy gold-plastic frame, embellished with leaves, held the image of a filigreed carriage rolling across a vine-laden stone bridge. Tall glass candles were wrapped in comic art of Mary and the apostles, standing near a stack of colored cloths. Brock took one of these, unfolded it into a large shirt featuring a jagged-edged logo: JESUS SAVES.

The next shelf held classic readers, biographies, math trainers, social-studies primers. A biography of Augustine was etched with more scrawls, the writing illegible. Whole pages were torn from a book of children's fables.

"He not make much income?" Jason scraped his hand over an empty white wall.

Brock sighed and returned the children's book. "Alexander came from a Colorado family, third of five children. His mother Roberta taught private school. His father ran an optometry practice." Dr. Christian Moore had self-published his own works about doctrine and family, a side interest that Alexander must have appreciated despite himself.

"How did you meet him?"

To find any resolution and to ignore these pains, each inflicted by Alexander one way or another, Brock was more than ready to share his mental notes.

"We met when he came to CIRCLE, alone. He once told me the Moores were third-generation Christians, and I replied that I could trace my line back to the father of Caleb Rivers, which made my family more holy. He seemed to think that funny."

Alexander had claimed his middle name, Graham, came from the famous evangelist. Later he had also said his parents gave him both names to honor the inventor.

Jason found another object, a stuffed lion with side stitches. "Childhood favorite?"

So that part of Alexander's stories was true. "He liked to take apart synthient stuffed animals. Then he gave them new personalities. His mother was horrified. She shut down the creatures and threw them away. I'll guess her actions were inspired by the family's latest church. Alexander must have saved this toy."

"Latest church?"

At least twice in those early years, Alexander had returned to complaints about this, and Brock had done his best to offer counsel. "Based on what he said, his family sampled churches. Dr. Moore wanted only the best church. So they never stayed in one. The pastor would misspeak. Or the musicians would mess up. A teacher would seem rude."

Jason returned the lion to its place.

"Alexander wanted consistency, so he applied for a CIRCLE scholarship and sent a personal appeal to Grandfather. But the campus staff declined, saying he needed more references beyond . . . well, his isolated family. So he broke with his family and moved from Colorado to the CIRCLE preserve. At church, he met Grandfather, and in class, he met me."

Jason inspected the books, as if seeking out anything unorthodox.

"Alexander and I often talked about how our people had abandoned the world. We liked to compare the antagonists of the Bible to the Christian villains we didn't like."

"Villains."

"That is my word." Brock lay one hand on the back of a chair, leaving a dust print. "Alicia was first to see the problem. She told me her concerns. The next day at church, I felt led to repent of my anger. And that same Monday, I told Alexander about my change of mind . . . that I was not controlling my tongue. We argued. Later, I learned the elders had already confronted him, and he hadn't taken it well. That summer, he left CIRCLE. He only returned after Alicia and I left Earth. I thought he was better, even restored. We all did."

Brock moved to the main room's inside wall, bordered by the desk whose polished black surface held scattered sheets. Jason approached and the desk detected motion. Tiny viz emitters shone three aerial screens in an inverted triangle.

A sheet lit with keys, which Jason tapped. "Yeah, encrypted."

Brock voxed Michael Starr, who sent adaptive anti-pathogens that opened access.

Jason sniffed. "Don't suppose he left a confession." They found no such blessing, only an outer layer of old pinholes into the Epicenter. "That one's dated May."

"May of 2123," Brock clarified for the record. So the traitor had begun corrupting CIRCLE long before he began work at headquarters. "Here, these are the links to *Alpha Omega*."

"He needed to stay aboard to help Templeton talk with Mahdi . . . no, Aziz."

"Or else he baited Templeton to the ship so he could redirect blame to him." Here was something—a script written in Shale Basic for scheduled transfer of data packets. More commands in that same languagewould open a signal at the same time. The last transmission, to an encrypted recipient, was done at midnight Sunday, July 22, earlier today. CIRCLE's embargo had not blocked this.

Brock cancelled the transfer. "I wonder if they can now end the embargo."

Jason pointed. "This log says he already sent stuff. Most encrypted."

Well, they had a man who could likely decrypt all their information, perhaps direct reports to the enemy. Each packet had released at midnight. Some contents were automatic, but Alexander had added more, sourced by his personal com. He had sent Templeton the note telling him to contact Aziz aboard the ship. One document gave a plain transcript from vox, dated yesterday.

> A: Prove it's you.
> B: Yes. We have three children not one. No that's not enough. Prove it's you first.
> A: I'm wearing the magenta blouse with pointed sleeves.
> B: And what else?
> A: Your favorite. Black. Now you.
> B: At age five, you first visited that butterfly garden, and a monarch landed on . . .

Alexander had stolen her words, then worked with the enemy that had stolen her away from Brock and out of her homeland. Somewhere out there, Alicia was waiting for him, but thus far, they didn't know where. After his arrest, Alexander had broken his silence only to repeat for investigators what he told Brock—that he could not tell them where Aziz's men held Alicia.

These records could reveal that answer on his behalf.

All this time, Alexander had recorded them all, using this for *vox persona* voice-impersonation tricks. And he had tracked them all . That had given his new leader the power to speak so prophetically, even about Brock's and Alicia's three children.

Yesterday's package contents were meticulous. Alexander had even enclosed transcripts of short notes with the men who had invaded campus. He never identified them, only the registry of their false Ministry vehicle. Jason traced that number to someplace in a British Columbian preserve and filed this for later investigation.

Next, to tie Alexander to his greatest crime, they needed one specific proof.

Derek had provided the destructive auditor's code. Brock searched the system for this and found the returns. Alexander had used his own schematics to forge seven total auditor devices. Each was attuned to listen within thirty meters for one set of sound patterns, the *soli Deo gloria* song, and respond with unique sets of commands. Three of these devices were forged three days ago, July 19. Alexander had affixed these to port reactors on *Alpha Omega*'s labor deck, with commands to overload the reactors.

One other device was forged July 16, then attached to the ship's fuel-tank membrane.

Two more devices were forged June 10, two weeks before Grandfather's address.

Brock's arms hit the desk. Viz blurred around his hands that pressed to his face. This foolish, evil young man had truly gone this far, worse than apostasy, worse than . . .

Why on Earth had he done this?

They might never know, but Brock couldn't leave without some explanation.

39

BROCK SANK INTO THE APARTMENT SOFA. WHETHER the man moved to a small campus detainment facility or some other private prison, preserve or secular, he would never return here for rest or plotting. He had committed assassination against his own future.

Oh, Lord, heal my exhaustion, even for a moment.

Jason had taken over, sorting through Alexander's early Shale programming for the auditor aboard ship, complete with detailed schemes for *Alpha Omega*'s cascade failure. He had made the ship spawn false alerts and suppress true alerts, calling evil, good, and good, evil. Apparently this let him play his part while letting everything else play along.

"Jason, did you find anything about Alicia or the enemy's location?"

"Nil. Only stuff that's way too self-obsessed."

Brock stumbled to the kitchen, where he retrieved a cup from the silver spigot. Fresh liquid chilled all the way down to his stomach. Even a traitor's hideaway could offer relief. "Jason, has Maxwell responded?"

"Nah. Guess they're waiting on Michael. You fine?"

"I will be, eternally speaking."

They could hope Alexander had deceived only them, and not recruited others.

Jason withdrew objects from under the desk. "You ready for this now?"

He meant all those unlabeled plastic shoeboxes filled with printed sheets. Brock moved a chair to the desk, where Jason opened one box. A first page showed one name, *Al-Haqiqa*, but written by another person, addressing Alexander by a pseudonym:

19-02-2117 | Thank you for your thoughts, The Truth. Your given name is like the name of our people in Arabic. We will not argue with you that Islam is the superior religion, but you speak as someone safe from many evils. Have you known the suffering that we know since the Last War? Have you been tempted as we have and yet crossed this burning lake with tears and cuts and blood, only to cry out for Allah's truth anyway?

Over the next several months, Alexander had hand-copied his opponents' points before writing his responses:

29-08-2118 | I don't agree with your false, evil religion. The Bible gives "salvation in no one else, no other name given among men by which we must be saved" Acts 4:12. Thank you for your respect. That is more than I see from so-called "Christians"! I agree that preserves are evil devices. They keep The Truth locked in while the world believes lies. We disagree on The Truth but we agree on one thing: the preserve system is a lie, and we must overthrow them any way we can.

So the name *Al-Haqiqa* also meant *The Truth*, not a single speaker, but a group of Islamic devotees Alexander had found. Later records showed him wading in deeper. His new friends spoke his language and could engage with the Christian Bible, despite its corruption as they saw it. They also knew native Arabic, so they could read the true Qu'ran. Alexander wrote:

17-12-2118 | Jathiya, thank you for sharing this with me away from commons. Be assured I will honor and respect you and the other men Allah has put in your life. I am available almost every evening and all day on Saturdays and Sundays. I hope this works with your time zone and adhan duties.

26-03-2119 | My studies have gone well so far thank you. Roots are overwhelming me. Yes, if you want, you can pray that Allah will aid my mind. I would be glad to speak with your friend if she too learned Arabic later in life. In the new month I am changing jobs so hope to have extra yun to install a reconditioned firewell as best I can. I want to try saying the shahada out loud even though I know you will not believe it saves me. Would your fathers allow us to visit in person?

15-01-2120 | Jathiya and Hajar, thank you for your prayers. I have found the adhan as exhilarating as you said. I have meditated more about Muhammad (SAWS), and I even use the wares you sent to find the exact direction of Mecca for prayers. By now you may know that your fathers have been writing with me, and they have offered to introduce me to the Guided One himself sometime. Please, if we can use the firewell once more, then I will show you how well I can speak the Shahada and the two Surah I have been memorizing. This way I can better greet your imam.

· · ·

BROCK
9:28 PM EDT, SUNDAY, JULY 22, 2125
CIRCLE PRESERVE, CINCINNATI

At 9:28 PM, dull aches twisted at Brock's temples. He looked for medications in the kitchen cabinets, but Alexander kept no drugs or caffeinated drinks.

One curious but quiet building staffer arrived with a groundline relay. Less than an hour later, two CIRCLE Security officers swept through Alexander's apartment, taking photos and copying data, but otherwise disturbing little. Following counsel by Brock and Dr. Templeton, they said they would wait for more data to be decrypted.

Michael arrived and joined Jason, adding personal viz to the desk displays.

More personal searches revealed a top player in Alexander's dialogues. Most of his conversation partners spoke from cities ruined by the Last War—Baghdad, Riyadh, Cairo, and Mecca itself. They revealed their pain at losing their people's heritage, but from their hadith, they found hope from Muhammad in predictions of a future savior. Men from Al-Haqiqa spoke highly of one particular imam who held influence above all: Aziz.

At any other time, Brock could see them as victims of real suffering.

Michael asked, "If Alexander converted, why not leave CIRCLE?"

"You see any records of his first conversation with 'Mahdi'?" Jason said.

"None yet."

"I think we won't," Jason said. "He only mentions that conversation while talking with his niche. Those sheets, there. He says Allah wants him to stay in his preserve. Months later, he meets up with the Sola Cathedral elders and signs back up with CIRCLE."

Brock pulled at his hair, now damp with the night's prying humidity. "By the time he graduated, I wonder if he wanted to put his secret interest behind him."

If that were true, one could guess at what happened. Alexander had tried to pursue a young woman from his church. It had not worked out. He had returned to his Islamic friends, probably even more eager to embrace another faith.

"Last May, he abused the Epicenter system," Michael said. "On June fourteenth, he accessed your grandfather's personal records."

At that time, Grandfather had found the Heritage time capsule and secret funding. Alexander would have learned about the Space Mission declaration. By then, this professing Mahdi had also contacted Templeton under the name of *Dr. Mahmoud Aziz*.

""Brock, this is a success," Michael said. "We have freed all your coms, the Epicenter, and the *Alpha Omega* from Alexander's infections. I can officially suggest you lift the com embargo."

We have freed, Michael had said, rather than rightfully taking this credit. But if CIRCLE lifted the embargo, Aziz could learn of Alexander's arrest.

"One more thing," Jason said. "I found the first package of many that he sent daily. This one's from . . . yeah, June twenty first, 2125."

Brock accepted the record and glimpsed the first few lines. "Excuse me."

• • •

BROCK
9:47 PM EDT, SUNDAY, JULY 22, 2125
CIRCLE PRESERVE, CINCINNATI

Walking slowly, Brock crossed through the broken threshold into a quiet dormitory hall. Here the cooled air clashed with hot humidity escaping from outside. One alcove of cushioned chairs, between a vending station and drinking fountain, provided some refuge.

Brock read these records twice before settling himself to start a static vox.

"This is for Maxwell Adams and CIRCLE Security. I submit this as evidence to reopen the Jerome Rivers death investigation. Please see the affixed documents."

He sounded so professional, but any listener would discern more.

"At 7:57:20 PM Eastern Daylight Time, on June twenty-first, 2125, Alexander Moore murdered my grandfather, Jerome Dwight Rivers."

His words landed against a wall mural that showed a bright countryside.

"As CIRCLE's new com chief, Alexander helped my grandfather write his speech. He encouraged Grandfather to add the prayer he had quoted for years: *soli Deo gloria.*

"On June 10th, Alexander accessed the Harding School of Engineering, where he forged two identical auditor devices. He gained access to CIRCLE storehouses and attached one device to one of the port reactors. Working with the committee, Alexander prepared Heritage Hall for CIRCLE's conference. He sent false reports of a compromised prime reactor to our maintenance staff. He ordered a port reactor installed as backup.

"That night, Grandfather gave his speech. His last words were captured by the auditor device, which signaled the port reactor to overload. That triggered a cascade that broke through all reactor safeguards, erupted into Heritage Hall, and destroyed him."

40

BROCK
11:55 PM EDT, SUNDAY, JULY 22, 2125
CIRCLE PRESERVE, CINCINNATI

BROCK PULLED OPEN HIS EYES TO REVEAL A BLURRED
and looming shape before him.

"Captain." Jason was nervous. "About midnight. Need you now."

Dark blotches crossed the world as Brock stumbled back to the desk, where Jason pointed to the main screen. "If the embargo ends, we can let Alexander's scheduled report go out tonight. But to keep Aziz from learning we exposed him, we made some edits. The packet confirms some facts, like the Harding quantum vault being destroyed yesterday. It has the campus death count. But we're showing Dr. Woodford *and* you still in the hospital."

"And what of Dr. Templeton?" Brock asked. "Alexander deflected blame onto him. He attached the elder's name to the launch script and the Heritage Hall port reactor request. Aziz likely wants to know if that plan worked."

"Maybe we falsify that too? Act like I really got Templeton arrested?"

Michael said, "Alexander often sent records dated before noon that same day. We have done the same, hoping their leader does not see a difference in the pattern."

"One other thing," Jason said. "Alexander talked with Mr. Mahdi aloud. Over live viz."

And from here on a Christian campus. Would the enemy expect the same tonight? "What if we use Alexander's own *vox persona* trick to answer Aziz? We can suggest that he found a way to avoid the com embargo, but only for vox."

"Maybe. We got plenty of voice samples from Alexander's records. He talked a lot."

Brock scratched at his roughened face.

More quietly, Michael asked, "Why would he want to kill Jerome Rivers?"

Moments ago, out there in that quiet alcove, Brock had considered the same.

Aziz, calling himself the Mahdi, saw CIRCLE as a leader of Biblical Christianity. Killing its president would leave the Aziz faction free to influence CIRCLE, buying into the resources and prestige of any space outreach.

Jason called his name. Brock opened his eyes and returned to the room.

"Do you want to play the part of Alexander? You knew him best."

Play the part. One time, Brock had privately mimicked him for Alicia, then felt bad. But here Brock need not imitate the voice, as if mocking him. He need only speak as if—

The desk rang two low notes, like a clock tower.

"Aziz says he wants vox *and* viz communication," Michael said.

Without aching desperation, Brock might fold over. "Share the vox. I'll try to cover. Michael, do whatever you can to find the com's origin. If that is even possible . . ."

He stood in the firewell corner. Intangible flames drew beside his shoulders until they surrounded his face in burbling crimson. Then all faded to black. For all his previous meetings with Alexander, Aziz must have wanted his servant free of distraction.

"Aqil." Out of the dark spoke the same enemy. *"Masaa al-khayr, as-salamu alaykum."*

This would fail if Aziz spoke Arabic the whole time. *Lord help me. Lord help me.* The first word was Alexander's new name. That last phrase was a greeting. *Peace be upon you.*

Brock's religion classes had taught this. *"Wa-alaykum as-salaam."* *Peace upon you too.*

No simulated voice echoed his own. For all he knew, he had just spoken into the void as himself. Nothing replied from the lukewarm darkness.

"Your spoken Arabic improves. I am glad."

Mimic his inflections, but speak normally. "I hope you received my report."

"I did."

The filter gave no delay. "Because of the embargo, I'm not yet free to use full viz."

"I understand." The enemy paused. Did he want Alexander to say more, or repeat some ritual? Finally he said, "Why could I not contact Dr. Templeton today?"

What was the cover story? "I am sorry. After I planted my evidence, Jason Cruz came aboard to accuse Dr. Templeton. But now the elder has been detained."

"Ah. Good work." Aziz spoke warmly, like a father with genuine praise.

Many seconds later, the vox held silent, possibly as he reviewed the fake report.

"Imam," Brock said. "The com embargo should lift soon. At that time, how can I best serve you?" His voice cracked, like Alexander's. "Will you give our demands to CIRCLE?"

"If I can't speak with Rivers or Templeton, whom do you suggest I contact?"

"I think . . . Mr. Rivers, when he is released. He wants his wife and will be most willing to hear you." Brock used a false voice, but this part was the truth. Now to share the untruths. "CIRCLE Security will investigate Templeton but find no evidence to support accusations. They may detain *Cruz* for menacing behavior and false accusations against Templeton."

"Then if Templeton is released, I will approach him as leader of CIRCLE. I want him to preserve the space program for us. I want you to make this happen."

Aziz wanted to keep the mission? "I will," Brock said.

"Rivers follows his grandfather. I will not allow him to take power at CIRCLE."

So there it was. During those Epicenter meetings, Aziz had tried appealing to Templeton's openness, but Brock had opposed him. From that day forward, Aziz must have chosen to target him. He, therefore, was not trying to destroy the Space Mission. He wanted it for himself—the concept, the resources, perhaps even the starcraft.

For years he could have been acting like a messiah figure. Had he also sent the Cairo hard-liner hostiles, then, and for this reason? One of those men living in the garbage had mentioned *Mahdi*. The enemy could be recruiting many people for his faction.

And could anyone blame him, if even CIRCLE was so vulnerable to such evil?

"Until then, arrange a meeting with Cruz. I will tell him they must return the ship to Cairo by midnight this Wednesday. If not, we end our mercy to the woman."

Return the ship. That's what they wanted. *Mercy to the woman.* So she was alive.

"Yes, imam . . ." How would Alexander ask him for Alicia's location? Brock glanced to Michael, who shook his head.

"Thank you, Aqil. *Allah ysalmak.*"

The vox cut. Black clouds cleared and left him blinking in the murky light.

"Yeah, he's gone," Jason said.

"Michael, is there nothing . . . ?"

"Overseas." Michael looked up and nodded. "It looks like northern Africa."

That location would align, especially given their Cairo conflict. "But no specifics?"

"I am sorry. He uses too many relays. I would need longer synthient analysis."

"Then save—" Brock coughed and retreated. "Save these records. Do you think—"

"He bought the Alexander persona?" Jason said. "Sounded like it."

What would they have done with her location anyway? Notify local authorities? Tattle on them to CAUSE? Brock may collapse back on the sofa, which offered no comfort from the simple truth he had to share. "If he does vox me, then for my part, aside from whatever Dr. Templeton says, I am . . . prepared to hear terms. I'll brook no debate on this."

Michael did not respond. He continued his work in silence.

Jason, however, lifted eyes to face Brock directly. "Can you step out a moment?"

• • •

JASON
12:30 AM EDT, MONDAY, JULY 23, 2125
CIRCLE PRESERVE, CINCINNATI

They walked far from that wretched apartment, enough time for Jason to rehearse his words. Past midnight on a weekday, all the campus slept. Night air hung wet and hot.

Two apartment buildings later, he and Brock reached a restroom hut for the big outdoor amphitheater. Jason stepped into a pool of lamplight, and his shoes scratched pavement. "Captain. Please *don't* surrender. Not the ship, not God's mission, not one jot."

Brock drew up his shoulders. "Then the Lord wants my wife to die."

"That's not what—"

"And how did you become so spiritual to determine the Lord's will?" Brock lifted his hand. "Please don't say *all things work together for good*. No verse tells me, *thou shalt do missions none of your people want and shalt sacrifice your family to the enemy*."

Jason tightened his fingers. "I helped protect your family."

"Thank you, truly. Now do you think our people will do the same for you?"

Even tighter. "Devils in a wicked preserve already stole my family."

Brock's face softened, but barely. "I'm sorry to hear that, and yet . . . let's say you had them back. Even if I sacrificed my life. I won't sacrifice women and children."

"So we sacrifice the mission instead?"

"You can save the mission if you want. As for me and my house, I'm done. The enemy wants the mission, wants the ship, or both, and they are willing to kill to get them. I am not willing to surrender Alicia's life or my children's lives to resist their evil."

Jason's ears burned. "We can still fight."

"For who exactly? Our religious freedom? Our rights to live normally in a world that hates us?" Brock swept his arm over the navy sky and campus lodges. "Alexander had a logical philosophy. If the world attacks, you have two choices. You can fight for your own rights, not caring how your allies abuse those rights to serve their own sin. Or you can surrender those rights, even your people's lives, pretending like you're some dying messiah. I hate both options. I don't blame Alexander for refusing either one."

"And where did that get him? Are you defending—"

"Was his choice not rational? Choice one kills your holiness, and choice two kills your people. Why shouldn't Alexander, in his foolishness and desperation and pain, try another god who makes false promises that sound so comforting?"

"He betrayed Jesus. Not just His people. And his kind of violence isn't our strength."

He'd left an opening, and Brock jumped into it: "Any *strength* we would need, violent or otherwise, is driven by pride. I've been prideful for most of my life. God wanted to rescue me from my old foolishness that made me ignore our limits and treat my own people like fools. I won't fight my Lord. I don't want to fight at all. I want back . . . my best friend."

"You expect us to fight for that, when you're first to flee the ship?"

• • •

BROCK
1:01 AM EDT, MONDAY, JULY 23, 2125
CIRCLE PRESERVE, CINCINNATI

Brock drove his fist—against Jason's instantly raised forearm. Jason grunted, but he had taken that blow, without hint of striking back in defense. Instead a muscle spasm took vengeance on Brock from just beneath his ribcage, making him fall back. Jason had not done this to him; the pain was from Brock's earlier damage. But showing his wrath against this man felt so right. Oh, how he longed for this *freedom*. Such a contradiction was powerful, and he could delight in the absurdity, which meant he mustn't think more about this sense in words, or he would regress—

Too late. His pretense was gone. He would devolve into that weak version of himself, as if stepping outside his own body of flesh and staring back in self-judgment. What a cursed gift, and yet, oh, how he hated that evil in himself, even more than he hated the weakness.

He couldn't hate Jason, or any of his people, not even the foolish ones.

So he surrendered and collapsed to the damp sidewalk. His moans escaped into sobs that tore at his throat. "I can't. Jason, I cannot do this." He must say more. Anyone deserved that. "I thought I had completed my hardship . . . for seven years. I wanted a reward at last. What is the worst sacrifice I'm called to do to find my place in whatever *He* wants?"

By now all of campus could likely hear them.

Jason said, "You don't need to—"

"Surrender the mission and return to exile? Or keep the mission and surrender Alicia? If the worst happens, it's Heaven for her, but must *she* first suffer Hell?"

Jason didn't talk, and that was wise.

"I'm sorry. I'm sorry. You've suffered before. Your own family. I haven't asked."

Jason breathed. "We saved your children. I still haven't saved my daughter."

Brock must hold onto this compassion, thinking first of his brother's needs. He made himself stand and approach a steel bench, where he sat down, arms falling to his lap.

Jason stood near. "Any saint would've come at me then. I pushed you too far."

No, he had not.

And for several moments Jason waited, giving Brock his space. "When you're ready, I have some thoughts on how to find her."

Brock pulled his breathing into even patterns.

"If they want to control CIRCLE, they've kept her alive. That's still your sacrifice. But maybe we don't need to sacrifice *her*. We can fight for her. Fight for the mission."

"Jason . . . I'm exhausted, I can't . . ."

"But I can. You listen. Back in the apartment, we lied to Aziz. I think he believed it. With his traitor arrested, we've limited his power. So maybe we give him what he wants, while we look for his location. Michael's already trying to trace that."

They dare not deceive themselves. But rational thoughts formed like dim viz cast into the night. "So we can pretend that Aziz's mission did succeed, like his schemes to frame Templeton, or his plan to return *Alpha Omega* to Cairo."

"Yeah. We'll do some tactical deception, to save the mission and save Alicia."

ALICIA
UNKNOWN TIME AND DATE
UNKNOWN LOCATION

EVERY TWENTY SECONDS, THE OLD CEILING CYCLED
its glimmering bronze-and-gold swirls, mingling with lumen threads
that cast the room's only light. Alicia could imagine this as some strange
artwork come to life. Not long ago, she had nearly slept on this flat floor
cushion. If they kept her in here much longer, this room's faint stench
might seem less repulsive. A few silent fans circulated air with its odor
of sweat and cheap perfume.

Behind the solid and lukewarm walls resounded loud hums and
clangs, like some vast machine that regularly opened and shut its
compartments. A single wood-and-steel door marked one wall of this
roughly square-shaped room. There were no windows, but she had a
small corner privy surrounded by a wispy green curtain.

So far, this boredom would seem the worst torture, if not for her
recent memories.

Brock had fallen so hard. He lay dead or dying, sprawled on the
stairs as she was whipped away into the storm. These people had come
to CIRCLE, intending to kill someone. Now they had her and would
surely use her for leverage.

Brock could not save her, and that guilt would make him suffer
worse than she.

The abductors had pulled her from the receiving vault and flung a
hood over her face. They'd shoved her onto a smooth floor with Earthen
gravity. She'd heard no distant hum to denote a ship. They pulled her
through voice-echoing corridors, then into this room. They stole her
clip and cleared her pockets. Otherwise, they had not touched her.

The facts felt like boxes of abstract data, but hours ago, they'd made her weep.

Searching the room gave no sign of their identity or purpose. She had found water bottles and three sealed packages, which when torn revealed packaged meals resembling turkey dinners. The first proved self-heating, but tasted like unfiltered dishwater.

Would they replace the supplies? How long would they keep her in this place?

Alicia prayed again, by name, for Brock, Adam, Emma, and Daniel. Jason Cruz, Alexander, the Starrs, Tameria, the new crew she didn't know well, and the council elders.

These prayers helped her feel like a Christian. She could act like a saint.

But she had yet to pray for her captors.

"Lord Jesus, no." She spoke aloud, making herself honest. "I don't want to do that yet. But I don't even know if I hate them. I don't know enough to feel that temptation."

Were they listening? She almost wished they would—

Noise shuddered. The door issued high beeps, then whirred as if turning gears. Her muscles locked tight as if ready to spring. Better this than grief or panic. Could she fight someone? She had no weapon. Try to escape? Either choice was bad.

The glowing ceiling faded like embers. New light split a gash between the door and frame. A dark shape intruded, then divided into two flanking figures, like guards. Their arms moved as they bowed to the center. They were preparing for something.

A third figure appeared in the doorway and strode forward.

Lord Jesus, protect me.

This must be the leader . . . Aziz. He stood at average height, wrapped in the silhouette of a single garment. His presence could remove all her impulses for escape or reaction.

"Alicia Rivers. You are doing well."

He sounded strong and melodic. English wasn't his first language, but a close second.

And he might expect a compliment. "I am surviving."

"Does this surprise you?"

"Truly. I assumed you would've hurt me more."

Silently he advanced, likely wearing soft shoes. "That is not our intent. In fact, we hope CIRCLE's leaders, unlike many Christians, will see the truth of Allah."

Then this *was* the ghost behind all the plots.

"I hope your leaders choose wisely, for your sake and for all who submit to him."

"Who are you?" she asked.

"I told your husband my title. You may know the meaning."

He was waiting for her to speak. "You follow the Islamic savior for the end times."

"I am the Mahdi myself. Allah raises me to break the chains of the religious preserves and the Cause. Allah gives to people of the book one choice. They may follow me to convert to the holy faith or join with the antichrist."

Chills crawled over her arms and neck.

"My people have suffered since the Last War. Their blood cries out. The bombing of Mecca. The raiding of holy places. This suffering has brought you and me to this place. Only by Allah's will could I become Al-Mahdi. Only by his will could the Russian attacks have spared the holiest section of Mecca. Only by his will could I publicly appear, as foretold, between the corner of Kaaba and the station of Abraham to be witnessed by the people. Now the people of the book may witness me, to join the uprising against secular rule."

He truly believed all this. "Your people attacked my husband in Cairo, Aziz."

"I am Mahdi, and the old hatreds will die when all true followers serve the eternal caliphate. Mrs. Rivers, this is not bad law or unjust restriction. It is true peace on Earth, good will toward men. Do your people flourish? Allah gave your husband a sense of conviction. Did he follow the truth? Seek the final prophet? No. He fled with you into the sky. What is the biblical story? Like the untrustworthy servant, he would bury his talent in the sand of Mars."

This stranger knew nothing about them.

"But his work is still useful. He found the ship and knows how to fly. I'm reminded of the words of St. Paul. Every working body will need eyes and ears, as Brock has shown—"

"Stop quoting. Stop doing that."

"Oh?"

She shouldn't have revealed that he had provoked her.

"I've read your Bible, corruptions and all. And I watch your world from afar."

"You claim to *know* people there very well," Alicia said.

The man smiled in his darkness. "Truth is truth, for all people. Here is another truth: My faith honors women. We train them to study. We do not forbid them to teach."

"You . . . have no idea who we really are." *Stop.* This was no campus debate, and Aziz was only faking his respectful tone. "You've watched us from a distance. You've read our com messages, maybe worked with some insider, someone who already hates us. That means you see distortions. That isn't *the truth*."

"Be still. We both know your preserve invites corruption."

"Then you'd better leave me alone, lest you get corrupted too."

Aziz was concealed by his own silhouette. "I am incorruptible. Are you? Are your people? One of your own friends has falsely accused an elder of being our spy. Your people rise up to oppose missions. Your leaders' weakness invites violence."

Violence that you caused, she could say.

"Your preserve is in chaos. My people are ready. You must prepare for the worst."

If only she had ways to warn them. "The incorruptible messiah is threatening me."

"It is mercy." Aziz lifted his head. "Have you heard the account of Abu Talib?"

If only she had, so she could repeat the account to him first.

Aziz stepped forward. "Abu Talib was uncle to the prophet Muhammad, *sallah allahu alaihi wa'sallam.* He loved his nephew and protected Muhammad from his enemies. In return, the prophet cared for his uncle. But as the years passed, Abu Talib fell into poverty. And when Allah chose Muhammad to be his messenger, Abu Talib did not embrace Islam.

"Ten years after the prophet began his work, Abu Talib was nearing death. The prophet begged his uncle to speak the Shahadah in truth so he might enter paradise. Muhammad also pleaded with Allah for his uncle to be saved. Finally, Abu Talib died.

"The accounts are not certain. Did Allah listen to the prophet's prayers and spare Abu Talib? I never learned, until after I left my home for training. My teachers showed me the older writings once thought lost in the Last War. In one hadith, narrated by Said ibn al-Musayyib, I learned the truth of Abu Talib. That is how I learned what true mercy is.

"One follower asked the prophet: 'Did your prayers help save your father's brother?'

"Muhammad replied, 'Yes. If not for my prayers, he would have gone to the lowest place. But now Abu Talib dwells in a shallow place of the fire.' To this day, in Hell, Abu Talib suffers. He stands in shallow fire like shoes that boil his brains."

The room gave her no place to hide. These blankets offered no covering.

"If Brock fights me, he will die in fire. If you also resist, we will use the old ways."

Aziz turned and vanished through the door.

42

JASON
7:13 AM EDT, MONDAY, JULY 23, 2125
SOUTH CINCINNATI

JASON RETRIEVED A FRESH DERMAPATCH FROM ship's stores and stuck it onto his bruised forearm. His new captain had repented, three times, and Jason had forgiven the same amount. But they were brothers. Lord willing, they would stay that way after all this was over.

Viz flared. A note arrived from CIRCLE's enemy, addressed to him and Brock.

> UNKNOWN, 7:13 AM, 07-23-2125 | You have seen the power of the Mahdi. Receive his word and obey. As soon as ship repairs are finished, you must launch the ship. Bring the ship back to the Khaldun Concern preserve in Cairo. Land by midnight local time within two days, on July 25, 2125. If you do not, we will kill Alicia Rivers.

Fine. At least he'd given them forty-eight hours for those emergency repairs.

Jason paced his cabin and relayed this note to Brock, Michael, and everyone who knew the plan they'd assembled last night. Today they still had CIRCLE's com embargo for cover. That gave them more time to beg Navistar for rapid repair turnaround, and to script a working narrative complete with fake records.

Yes, it was deception. To save not just her life, but also thousands of their people.

. . .

JASON
10:30 AM EDT, MONDAY, JULY 23, 2125
SOUTH CINCINNATI

Hours later, Jason found late breakfast in the commons and read their first lie.

> CIRCLE SECURITY, 10:25 AM, 07-23-2125 | CIRCLE officers have arrested Jason Joshua Cruz (male, 30, RP-BC-Va-87), engineering teacher at Freedom Hills College. Cruz faces two charges of armed assault and terroristic threatening. The complaint was filed by Dr. Harold Whitehall Templeton (male, 55, RP-BC-Oh-1), elder of Sola Cathedral and member of CIRCLE's elder council. A hearing date will be set.

Next, Jason sent a real message to someone who probably remained their ally.

> JASON CRUZ, 10:31 AM, 07-23-2125 | To Nabil Sadat. Our people have been invaded. We think they're allied with hardliners. Now they demand we return the ship to Khaldun. But can we land the ship in your preserve tomorrow, one day earlier than deadline? We won't presume on your hospitality. But we need help. Please reply.

That afternoon, Jason stopped by lowbridge to confirm Mike was building the new facsimile. So far, the fake ship looked good. So did the captain's overly polite reply to their enemy.

> BROCK RIVERS 1:27 PM, 07-23-2125 | Mr. Aziz, I am recovering from my injuries after your attack. We agree with your terms. CIRCLE will deliver our starcraft to the Khaldun Concern preserve by midnight Egypt time, July 25 (6:00 PM EDT, July 24). We demand the

safe return of Alicia Rivers. Then we will vacate the starcraft. We await word from Khaldun Concern to see if they agree to serve as a neutral location.

OFFICE OF THE PRESIDENT, CENTER FOR INTERNATIONAL RENEWAL OF CHRISTIAN LIFE AND EDUCATION, 03:30 PM, 07-23-2125 | Greetings. CIRCLE elders have voted to lift the embargo on our external com systems. This was a divided decision. We believe this change is necessary to share an update with sisters and brothers around the world.

Two days ago, enemies of CIRCLE invaded our campus. They attempted to kill our president, Dr. James Woodford. Vice President Dr. Gregory Hendricks was wounded and died the same day. We grieve with his family and condemn this evil attack.

CIRCLE now faces threats of further violence. We wish to encourage a spirit of "power and love and self-control," as the apostle Paul encouraged his student, Timothy. Still, we must also take precaution. So we urge residents to evacuate from the preserve. Find friends and churches who might host you elsewhere.

"Now may the God of peace . . . equip you with everything good that you may do His will, working in us that which is pleasing in His sight, through Jesus Christ, to Whom be glory forever and ever. Amen." (Hebrews 13:20–21)

Dr. Harold Templeton, CIRCLE acting president

ALEXANDER MOORE, 12 AM, 07-24-2125 | My Imam, peace be to you. Tonight I cannot speak with you alone. My job requires late hours to help with preserve evacuation. Praise Allah for casting CIRCLE leaders into fear. Dr. Templeton is released. Jason Cruz has been charged with assault. Brock Rivers is still in recovery. What do you plan for the ship? Should I go with the crew, as I did during the test flight? Should

I manually overload the port reactors? I stand ready to continue as your servant and have never stopped praying in accordance with Allah's will.

Allah ysalmak

Aqil

. . .

BROCK
9:45 AM EDT, TUESDAY, JULY 24, 2125
SOUTH CINCINNATI

At 9:45 AM on Tuesday, July 24, nearly 31 hours before Aziz's deadline, Brock made himself stand and walk in the captain's cabin, and he sighted for a new static vox.

"To my brothers and sisters, I'm Brock Rivers, and I'm truly sorry."

No skies or space flowed beyond that window, only the faintly glowing wall of Reformation Hangar Bay 1..

"I hoped to share the gospel of Jesus beyond our preserve. Instead, I've brought the world's evil into my home. As a result, I'm forced to deceive my people by lying about certain details, such as my brother's supposed arrest. I confess I have personally chosen to support this scheme. Someday, I might see this moment more clearly. Today, I cannot . . ."

Shadowed walls hid the gently roaring fans that drew frigid air into his cabin.

Pause. He cleared viz. Hours ago, he had lain still on his bed. Acting like a ship's medical officer, Elizabeth Starr had suggested he rest and pray. He had failed at both. Lawrence and Julia might help with the prayer after they finished their tasks.

What was left undone? Of course, at Maxwell Adams's suggestion, he should contact one other man. He voxed Dr. Josiah Busche and heard a message prompt.

"Good morning, pastor. I want to thank you for the care you've shown, especially for my children and Rachel Starr, despite your differences with me about the mission. I must ask this. Please do not trust all you hear from CIRCLE news this week. Godspeed."

He sent the message, just as Jason's vox arrived. "Captain, we're ready."

Brock straightened the bed covers. He donned his boots and the same gold-trimmed navy jacket Alicia loved. He departed his cabin and headed through the hall, then up the ramp to the ship's main levitator. A short drift upward took him onto command deck.

Michael and Elizabeth Starr waited in the starboard lowbridge. Julia and Lawrence Peters emerged from the commons. Tameria and Derek walked up the starboard ramp.

Brock approached the highbridge.

Jason met him. "Captain, Navistar staff finished inspection thirty minutes ago. They gave the ship a C grade. Sumisawa issued a warning about the starboard base structure."

"Thank you, Jason."

"Sadat's not answering. I set my clip to vox him every fifteen minutes. That really bothers me. But even if he delays a day, we can reach Cairo before deadline."

Brock moved into position for this launch.

They had no need for declarations and stagecraft.

He switched on bridge mirrors and confirmed their clearance. Hangar gates opened and moorings released, while port control sent permission. He cleared nav boards and set their new course: a near-reversal of their flight from Egypt about one month ago.

Jason activated gravity spectra.

Alpha Omega lifted until she cleared the hangar walls and their viz reflections. She would fly into this late and humid morning, blanketed by clouds. As soon as the ship left the pad, Brock raised pitch to +60 degrees. Land and clouds poured down like a waterfall.

He released the yoke, and they flew onward, without alarms or objections.

"Michael Starr, have you prepared *both* of our ships?"

Michael arrived and placed two sheets on the console, copying their data.

ALPHA OMEGA (TRUE) showed the starcraft at current position, heading eastward, dragging her damaged-yet-sealed starboard arm. She carried two days' worth of fuel and supplemental power from three secure port reactors. Weak life systems were augmented by two emergency backups, hastily installed by Derek Soren and his Navistar friends.

Michael's second version, ALPHA OMEGA (FALSE), showed the same damage alerts, but with several changes. All systems ran in low-power mode. All three of the original port reactors stayed on board, with Alexander's auditor devices still in place. This version was not airborne, but grounded inside the Navistar hangar. Michael had even added scripts for random ship activities and human signatures, suggesting CIRCLE crew on board or Navistar staff making repairs—as if for a planned launch to Cairo, one day later.

He had made all this, even after their argument. "Thank you for your work."

Without a word, Michael retrieved the sheets and left.

Jason took his place. "In this world, Alexander Moore is free and obeys his Mahdi. Now the enemy can access the ship and see everything, but—"

"He will see the false version."

"Same timestamps, movements, everything but our active viz. Aziz can't watch us in flight. But he can see ongoing repairs that kept his little bombs aboard."

"Why the bombs?" Brock pointed to the port reactors. "He wants the ship intact."

"It's probably a failsafe. If he can't possess the ship, we can't, either."

Only the Lord knew what evils this would-be messiah could commit with a starcraft like this. Did he want to capture Space Mission resources to convert into his own currency? Would he ascend into space and attack CAUSE, hoping to start his own extra-orbital holy war?

"Meanwhile, acting president Templeton found an acting CIRCLE com chief. Bryony is all set up in the Epicenter. They're waiting to hear from Aziz."

Brock retreated from his station. "I will be downtube."

"Captain, I can watch the highbridge. I recommend breakfast."

. . .

BROCK
10:15 AM EDT, TUESDAY, JULY 24, 2125
EASTERN UNITED STATES

After a hot meal of fresh eggs, Brock stepped into the living deck firewell and cleared the Waters of Life display, the replica Alexander had mocked two days ago. All lines should still be open. "Michael, have you found Al-Haqiqa's location?"

"Not yet," came the vox reply. "I'm working with Bryony about their last contact."

Brock still needed to apologize to him. "What last contact?"

"She said Aziz called Templeton and asked for a meeting at six o'clock Eastern."

When did this happen? "I suppose he's still hiding his location."

"He may use scramblers or work with domestic preserve allies," Michael said.

"He does," Jason cut in. "Could be the same ones who sent men to campus."

"Yes, but if he ghosts into the Epicenter, he needs a relay, perhaps one in orbit."

"Mike, I fought his allies further out," Jason said. "Those men were Martian natives."

Regardless of whether CIRCLE continued the Space Mission, someone was already at work spreading religions beyond Earth. One way or another, in this generation or centuries from now, the Cause would face a startling truth about real humanity.

Firewell, open channel, full spread, CIRCLE headquarters meeting.

Emitters cast down rays of specs that swirled and assembled into outlines. Pieces of simulated Epicenter filled with color and gained dimension. Brock turned in all directions and saw the surrounding rows. Overhead, the firewell emitters were replaced by triangle-paneled skylight glass. If he moved his head far enough backward, he might discern the tiny wire that extended to fit into the head of his own "ghost," granting him this perspective.

Templeton appeared, standing by the elder table and staring over at Brock. "Oh . . . so it's you. I was afraid our enemy had come seven hours early."

Brock's one step made the room jump too quickly. "He wants to meet in private?"

"Because I'm now CIRCLE's acting president." Templeton nodded, walking around the table as if warily eyeing the open mouth of a volcano. Dark smudges ringed his rendered eyes.

"What does he want? We told him we'll surrender the ship."

"His note said he wants to resume his proposal for a joint partnership with CIRCLE, specific to the Space Mission or other projects."

After all that evil the enemy had wrought, what a notion.

"I realize you need me to play along with him," Templeton said.

Of course this gentle, optimistic soul would express doubt. "That's right."

"We're all doing it," came Jason's voice. "I'm taking that hit myself. Dr. Templeton, call it my penance for falsely accusing you. But if it helps CIRCLE . . ."

"Thank you. And I do see your reasoning, but don't accept this strategy."

"They gave us no alternative," Jason said.

Templeton turned away. "The world would hate what we do."

Or perhaps the real *world* paid little attention. Only certain Christians would care, blessed with the luxury of their shelters, safe from making such decisions.

• • •

JASON
1:16 PM EDT, TUESDAY, JULY 24, 2125
ATLANTIC OCEAN

Hours ago, Jason watched the North American coast rush under the ship, then pass far behind. Now the borderless ocean spanned in all directions, at first gray, then deep blue like the sky. His clock showed 1:16 PM EDT, or 7:16 PM Egypt time.

They had one day, five hours before Aziz's deadline for returning the ship to Cairo.

After that? Only the Father knew.

Jason checked their simulated ship, ALPHA OMEGA (FALSE), grounded in the Navistar hangar. The fake ship's fake repairs were going fine, thanks to the dedication of five false Navistar staffers testing the false prime reactor. Another simulated team worked on the mangled base. They'd probably fix it better than the actual ship repairs.

The enemy had already pinged this fake ship, but they were untraceable—so far.

Jason stiffened. Someone approached the highbridge. Her sandy-blonde hair blurred through mirror viz. "May I . . . ?"

"Yeah, fine."

Tameria stopped by the console and stared to the ocean, twelve kilometers beneath. To this moment, he'd wondered about the wisdom of inviting her aboard. They had no idea what they were flying into. Sure, none of them were trained for this. He barely was. But she was meandering up here as if uncertain whether to ask favors of a stern parent.

"Ma'am, I don't mean to intimidate you."

She rested her arms to her sides. "I'm only a little confused. Alicia's been good to me. I'll do anything to help her. But I . . . I'm not an engineer. Or soldier. Please don't say I'm the prayer support. I could do that anywhere."

So the captain hadn't explained this in full. "You put up cameras downtube, yeah?"

"I did. All over the ship. Even in the commons."

"And they're still recording, closed-system, no interface with *Alpha Omega*."

"You think they'll corrupt the ship?"

"No, ma'am, no." Did she want to be this skittish? "Just the opposite. What if we didn't clean out the ship like we thought? That's why you're keeping independent tools. You're here again for the same purpose as before—you're Space Mission posterity."

Tameria glanced back to the mirrored skies.

She was barely a friend, but . . . "Listen, the highest rank I have is SOAR castoff. Raised in a bad preserve. I came here out of nowhere, and I've got nothing like Brock's legacy."

Years ago, God had clearly worked in Jason's life, when Jason had first confronted the evils of New Zion and finally escaped the place.

But during Jason's time with SOAR, God went quiet. Only when Jason returned to the cult preserve, hoping to confront the abuse yet again, did his Father seem to return. He didn't speak aloud. Just worked in small ways, like a providential answer or a true friend's support. God helped Jason leave the cult, this time for good.

Apart from Jason's sense of a divine mission call, God switched back into silence.

All that nastiness in his old preserve was never publicized. Now all of CIRCLE knew Jason's name. They could accuse him of worse crimes than the fake ones.

"I never went near the *bigger* Christian groups. Then I tried the Cincinnati conference. I got in the Hall and heard the president call for missions. Then I felt like . . . Jesus was talking. Told me I should stop using battle scars to hide from His command. That's why I said *yes*. So now I'm back in a different kind of battle. I met Brock Rivers, that supposed prodigal son. But he's just a man who worked hard and loves the Lord. I feel like Jesus is getting loud again, even through that man. Even against this enemy."

"I didn't know that," Tameria said. "The way you work together . . ."

"Eh. It hasn't been long. But he knows me better than CIRCLE people. Now some of them may think I attacked an elder or that *I'm* the traitor. People are people. Christians can be worse. Especially if our leaders let the lies spread far." Jason raised a finger. "That's what you're for. No, I can't promise you're safe. But we need you to help fix the lies."

"What do you mean?"

"The ones we're making up. That I'm viewed as the traitor and we're surrendering the ship to Mah—Aziz. But we're entrusting you with *the truth*. Whatever you see, we want everyone else to see, later, when this is over. That way the lies won't be permanent. People can know the real story and judge for themselves what we did. That will also help exonerate me. You're recording this conversation now, aren't you?"

Tameria broke her reverie and nodded.

Deeper talk was done. They chatted over lunch items and how the galley needed restocking. She departed, just as Jason's com buzzed. NABIL SADAT. After all this delay?

"Mr. Jason, I'm sorry. Your earlier notes were lost. I try to ignore coms after six."

Jason filled in the explanation.

Sadat swore. "So your enemy gave you a deadline of tomorrow. Why come tonight?"

"We hope to avoid surrendering the ship. And find Al-Haqiqa instead. I apologize, sir. We hoped to reach you long before launch."

"It's well. But I do not know this militant group or its location."

His denial sounded pleasant, so Jason needn't feel that old suspicion. "This leader spent months infiltrating our preserve. He's killed our people. He calls himself *Mahdi*."

After many seconds, Sadat muttered in Arabic.

"You know this man?"

"I think we do. We heard of him in the last month, soon after I returned from your preserve. The hardliners have rumors, or propaganda. We hear *Mahdi* this or *caliphate* that. Some signals come to us, telling us . . . to stop committing *shirk* and follow Allah."

Jason should relay this to Brock, as soon as the captain returned from his cabin.

"Otherwise the hardline area has been quiet, after we repelled their last assault."

"They're waiting," Jason said. "Their new leader might give them orders."

"Are you then familiar with the *Mahdi* belief?"

"Yeah. He'll fight Satan at the apocalypse and kill my people if we don't join."

"Mr. Cruz, that is not my people and not my religion."

"I know it's not, sir."

"We will help. You may land your ship in our preserve."

That would help. "But last time, we made your home into their target."

Sadat considered it. "This is the reality. To me, we are allies in the struggle. If you have spoken with Mahdi, I need to know about this threat outside my gate."

. . .

ALICIA
UNKNOWN TIME AND DATE
UNKNOWN LOCATION

By herself in the darkness, Alicia recalled all of the major prophets, Isaiah, Jeremiah, Lamentations, Ezekiel, Daniel. They were the messianic one, the weeping one, the weeping one part two, the weird one, and the fun one. Then came the minor prophets—*miner*, because you went deep to find their treasure. That old school line might still be funny.

What about Isaiah? First came his visions and prophecies about the Lord raising his holy mountain for Israel. In the year that King Uzziah died, Isaiah saw the Lord on his throne, flanked by seraphim. She could recite that sublime scene, aloud, that had so fascinated her since childhood, even inspiring her first serious compositions.

"They called to another and said: 'Holy, holy, holy is the Lord of hosts; the whole earth is full of His glory . . .'" That last word drifted away into the darkness.

Next came prophecies about a virgin and invasions. So many invasions. Bad people always punished Israel on the Lord's behalf, because of Israel's sin. Did this pattern continue with the Church? Hadn't Jesus fixed this by saving people's hearts?

"For behold . . . I create new heavens and a new earth, and the former things shall—"

Crash. Her heart leaped and she rolled over, looking to the door.

Machinery ground inside. The door moved, splitting open, shedding light over human shapes and revealing long-sleeved garments of black and beige.

Men approached her, surrounded her, and clutched at her arms.

She wilted, unable to react. Maybe they used some numbing agent, or she was trapped inside her own body's panicked response.

Fight them. Give a demand. What if they did worse to her?

They let her walk. Alicia's legs could move. She glimpsed some portions of this place, high ceilings and gray crete walls, without windows, with silent floors.

Corridors fell into darkness. New prying light stabbed her eyes, gold and musty like sand. A new room's walls were flung far away. Men had gathered here, some wearing turbans or wrapped in robes, many clad in the same military-like apparel as Alicia's guards. Desks and shelves lined those walls. Colored objects hung beside maps and framed pages. Taller desks glowed with viz. Was she onboard a ship after all?

Her guards halted against a platform with consoles. Many meters ahead, a curtain of viz showed a telescoped room with red-carpeted floors and encircling rows of chairs.

So they had brought her to the Epicenter? Would her captor appear as a ghost or use his true form? Aziz might show her to prove his cruel bargaining authority, assuming he still wanted to manipulate CIRCLE. Or he might still have power for a more terrible attack.

43

BROCK
11:50 PM EEST, TUESDAY, JULY 24, 2125
MEDITERRANEAN SEA

"CAPTAIN, IT'S JASON. YOU AWAKE? AZIZ ARRIVED early in the Epicenter."

Brock's clip viz showed 4:50 PM home time, 11:50 PM Egypt time—about 24 hours to Aziz's deadline. "I'm here." He stumbled to the bathroom, blasted cold sink water into his dry eyes, and shuddered. "Everyone, stay clear of the living deck firewell."

He took his cabin stairs and sighted a new letter from DR. JOSIAH BUSCHE.

> Mr. Rivers, we're family in Jesus. I will pray. Hannah
> says the children are a joy to care for. You and the Starrs
> raised them well. We're happy to bear your burdens.

That man, the bearded preacher from the campus protests, was not even a preserve resident. He had stayed after the conference to help counsel grieving residents. And now, after hearing at Sola Cathedral about the sudden need for these four children, Busche and his wife had been first to cite their overqualifications and offer their rented condo.

Whatever the preserve's troubles, may the Lord preserve any of His saints.

Brock made himself leave the cabin. Past the alcove walls, the firewell was still wrapped in viz that reflected another reality, compressed-reversed, with no human shapes. *Firewell stats, outgoing.* He muted all firewell sound and shut off cameras.

Jason said, "Five minutes to the Khaldun preserve."

Beyond the firewell and living deck floor, littered with stray furniture, the ship's night-filled window showed no sign of movement. Gentle humming reminded him this was a flying ship, over the land of Egypt, so far protected from plagues.

What if Aziz knew all this? Was he lurking out in the night, watching them?

"Hello, is this the ship?" came Templeton's voice.

"Yes. I am Michael Starr. Aziz sees the Epicenter and is probing our false starcraft."

Creator God, blind them. Brock gripped the bulkhead's edge.

"I heard from Aziz," Templeton said. "He demands a meeting with me and Brock."

This was a complication. In their false version of events, Brock had stayed in Cincinnati. Was he still recovering, or would he have moved to the settlement, fifteen minutes from the CIRCLE preserve? Either way, he should "obey" Aziz's orders. "Michael, can you integrate this true firewell with our false version of the ship?"

"I believe so."

"Dr. Templeton, tell Aziz I can meet you by phasing into the Epicenter from here."

Lawrence and Julia emerged from the hall. He waved them back from the firewell. "Aziz is here," Brock told them. "He wants me to appear, so I will, to maintain our story."

"So in the ship," Lawrence said, "inside the hangar, are you helping with repairs?"

"I suppose . . . yes."

"Then you need to pull off that jacket."

Julia nodded. "And roll up your sleeves."

• • •

JASON
12:00 AM EEST, WEDNESDAY, JULY 25, 2125
KHALDUN PRESERVE, CAIRO

Jason's clock shifted to midnight. Derek Soren, his acting ship's regent, loudly reported that Khaldun's preserve had no aerial traffic this late. *Not bad, big man.*

Sadat returned to earspace. "We see you, Jason. Please approach landing pad M."

"How are things down there?"

"We remain on alert, but the hardline is quiet."

Pad M coordinates arrived. Jason conveyed them to Derek to mod their course.

Sadat added more in a whisper.

"Sorry, what was that?"

"Not you, Jason. I was saying goodnight to my wife."

Jason had seen that mauve-clad woman on Sadat's belt viz, teaching her preschool.

"I would like to come aboard. Can we compare notes about the *Mahdi*?"

Only if you share with us too. Or did Aziz hide in *this* preserve, working with Sadat all this time? Why else would he choose this place as a meeting location? But why then would Sadat have protected Brock and Jason or sold them the ship?

If Mr. Sadat knew the ship had come a day early, Aziz would soon know it too.

Still, even a heathen king could help God's people. "Yeah, come up. I'll open the bay."

"Regent!" Mike called from lowbridge. "Brock entered the Epicenter."

. . .

BROCK
12:02 AM EEST, WEDNESDAY, JULY 25, 2125
KHALDUN PRESERVE, CAIRO

Jason called, "Captain, Aziz is already there, yeah? If so, Mike, can you trace his link?"

"I will try when Aziz ghosts into that room," Michael said.

Brock stepped back into the simulated Epicenter, letting his view sharpen and stabilize until the illusion was complete. As he moved across the room's center platform, both upper doors opened fast for Templeton to charge down the main ramp to the center table, as if he were late for an appointment. Aziz had not yet manifested his ghost.

Templeton removed his pine-green jacket and laid it across a chair. He pinched at his own silver hair and turned toward Brock, or rather, to Brock's ghost.

On the table, a sheet flashed. Templeton retrieved this and thumbed a response.

Another ceiling probe lowered, bringing the fog of specs that bent into angles and curves and then shapes that filled into surfaces—a human being with vague limbs, crowned by a smaller head-like shape. Pale film distorted all edges of the hovering figure.

"Brock Rivers and Harold Templeton, good evening."

Aziz had kept his viz filter, but let out his true voice. Brock stood on the platform, nearly eye-level with the ghost, while Templeton kept to one lower step, looking upward.

"Soon your CIRCLE will confront a great change. I come to promise security. Your people need not evacuate as you've been doing in fear. You will suffer no further attacks. There is no safer place than complete submission to Allah."

Templeton said, "Mr. Aziz, can you assure us that Alicia Rivers is safe?"

"You will address me as the Mahdi. Do you understand?"

"I . . ." Templeton stiffened but nodded. "Where is Alicia Rivers?"

The ghost shifted and raised its head. He lifted an upper appendage.

Alicia was there! She stumbled beside the enemy, cast in fierce light, her perfect face flushed under disheveled hair, her magenta blouse dirtied and torn.

Her eyes flared, and she mouthed Brock's name. She could see him. Could he speak to her?

Something else changed. Aziz's form was sharpening. Shadowy film slipped off like a cloak to reveal the middle-aged man they had first met, now standing taller than his ghost. A thick white turban encased his broad forehead and restrained his curled black hair, which fell to the sides over stern, tight skin. Dark eyes shone under black brows. His beard was rendered black and trim, dropping many inches over his chest, which was partly bare from the curve of his beige tunic that showed black and red accents.

"Alicia, this is Dr. Templeton. Are you well?"

She did not reply. They wouldn't let her listen!

The elder steadied his voice. "Mahdi, you must let us talk to her."

"Not now, Harold. She lives by our mercy."

"Will you show mercy after we surrender the ship?" Brock said this with full force of doubt, fighting to keep rage from smoldering onto his face.

Those eyes fixed on him, their sharpness doubled by Brock's own ghost effect. "Mr. Rivers, in truth, I did not lie when I met you that first time. We want to work with you. We will share truth and go above the Earth into the heavens."

Alicia stared straight ahead of her, vaguely in Brock's direction.

"Here is more truth. You would save men for Jesus. I would conquer the world for Allah. Why hide this truth from each other? As we battle our shared enemy, my people will call for your conversion. If you turn, I will protect you. We will rise against the preserves. We will war against CAUSE. Wherever this justice begins, on Earth, the moon, or Mars, our united peoples will bring peace to a new frontier."

• • •

JASON
12:15 AM EEST, WEDNESDAY, JULY 25, 2125
KHALDUN PRESERVE, CAIRO

A ringing bell signaled Sadat's arrival outside *Alpha Omega*'s bay gates. Jason hated to mute the CIRCLE vox, but he did. Brock would handle it. "Derek to the highbridge."

Michael stood from his lowbridge station. "You are listening?"

"Yeah. Enemy's getting honest."

Michael spun about, staring through his face-full of images. "We are not the only viewers. He reflects this viz elsewhere. I find Vancouver, Detroit, San Francisco, Sydney, New Dubai, London, Madrid, Berlin, Babylon, Baghdad, Damascus, Istanbul, Kabul, Riyadh—"

"Cairo?"

"No, but to some smaller receivers near Cairo."

So this Mahdi had followers in many preserves. Maybe hundreds. A thousand Alexander Moores, sick of their household gods and longing to try a new one. Maybe one of those relays was boosting the enemy's message across orbits to the red planet.

"Mike, is this a mirror or relay? Can we probe the Cairo receiver?"

• • •

BROCK
12:18 AM EEST, WEDNESDAY, JULY 25, 2125
KHALDUN PRESERVE, CAIRO

Aziz spoke the truth as he saw it. If CIRCLE surrendered to him, they would gain an impossible choice, not between safety and space missions, but between one mission that brought enemy attacks, and a "safer" mission that would sabotage Brock's people.

If CAUSE ever heard this, they would rightly charge CIRCLE with insurrection.

Sweat clung to Brock's arms. Though he stood in the recreated Epicenter, his real temperature came from the ship's living deck. "Aziz . . . if you stay true to your religion, so must we. Christians are supposed to die before we deny the Lord Jesus."

A bold witness should say this. *Lord, make it true of us.*

The ghost approached him, taking steps onto the air. "Brock, where are you?"

He liked his rhetorical questions. "Dr. Templeton told you. I am aboard the ship."

"Where are you?"

Why speak as if he had not heard? "I am aboard the ship, using our firewell."

"Brock. Where. Are. You."

Something was wrong, perhaps desperately so. "I don't understand."

"Where is your ship?"

"We are making repairs in our reformation hangar, in southern Ohio."

"*That* is a lie."

• • •

JASON
12:20 AM EEST, WEDNESDAY, JULY 25, 2125
KHALDUN PRESERVE, CAIRO

Before the *Alpha Omega* bay gates finished opening, a new craft edged close. It shone gold over dust-toned metal. Blunted protrusions like claws made it resemble a sand crab. When it grounded next to *Legacy* and the Navistar shuttle, half the crab's face opened. Sadat climbed out and stuck to the floor. He lifted two hands to take Jason's arm.

"Mr. Sadat, welcome aboard *Alpha Omega*."

Their guest blinked, either from the bay's glare or this late hour. Jason led him to a levitator and explained the updates as best he could, leading to Alicia's capture.

"Your enemy has abducted Brock's wife? I am so sorry."

"Regent?" Michael breathed fast. "I'm trying to trace Aziz. But he is tracing us. He knows we left Cincinnati, and I think he will expose the false ship."

• • •

BROCK
12:20 AM EEST, WEDNESDAY, JULY 25, 2125
KHALDUN PRESERVE, CAIRO

Had the crew ever held control over this situation? Brock tightened his voice. "Sir, that's enough. I can't answer false accusations." The enemy must not see his quaking hands. If only Brock had kept wearing his long-sleeved jacket. "We will meet your demand. In the twenty-four hours we have left, we're hurrying to get the ship in some airworthy—"

"Do not tell me *enough*. You think yourself a man of truth, while you treat my people as fools? Who can't see through your image and hear the delay in speech?"

See through his image. But he would see only walls behind Brock.

Delay in speech. This was the error. Brock had not used a quantum connection, so he perceived himself interrupted by split-seconds of com delay, yet in Aziz's perspective, any savvy technician would see Brock's feed showing twice that delay.

"You are nowhere near CIRCLE campus. So where are you?"

No one else replied, while Brock fought to imagine any rational cover story.

Aziz whipped down his arm. From his robes he withdrew a small object, some unfamiliar tool or else a weapon. He seized Alicia, held her close, clenched his right arm over her chest and pressed the copper muzzle to her throat.

Jesus, Lord God almighty, please save her. Do something.

Brock could not be silent. "We have taken the ship to Cairo."

"Good. Now, tell your crew to remove the false information."

. . .

JASON
12:25 AM EEST, WEDNESDAY, JULY 25, 2125
KHALDUN PRESERVE, CAIRO

Jason landed hard on the lowbridge. "Mike, kill the ship facsimile."

"But . . . I cannot do that, not without surrendering . . ."

"If we don't, he kills Alicia."

Elizabeth said, "Won't the removal expose the ship's cleanup and repair?"

"It will," Michael said. "If the enemy sees we removed the sabotaged reactors . . ."

"Regent," came Brock's calm voice on vox. "Please remove the facsimile."

"Michael, what about the first version of your fake ship?" Elizabeth said.

Jason cleared viz. "What first version?"

"That was a draft," Michael said, "based on earlier data before the ship's crash."

Brock shouted, "Jason?"

"Hold, Captain! Mike, does that old version show port reactors rigged to blast?"

"It does."

"Then use that, *behind* the current facsimile. But keep our real location. If he knows we've already landed in Cairo, that's more believable. Brock, you hear this? Stall him."

. . .

BROCK
12:30 AM EEST, WEDNESDAY, JULY 25, 2125
KHALDUN PRESERVE, CAIRO

"My crew is removing the facsimile." Brock could not move without provoking the enemy who held onto Alicia. Her arms hung limp, and her eyes clenched with terror.

"Mahdi, we will do what you ask," Templeton tried. "Have you no mercy?"

"Mercy? You tell people to follow Jesus or face your God's judgment. How is my call to conversion or else death any less merciful? Would you do anything to save her? Then we are alike, because I would also do anything to save my people from death."

No, he would not, not *anything*, and neither would Brock, not even tonight.

Words came to mind. Each sounded like a veil over this violence before him, or else a distant resolution to this evil, and each was an ancient truth that he could truly know. "Aziz, I don't know about your beliefs in god. But mine is Jesus, the One Who mercies and hardens whomever He wants. Here is truth. I cannot do *anything* to save people."

Aziz's face turned away, as if hearing someone else.

He released Alicia, and she fell to her knees, rasping and shaking.

From somewhere on vox, Michael said he had removed the false ship.

The enemy lifted his chin. "So you landed in the Khaldun preserve. You did obey my commands, but one day early." He added an Arabic phrase, then stepped partly out of the field; his right arm blurred off, then reappeared as he returned. "Brock, you have sang out words you think honor God. But tonight the true god will expose how these words destroy your people. For one last time, say these words you believe."

Alicia watched Brock. She could still see him, which meant she would see . . .

Perhaps the enemy meant to do this. He had always wanted to destroy the ship.

Brock strained to speak the words, almost as a song. "*Soli . . . Deo . . . gloria.*"

This phrase would not be heard by secret auditor devices that would overload the port reactors and destroy this ship. In reality, Navistar had removed those machines. That meant Aziz would see the failed sabotage and murder Alicia before them all.

Aziz smiled warmly, as if Brock had just passed some test to enter Heaven.

"Everyone who watches, you see that the infidel condemns himself and all like him. The grandfather's words brought death. His grandson now brings judgment to his people and his ship. Behold the wrath of Allah, through me, on those who rebel against him."

Aziz gave a command.

Over the vox, Jason shouted.

Like conditionals in a com script, every screaming thought flowed into one. The enemy never wanted to capture the ship, only to destroy it by a public showcase of power.

Thunder struck *Alpha Omega*. Hard floor met Brock's knees; his legs vanished under simulated carpet. He needn't even pretend. "Jason, talk to me! What is wrong?"

"Captain, bridge alert. I'm sorry, he's done it, he's overloading the port reactors."

Brock turned toward the flames and Alicia's image. She forced open her eyes and lips, lifted her quavering palm toward him, and bent down her two center fingers.

He pointed back, returning their sign: *I love you.*

Flames fell apart. Aziz, holding Alicia inside that living Epicenter image, turned into glassy mud, collapsed to the floor, and streamed away like dust evacuated into space.

44

BROCK
12:45 AM EEST, WEDNESDAY, JULY 25, 2125
KHALDUN PRESERVE, CAIRO

COMMAND DECK'S GRAVITY RESISTED EACH OF Brock's slow and automatic steps toward the highbridge. Jason and Derek stood, waiting before the vast canopy, and there was Michael working steadily in the starboard lowbridge, all alive and well.

They had come all this way, only to deceive no one but themselves.

Could any of them fathom the suffering they had just caused Alicia? His beloved, in captivity, had just watched while the starcraft—along with Brock and their people—was destroyed by a madman. His despair was nothing compared with hers! If not for any hope of finding and rescuing her, he might rage against the world and God.

Brock stepped down into the starboard lowbridge.

"I have cut his link to the false ship, and our true firewell," Michael said.

Over open vox, Templeton whispered prayers, as if he also believed their enemy had destroyed *Alpha Omega* in Cairo. All the better, then, for his authentic despair. But for Alicia, Brock could not reveal the truth within moments of the lie.

"Dr. Templeton," Aziz said. "Gather your elders tonight."

"I can find . . . six or seven . . ."

"Use the documents I send you. Contact the men I invite. Tell them my name."

"I can try."

This must be a performance; even Templeton sounded too willing to appease.

"I will return in three hours."

The vox went silent but for Templeton's labored breathing.

Finally the elder said, "Mr. Starr? Mahdi has left us. Have you really been . . . ?"

So he suspected otherwise. "Sir, we are safe," Michael said.

"Thank the Lord. I heard noise like explosions. For a moment . . ."

"Had to rev the engines a bit." Jason palmed his temple. "Added the effect."

"Then you're secure in Cairo. Oh, no . . . Alicia saw this! Brock, I am so sorry."

The lowbridge wall pressed firm on Brock's shoulder. "Michael, the trace?"

"The trace is done."

A tiny shard of hope drove deep into Brock's chest. Michael brought a grid into his console's tiny well. "He is indeed nearby, somewhere in Egypt, but not this city. The ghost comes from unclaimed lands, west of Cairo."

"That's raiding territory," came a woman's voice, then Tameria descended to the lowbridge. "I mean *raid* as in radioactive. In the Last War, Russians put missiles all over western Egypt. It's no-vault and no-fly. In fact, it's one of the world's least livable areas."

Brock pressed his fist against his eyelids. "Aziz looks healthy to me."

"Maybe it's a wartime shelter," she said. "Many countries built those."

"I can probe more." Michael took to his feet. "Elizabeth! Let's find any public data about that area, including mapped settlements, even abandoned ones."

"Mike," Jason warned.

Rather, they should let *someone* enjoy this. "Jason, Mr. Sadat, join me on highbridge."

The two men climbed the steps to displace Derek, who bowed and stepped off.

"If I want to fly out there," Brock said, "can we guard against radiation?"

Sadat considered this. "It is not much worse than space travel."

"But with a damaged starcraft arm, yes, it is."

"What about optics?" Jason said. "Aziz just 'destroyed' us."

"He may also have followers watching my preserve." Sadat glanced to his com belt. "If we do not publicly report an explosion, your ruse will not last."

"Agreed," Brock said. "Do you know about this radiated area?"

"Your crewwoman is right. West Egypt has much hazardous desert, even before the war. For thousands of years, Egyptians have kept to the Nile valley."

"I can still set course to Michael's coordinates," Jason said.

Sadat took a signal, then excused himself from the highbridge.

"I think I found the enemy's origin," Michael called up. "I can probe this, using the same reverse pathogen I sent with Aziz's ghost vein to the Epicenter."

Brock leaned over the console. "Can you find thermal readings, radio, visuals?"

"I am sorry. We have no way to know those."

Jason dropped his voice. "Another problem. Aziz brought us here to Khaldun, then thinks he bombed the ship in the middle of it. He said we obeyed him, but a day early."

"Agreed. So in his mind, he has punished us for disobeying him."

"Or never wanted the ship. So why bring us here? Why not destroy it back at home?"

Brock stared down to the scanboard that showed no threat thus far. "What?"

Aziz had waged his war on two fronts. First, he sought to influence and then take over CIRCLE. Second, he was preparing his next move on the Khaldun preserve.

Jason prodded, "Captain?"

"He wanted to destroy us as a sign for his followers." Smooth blue metal cooled his bracing hands. "And he wanted the explosion to cause chaos to the Khaldun preserve."

"Like the Heritage Hall blast." Jason swore. "This time, against Khaldun."

"One ship and one wealthy preserve isn't enough for him. He wants these people and their wealth, manufacturing, weapons, vehicles, and many more ships." Brock stepped back. "If I'm right, our early arrival also forces the attack one day early. Tonight."

Brock crossed the floor and dropped through one levitator into the cargo bay, where Sadat was just climbing into a shuttle that resembled a spiny ocean creature. "Sadat!"

The wide-open hangar gates opened like a cliff over this world.

Vast land dressed in silver-matte crete reached halfway to the horizon, interrupted by the great wall, like a castle's tower-bearing keep, facing the lands outside Khaldun territory.

Beyond that barrier waited unbroken starless night. Dusty wind pricked at Brock's nose, catching his sleeve. This preserve slept, with thousands of parents and children.

The sky broke. Lights over the land sparked like tiny fireflies.

Sadat turned and shouted in Arabic. Those little shapes drew nearer, coalesced, and formed one long widening streak like a meteor that swept into an arc, then peaked, and dropped into the preserve. A great report shook the ground and *Alpha Omega* trembled.

Brock had been right.

More streaks arrived. Searchlights erupted from preserve walls. Vehicles thrummed and distant men shouted. Wall turrets activated and began returning fire.

"Lord preserve us." Brock retreated from the gateway's edge.

Jason cast out viz to reflect *Alpha Omega*'s scanboard. Two red clusters spawned in the northern hardline area, while a larger swarm formed in the west like a storm front.

Sadat switched to English. "We have never faced an attack like this."

"What'll you do?" Jason said.

"We evacuate. First, my family."

If the ship had landed elsewhere, they would not have attracted Aziz, certainly not tonight. This monster had taken Brock's wife. Next he would invade this preserve and attack more people.

Sadat shouted for defenses. Beyond the great preserve gates, small Khaldun crafts launched into the air and rushed toward the northern border. They would face attack from two or more directions. How many other hardline fighters did Aziz already control?

Under C-grade repairs, *Alpha Omega* had journeyed halfway across the globe, but even an A-graded ship couldn't withstand projectile attacks. Unlike a CAUSE ship, this former luxury starcraft wasn't equipped to return fire. Once she had carried many of these same people, and she could do it again.

"Mr. Sadat." Brock found the man's eyes. "We will help with evacuation."

Jason took that in. "But you, Captain? Take a shuttle. Find the enemy."

"Thank you, Brock," Sadat said. "I pray you find your wife. You must take my van."

"Why that vehicle?"

"Because it has something no good Muslim should have, but that you may need."

• • •

BROCK
1:20 AM EEST, WEDNESDAY, JULY 25, 2125
KHALDUN PRESERVE, CAIRO

Brock retrieved two glazers from his own cabin and ascended uptube. He found Michael in the lowbridge, still trying to scout the enemy origin. He and Elizabeth had already risked so much. But he alone had the gifts to do this, so Brock must ask.

"Michael, I'll not pull rank, but I ask you to join me, flying out to that area."

When he returned from the kitchen with rations, Michael was embracing Elizabeth.

Back in the cargo bay, open gates revealed white flashes and distant rumbles like a thunderstorm. Sadat's promised van had arrived, and Brock climbed into its luxurious cabin. There he linked personal viz and entered base coordinates into the autodrive.

Michael opened the other door. "We are paired with *Alpha Omega*'s scanboard."

"Thank you." Brock sealed them in. "Liftoff."

One long push on the yoke drove *Alpha Omega*'s open gates far beneath, dropping away with the land. Brock reversed and blasted the van higher into dark skies, underscored by a wider horizon that carried the same faint ridge of trees where he and Jason had first seen the starcraft. Fertile rows bordered the distant Nile River and birthed the Khaldun Concern's capital palace of ice and steel, shining like a holy city.

"Jason, we're clear, hopefully small enough to avoid detection." Brock spoke like the soldier he must not be.

With each new hundred meters, the van gave a shudder. In seconds they would rely on pressurization. Michael gazed out the window, looking fairly comfortable. Days ago, he had helped Jason and the Rivers children escape Mars. Even after Michael pled with Brock not to abandon the Space Mission, he remained quietly faithful.

Brock sighed and released the yoke. "I'll check the cabin."

Something no good Muslim should have. Was this a pile of idols? Perhaps a Bible?

He pulled aside a corner curtain to expose a refrigerator-sized object. Viz beams lit this machine, wrapped by steel and glass, a very small but usable quantum vault.

• • •

JASON
1:30 AM EEST, WEDNESDAY, JULY 25, 2125
KHALDUN PRESERVE, CAIRO

Over half a kilometer from the ship, Khaldun defenses engaged the enemy. Jason couldn't identify the ordnance types. Sadat's forces would likely respond first with synthient drones, but these wouldn't last long, not if Aziz pulled in more waves.

"Sadat, when are we getting evacuees?"

"Soon," came the reply. "First, my wife and children. Please see to them personally."

"I will. What about Mr. Khaldun's family members?"

"Do as I say. Please, Jason."

They had never met or seen this *Mr. Khaldun*. Only the one man, Sadat. Only he showed a leading role in this preserve, not to mention personal attachment to this ship. This was starting to make sense. "I'll guard them, sir. How many do you expect next?"

"All women and children in the preserve. Thousands."

Could the ship handle that weight and still take off? They had two days' fuel for fewer than ten people. What about food, water, supplies, infrastructure, order? "Have them bring limited stuffs. And I need rankings for who gets cabins first."

"Jason, I command the defense. My wife will meet you."

"Fine. Out."

Jason was also in command, so he should give commandments. *Shipwide vox.* "Acting crew, as you've seen, our shared enemy is attacking the preserve. We can't fight back. But we will help. Per the captain's orders—guess this is our first missionary journey." He headed for the cargo bay. "Lawrence Peters and Julia Peters, you're at com. Use translators. Run arrivals and lodging. No evacuees are allowed on command deck. You good?"

"Praise the Lord," came Julia's voice, then louder, "Yes, sir."

"Derek Soren, ready the vault for multiple use." In an emergency, folks should ignore their fears of vaulting. Derek may persuade them. CIRCLE could pay for it.

"I'm on it, soon as you're back on highbridge," Derek boomed.

"Tameria Lightheart, please handle food and supplies. Work with Julia."

"My gosh, yes."

"Elizabeth Starr, we may have injuries. You're now acting chief physician."

"What? Mr. Cruz, I'll try, but I'm not trained for rescue, let alone in this gravity!"

"And ma'am, I've never commanded a starcraft. You can do first aid?"

"Yes—"

"Then get to the infirmary."

Another wide craft landed in the now-crowded cargo bay. One male driver exited and opened a side door. He ushered out a dark-haired woman clad in dark purple. She held two babies and led four more children, two boys and two girls, none wearing hijabs.

Jason fetched his Arabic inscriber. "Mrs. Sadat, welcome." She read his viz-projected letters. "Here is my code. Send me any needs."

Boom. A closer thunderclap made the ship shudder.

Derek called, "Aye! I see big projectiles inbound from the west."

"Lift the ship and face that direction. Keep the stern away from danger!"

"Acting captain," came Sadat's voice. "Is my family onboard?"

Jason found his highbridge relay. "Yes, sir." Where was defense system access?

"Can people come aboard through the ship's bases?"

"Only port side and able-bodied. Use the levitator." There, Jason found hull repellant. This would deflect small fire, but draw from the ship's limited power.

VOX FROM HAROLD TEMPLETON. "Yeah, hello?"

"Jason, have you found Alicia?"

"Trying." Something flashed on the western horizon. "We're occupied here."

"Is this true that she was taken to the moon?"

That made no sense. Had the enemy told him this? "Where'd that come from?"

"Bryony says the news and rumors about Alicia have spread over campus."

Jason scowled. "I thought your people weren't sharing the details."

"We didn't. But however they found out, churches are gathering to pray for Alicia's rescue, from the moon or otherwise, and for the strength of Brock Rivers."

• • •

BROCK
1:40 AM EEST, WEDNESDAY, JULY 25, 2125
WESTERN EGYPT

Brock's quick tests showed that Sadat's absurdly tiny vault would work. Michael would need to stay in the shuttle. Only one of them could pack himself in there to vault out.

He returned to the pilot seat. Dark skies quivered over the thermal-illuminated gray earth that blasted fiery winds against their approach. Michael's data showed the enemy origin: a rough elliptical outline, red on black, about 350 meters wide, with no other information. This place might hold thousands of people.

This was a quiet moment, so Brock must say this. "I'm sorry."

Michael watched the trembling land.

"You have known Jesus for less than a year, and I've led you into this hell."

"Well. Maybe I would disagree, brother." Michael loved to try on his Christian-language for size. "Were we not going to Hell before? Yahweh wants me to know this truth." He looked down to his right hand. "When Elizabeth and I came to Port Ares, we had our good home. We had Rachel. We had financial security. But I soon felt I had stopped learning, not about com systems and the Cause philosophy, but about the true world and a man's purpose. Yahweh brought you and Alicia to teach us, first about your people's ways, then about Himself."

Brock was grateful to help a brother, but this mustn't change his decision. "The Lord can keep teaching us, while we live on Mars."

"You would give up the mission," Michael said. "But I would give up my old life for this."

Brock would have spoken this way ten years ago, in those heady days when the *mission call* felt so inspiring, a self-destructive summons to forsake the ordinary for a life of spiritual adventure. "I know. And yet I can make room for you at our skiff. Reyes might—"

"We've arrived."

The altimeter reached 120M, lapsing the van into auto-descent. They should stay above any radar from the surface base, especially if this were an old military shelter.

Michael leaned forward and whispered to himself.

Far below awaited a wasteland, not just desert, but the shredded remains of Earth, like some titan had targeted solar flares against the surface, vaporizing all life and etching mountainous gashes against the sand. Jagged lines of rock had re-molten. Vast craters punched the terrain, as if this van had entered a spatial rift and emerged on Mars.

People lived here, in a land worse than the garbage dunes of Cairo?

So far the van's limited imaging showed nothing on the ground, except that one elongated structure, like a skyscraper-sized javelin cast from the heavens.

Michael pointed. "That is . . . a piece from a Russian spacecraft carrier? *Drotik* class."

And left abandoned? "Perhaps it fell during Sixty-Eight Thanksgiving."

Red light danced against the scanboard's edges.

"This is not radiation," Michael said. "We should be safe. Other vehicles would..."

Brock found the tab to douse the van's external light. On the tiny scanboard, seventeen to twenty red specks glided over the desert, their line undulating like a serpent. They were vehicles, but traveling slow. Any militants inside might expect to do simple cleanup after Aziz's first waves overwhelmed Khaldun.

Soon the enemy caravan departed the van's scanboard. Brock allowed one more minute for safety, then gained altitude, closing their distance to the base.

One kilometer was left. Three-fifths. Now half. The land surface was crumbling.

Brock descended, heading to port to avoid flying across this new horizon, whose shadow didn't register on their map, but stretched on like a canyon, darker even than the sky. This was no natural chasm, but a massive crater, as if a meteor had struck here. Further to the west, there . . . the scanboard revealed one small elliptical edifice sunk within the crater. Through the window, the object was invisible, without lights or nearby features.

Brock fingered the two gloves curled inside his jacket pockets. "I don't suppose you can take thermal reads, open doors, de-power systems, or access security."

"I'm afraid not," Michael said. "My pathogen found size, location, and a few systems."

They would need a way inside without being seen, stopped, or killed.

"Based on energy use, we can guess people count. Their security is the radiation."

• • •

JASON
1:50 AM EEST, WEDNESDAY, JULY 25, 2125
KHALDUN PRESERVE, CAIRO

Jason's viz showed 52 refugees had cleared *Alpha Omega*'s bay, excluding drivers making return trips to fly in women with children and elderly. Derek had rotated the ship so that *Alpha Omega* faced the east. One tiny projectile like a firework exploded in midair and rained pebbles against the hull repellant field. Jason flinched, but the attack barely showed on the scanboard that mirrored most of the preserve's western wall.

"Regent, cabins are filling fast," Julia called on vox.

"Take my cabin and move my stuff to Brock's quarters." If the attack got bad enough, where would they take these people? Back to CIRCLE? Where else could they flee?

Out there in the battle, that "lifeform" looked so familiar—tiny swarms of flickering red locust drones, as if some munitions lab was reenacting the Exodus plague. These hadn't registered on scans until enough bugs gathered in a horde, then, *blip*, appeared. Ordinary defense systems would react too late, but Sadat's men clearly knew better. As soon as the red swarms appeared, tower-mounted sonic weapons—those coned dishes—spun about and blasted them. From higher up, more attackers launched small missiles or fiery streams versus the towers or versus Khaldun pilots who swept into the night to engage them.

Thunder cracked. One craft split into lava and debris. Whose was that? Should Jason grieve or clench his fists in victory? Either way, people were dying.

"Jason! Do you hear this?" Sadat sent an Arabic glyph, which Jason sighted. Syllables filled his earspace. *Translate.*

"—vengeance brought by god," came a flat agent voice, an automatic signal. "He has sent us in his wrath and great will be his justice. You will surrender the Khaldun preserve. The Guided One will take possession by end of night. Men will not resist. Convert to god and Muhammad his prophet or suffer judgment." A long pause. "Greetings. In the name of god most merciful and Muhammad his holy prophet, we have been entrusted with vengeance brought by god. He has sent us in his wrath and great will be his justice . . ."

New red clusters pressed like ants against the preserve walls—enemy land forces. By now Aziz may have recruited all the hardline. All those people living in garbage, who had been feeding them? Teaching them? Helping them survive today while giving them hope for paradise? One wicked strongman. That's all they needed.

Alpha Omega trembled, tipping Jason's boots off the floor.

Alarms blared that enemy fire had struck the ship, not stray, but aimed.

"Sadat, we're taking hits."

Sadat went quiet, then said, "If I signal, you must lift and fly south."

Saving people, but leaving preserve troops to face the enemy? "Yes, sir."

If only Jason could fire back. An eye for an eye, a plasma stream for a plasma stream.

This enemy was killing innocent people.

Boom. No repellent field shook that off. Screams echoed and scanboards showed an impact in the upper bow. No damage? For now, their hull had absorbed the hit.

This enemy had threatened the Cause. Did his militants travel across civil space?

Two hundred klicks north, in Port Alexandria, was the SOAR base he knew. Just like Jason's own people, they had eventually cast him out. One signal up there would summon CAUSE's defense force to engage this enemy—and also drag CIRCLE into a nil-win scenario. If they surrendered to Aziz, they would lose, and if they reported the enemy, this incident would blow up. CAUSE would use the excuse to fight anything left of the Space Mission.

Still, he had enough data to call in the cavalry. In case the captain approved.

• • •

BROCK
2 AM EEST, WEDNESDAY, JULY 25, 2125
WESTERN EGYPT

Brock read quickly over Michael's scraped-together data. That domed shelter was built to survive wars. External reads showed energy support for at least 750 people, unless they operated in low power. How had they brought Alicia inside? Perhaps they used that Cairo quantum vault, the lobster trap. The closest CAUSE ports were in Tel Aviv or Amman, and of course monitored. Otherwise, the base might have its own machine.

"Michael, can you find any energy signatures matching a vault?"

"Oh? They might have one."

"Captain," came Jason's voice. "Found her yet? Getting hot here."

"Regent, listen closely. I will try to vault into the base." Brock must say the rest as pure, inalterable facts. "If something happens, I want you to copy that last conversation between Aziz and Dr. Templeton, and send that to any local authorities you can find."

Jason paused. "Yeah. That helps me with something. How long till I hear from you?"

"Give me thirty minutes."

Michael lifted his hand. "Brock, I may see a vault. You cannot go there without—"

"We have no other way. Can you trace a code?"

Michael muttered about a nomenclature to mask signatures. "It's here."

"Send this to our vault, and give me any details."

"I can try to trigger auto-reception down there. I can't know if anyone waits nearby. Their vault could have countermeasures to lock you inside or jam your signal."

Brock slipped on both his gloves. Over vox Jason said, "Godspeed, Captain."

Brock had to drag open the vault door. The inside provoked mild claustrophobia, caused by cramped walls that pressed his arms and the low ceiling scraping his head. Drawing from the van's limited reactor, could such a tiny machine even generate bonded space?

He lifted his hands and readied the vault sequence.

Michael gave the order.

45

BROCK
2:10 AM EEST, WEDNESDAY, JULY 25, 2125
WESTERN EGYPT

A HURRICANE OF FIRE HURLED INVISIBLE FORCES
from all sides, like spirits punishing him for this rebellion against
physics. Claws tore at his clothes and limbs, ceaseless and brutal—then
released Brock onto a burning floor that hardened into cold clay. His
knees and elbows struck hard. Air caught back into his gasping lungs
and dust coated his tongue. The sequence was finally ended. What
place had he vaulted into?

He summoned viz and shone out his light. These walls allowed a
little more room than the van far overhead. They were not made of
glass but of opaque metal. He could breathe, focusing on his inner viz,
which flashed null signs. All shared vox was gone, smothered by this
mechanical gurgling. He had landed inside another beast.

Throm-throm-throm. Throm-throm-throm.

Brock lifted his hands, fetching infrared scan, turning the world
into muffled flames. Then he lowered his arms, clearing the fire. That
glimpse had shown no human shapes. Feeling about in the dark, he
found the door seams, then a manual handle. He pressed his back to
that wall. There the triple-pulsing thickened, shaking his body.

He pushed the vault door. The resounding *clank* was surely too loud.

The outside afforded no cover. This vault stood against the wall of a
huge oblong room, like a hangar. A few tubes gave dim light, revealing
machine parts lining shelves and towers of stair-stepping crates.
Haphazardly grounded vehicles sat dark. Other vehicles were splayed
open for dissection. He stepped around a red tarp hanging from wires
and found floor pads under racks of large weapons, cannons, and
smaller weapons like rifles.

One doorway led him to a passage, formed of rough crete ridges and lined with faint red lumen threads. If this was a military base, the militants were gone or sleeping. Or he'd found the wrong location. Either way, any leadership would stay in the center of it.

A voice splintered like glass and whispered.

He pressed his back to a wall. No human shape entered this place. The voice came from ceiling emitters, speaking in Arabic and mentioning the name *Khaldun*.

"We prepare division in Riyadh," his agent translated. "Glory to god. Proceed."

Red light blinked ahead, not a lumen thread, but a shadow, and its source came closer.

. . .

JASON
2:25 AM EEST, WEDNESDAY, JULY 25, 2125
KHALDUN PRESERVE, CAIRO

More bolts off the port bow rattled *Alpha Omega*. Someone must have seen the ship and ordered direct fire. Khaldun was sending defense drones to intercept—not too close, lest they expose the target's value, and not too far, lest they ignore the target.

Scanboards added red gashes. No ship could self-repair that fast.

Jason could only watch.

"Over two hundred guests have boarded," came Julia's voice.

That many could sink their life raft. "Michael, is Brock—"

"He vaulted down minutes ago, out of our range."

But not before giving Jason clear orders.

More punctures. Enemies may have found the bow's weakness to target.

"Sadat, I'm relocating *Alpha Omega*." Jason pulled the yoke, adding gravity and repelling the land. Over vox, Sadat shouted orders whose rough translations scrolled at Jason's top viz. Squadrons C and Q would protect the ship at a distance. Squadron I would guard west towers 1-C through 2-D.

Scanboards lit with multiple bolts—even Jason's slow movement might provoke the enemy. Khaldun drones responded, moving closer and increasing fire. There to the east, more enemy aircraft swept inward like a single curved arrow. Defense drones were pivoting that direction. A third attack trajectory? He eased into faster retreat.

One lightning streak cleared the drones, then dove into a building cluster, the lodging place where Brock and Jason had stayed. Fire and debris carved into the structure.

They didn't attack the manufacturing district. Aziz likely wanted to capture that.

Jason steered that direction.

Khaldun's drones neared *Alpha Omega*, tracking with her course, firing outward.

His board showed a single flaming arrow. Now it appeared beyond the ship's canopy, resolving into a fleet of vehicles—and swept on, toward that bright patch in the southwest. Khaldun's palace. They would strike it like a hailstorm.

Out of the palace gardens, two drones rocketed up and threw hellfire against hellfire. Other cannons burst stone pellets into the sky, forcing apart five enemy ships. They evaded, dodged, regrouped, poured down missiles and plasma torrents. Among the trees, artificial lights flickered and snapped as the palace began crumbling.

But Khaldun's little ruling family was safe aboard *Alpha Omega*.

Only for now. Even if they survived, their preserve would not.

"Jason!" Tameria called. "CIRCLE says Aziz phased back into the Epicenter."

• • •

BROCK
2:30 AM EEST, WEDNESDAY, JULY 25, 2125
WESTERN EGYPT

Brock hurled lightning that scorched into the wall. His second blast caught legs and threw down a dark figure. It lay still on the floor.

He risked more viz light, revealing the shape snarled inside blue fabrics, with smooth feet and hands, and a curving body that led to a bare face with dark-brown eyes that stared with dwindling consciousness. She blinked, and her lips stirred.

He had hurt this woman. Even if his viz translated an apology, she wouldn't understand.

"Where is he?" Brock knelt closer. "The man *Mahdi*?"

Her eyes lifted to the hall from which she'd come, then she lay still.

Her pulse held, thank the Lord. Brock hoisted her body over his shoulder. This corridor narrowed, exchanging dim orange lumen threads for pale white ones that drew gentle swirls and curlicues on the walls. Here were hung several bronze frames that held abstract paintings without any human forms, interspersed with deep velvet curtains.

With a groan, he carefully set her down and wrapped her inside the fabric.

Lord, preserve her life and forgive me.

Vox crackled and Aziz himself spoke. Brock's agent tried to translate, offering phrases about three men overseeing an attack, targets of the Khaldun palace, apartment towers, homes, commons, export center. His victory seemed to be nigh . . . then the vox cut off.

• • •

JASON
2:40 AM EEST, WEDNESDAY, JULY 25, 2125
KHALDUN PRESERVE, CAIRO

"Dr. Templeton," came their enemy's welcome on Jason's vox. "Who are these?"

"Mahdi, these are five CIRCLE council elders."

"Perhaps one of you can tell me about the *Alpha Omega* ship."

Father God, don't let them find out.

Khaldun defense crafts formed a wall between the starcraft and invaders. There was no question the enemy had seen the ship, larger than all others, wounded in the leg, but not destroyed. Aziz may have shown his people the images and told them to look for wreckage.

"You destroyed our ship." Templeton sounded truly grief-stricken. "We never—"

"Such a lie. The ship survived. We see it in the Khaldun preserve. How did you do this?"

Jason swore. The secret was out. They had used up their technical trickery.

"No matter." Aziz sounded tense. "I have the woman, but I have no more patience."

"Sir. Please. You asked us to gather. You promised—"

"No. Enough! I showed you mercy. You denied the truth and lied to me. Now I will show you the consequence. I will destroy CIRCLE and take everything you have, before the sight of all the preserves, but only after I behead Alicia Rivers."

"Sir, we have no way—"

"No way? No way? Let us see the woman again."

Aziz would kill her, and that broke the impossible choice wide open.

Jason fetched his data package, with all time and place markers lit in red. He only needed add the SOAR emergency address for this area. Atop his note, he'd put the critical line: WE WILL RISE AGAINST THE PRESERVES. WE WILL WAR AGAINST CAUSE. WHEREVER THIS JUSTICE BEGINS, ON EARTH, THE MOON, OR MARS, OUR UNITED PEOPLES WILL BRING PEACE TO A NEW FRONTIER.

Father, forgive me. He added the SOAR address and fired off the signal.

46

A BROADER DOORFRAME LED BROCK INTO A VAST common area, washed in rusted glows from old garden ridges. Pillows and short tables lay strewn over its long floor. At the back was an open kitchen of decayed countertops between ancient refrigerators and ovens.

Someone was there.

In the corner slumped a single figure, atop his own pooled robes. The head rolled back against the wall. His yellow cap contained sparse gray hair, and his beard gently lifted and fell over his chest. This one couldn't go out with the fighting forces.

Brock approached more doors, each closed against this hall. That mechanical *throm-throm-throm* faded with distance. One door had been left ajar, so Brock peered inside. The room was small, packed with many people. They lay in sleeping bundles, not soldiers, but civilians at rest. While their Mahdi waged his war, he'd kept this place as his own preserve.

Again the hall turned, revealing open doors that let muted noises drift from ahead. This passage ended in a narrowed square doorway edged with copper.

Brock's chest heaved. He moved through the frame, closer to a man's echoing voice.

He cast soft light about a new room. The ceiling lifted into shadows, borne by walls that held many objects, including many national flags—an old green standard with Arabic script in white, a red-white-and-green-striped one with the Islamic crescent, an ominous black one with gold lettering under a red spear and sword. Shadow-boxed frames held relics—a scroll, a book, a scimitar. Printed maps showed foreign lands, pinned with notes.

Another doorway to another room brought that voice closer.

Shallow platforms lifted to ankle height, like lap desks. Taller wall shelves were crowded with books and binders, some labeled in Arabic.

A distant voice shouted. Shadows sprang into the room. Brock shoved forward—making one shape tumble—then he flew to a second man, caught his hand, threw its object aside. Matching strength resisted Brock's right arm. Enraged black eyes set against him, then cast down to see Brock's gloved left hand. Close enough! Brock opened his fist to clench at the neck, releasing steam from burning flesh, and held fast while the other man shuddered.

This anger was righteous. They had come to Brock's homeland to make them suffer.

No. Enough. Brock withdrew his hand.

The other slumped, his limbs temporarily paralyzed as he slid down to the floor.

No more men advanced. Two newly opened doors allowed faint light into this room. Brock pressed against that doorframe, readying every adrenaline-charged muscle.

Another sound filled the next space, something buzzing against shelves that grew like vines against curving walls. Books shone with neatly labeled covers. More memorabilia clung to the walls: aircraft schematic sheets, maps, missile and drone models, folded uniforms. A dominant viz-illuminated map had edges flowing with Arabic words.

Freestanding shelves formed a center wall, with big books of oddly familiar colors, like that crimson-and-gold-colored spine with an English title. No, this couldn't be right.

Peculiar People, Caleb Rivers, the old 2056 edition.

Into the Heart of Jesus, 365/Year, volumes one through eleven, Savannah Rose.

The CIRCLE Study Bible, general editor, Jerome D. Rivers.

"Men, I am followed by thirty-nine other preserves. They will behold my wrath."

Now the echoing voice spoke plainly, only meters away, from beyond these shelves and beside a central platform, against the wall opposite Brock's entrance point.

Over there, flowing viz curtains surrounded the voice. Inside, shapes wavered as if through a burning cascade, atop a red floor that supported narrowed human figures.

"You will see the anger of Allah against the infidel who . . ."

Did he mean *Alicia*? Brock reached the epicenter, but found only one man. There were no more bodyguards, and this room had only the single entrance.

His heartbeat thrashed as he simply . . . stepped onto the platform, where lukewarm flames engulfed him. Specs swept away, desperate to re-form their images, to reveal one solid figure in full resolution, this man standing in *the* Epicenter. He lifted shoulders and arms, spilling out beige sleeves edged with black, and leaned back to stare at Brock.

"Where is Alicia?"

Aziz held himself like a paused image, a smile playing under his beard. "My forces have surrounded your Khaldun allies. You are a liar. Now you've returned to see her die."

He assumed Brock was part of the viz.

Brock found words. "Aziz, we are reporting your violence to CAUSE."

The enemy took one step. "Let them try. I will break the preserves. I will cleanse the lands and fill the Earth with Allah's power, you might say, as the waters cover the sea."

A strange thought flared in his mind like viz: *Never. That place is for His glory.*

Brock lifted his right fist. Energy surged under his skin, as if he'd turned the glazer upon himself. This wasn't adrenaline, but real power, a sense he rarely felt over another person. No official on Mars or elder on Earth had been so vulnerable to him.

"Well then, behold the great Mahdi. He dwells in his holy shelter. His people fight while he leads from his fortress, too 'pure' to walk in a wicked world." Brock spoke as steadily as if he had rehearsed this.

"And where are *you*, Brock Rivers? Hiding in your ship to plot more lies?" He lifted his right arm. "Stay there. I have just sent for your woman, to behead—"

Brock's two hands seized his neck.

Aziz choked. He fought to retreat, crying out, staring in fear, weak as any man.

Brock released one hand and punched hard. Blood streaked over Aziz's face and beard. The enemy stared back, then roared and wrenched away. He doubled forward, grappling for the glazers Brock had yet to use. Brock fired bolts. Without thermal viz, they scattered in the room.

He had lost control.

Aziz swatted his arm, bringing pain too little and too late. The next bolt stung the enemy's hand, making him clutch at his own petrified fingers. An opening—Brock drove new punches against Aziz's chest and shoulders and arms. Now the enemy fell headlong, streaking his blood on both gloves.

Brock's knees struck tile floor. He pressed two fingers mere inches from Aziz's face. These fingers pressed so close against hot skin and black hair just beneath the turban.

One bolt. It would be lethal. So close. So close as this. *Think. No, do not think. Think!*

"Where is my wife."

A stone face turned against him, anguished yet defiant. Brock's gloved hands clenched hard around Aziz's skull, power crackling at his fingertips. The enemy's head twisted. Eyelids shut. He cried out for two bodyguards who couldn't help him.

That face, even with such evil eyes, reflected *imago Dei*.

Never surrender that truth. Not even when you need to strike that reflection.

Now a small voice infinitely more ancient than Jason Cruz was quoting the Lord's very word: *Give place unto wrath, for it is written, Vengeance is mine; I will repay.*

"My wife."

His defeated enemy pointed past the firewell, back to the single doorway. Brock released the head. Thermal scans showed no upright figures in that direction.

Inside the recreated Epicenter, men shouted. They were half of CIRCLE's elder council—and not just them. Screens showed people watching from 39 preserves.

Jesus save me.

Brock removed his grip. Exhales convulsed in his lungs. He de-powered his gloves.

He clung under those arms and fought to drag the fallen man off the platform. Flames parted to reveal the Epicenter's interior along with the six motionless CIRCLE elders. Scrolling gray text indicated those 39 preserves Aziz had cited, all watching.

Translate, Arabic, ex vox. "To all of you . . . allies of Al-Haqiqa." Waiting for translation gave him time to plan this. "I did not come here to kill anyone. That is not my calling. But your leader sent his men to kill my people and attack my family. What I've done tonight, I've done with the single purpose to save them. I'll do no more than this."

What absurd platitudes. As if the sun had turned into ice or weakness were true strength.

As if men could be raised from death.

"God's wrath is good. Mine is evil. I will not avenge. Only my Lord and Savior does."

These words would be used against his people, or else to defend them.

"Let us talk as men. Not destroy. But stay out of my world. That is your choice."

Brock tagged the firewell stat. This simulated world collapsed into sludge until he stood on a naked stage, alone but for this messiah who lay slumped like a dead body.

On his own skull his violence descends.

Brock left the enemy and entered the hall, finding a side passage. Two broad doors blocked IR signatures. He pressed hands against one door, then the other. Something clicked and set mechanics in motion. The door split and pivoted out from the frame.

Another small room showed four corners and a low ceiling that glittered like a cave roof. There on a floor mattress lay a form, wrapped in a chrysalis of violet fabrics.

Had he dreamed this image?

Brock knelt beside her. He lifted his hand over her form and felt . . . oh, her warmth. She was not dead, only sleeping. "Licia." He touched her arm. "*Licia.*"

Her eyes opened to blink, and blink again.

"I'm here."

Alicia cried out, clung to him, buried her forehead into his neck, shaking with sobs.

"But the ship—you were gone. All of them in the blast. The crew—"

"All alive. We had to let Aziz appear to win. I'm so sorry. Lord willing, it's over."

"Your hands . . ."

They were covered in Aziz's blood, and possibly his own. "I'll tell you as we go."

• • •

JASON
3:10 AM EEST, WEDNESDAY, JULY 25, 2125
KHALDUN PRESERVE, CAIRO

Al-Haqiqa's forces stopped firing against *Alpha Omega*. Now they hurled themselves against Khaldun defenses, tangling into fiery airborne debris. Had they used up their energy or gone suicidal? It didn't matter. They were overwhelming the preserve.

Jason's earspace filled with shouts of the dying or despairing.

Sadat kept repeating syllables that sounded like *Allah, Allah, Allah*.

Another blast slammed the ship. Scanboards creased with red cuts—hull breaches. Lumen threads popped. The domed ceiling buckled, and alarms panicked. Whether from weight or lapsed energy, the vessel's synth grav had given way. Another crash and violent shudder confirmed *Alpha Omega* had slammed to the ground.

Yeah, Jason hadn't evangelized anyone, but he'd kept the helm like a good captain.

Father. Tonight, did we win anything? Or anyone to You? Please help Brock find his wife. As for mine . . . my precious Hope, and little Grace, I love you. I'm sorry I could not.

Rumbles overwhelmed the ship. His eyes reopened.

This was some new evil, or else Jesus might return at this exact—

But the heavens really had opened. White light filled the sky, cast from a platoon of flying ships. How high? They had kept shielded until they'd crossed into the preserve.

One more explosion of entangled enemies lit the horizon.

Al-Haqiqa's forces turned away. Over vox, Sadat began repeating the name SOAR.

Sleek birds swept over the world. Like robotic bugs, the Al-Haqiqa crafts shot up against them—into intercepting pillars of light. The enemies locked in midair, tumbling like toys in a maelstrom. Their lights drained, and fiery bullets stopped. Had SOAR used null beams? Harmonized electromagnetic pulses? Zero-gravity generation? Other tech CAUSE wouldn't name or reveal even to these supposed defenders of Earth?

Well, tonight they did actual defending. Behold the might of the human image.

New vox came in: "We are Strategic Orbital Armed Reserve, Alexandria division. Residents of Khaldun Concern preserve, stand down. Aggressors of Khaldun Concern preserve, you are violating the One Humanity Accords. Surrender."

SOAR crafts reached land. Enemy fire upon them was simply absorbed.

A swarm of smaller enemy locusts tried to form, yet fell apart.

Two more beams, perfectly targeted, brought higher enemy crafts plunging to Earth.

Jason called for a downtube report. Julia told him the refugees were stable, but children were crying and some elderly were struggling to understand any of this.

"Jason!" called Sadat on vox. "What news?"

"Holding together. Thank you for the defense. We took some damage."

"How are the, ah, Khaldun family members?"

Over a public channel, Sadat needed to speak this way. His was a story to hear later.

"They are well. They may appreciate their old cabin."

Elizabeth Starr labored to the lowbridge, her slender face flushed with exertion yet relief. "Michael just came back to the vox. People were crowding him out."

Jason isolated the channel. "Mike, where are you?"

"The same as before. Alicia returned to the van. And now Brock is here."

Jason had heard right. Elizabeth heard, too, and began thanking Yeshua.

"Jason . . . we're here. Aziz is alive. Only just."

Then the captain had done better than Jason would have.

"And the crew? The ship?" came Alicia's faint voice.

"Ma'am, it's good to have you back. We're alive. SOAR is routing the enemy."

So far, they weren't saving souls for eternity, but they could save them for today.

"Jason, as soon as the battle clears, and SOAR gives us permission, we're returning."

Whenever the captain could resume command, Jason might fall to the floor and sleep for hours. He'd awaken to the new threat of the legal mess. For that they might need more miracles.

47

BROCK
7 AM EDT, TUESDAY, JULY 31, 2125
CIRCLE PRESERVE, CINCINNATI

GENTLE AIR FROM MIDSUMMER WIND WARMED
Brock's face, lighting his outer eyelids with radiant gold, bringing flowing scents over the CIRCLE headquarters rooftop garden.

He leaned back in his chair—for now, able to rest in this glorious homeworld.

Later he would prepare for the next journey. By Jason's account, the attack on Mars had left Brock's skiff sealed of its large ruptures, but otherwise in a terrible state. Once he returned, he would stay busy with repairs. With discipline he could embrace such a life.

In fact, he would have plenty of time, given the order sent to CIRCLE this morning. Elders would deal with that mess. He needn't review it again . . .

Brock leaned forward and drew the sheet from his table.

> To the leaders of Religious Preserve–Biblical Christianity–Ohio-1, greetings.
>
> Your preserve is hereby placed under criminal investigation according to the full Coalition enforcement of global and interplanetary law. This includes but is not limited to: restriction of communications, restriction from economic trade beyond legal limits, restriction from new economic trade with other preserves, and further penalties per any confirmation of felonies and high crimes under civil law.
>
> Per witness of Port Augustine Gamma Radomil Cherek, charges versus RP-BC-Oh-1:

- Suspected affiliation with radical known as "Mahdi," former leader of rebel faction Al-Haqiqa, waste territory, western Egypt, no preserve designation.
- Suspected illegal acts and subversions, joined by other preserve(s) and settlement(s), including but not limited to: Japanese Refugee–Resettlement District–Northern Kentucky–3, Religious Preserve–Eastern Islam–Cairo–28.
- Failure to report violations of civil law within a religious preserve, including but not limited to: assault with weapon, death of preserve resident caused by assault with weapon, death of preserve guest caused by assault with weapon, obstruction of accident investigation, provocation of inter-preserve warfare.
- Repeat incursions into public airspaces by spaceworthy aircraft without commercial intent or flight plans, related to the investigation of subversions against CAUSE and illegal acts contra One Humanity Accords.

The Ministry of One Humanity in conjunction with the Domain of Public Affairs as ordered by CAUSE hereby restricts all RP-BC-Oh-1 residents to certain confinements within the preserve. All non-preserve commercial airships are barred from leaving or entering preserve territory, pending the investigation. Residents and guests of RP-BC-Oh-1 must cooperate with Ministry and CAUSE investigators for restoration of preserve integrity, the preservation of global law, and the protection of human dignity.

First Minister Salome Rochelle, Ministry of One Humanity CAUSE Domain of Public Affairs, Port Cincinnati, Ohio, United States, Earth

"Captain." Today, Dr. Woodford's voice was even warmer. "Good to see you here."

Brock returned his page to the table. "Wouldn't miss a beautiful day on my world."

The president eased into the opposite chair. "I come here often, not just to escape the system downstairs." He leaned back and gazed to the sky. Sunlight glistened on his face and golden monitor clip, which glowed against the cast on his right arm and shoulder.

"You wear the battle well," Brock observed.

"Real doctor's orders, till I'm done healing. Ah, but this time I made it up the stairs." Woodford sighed. "So you've seen the newest order from CAUSE."

"Frankly, I'm more afraid to see our people's responses."

"Some of our people may appreciate the Causians enforcing *our* law."

Brock released a sigh. "So long as that ends the Space Mission nonsense?"

"Some would say yes. After the evacuation, I think some chose to leave our preserve for good. Dr. Templeton said five families are transferring from Sola Cathedral."

"That many." Lord willing, Brock wouldn't know their names. Part of him still hoped everyone at his former church would support the Space Mission. Even if they never helped fund the effort, they could speak well of it or avoid speaking against it.

"Did Bryony tell you about our migration requests?"

"She didn't."

"The ratio looks like 50:50. Half want to leave this preserve. Others want in."

Brock shook his head. No doubt this was wishful thinking, even from Woodford.

"It's true," Woodford continued. "They're emigrating from many preserves and denominations. Many are seminary students, but several are PhDs. They say they feel called. They're asking how they can join the mission. A few elders said our churches and apartments—"

"What does this matter? This CAUSE ban would stop our migrations."

"Oh? The ban applies to commerce, not residents relocating." Woodford sat up and returned his feet to the floor. "'They went out from us, but they were not of us; for if they had been of us, they would no doubt have continued with us.'"

That reference wasn't about true Christians, but false ones.

Woodford's smile was almost a smirk. "Not quite the meaning, I know. Still, I think God may have plans for our critics elsewhere, like Barnabas away from Paul."

"How did you know I was thinking—"

"Executive privilege. Your grandfather, too, only *thought* he hid his thoughts."

That was fair.

"I know you feel that call. As do I. But, Captain, don't despise people with other calls."

Woodford kept calling him *Captain*, without subtlety.

Brock gripped his armrests. "We planned to use the commerce loophole for space travel. The Lord's calling won't matter if CAUSE grounds the ship."

Woodford laughed. "This was no surprise to the Lord. Dr. Sheldon also expected this, so he's massing our legal department. I see this CAUSE reaction for what it is. They are shaken. They know that SOAR, for all its power, could not have helped in Cairo in the way God let *us* help. Your crew's joy is infectious. That man you found, Mr. Soren? He's sharing the story on viz. My grandson showed me. He's excited. So are many."

The man was inspired, just as Brock had been, under all his motives, years ago.

Brock shut his eyes and planned his evasion. "Sir, I long to believe that. But that same God allowed death. Dr. Hendricks, Constable Longoria, and my grandfather, destroyed by sin that we let fester in our own body."

Woodford touched his hand to Brock's arm.

"I broke the seal, doctor. I let in the poison that attacked my people."

The president gripped tight. "And now the body needs antibodies to heal."

• • •

BROCK
10:58 AM EDT, TUESDAY, JULY 31, 2125
CIRCLE PRESERVE, CINCINNATI

Guards met Brock at the front desk. One of them recognized him but still asked for his name. They made him surrender his clip and tool belt, then ushered him through an old device like a mirror frame. Apparently this proved he carried nothing dangerous.

A uniformed man with curly hair requested the reason for his visit.

Decades ago, this place housed CIRCLE administration, with this tiny room serving as the original reception area. Now it was remade for very different use, denoted by a wall emblem: CIRCLE SECURITY, EST. 2076, subscripted by ROM. 13:1. Every preserve needed police.

"Mr. Rivers, you're cleared."

He led Brock through cramped and cool halls that forced Brock to hunch under low-hanging light panels. They entered the detention area, lined with newer doors of steel and glass. Offending residents were kept here, pending tribunals for various accusations.

This man's tag read CONSTABLE I. LONGORIA. "By chance did you know—"

"I'm Ivan Longoria. Sergio was my father."

He shared the soft-brown eyes of that rough-mustached man, who had fought a first and last battle to protect CIRCLE against invasion. Brock must speak to this. "I'm so sorry for your loss. I was there. If I'd known our mission would bring this consequence . . ."

"Sir. No, sir. I don't blame you. I blame the enemy. I blame the traitor."

At this new corridor's end, he buzzed another door, revealing a three-meter-by-three-meter space, with one small window permitting natural light. One twin bed, turned on its end, was shoved near the water closet to make more room.

Against the far wall sat Alexander. A brown burlap hood concealed his blond hair, leading to white robes. A red sash poured around his neck as he faced the floor.

Brock entered, and Alexander glanced up, then looked back down, dragging shaggy growth from cheeks and chin. His bare foot nudged closer to one large open print book, a Qu'ran. It rested atop many scattered pages and other closed books.

The young apostate must *want* to look this way, all a conscious choice.

"Alexander. I think you show great dishonor to your new holy writ." Brock pointed to the floor. "Touching it with your foot brings twice the insult."

The other didn't move his leg.

"You should know that Al-Haqiqa is over. After our mission in Egypt, the Reserve captured every surviving militant in Cairo. Hours later, they arrived in the wastelands to find the refugees and capture your imam. Mahdi is a false messiah. That is the truth of him."

Alexander blinked, holding his hands near his stomach.

The man was charged with murder, attempted murder, and sabotage of an airborne vessel. Soon the preserve tribunal would add charges for Heritage Hall's bombing.

"You grew to hate the old Christianity. But your new gods are dead, while Jesus lives."

That stubborn silence was a farce. Soon Alexander would be forced to speak.

"And now, congratulations. Thanks to CAUSE and all its Ministers bearing down on us, you've shut the borders tighter. Even then, we're free. Dead gods won't save you from self-imposed slavery. You can stop pretending you're some good Muslim."

"I am a good Muslim. A better Muslim than I ever was a Christian."

There it was. "You are neither. You an *Alexander-ist*. Any other name or religion, Christian, Muslim, whatever, is just an altar for your own idols."

"Says the man of privilege." Alexander glared. "The man with all the gifts."

"Ridiculous. We've both received much. Grandfather loved you. I befriended you."

Brock should quote the Scripture, not his own anger. The apostle had written, *Idolaters, revilers, swindlers . . . but such were some of you.* That's what he had come to say.

"Alexander." He leaned back on the wall. "I'm repeating your name, as if to remind myself that it's you truly in there. Lord help me, I don't want to cast you out, even after all this. We will never again be friends on this Earth. I wish you had not turned against us."

This may be the Spirit working over Brock's heart. Perhaps he truly was a missionary.

"If we could practice capital punishment, I might testify before a judge to demand *your* life for Grandfather's life. That's the truth of it. But so is this. The apostle Paul himself once helped murder a beloved saint. Even now, Christ wants you to do as Paul did. Repent."

Alexander murmured.

"I didn't hear you."

He drew his leg under him. "I will get transfer to a Muslim preserve."

"The judges will decide that. It's the final Judge who—"

Alexander's arms trembled and he lifted his chin. "*La ilaha illa'Allah. Muhammadur Rasul-Allah. La ilaha illa'Allah. Muhammadun Rasul-Allah.*" He fixed his eyes on Brock and enunciated, "*La ilaha . . . illa . . . Allah.*"

Their time was over. But for today, this had been Brock's mission field.

Deliberately, Brock gazed to the floor until his enemy also looked there. Brock lifted his left foot, then the right, to shake imaginary dust from his boots.

He faced the room's camera and raised a hand. The door buzzed, and he departed.

48

ALICIA
2:04 PM EDT, TUESDAY, JULY 31, 2125
SOUTH CINCINNATI

SOMEONE HOWLED OVERHEAD. ALICIA BOLTED UP the steps to the cabin's upper level and found Daniel sprawled face-first on the floor. Rugburn glistened under his tears.

"He jumped off the couch," Emma cried.

"He thinks like we're still back on Mars!" Adam shouted.

They hadn't budged from the larger sofa, so engrossed in their real hardback books with color images. Nearby, Rachel Starr busied herself with stringy goo.

"Daniel, come to the galley. We'll fix the hurt. But you can't do that anymore."

"*Whyyy noooooottt?*"

"Because this is a different world with different rules." After she sprayed his burn, he only cried louder. Of course it would sting.

"Can we go play in the dry fountain?" Emma called down.

"Not yet. Stay upstairs until I'm done working."

"Someone's knocking," Adam said.

That new fear stabbed at her chest, quivering into her shoulders. She took one step upward to see the floor. *Lord Jesus, help me heal.* CIRCLE counselors were also helping.

For now, all was well. "Adam, let them in."

Elizabeth descended to the galley. She wore that official-looking green jacket Alicia had ordered. "My two-thirty rescheduled, so I'm on break. I can take back Rachel."

Alicia found a wafer to bribe Daniel. "I'm fine. You kept my kids for a week."

"Wish I could be ship's backup doctor and mom at once," Elizabeth said.

They had talked about enrolling her with CIRCLE medical classes—that is, if Elizabeth and Michael were serious about staying.

"And has our captain changed his mind?"

Alicia ascended a few steps. "Our captain has not."

Logic alone helped her support that choice. Only days ago, the enemy had held her captive. Aziz had threatened to kill her—Brock never told her how—and Brock had been forced to make her believe that he and their friends had been destroyed in the ship. Now he would surrender his dream to protect her, and any mission would continue without them.

"Also," Elizabeth said, "Jason said he and the others were planning something?"

• • •

BROCK
2:30 PM EDT, TUESDAY, JULY 31, 2125
SOUTH CINCINNATI

Brock entered the captain's cabin of the *Alpha Omega,* perhaps for a final time.

How he'd loved this ship with all its provisions. Beyond this private family cabin, larger than all his other dwellings, the ship had enclosed a world of coms, potential gardens, storehouses, and simple glory. In mere weeks, they had invested so much in her. No doubt Navistar executives felt even happier after taking more of CIRCLE's secret gold-spun-into-yun and finishing a new set of C-grade repairs. Now, having stewarded the ship as best he could, *Alpha Omega* bore well her wounds. He could release her back to the Lord.

Alicia met him on the cabin stairwell. "Hi."

He kissed her deeply, another gift they had fought to enjoy this week. "Dr. Woodford and the elders have paperwork to finalize the ship's captain transfer to Jason." And to reorganize the Space Mission, should the elders choose to move ahead with it.

Alicia gripped the stair rail. "I found another freight vault. It's pricey, but legal."

"One last draw on the secret gold." Brock found a smile.

Their family could survive in the quev, or perhaps sublease the Starrs' old apartment, until Brock finished skiff repairs. Either way, they needed to visit Port Ares so they could pack the Starr family's possessions for shipment to *Alpha Omega*.

It would be a long struggle to restore communications with the Reyes Syndicate, but Brock could fight for his place repairing the Martian frontier. All this would aid his grief while he recovered from spiritual hubris. No more surrendering his family for a "calling." He and Alicia would live their lives, raise a family, and try to support true missionaries.

"Packing won't take long. I'll only add books, and the children can take theirs."

Alicia crossed the stair landing. "Actually, that may take longer."

She switched on the study room light.

Dozens of boxes lined the glass wall, many already opened as if ready for a move, and new objects lined the corner desk Brock had once planned for a personal workstation. Twin recliners held books and sheets, laid out for display—his pages from school binders? Many sheets were loose, others clipped together, but all showed his handwritten notes, some barely weeks old. There on the main desk rested his own print Bible of ten years.

And there was the octagonal crate that carried all their memories before exile.

"How did this get here?" Brock hadn't meant that to sound so disturbed.

"After the skiff attack, Jason thought the enemy might return. So they brought it all. This morning they moved these in from the *Legacy*. All our clothes. And the children's toys, and Daniel's favorite cup and bowl, and that quilt you gave me for our anniversary . . ."

Her voice broke.

"Why did they do that?" Could his quev handle added weight? Or could they ship everything back when their budget allowed? "I appreciate the gesture, but we need—"

"My love. They wanted to help you. To support the Space Mission."

"But they knew I was leaving, when they moved all this into the cabin."

"Same reason."

Beyond this window loomed that solid wall, blocking any wonders waiting outside.

Alicia took his arm. "Jason didn't tell you, but he used his life savings for quantum vaulting to Mars. Michael and Elizabeth are ready for this. Their care, and friendship . . ."

This wasn't right. "I can't repay those sacrifices."

"No. We can't."

"They can still join the mission. I commended them to CIRCLE."

"Will our leaving serve *them*? What about our children? Adam couldn't stop—"

"We don't know if Adam can stay here. If we don't launch in time . . ."

Alicia pulled, and he resisted. She held her place until Brock faced down to her.

"Listen to me. Please." Those beautiful hazel eyes would not let him go. "Whatever you think now, whatever secret hopes, under all doubts and realism, those dreams are not your sin speaking to you. I think the Lord's given me wisdom to say this. You have *good* dreams.

"Whatever your decision, I will honor and love you. Yes, the grief and fears are real. But so is the joy. I've seen the preserve migrations and the missions mailbox. It's now filled with more questions and prayers for us. People expect *you and me*, by name, to lead the Space Mission, and not just because we're some celebrity couple. It's because people heard in their church meetings that we were willing to suffer for this calling."

Brock pressed his hand to his forehead and found some glimpse of absurdity in this.

If the evil one attacks, and your leaders halt all coms, simply use a prayer group.

"*My* calling also counts, love. Please. Let's come home. Let's oversee the mission."

This was no posture. She had broken their code of silence and confessed her own dream. But he dare not hope, no matter her intentions. This was impractical, dangerous . . .

"Alicia, I can't lose you again. I can't go through that."

"Then, with respect, we would be treating ourselves as better than our neighbors. If the Lord truly wants this mission to reach others, why would we *not* risk so much?"

Alicia relaxed her head on his shoulder, just as she had during their slow and cautious walk across the enemy's shelter in the wastelands. Even then she had supported him. Now she was doing the same, by trapping him in an argument.

He found one rebuttal. "You've already written my resignation . . ."

"Actually, I wrote two documents."

Brock pulled back and stared to her.

"In one, you give the update and introduce the crew, then resign and transfer your role to Jason. But the other has only the first parts before you announce that we . . . we stay."

We stay.

No CIRCLE elder or church leader had counseled Brock to leave. So why assume Jesus wanted him to? If anything, if he rejected this call, he might be failing to obey.

Go therefore.

The choice was already made, like a divine decision on his behalf.

He embraced her, kissed her, lifted her to spin about. Even in this gravity, he could do this and perhaps even laugh, surrendered to joy. Yes, the suffering was real and lasting, but so was this happiness, like that day when he'd stood before the mobs to quote the Great Commission, or the day he had flown up through the hangar to the ship.

After one more spin, he set down Alicia for another long kiss—

In full view of four children who stood staring from the opposite rail.

Matching his grin, Alicia glided back to the study desk and fetched his pages.

He read them and wiped his eyes. "So I should choose . . . your speech version *alpha*?"

"Mm, and wear the navy jacket. You'll be the handsomest captain I know."

• • •

BROCK
3 PM EDT, TUESDAY, JULY 31, 2125
SOUTH CINCINNATI

Like tiny hummingbirds, three cameras hovered before Brock, while their trainer Bryony paced nearby. Two meters behind her, Tameria Lightheart beamed as she guided two larger floating cameras across the stairwell.

Future historians and theologians might debate this choice of publicity before the world. But for today, this event would serve Brock's family, his true people.

At 3:00 PM, the signal began. Bryony's prime hummingbird shone a faint glow.

He didn't need a script here. "Hello. I'm Brock Rivers, overseer of the Space Mission."

Bryony moved closer with her hummingbirds, followed by Tameria's duo.

He lifted his hand toward the shelf of newly placed mementos. "This is a tiny model of our homeworld. When I was a child, my grandfather said he received this model from an old missionary. A *missionary*, he said, is another name for a Christian. I asked where this missionary had taught, at a seminary or church? 'Not this one,' he said. 'Years ago, missionaries traveled to other lands to reach people who don't know Jesus.' This missionary he knew had worked secretly in China before the Last War. Grandfather told me, 'Perhaps someday, the good Lord will call new missionaries out of preserves into a world that needs Jesus.'"

Brock spoke directly to Bryony, and she smiled with encouragement.

Viz showed they had 843 VIEWERS.

"This is the original document found in our time capsule, left in the year 2075 for us and signed by my great-grandfather, Caleb Rivers." Brock lifted this next one closer to the cameras. "Here is a single gold bar, part of the inheritance from CIRCLE's founders."

Some elders had objected to this next part, but Brock had insisted on saying it.

"This treasure will fund the outreach Grandfather entrusted to us— the CIRCLE Space Mission. We want to restore obedience to our Lord's great commission, sharing His gospel beyond our preserve with our secular neighbors, above our planet."

On that cue, Tameria and Bryony retreated, and he followed them.

"Yes, CAUSE will oppose this, but we will defend our actions before civil authorities."

Alicia emerged from the stairwell to join Brock, and whispered to the children.

They veered every direction except the right one, until Bryony chirruped. Before the sight of thousands, the kids didn't act perfectly, and they didn't need to.

"This is my wife, Alicia. These are our *three* children, Adam, Emma, and Daniel." They all passed through the living room, out of the cabin door, into the hallway. "I've fought to guard my family from evil. Yet I know I'm called to spread the gospel."

Bryony and Tameria pulled back, showing Brock and Alicia standing at the firewell.

2,386 VIEWERS.

"Seven years ago, Alicia gave birth to Adam under secular law. We were forced to leave you for a time, to be cut off from our people. That broke my heart. When we returned, I wanted to guard you from evil but also to spread the gospel. How could I do both?"

His children were distracted by the viz fountain. Adam and Emma drew their hands through stones, while Daniel scooped out animated water that would not make him wet.

"I didn't know. I only knew that all power is given to my Savior, Jesus Christ."

With Alicia, he stepped onto the platform between ambulatory ramps—
Lord, thank You for this.

Beyond this great glass canopy, the hangar wall was gone, replaced by glorious blazing blue skies that teemed with clouds. *Alpha Omega* was already lifted into flight.

Cameras might capture his glimmering eyes. "Before any other missions, my first calling is to serve my people. In my zeal to reach the world, I neglected to love and share gospel truth with *you*. I hope to earn your trust by ministering to *you* through the Space Mission, suffering like Jesus, and inviting your support."

8,722 VIEWERS.

Bryony with Tameria and their cameras moved first up the port-side ramp, walking backward, while Brock walked after them, Alicia pacing beside him, the children following.

"I am my own religious preserve. I have my own boundaries and little systems. But I believe in a Creator God who tells us to make straight highways in the desert, terraforming worlds. We will do this upon mountains, in cities, and beyond. He sits above the circle of the Earth, and he promises His glory will fill the whole planet, as the water covers the sea."

On the command deck, Brock led his family up the highbridge stairs.

His heart pounded. From this place, he could see no earthly horizon below the glass canopy. As planned, Tameria and Bryony moved closer. This would give viewers glimpses of the ship while keeping them from seeing her vast window.

On lowbridge, Michael and Elizabeth waited. On highbridge, Jason stood to attention.

"As mission overseer, I've served as starcraft captain. This is my regent, Jason Cruz, acting ship's captain, and my brother. Sir, thank you for your service."

He returned Brock's handshake.

"And for the service you will continue, if you're willing, as ship's regent."

Jason's grip tightened. "Captain. Yeah . . . yes. Thank you, sir."

10,398 VIEWERS.

"Our ship has nine crew members, and may gather more in the near future. When we first opened recruitment, we had restrictions. We wanted—I wanted—to find 'super-apostles.'" Brock allowed a gentle laugh. "Perhaps I loved the idea of exploring other *worlds* of people, but only if they could breathe in my world. Now I shall truly learn to breathe in another's world, starting with my homeland. Therefore, CIRCLE will expand recruitment for the Space Mission. Anyone from every Biblical Christian preserve can apply for this outreach. Bring us your gifts. We need all parts of the body."

21,709 VIEWERS. Lord willing, they would reach many more.

Now to try some greater courage.

Bryony and Tameria watched him atop the highbridge. Behind them waited every crew member and nearly half of CIRCLE's elder council. If only Grandfather could be here.

"When our enemies sabotaged our test flight, some of you may have glimpsed our starcraft, even if you didn't know it. I want to thank Navistar Corporation and our friends with Khaldun Concern in Egypt. We do not share a savior, but we do share humanity. These groups have found common cause enough to restore this vessel for today's test flight."

Bryony and Tameria drew back, letting their birds reveal the highbridge.

Brock took position over the console. Far below the ship lay their home preserve, so green and blue, shining in clear sunlight. Ark Hotel lay like a single great beam beside lake waters, surrounded by campus buildings and dorm complexes, the homeworld where Brock had grown up, struggled, left in disgrace, and now returned to help lead.

Down there was the torn side of Heritage Hall, where Jerome Rivers had sung his last *sola* in this age. One day he would return. Perhaps then, Brock could share with him true stories of new missions, not only into the nations but into colonies above the homeworld.

Go therefore.

Soli Deo gloria, for the glory of God alone, he would be a missionary.

"My family in Christ, welcome aboard the *Alpha Omega*. You can see the starcraft behind me. Yet for everyone in my homeland watching this viz, I'd like you to see this ship for yourself. For just a moment, step outside your homes and offices, your classwork and church labors. Come out from your preserve and look above."

ACKNOWLEDGED

No great starcraft can challenge gravity without the God-given talents of her crew.

Long before I found Lewis and Tolkien—or the heroic worlds of Spider-Man, *Star Trek*, or the DC "Snyderverse"—Phil Lollar and Paul McCusker were creating the Christ-exalting drama *Adventures in Odyssey*. I thank them for this place of wonder, excitement, and discovery.

Next, I'm grateful to those movie marketers who put that 1999 prequel space hero on the pizza box. Their simple promotional act prompted this homeschooled teenager to ask the highly original question: "Hey, why aren't there science fiction tales, but, you know, about Christians?" 'Twas such a loveable start for a young storyteller. Lord willing, the results clean up better.

So many Christian fantastical works inspired this venture. Pioneers like Frank Peretti, Bill Myers, Jerry B. Jenkins, and John B. Olson/Randy Ingermanson shared early fuel sources. Across closer creative spaces, Jill Williamson, Kathy Tyers, Kerry Nietz, Ronie Kendig, Mike Duran, Sharon Hinck, and James R. Hannibal gave encouragement. Secret agent man Steve Laube wisely held this launch until the right time. And all the Enclave crew—Lindsay, Nadine, Sarah, Trissina, "Captain" Kirk, Julie, Jamie, and beyond—took this ship and helped it shine.

Nasser al'Qahtani and Andrew Benyamin helped with the finer points of Arabic spelling and pronunciation. Philip F. Pugh assisted with Latin phrases. And, although they know it not, the Goddard Institution for Space Studies (and many other Mars buffs and math wizards) saved me a *lot* of spreadsheet time thanks to their data-collection and program-creation.

Scott and Becky Minor invited me to their own mission in 2013. Realm Makers has since marshalled thousands of Christian fantastical creators. At last, we're connecting the circles!

Team Lorehaven gets exclusive assigned crew quarters: Elijah, Josiah, Jenneth, Marian, Laura, Ticia, Andy, Daniel, Jessica, Shannon, and everyone who has written or reviewed for Lorehaven.com. Up there in the starboard commons, we'll always keep our dedicated table.

A special shoutout goes to Zackary Russell, the fantastical and truthful Lorehaven podcast engineer who's also a burgeoning future cyberpunk missionary. *Tsugi wa kimi da!*

All this subcreation, however, may be meant to impress a girl. So for my Lacy Rhiannon, the only mission specialist on my highbridge, let's engage the next stage of this Adventure. Today, the science fiction. Tomorrow, the real-life starcrafts soaring from New Earth.

Ultimately, I thank You, Jesus, the Author of life who holds all the worlds in His hands. Even in this groaning era, the heavens declare Your glory. I can't wait to see Your sequel.

ABOUT THE AUTHOR

E. Stephen Burnett creates sci-fi novels as well as nonfiction, exploring fantastical stories for God's glory as publisher of Lorehaven.com and its weekly Fantastical Truth podcast. He is coauthor of *The Pop Culture Parent* and other resources for fans and families. Stephen and his wife, Lacy, live in the Austin area and serve in their local church.

IF YOU ENJOYED

ABOVE THE CIRCLE OF EARTH

YOU MIGHT LIKE THESE NOVELS:

www.enclavepublishing.com